The Dead Saint

Other Books by Marilyn Brown Oden

FICTION
Crested Butte: A Novel

NON-FICTION
Hospitality of the Heart

AbunDance
Joyful Living in Christ

Manger and Mystery
An Advent Adventure

Through the East Window
Prayers and Promises for Living with Loss

Wilderness Wanderings
A Lenten Pilgrimage

Land of Sickles and Crosses
The United Methodist Initiative in the C.I.S.

The Courage to Care

Beyond Feminism
The Woman of Faith in Action

The Minister's Wife
Person or Position

MULTI-AUTHORED BOOKS
Compassion
Thoughts on Cultivating a Good Heart

365 Meditations for Grandmothers

365 Meditations for Women

At Home with God
Family Devotions for the School Year

THE DEAD SAINT

A Bishop Lynn Peterson Novel

Marilyn Brown Oden

Western Reflections Publishing Company

All characters in this book are fictional and not meant to represent any real person.

Second Edition

ISBN: 978-1-937851-37-8

Cover Design by FluiDesigns, Steve Smith

Western Reflections Publishing Co.
P.O. Box 1149
Lake City, Colorado 81235

www:westernreflectionspublishing.com

In memory of
my father,
who gave me wings

PART I
The Sniper

Wednesday, 10:17 A.M.

Everything begins in mysticism
and ends in politics.
—Charles Peguy

1

AT 10:17 ON WEDNESDAY MORNING, THREE MINUTES BEFORE A BULLET whizzed through the French Quarter and severed her sheltered yesterdays from her sinister tomorrows, Bishop Lynn Peterson sat at her favorite outdoor table at Café du Monde. She was incognito behind sunglasses and dressed like a tourist in a teal knit shirt that matched her eyes, khaki walking shorts and sandals, with her black hair swooped up under a straw hat. She'd escaped her office to read over her lecture for the conference in Vienna. No phone calls. No "emergency" appointments. No interruptions. She smiled.

Lynn sipped *café au lait*, resisted the third *beignet* and listened to the calliope's happy tune drifting from a paddleboat on the river. Nearby a wannabe king of jazz improvised on soprano sax, playing the music like it should've been written. Feet tapped to the beat. She loved to sit here. Loved New Orleans. The city suited her.

She heard Bubba Broussard's laughter resound like a bass solo from half a block away. The six-five, 250-pound ProBowl linebacker for the New Orleans Saints ambled down Decatur Street, green polo shirt stretched over his biceps. Elias Darwish sauntered along beside him, the never-miss place kicker who hailed from Sarajevo and helped turn the "Aints" into the Saints. The two, built of rock-hard muscles and soft-touch hearts, often helped Lynn with benefits for kids in the Projects. Their friendship deepened while working together during the aftermath of Katrina. The Saints had also helped clean up after the BP oil spill. Elie and Bubba were heroes on and off the football field. Hurricane heroes abounded, but hoodlums stole the headlines. The renovated Superdome rose like a vivid symbol of hope: the Big Easy refused to become the Big Empty. The Saints had more at stake than winning now. They played for a city's soul. Katrina still spins in the shadows of our minds, thought Lynn, then we remember to forget.

Determined to remain incognito, she didn't go greet her friends. She felt secretive and didn't like the feeling. Another point for her lecture. She grabbed a napkin J. K. Rowling–style and scribbled quickly: Secrets make us sick. They do indeed, she thought, giving in to the third *beignet*.

Lynn scanned the buildings that told stories from another era. Ferns and ivy draped the fancy ironwork on their second-story galleries. Sunlight bounced off the triple steeples of St. Louis Cathedral. Banana trees guarded the gates to Jackson Park. A clown twisted bright balloons into animal shapes. Strangers from all parts of the world meandered along in a friendly fashion. No one worried. No one hurried. Only the red-wigged mime stood still, a human sculpture standing on a box, backed by the iron fence around the park.

Two little boys tap-danced on the slate sidewalk, the soles of their sneakers rigged with metal. A tourist eating a praline slowed to watch. His black leather fanny pack protruded from his paunch and pecan bits dropped on the camera that dangled around his neck. A teenager hustled him. "Betcha a dollar I can tell where you got them shoes." The tourist swerved to avoid him and stepped in front of a blue surrey. The bored mule cocked his head, tilting the red and yellow flowers in his straw hat.

A red light stopped traffic. One taxi raced through it. The second squealed to a halt. People strolled across Decatur, confetti in motion. Bubba and Elie crossed with the crowd. Bubba's laugh resounded like a bass fiddle with a melody solo. Lynn smiled, enjoying his joy.

Elie lurched. Grabbed his chest. Dropped to the street.

Bubba looked down. A growl of agony ripped from his throat. A woman screamed, and the crowd panicked.

Lynn ran toward them. Bubba knelt beside his friend. "Someone call 911!" Lynn put her hand on his shoulder and turned on her cell phone.

The Saints kicker lay still and silent. A circle of blood widened on his white T-shirt.

2

A MACHETE HAD SLICED THROUGH TIME, SEVERING IT INTO THE *BEFORE* and the *after*. As still as death Elias Darwish slept, his soccer foot splayed on the gritty, oil-slick street, his face distorted, his body twisted. Numb, Lynn stood beside Bubba with her hand still on his shoulder. He kept a soft running monologue near Elie's ear. If Elie could hear, he'd know Bubba's voice. If he opened his eyes, he'd see his face.

For an instant Bubba drew a few inches away and shook his head slowly. "I don't understand." Pain filled his James Earl Jones voice. He looked at Elie's broken neck chain. It hung loose, split by the bullet. He scanned the dirty street around them, and his big hand closed over something small and shiny. He clutched it in his fist.

The French Quarter police arrived on foot in minutes. The somber crowd stared silent and subdued, the carnival now a wake. A hundred onlookers had witnessed the crime. But no one knew what had happened. An image tugged at the edges of Lynn's mind—the red-wigged mime had disappeared.

It took a long time for the ambulance to make its way through the crowded, narrow streets. Too long. The paramedics bent over Elie. They glanced at each other, then put him on a stretcher and lifted him into the ambulance. Bubba stooped to climb through the rear doors.

"Sorry, mister." A paramedic slammed one door shut. "It's against the rules."

The linebacker glared at him and jerked it back open. The force jarred the ambulance.

"Careful, Bubba," called the driver. "You can ride up front with me." She thumbed toward the paramedic. "He's a Yankee. He doesn't understand that rules in New Orleans depend right much on the situation."

Bubba jumped in beside her. The siren blared and the ambulance pulled away.

A police officer shook his head. "They don't need the siren. That Saint is dead."

3

THE DENIZEN OF CHAOS SAT IN HIS DC OFFICE AT A MAHOGANY DESK, ITS black leather inset clutter-free. He wore a custom suit and shirt, initialed Tiffany cufflinks, a conservative silk tie, and gleaming Italian shoes. Two centuries of presidential memorabilia dominated the décor, a silent testament to his patriotism. The secure green phone rang. Green for *go*. *Stop* was not in his vocabulary. He clutched it in his long, El Greco fingers. The familiar voice spoke two words. "Problem solved."

"Good work, as expected." He punched *End*. Elias Darwish was dead. Tragic but necessary. He frowned and moved thoughtfully to the window. The sunless sky cloaked the city in gray. It matched his mood, for he preferred to avoid fatalities. Darwish would still be alive if he had not woven his own noose by connecting too many threads. An attempt to identify the Patriot was suicide. Not murder.

The *Patriot*. He smiled, fond of the self-dubbed sobriquet. It fits me, he thought. No American loves this country more than I do. No one stands straighter to salute Old Glory. Or mourns more deeply when her honor is spattered. *Patriot*. The word evoked an image of discipline and power—essentials in his highly complex *modus operandi*. Justice drove him. It had since his sixteenth birthday when his father was killed. It would always drive him. Words from Deuteronomy echoed in his ears: Justice and only justice, you shall pursue. One definition said it all: the quality of being righteous. He stood proud, a man of justice, a man of righteousness, a man of power.

He watched the people below scurry about importantly. Locals used cell phones and tourists aimed cameras. His charming public persona connected him to both groups. How stunned people would be to find that his persona masked the unrelenting fire of the Patriot's native forcefulness, a fierce desire to win at all costs, and the capacity to bring harm when needed—traits that served him well as a covert arms dealer, unidentified and unidentifiable. He thrilled at the challenge of this game of masks.

A rain cloud blew slowly across the sky, further darkening the view. He thought of chaos theory, recalling how a butterfly on one continent could flap its tiny wings at the right moment and create a disturbance that influenced the winds on another continent. Perhaps a butterfly in Brazil had caused this drifting cloud. He too could manipulate small disturbances that rippled into large ones. At first he had done this for the poor or, in another meaning of the word in Hebrew, for the *little people* of the earth, the ones discounted and overlooked. In time God rewarded him with a means to wealth: disturbances create a market for arms, and the destruction creates a market for new infrastructure. The more money he made, the greater his generosity and thus the wider his influence. His beneficence evoked trust and frequently bought respect and privilege from the politicos on both sides of the aisle. Feeding their egos and campaign funds gained him power for his righteous pursuit of justice.

He glanced down at the noontime traffic, then shifted his gaze to the Pentagon in the distance. He still seethed when he thought about Osama bin Laden's attack on the financial and military symbols of U.S. superiority. He had destroyed more than precious lives and prestigious buildings. He'd shattered the country's fearless self-image. Manifest destiny had been struck down. The Promised Land had lost its promise, at least temporarily. The country roamed through the wilderness of fear and suspicion, and he longed to be the new Moses. He hated bin Laden, but he had learned from him. Repugnant but necessary.

He gazed down again at the cars stalled in D.C. gridlock, drivers honking to no avail. No mental gridlock for him. Let those with less at stake practice the Golden Rule. He would live by the Platinum Rule: Zero tolerance. So . . . Darwish was dead. He shrugged, turned away from the window, and locked the door on remorse.

4

Lynn got off the streetcar that ran down the median of St. Charles Avenue. The late afternoon sun cut long shadows on sidewalk and soul. She climbed the steps of her episcopal residence, a Victorian home renovated after Katrina's assault. The house suited her: a white-railed veranda with friendly white rockers and hanging baskets of fuchsia bougainvillea, a welcoming door with a brass knocker, and large windows that filled the rooms with light. But this inviting image couldn't erase the big-screen view of Elias Darwish prone on the pavement.

The security alarm hummed as she entered. She punched in the code: *Twelve-ten.* December tenth. Precious Lyndie's birthday. A familiar bolt of pain stung her heart. We can guard against molesters and kidnappers but not car wrecks. Lyndie's death would always gash her soul. And Galen's too. Parents are supposed to die first.

She closed the door and leaned against it for a moment, almost paralyzed. The crystal vase on the table caught the sunlight, and the mirror doubled the dozen red roses that perfumed the entry hall. But it was the image of Elie that she saw.

Habit claimed her, and she shuffled through the letters and catalogues that lay in a heap below the mail slot. An American Express bill, a letter to Galen Peterson, Ph.D., and three for Bishop Lynn Prejean Peterson. The return address of one caught her eye: THE WHITE HOUSE. She held it like a treasured piece of Tiffany glass. President Helena Benedict was steering admirably through her bumpy first year, adroitly dodging stones cast by her opponents. Lynn had written her a note of appreciation and had asked the President's former pastor to send it to her directly. She hadn't expected a reply. She read President Benedict's letter through twice, astonished that it was not a computerized mass-produced reply but dealt directly with her comments.

Evidently she employs an excellent correspondence staff, Lynn.

She resented this annoying Inner Voice. I.V. *Ivy*, she'd dubbed it. The nickname gave her a sense of power and control over the voice. She liked the feeling and continued to bask in the illusion that the President herself had written the letter.

Again the image of Elie invaded her mind. Again habit prevailed. The same routine every afternoon: first the mail, then the voice messages. She stepped into the library to check the phone. She'd been careful not to convert the spacious room into a cluttered museum of relics and riches and egocentric evidence of honors. To a large extent the decorative aspects changed with the seasons. She took turns with some objects and rearranged the ones with special meaning or beauty. These changes prompted a fresh view, better than giving in to her expedient get-it-right-and-that's-done nature. The one exception was Lyndie's portrait in its prominent place on the mantle.

One message was from Fay Foster, her assistant, a talkative and loyal woman she'd grown to love:

> "Bishop Peterson, Fay here. I know this call isn't needed, but I want to do my duty and remind you of the banquet tonight at Windsor Court. It's unnecessary, I know—what with the Vice President speaking and you giving the invocation and all. You've probably known for weeks not only what you're going to say in your prayer but also what you're going to wear. I bet you're at the hairdresser's right now. Have fun tonight."

In the chaos Lynn had forgotten all about the banquet. Quickly she showered and washed her hair, savoring the scent of coconut shampoo—one of life's small pleasures before the machete falls. She put on makeup, conscious of the mess she'd made of her skin by being in the sun so much. Her friends had those beautiful southern complexions of smooth ivory or dark satin. Friends. Elie was dead. The tears came.

5

GALEN ARRIVED AS THE CLOCK CHIMED SIX. LYNN'S CONSECRATION AS A bishop had changed their lives. Some of the changes good. Others not so good. She was grateful that with their move had come Tulane's invitation for Galen to fill its most prestigious chair in the area of history. He often traveled with her across the pond, taking advantage of opportunities to participate in different cultures and do research in libraries all around the world. The years had grayed the temples of his sandy hair, but he retained a remarkable semblance of his USC quarterback physique. Intense brown eyes that pierced façades dominated his handsome face. Though he was fastidious about his appearance, she noted tonight that he could have been leaving for work instead of returning.

"Hi, Love." She zipped up the back of her black dress, realizing she'd eaten too much bread pudding since the last time she'd worn it.

A foot taller than she, he bent to kiss her. "What a day!"

What a day! she echoed mentally.

He tossed the *Times-Picayune* on the bed. "Faculty meeting. Translation: forum for pompous professors to exercise their predilection for pugnacity."

A scholar, she thought fondly, who enjoys alliteration and speaks English from an unabridged vocabulary.

He turned on TV and looked at her, his eyes sad. "Did you hear about Elie?"

She nodded. The dam that held back her feelings threatened to break.

The murder scene flashed on the news. "Lynn! That's you!"

She stuck her thumb in the dike, desperate to distance herself from reality. She had managed to hold herself together through the long aftermath of panic and police and reporters. She willed herself back into control.

"Did you go to the Quarter alone?" Her profession was hard on his Gentleman-of-the-South upbringing.

"I had to. No one called to hire me for a bodyguard."

He didn't laugh. "You were present when it happened!"

"But it was OK. The mime wasn't aiming at me."

"The mime?"

"There wasn't a butler." She fought the tears that would flood if the dam broke—and she would give the invocation with red, swollen eyes.

Vanity again, Lynn!

"Be serious. This is not a time for badinage."

"I was perfectly safe, Love."

"A sniper assassinated my friend in the proximity of my *wife*! I don't call that *perfectly safe*."

Her defenses nearly collapsed and she saw the scene again. Crawfish crawled through her stomach. She willed herself to focus on Galen.

"I see our speaker has arrived," he said as the local news switched to the Vice President's landing half an hour ago.

Lynn watched him wave at the cameras, armed with his propensity for appearing sincere. "We're sitting at the head table with him tonight."

"You'd have an enviable office if the stress didn't accompany the symbol."

"True," she agreed. "Isn't that John Adams in the background, Love?" He was a distinguished-looking man and a frequent guest on TV talk shows. Lynn had often heard him express pride that BarLothiun was a private company, allowing him the advantage of looking ahead long-term instead of having to satisfy investors quarterly.

"A man almost as well-known as the original John Adams."

"What an honor to be invited to ride with the Vice President!"

"I read somewhere that they're good friends." Galen turned from the TV and looked her over. "You are stunning tonight, as always. Bishop or no, you're still my raven-haired beauty with aquamarine eyes."

Raving-haired was more accurate in Louisiana humidity. Yet it felt good to hear that fond phrase from dating days. She wondered if today would widen the gray streak in her widow's peak.

That trait portends early widowhood, Lynn.

Ignoring obtrusive Ivy, she reminded herself that she didn't believe in superstitions. But the machete came to mind. "I love you, Galen."

He put his arms around her. "I don't know what I'd do if something happened to you."

"It won't. Life with you is too interesting to miss." She nestled against him, savoring his protective embrace, which kept the world's chaos at bay. The phone broke the precious moment.

He answered with his customary, "Petersons' residence. Galen speaking." . . . "Yes." . . . He listened, looking puzzled, and finally replied, "We would be honored." He hung up, still staring at the phone.

"Who was it?"

"Vice President Parker's staffer. She said he would like for us to ride with him to the airport after the banquet. He wants an opportunity to speak with us."

6

The evening at Windsor Court began with paying the taxi driver, followed by Galen's refusal to walk up to the twenty-third floor as Lynn wished. She wondered how anyone as logical as Dr. Peterson could trust little cords to hold crowded elevators and ski lifts! He was wrong. She didn't have a phobia, merely sound judgment.

The chef stood proud in his spotless whites and announced the five-course menu like a diva offering an aria dedicated to the Vice President. The feast raised the bar even by New Orleans standards, placing the after-dinner speaker in the awkward position of being anticlimactic. A drizzle of rain pattered against the windows during the mayor's long, egotistical introduction. When he finally released the dais, Vice President Parker thanked him and asked for the personal privilege of inviting John Adams to stand. "You who suffered so much from Katrina know firsthand that many contracts to rebuild the infrastructure of New Orleans were a fiasco. You also know that those given to BarLothiun, under the leadership of John Adams, always met the timelines and there was not a single accusation of wasting taxpayer dollars." Spontaneous applause resounded. "We all know that BarLothiun steers clear of lobbies. Every government contract it has received is because it offered the lowest bid. I invited John to come with me tonight because of all he did for New Orleans after Katrina." When the second round of applause ended, the Vice President told a joke and began his address.

Galen pulled out his BlackBerry and took abbreviated notes, a habitual custom. The speech concluded with an expected standing ovation for the Vice President and an unexpected text message for Galen. It was from Tulane's president, Thomas Turner, via Fay Foster, who, though Lynn's assistant, congenially helped Galen also when needed: You are needed immediately at Tulane University Hospital. It is an emergency regarding one of your students.

He told Lynn about it while texting Fay his thanks for helping him.

"You're leaving now, Love?" Even as she asked, she knew the answer. His students always took precedence. No exceptions. Not even an invitation from the Vice President.

"I trust Tom's judgment," said Galen. He offered his apologies to Vice President Parker, who said something Lynn couldn't hear. Galen nodded and turned back to her. "He'll have a car take you home from the airport."

7

AS LYNN HURRIED OUT WITH A SECRET SERVICE AGENT, SHE FELT PARTY to intrigue in a surreal world. The agent rushed her through back halls to the alleyway off Tchoupitoulas and provided an umbrella as she scooted into the black limousine. She waited in the dim light to the soft sound of Mozart and the smell of leather. Thunder rumbled its anger over Elie's murder, and the sky rained tears of mourning upon the city.

As soon as Vice President Parker arrived, the motorcade pulled out. Escort sirens blared, adding shrieking soprano to thunderous bass. He campaign-poster smiled in the dimmed interior lights invisible to the outside world. "Thank you for riding to the airport with me, Bishop Peterson."

"I am honored, Mr. Vice President. Galen regretted being called away."

"It was necessary." Mozart's *Symphony in G Minor* rose in the background. "The President asked me to convey her greetings to you. She appreciated your kind note."

Startled that he knew she'd written, Lynn mumbled, "I received a gracious reply."

"I suppose you know that the President and her husband are members of your denomination?"

"Yes, sir."

"She recalls meeting you on a campaign stop here in New Orleans. She is aware of the significant international work you and Dr. Peterson have done, especially in Russia."

Stunned again, Lynn said nothing.

He smiled, this time natural and easy, warmer than the poster smile. "You are surprised. She surprises many people."

The lights around the Superdome reflected in the drizzle as they passed by. "The home of the Saints," he noted. "I was told that one was killed today."

Lynn remembered vividly. Too vividly.

"A kicker, I understand."

"The best. Elias Darwish from Sarajevo."

"Did you know him?"

"Yes, sir." The symphony filled the silence that followed. She felt scrutinized.

"Your note mentioned that you and Dr. Peterson are going to the Balkans on a peace fact-finding mission. Are you afraid?"

"Somewhat." With a grin she added, "But I have to go to protect Galen."

No grin from him. "The current trouble there was predictable. Dysfunction perpetuates itself. But you know that—you've done work in Russia."

"Yes, sir."

"And you wrote a book about the experience."

"Yes, sir." Is there anything he doesn't know?

"You and your husband both graduated from Harvard. He has a doctorate in history and you in theology."

"Yes, sir." She didn't talk about that and certainly hadn't put it in the letter. She'd found that both "Harvard" and "doctorate" could be barriers to building relationships with others.

"Russia is not the only country where you have met with national leaders. South Korea, China, Israel and Palestine, and Zimbabwe, for example. Is that correct?"

She nodded, puzzled. He'd probably used plane time to study the brief on prominent people attending the banquet, but she'd only given the invocation. These details were unlikely part of any briefing; none of that was in her letter to President Benedict.

"You've also met with religious leaders from Judaism and Islam as well as Pope Benedict, the Archbishop of Canterbury and the Dalai Lama. Also correct?"

She nodded again and answered her earlier question: No. There is nothing he doesn't know about me.

"You have participated in peace delegations in the Middle East and the earlier Balkan conflict. You've been in some forty countries and on five continents. Also correct, Bishop Peterson?"

"Yes, sir."

He began talking faster, evidently feeling hurried. "When you leave the country Saturday, you will have a stopover in Frankfurt and connect to Vienna for the International Conference of Bishops? I understand that you are the keynote speaker."

Absolutely nothing he doesn't know. "Yes, sir." The phrase was beginning to sound robotic.

"President Nausner has invited the delegates to a reception Monday afternoon."

She didn't understand his obsession with their itinerary, but she wanted to be helpful. "Ambassador Whitcomb has invited some of us to dinner that evening."

"And you leave the next day for Skopje."

She nodded, beginning to feel wary about all his information. Maybe she shouldn't be so helpful.

He leaned forward and lowered his voice almost to a whisper. "Let's speak hypothetically, Bishop Peterson. Suppose a president became concerned about an emerging pattern in which the receipt of confidential information was followed by heightened chaos and conflict in those very areas. Suppose a president, therefore, began to suspect breaches of trust at high levels."

Lynn sat absolutely still, barely disturbing the air to breathe.

"Under those circumstances a president might feel compelled to avoid official channels in certain situations and, therefore, desire the aid of an outside volunteer."

Lynn stared at him.

"For a safe task, of course," he added quickly. "Say, as a letter courier, for example."

"The President must be desperate."

"Remember that I am speaking hypothetically. This volunteer would have to be someone with integrity who travels around the world for nonpolitical and noneconomic reasons. Someone who has no vested interest except the common good. And, above all, someone totally trustworthy."

"Your hypothetical situation seems to have a hypothetical Galen in it."

He hesitated. "Dr. Peterson does have those characteristics. What if he were asked to assist the President? Do you think he should?"

"Absolutely."

"Thank you, Bishop Peterson," he said as they turned in at the terminal. "However, that is not what the President has in mind."

She felt relieved that Galen wasn't going to be involved, yet even more puzzled by this strange encounter.

"I want to remind you that the purpose of my visit is to bring you and Dr. Peterson the President's greetings and appreciation. The hypothetical part of this conversation will, I trust, remain confidential."

"Certainly, sir."

His eyes held hers in the dim light. "Totally confidential. For your ears only."

The motorcade stopped, and the Vice President's poster-smile returned. "You see, it isn't the good historian the President has in mind. It's the good bishop. Lynn Prejean Peterson." He thrust an envelope into her hand and stepped out of the car.

8

LYNN DASHED UP THE VERANDA STEPS IN THE RAIN, STILL STUNNED. MAKING out Galen's form in the darkness, she flopped in the rocker beside him. They both liked to sit outside during storms and watch the rain dance with the city lights. "I'm surprised you beat me home, Love."

"The message was fake."

"*Fake?*"

"Tom didn't leave it. There was no hospital emergency."

"That's weird."

"Maybe it was just a sick prank, Lynn."

"But why?" As lightning streaked, she saw the why. The call kept Galen from riding to the airport. The Vice President's words echoed through the rain: It was necessary.

Stop it, Lynn. This is real life, not a Ludlum novel.

He released a sigh. "What did I miss?"

"Vice President Parker was very nice." She started to pull the unopened envelope from her purse. Again his words echoed: *Totally confidential.*

"And?"

And what? How much should I say? The boards creaked in rocker rhythm as the rain pattered against the sidewalk. The scent of the river thickened the air.

"Lynn?"

She hedged. "He said President Benedict respects our work in the global community."

"She knows about us?" he asked, astonished.

"Especially our work in Russia. I'm sorry you didn't get to hear the compliment personally. Also, she appreciated my note."

"That's all? He invited us to ride to the airport simply to express thanks?"

The rocker creaks ticked off seconds of silence. She wanted to tell him the whole strange story. *For your ears only.*

"Lynn?" This time impatience edged his voice.

She debated telling Galen despite the warning. A safe task, being a letter courier. But *courier* will ring louder than *safe* and he'll drive me crazy worrying about me. If I don't say anything now, I always can later. But if I do, I can't ever unsay it. In the zigzag of lightning she scanned the face she loved so much and reached the end of her debate: if a problem occurs, I don't want him connected with it. Forcing a light tone, she asked, "Would you like a direct quote, Love?" She deepened her voice to imitate the Vice President: "The purpose of my visit is to bring you the President's greetings and appreciation." Galen seemed satisfied with that, but she didn't feel good about it. He trusted her.

Until this moment you were trustworthy, Lynn.

Technically I didn't lie, she argued back to Ivy.

You're hang gliding across a chasm of deceit.

It was a new experience to be less than honest with this man whose touch could uncloud her sky. She didn't like herself right now. It had been a terrible day. She reached up and brushed her forefinger across a bloom of bougainvillea, wishing its scent and soft petals could sooth her shredded soul.

A car approached, not unusual on busy St. Charles. But this one slowed down. It was too dark to tell what kind. Its lights flipped to bright. Raindrops bounced off the hood like silver confetti falling upward. Last night she wouldn't even have noticed. But last night she lived in a different world, one wrapped snugly in the illusion of tranquility.

Her cell phone rang. As she pulled it from her purse, her fingers brushed against the envelope. She winced at keeping it from Galen. Secrets make us sick. "Hello."

"Bishop Lynn?"

No problem recognizing that James Earl Jones voice. "Hello, Bubba."

"I wouldn't call so late, but I'm driving by and saw you and Galen on the veranda."

"Come join us. I'll make some coffee."

"I just left the Feds." His voice shook with rage. "They accused me of setting Elie up!"

9

THEY SAT IN THE DEN AT THE ROUND OAK TABLE THAT HAD BELONGED to Lynn's great-grandmother. The yellow roses in the center matched the walls. Usually a cheery room, tonight it picked up the negative energy of distress. Lynn reached around Bubba's immense, rain-dampened shoulders to pour his coffee, averting her eyes from the dark stain on his green polo shirt. The FBI hadn't even had the decency to let him change it!

Bubba circled the coffee beneath his nose, inhaling its aroma, and smiled at her. "Thank you." He took a sip and released a weary sigh.

"I'm glad you came by tonight," said Galen sympathetically. He was good at opening doors to whatever a friend needed to say.

Bubba's anger rested just beneath the surface. "How could the Feds think I . . ." He struggled for control.

Galen put his hand on the linebacker's shoulder. "Everyone in Louisiana knows the name Bubba Broussard is synonymous with character above reproach."

"But these Neanderthals aren't from Louisiana. I wanted to sack the—"

Talking to a bishop self-censors people from their most satisfying expletives, Lynn.

This time she agreed with Ivy.

"Chief Armstrong told me killing a Saint ranks right up there with killing a cop. He's like a mama gator trying to protect her nest. And me."

It was hard for Lynn to grasp that this tough Pro-Bowler needed protection.

He ran his palm across his shaved head. "I've replayed it again and again. We were on our way to autograph toy footballs for the Orthodox Church benefit."

"I saw the article in the *Times-Picayune*," said Galen. "Anyone who read the paper knew where to find Elie this morning."

"We just wanted to help folks. Now—" his voice cracked.

Lynn reached over and touched his hand. She wished for a way to comfort this large, in charge, no-nonsense man. Wished for more than worn-out words. Wished most of all that she had the power to erase this tragic day.

Bubba regained control. "You were there, Bishop Lynn. Did you see anything?"

"It happened too fast."

"She has a theory, though." Galen grinned. "The mime did it." His effort to lighten the mood failed. "I remember the last Saints game. All the fans looking down from the stands as he drew back his magic foot and kicked a 53-yard field goal. Electrifying!"

Lynn nodded. "The last time I was with him he taught me some Serbo-Croatian for the Balkans. What patience!"

"Why would anyone want to hurt him?" Bubba's voice sounded shallow, the words traveling around a knot in his throat.

Silence followed his poignant question. Lynn rose to pour more coffee, struck by the human capacity for savagery. It sickened her.

Galen glanced at his watch. "Time for the news. Maybe there's an update." He turned on TV and caught the lead story:

> "We take you now to Chief Martin Luther Armstrong of the New Orleans Police Department for a live report on the Kicker Case."

"The Kicker Case!" Lynn groaned. May that cutesy caption writer spend eternity scribbling it on the walls of purgatory!

Chief Armstrong, promoted from the ranks for his heroism after Katrina, stood confident before the cameras, as smooth and hard as a stone washed up from the river.

> "I pledge to keep the citizens of New Orleans informed about every step of the investigation into the murder of Elias Darwish, a hero on the football field and a role model for youth. He will always have an honored place in our hearts. Late this afternoon one of our friends from the homeless community in the French Quarter gave us an important lead. While rummaging through a trashcan in Jackson Park, he found a plastic bag that contained white gloves with powder burns. He gave them to a police officer he trusts in case they were connected to the murder. He has asked for a reward: three hots and a cot in an unlocked cell." A slight smile played at the corner of his lips.

Galen chuckled. "Knowing the chief, his 'friend from the homeless community' will get that free room and board."

Chief Armstrong held up a red wig and a white stretch mask with red circles on the cheeks. The camera zoomed in for a close-up.

Startled, Lynn leaned forward in her chair. "The mime wore those!"

> "The bag also contained this wig and mask. We believe the killer posed as a mime until Darwish came by, then shot him and scaled the Jackson Square fence."

Galen looked at her with surprise. "You were right, Lynn!"

"Then," she said aloud to herself, "he pitched his disguise and faded into the crowd. Ambling away. Or standing in the crowd to watch the aftermath." Little green lizards skittered up her spine.

"How did you know?"

"A hunch, Bubba. I walked past him on my way to Café du Monde. He had the hardest eyes I've ever seen—like cold gray marbles. After the . . ." The words wouldn't come. "While we were waiting for the ambulance, I noticed he was missing."

The chief leaned in toward the camera, speaking personally to each listener.

> "I want to assure each of you that nobody robs the good folks of Orleans Parish of one of our favorite sons and gets away with it! Finding his murderer is the NOPD's top priority."

The station cut to a commercial with a promise to return for live updates as the case progressed.

"The brother does a good job on TV." Bubba paused thoughtfully. "So do you, Bishop Lynn. I saw that interview about your peace trip to the Balkans. You mentioned Sarajevo. Are you still going? With all the escalation?"

She nodded. "The invitation was an intelligence test. We both flunked."

Bubba's laugh had a hole in it. "Be careful," he said soberly. "That's a dangerous place."

The image of Elie lying in the street filled Lynn's mental screen. "Apparently, so is the Quarter."

10

ON THURSDAY MORNING THE SUN ROSE IN A SPECTACLE OF MAUVE AND mango, lilac and lapis. The colors changed like a dance of veils. Lynn watched the performance through the semicircle of east windows in her study, a small room nestled in the second-story turret. Favorite books and photos of loved ones lined the shelves. Last night's envelope from the limo ride rested on her lap, still sealed, enticing her toward a strange new doorway.

One that might slam closed and lock behind you, Lynn.

She willed her mind to ignore Ivy and the envelope's distraction and began the day in her favorite way—silently centering herself, trying to stay grounded in a slippery society. A challenge any day but especially today, for the sun rose on a scarier world than yesterday. Just *yesterday*?

She poured a cup of green tea from the calico pot, the steam rising aromatically. She watched the small stream hit her blue teacup with a dainty splash. She'd chosen blue because Luwuh, an eighth-century Chinese poet, considered it the ideal color as it lent additional greenness to the tea. And he should know—famous for formulating the Code of Tea in *Chaking*. She took a sip and set the teacup on the glass-topped coffee table beside the white roses. They were her favorite flowers because they bloomed in the midst of thorns and offered a fragrance almost holy.

The table doubled as a display case for vanity. It held her certificates and mementos, her writings regarding the church, trinkets symbolizing honors. She'd left an empty space, book-sized, in the corner. A silly thing to do, but it symbolized her secret dream: writing a novel. Someday, when she had time. She'd completed the first and only word: *Secrets*. The display case was a private vanity since no one else saw it, but vanity nonetheless. Vanity, she thought, my worst habit of the heart. Some would say sin, but she'd deleted *sin* from her vocabulary. Sin led to guilt and guilt led to dysfunction. A habit, on the other hand, could be changed. It left room for hope.

As always, she focused for a few minutes on precious Lyndie at sixteen, the final photograph of their only child, whose smile brought the light of dawn. Taken from them yet always with them. Each morning at sunrise she held Lyndie in her heart while the silence played a symphony of cherished memories. Each year on Lyndie's birthday she added another candle to an imaginary cake and tried to add another year to her image, wondering what she would be like at this new age, nineteen now. Sometimes Lynn felt tossed about in an eternal sea of grief. Occasionally, she was strong enough to let the celebration of Lyndie's life overshadow the agony of its brevity. Evagrius, the wise fourth-century analyst of the human soul, came to mind this morning as he often did in these circumstances. She understood what he meant when he said that despair is rooted in the sacrifice of the past life for the present one.

She poured a second cup of tea, recalling Luwuh's words: The first cup moistens my lips and throat, the second cup breaks my loneliness. She sank back into the white wicker settee, curled up her legs on the dawn-colored cushions, and faced the envelope left by Vice President Parker. She'd been too drained to deal with it after Bubba left late last night. The envelope appeared harmless. No return address in gold ink. No presidential seal. No addressee in fancy script. No watermark of fine paper. It reminded her of the common envelopes at Walgreen's.

She picked it up. An ordinary item with an extraordinary impact. It seemed to generate its own heat, like an omen. "Oh, Lyndie." Her monologues with her precious daughter were common in this snug space so filled with her presence. "I dread opening it."

Rightly so, Lynn. It could lead you down an irreversible path to things you don't want to know and places you don't want to go.

Sometimes Ivy irritated her. Sometimes she offered wisdom, like now. But Lynn's curiosity won. As always. Inch by inch, her faltering hands unsealed the envelope. Fine splits tore along the flap demonstrating that this common envelope was not common at all, for it showed any attempt to open it. She heard the sound of her breathing and the pumping of her heart. Done!

She looked inside. "No white powder, Lyndie. No anthrax." Just another plain envelope, also unaddressed. She opened it also and found two items: a third envelope and a folded piece of paper. She knew without knowing that it would launch her into a new space. Her fingers trembled as she unfolded the brief note. It was handwritten in caps in an unnatural style.

Thank You in Advance for Delivering
This Letter To My Friend Marsh (With Nato)
At The Frankfurt International Airport When
You Change Planes For Vienna.

Nothing in it appeared clandestine. Nothing aroused suspicion. A common note without a signature. All she had to do was watch for a man named Marsh during their Frankfurt layover and give him the envelope. Simple enough. She was so relieved she almost felt disappointed.

How will you recognize this Marsh with NATO in a crowded airport, Lynn?

A worrisome question. She read the note again, recalling the Vice President's knowledge of her itinerary. How did they know it? What else do they know? She imagined a surveillance camera aimed at her windows and fought the impulse to pull the drapes. She decided to destroy the note like a good spy in a John le Carré novel.

She tore it into tiny slivers and flushed them down the toilet, watching them swirl away to the sewer. My first act as a courier, she thought, feeling sneaky instead of patriotic. She didn't like the feeling. Secrets make us sick.

"Well, Lyndie, how is that for being overdramatic!" She visualized her daughter smiling and wagging her head.

Her cell phone rang. She jumped like a criminal caught destroying evidence. "Hello."

"Bishop Lynn, this is Bubba." He skipped the customary Southern detour through preliminaries. "I've been thinking about something and have a favor to ask."

"Name it, you have it."

"Do you have any time this morning?"

Her photographic memory pictured her calendar. She could adjust her schedule until eleven. "Sure, Bubba, but I have to be at a meeting at eleven."

"Is nine too soon?"

"That's fine."

"Shall I come by?"

You know where you need to meet him, Lynn.

Against every instinct to the contrary, she named the place. His question. Her answer. Silence. Reluctant agreement.

Before she went downstairs, she hid President Benedict's envelope in a drawer like a good courier.

How do you know it's really from the President, Lynn?

11

THE MIDMORNING SUN STREAMED THROUGH THE OPEN, GRAY-TONED drapes and fell across the tidy surface of the Patriot's desk. He thought about his Platinum Rule of zero tolerance as he listened again to the recent phone conversation on President Benedict's secure line. *Secure!* Within a month of her election, his elite on the inside, code-named Lone Star, had provided him access to *all* of her communications. He smiled to himself, then frowned. Stealing another's privacy was a grave matter. Grave but necessary.

The President of the United States was the most powerful person in the world and therefore, he thought, the most dangerous. Unfortunately the power of this POTUS, like all the others, exceeded her judgment. He hadn't known what to expect from the first woman to hold that office, but it surprised him to find her to be less compliant than her predecessors. She discounted the basic principle of career politics: The top priority is reelection. Mind the money. It gave her unprecedented freedom from lobbyists and nonprofit foundations like his. She seemed willing to sacrifice the pragmatism of self-interest for the idealism of the common good. Her naiveté or altruism—he had yet to decide which—complicated his life, and he didn't like it. Or her. But, of course, he wouldn't show it.

What troubled him most at the moment, however, was finding Darwish's surreptitious report, if it existed. Over the years the Patriot had supplemented his D.C. contacts with a cadre of a dozen international specialists. World-class in their fields—and in their pay. For where your treasure is, there your heart will be also. Snipers. Bomb experts. Investigators. Tech prodigies. He founded his elite system on three immutable precautions: One, no one was permitted to know the Patriot's identity nor the identity or codename of anyone else in the cadre. Two, no one had access to more than one piece of the puzzle in any operation. Three, they were never given related assignments where their paths might cross. Since they knew nothing, they could reveal nothing. He also used totally separate and untraceable communication with each member of the elite team. Sometimes, as with the Darwish information, these essential precautions forced him to step outside his cadre and deal with less able people, even unsavory men like Cabrioni. Unpleasant but necessary.

Cabrioni's best man had beaten the FBI to Darwish's apartment and had searched it thoroughly. *Neat and complete*, Cabrioni had reported on the secure phone message. No computer. No flash drives. No names. No dates. Nothing. As clean as my daddy's liquor cabinet after Mama cleared it out when he died—God rest his soul.

Was Cabrioni lying? He wouldn't dare. *No one* betrayed the Patriot. Zero tolerance. He smiled. His exaggerated reputation gave him power beyond his means. Swiveling his chair toward the credenza, he rubbed his fingers across the cool bronze bust of John F. Kennedy. Many citizens continued to wonder whether the New Orleans Mafia was connected to JFK's assassination. That was understandable. How could a misfit with a twelve-dollar rifle from a mail-order catalogue take down the President of the United States! A Mafia conspiracy seemed more reasonable. He suspected that the Society of St. Sava knew the truth and guarded the secret both carefully and advantageously.

He also suspected that Elias Darwish was a member of St. Sava, his football career merely a cover. The Patriot's search for verification produced nothing. Yet the lack of proof itself was proof enough. Even the CIA had been unable to link anyone with St. Sava or, for that matter, find any concrete evidence of its existence. Invisibility was the trademark of the ancient secret society.

The bust of Kennedy faced toward Ronald Reagan's, appropriate pieces for the presidential décor of his office. They perched on tall stands at opposite ends of the credenza. A *fleur-de-lis* was carved on the front of each upper panel. The stands looked identical. But when he rubbed his thumb across the *fleur-de-lis* on JFK's stand, the panel dropped into the base, revealing bins for secure phones and SIM cards, passports, foreign cash, and a small secure laptop and flash drives.

His mind turned again to Darwish's information. Though nothing had been found, the existence of a report continued to haunt him. Someone wanted it! Had Darwish memorized the information, fearful of recording it? Fearful of the risk of someone finding evidence that he was more than a football player? Had he planned to deliver it personally? If so, he was a fool! A dead fool stopped in time.

An unwelcome question rose from his viscera and throbbed through his blood. Could Elias Darwish have been innocent? Unthinkable! He shook off the question and returned to the matter at hand.

He listened once more to the President's call to the Secretary of Defense. It seemed innocuous. Her request for a personal favor was not noteworthy. Neither was her desire to protect Lynn Peterson, a bishop in Benedict's denomination who was headed into harm's way in the Balkans. Nor was her specific request for Major Marshall Manetti, because, as she explained in her overheard words, He's a practicing Catholic and likely to be both respectful and comfortable around a bishop. He listened carefully for strain in her voice and found none.

But why did she use the secure line to make the call?

He intended to find out. But it would have to wait. Right now he had to prepare his strategy for the afternoon meeting. With a sigh he automatically straightened his red tie and faced the public side of his divided world. This afternoon he would don his charming public persona and join the Inner Circle at the Oval Office.

12

Lynn arrived before Bubba at Café du Monde. It was essential to return to Jackson Square. The sooner, the better. They had refused to let Katrina's tantrum force them from New Orleans, and no sniper's bullet would chase them from the Quarter!

The aura of déjà vu enshrouded her. She glanced at the corner backed by the fence where the mime had stood yesterday. Chilled despite the heat, she shuddered and locked her arms together across her chest. Her eyes carefully avoided the pavement where Elie fell.

Today was like every day in the Quarter. Nothing was different. *Everything* was different.

Cy Bill Bergeron, a mounted policeman, rode down St. Peter. He was another Katrina hero and one of the NOPD's most respected officers. He cut a dashing figure, wearing a black uniform from head to toe, sitting tall on his dark, shiny Percheron. Strong and agile like his rider, Ebony stood seventeen hands and weighed nearly a ton. Centuries ago his breed was ridden by knights in combat, and Lynn could visualize both Cy Bill and Ebony charging forth in chain mail. They knew how to put on a show just crossing the street. She wished he'd been patrolling Jackson Square yesterday morning. If anyone could have prevented the shooting, it was Cy Bill astride Ebony. At the very least, the mime wouldn't have escaped.

She saw Bubba in the distance, walking down Decatur like yesterday. But not like yesterday at all. He walked alone, head down, shoulders sagging. She knew that each painful step took far more courage than any feat on the football field. Cy Bill turned Ebony up Decatur toward the linebacker. He dismounted, leading his horse, and walked along beside Bubba. Folks need company on painful journeys.

"Hello, Bishop Lynn."

Lynn turned to the petite server, a porcelain doll in her white apron and cap with CAFE DU MONDE in green letters. "Good morning, Yoo-Sei."

She smiled and turned her head, pointing to the barrette Lynn had brought to her from her native Seoul. The hand-painted hibiscus looked lovely fastened around her long dark hair. "This is my favorite," she said in careful English.

"I'm glad you like it. I appreciated your teaching me those tricky Korean inflections before we went." Lynn smiled at her. "A friend's help makes all the difference."

"*Café au lait* and *beignets?*"

"Please."

"Make it two," said Bubba.

"How about three, Cy Bill?" Lynn asked. "Can you join us?"

"You know I'd love to. But I have to keep moving." Ebony came to attention as he remounted, his eyes looking into their souls. "I'm glad to see you both back in the Quarter." Touching the brim of his black hat, he nodded and moved on, the horseshoes clicking sharply along the street.

Bubba folded like an accordion into the chrome chair, shrinking it to child size.

Yoo-Sei's dark eyes grew large as she recognized the Saints star linebacker. "Please, Mr. Bubba Broussard, would you sign a napkin for me?"

"My pleasure." His haggard face and downcast eyes contradicted his smile.

Holding the autographed napkin as proudly as an Oscar, she hurried off for the order.

After passable Southern niceties, Bubba came to the point. "Before we get to the favor I mentioned, I want to thank you again for inviting me for coffee last night."

"We're always happy to see you, Bubba."

"When I got home, I had the strangest feeling that someone had been there."

"Oh, Bubba! You didn't need that. Not yesterday."

"Nothing was missing, and nothing specifically seemed disturbed. But . . ." He brushed his palm across his head. "I don't know."

"It wasn't quite right? I know that feeling."

"I wondered if the Feds searched my condo while detaining me. Or if someone was there connected to Elie's . . ." He lowered his eyes and shook his head, leaving the word unsaid.

An unrushed silence followed.

She didn't break it. He would say more when he was ready.

"Now, about that favor, Bishop Lynn." He opened his hand and revealed a medal.

She remembered the chain split by the bullet and the shiny object she'd seen Bubba pick up.

"Elie never took this off. I knew he'd reach for it first thing when he became conscious. And I'd be there with it, right beside him."

Yoo-Sei brought their order. Bubba closed his hand.

Lynn moved the napkin holder from the center of the small table to give her room and thanked her, "*Kamsahamnida.*" To simplify remembering the courtesy, she thought of it as two words—*kamsa hamnida*.

"Good accent, Bishop Lynn." She flashed a shy, admiring glance toward Bubba and turned away.

He opened his large palm again. The medal rested there as cherished as an infant in a cradle. For a moment they stared at it in silence, poignantly aware of Elie's presence in his absence. Two gemstones formed a pair of linked crescents like waning moons in the center of a silver circle. They slightly overlapped, one above the other. At first glance the gemstones looked sea green, but a closer view showed tones of mottled green and blue streaked with white. The unique medal drew her like a portent, triggering something in the mist of memory.

A man in opaque sunglasses caught her eye as he passed by their table. He carried a newspaper and black canvas bag to the corner table at the back. His navy T-shirt and jeans blended in with the relaxed camaraderie of the crowd. His demeanor drew her attention, not his clothes. He exuded intimidation. His brow was creased in a permanent frown, and his thin lips drew a tight line above his square jaw. Lynn's trusted yellow flag waved. Automatically she clicked a mental picture and filed it under *C* for caution.

13

BUBBA TOOK A SIP OF *CAFÉ AU LAIT* AND SET HIS MUG DOWN. HE TURNED Elie's medal over and ran his finger across an engraving on the back. "I wonder what it says."

The tough linebacker's tenderness pulled at Lynn's heartstrings. She peered thoughtfully at the letters. "It's his name."

"You can read that?"

"Not really. But I learned the Cyrillic alphabet for a visit to Russia, and I can figure out words." She smiled. "It's their meanings that stump me."

"You are amazing, Bishop Lynn."

She shrugged. "Not amazing. Just cursed with curiosity."

"Did you know that Elie's mama lives in Sarajevo? He told me she spent a good while in a refugee center."

"I visited a lot of those centers when I was there before. Not a pretty memory. War is only glamorous in fiction."

"He was sure his daddy ended up in a mass grave."

"Most of the women refugees had lost husbands, sons, fathers. I've been in some scary situations. But nothing like Bosnia." The sounds and sights vividly returned. "I can still hear the shelling and the roar of planes carrying bombs. Galen and I would eat lunch in the mess tent with soldiers and then watch them load into tanks and head into harm's way. And it wasn't a movie. It was real." Even now, just talking about it tensed her stomach and raced her heart.

"It's bad over there again. Aren't you afraid?"

"Yes. But there's also a sense of peace. It was the same way last time." Fear wrapped in peace—a puzzling and illogical reality.

"Elie sent his mama money regularly, but she didn't always get it. He said it's common for them to steal foreign mail." Bubba looked away. "He always hoped to bring her here." Grief enshrouded his words.

"My heart aches for her. Both her husband and her son." She thought of precious Lyndie and felt the familiar bolt of pain.

Stay in the present, Lynn.

"I've taken the long way 'round to ask the favor. It might not be possible, and I'll understand if you can't. But while you're in Sarajevo, would you try to find her and give her Elie's medal?"

"I can't do much for Mrs. Darwish, but I can at least do that."

When? Your schedule is too tight, Lynn. And how would you find her in the Balkan chaos?

Butt out, Ivy! "I promise, Bubba," she vowed. He passed the medal over with reverence. Its greenish-bluish crescents jogged her mind once more but still remained a mystery.

"Thank you." His eyes misted and he lowered them, fumbling to pull out his wallet, giving himself time to regain control. He removed five one-hundred-dollar bills. "I hope this will help her out until his affairs are settled."

"How thoughtful and generous." Typical of Bubba.

"I wrote her a note. Maybe someone can translate it." He folded the bills and put them inside.

Since Lynn avoided carrying a purse in the Quarter, she stuffed Bubba's bulging note in her skirt pocket, wrapped the medal in a paper napkin, and put it in the other pocket. A feeling of being watched swept over her. She glanced toward the stranger in opaque sunglasses. He appeared to be reading the newspaper. She tried to dismiss the feeling: more people know me than I realize, so it isn't uncommon to be recognized and observed. Besides, every Saints fan in New Orleans can identify Bubba Broussard. Her logic failed.

Alert and uneasy, she stood to leave. "When Galen and I return, I'll tell you all about Elie's mother."

"And you *will* return," he said, unfolding from the chrome chair. "Even this sinner will pray for that."

"You look like one of the Saints to me, Bubba." She reached up and hugged her friend goodbye. As she wove around the crowded tables, she glanced again at the man in the corner, her yellow flag still flying. The dark glasses that hid his eyes aimed at her. She moved her mental file on him from *C* for caution to *D* for danger.

Zigzagging through the tourists, Lynn headed for the corner of Canal and Carondelet to catch the St. Charles streetcar. Concerned about Bubba's money in her pocket, she walked fast but not fast enough to attract attention. New York was the place to rush, not New Orleans. A long line waited to board and pay as number 921 drew up. A new driver watched people clink exact change into the slot.

"Where's Louie?" she asked.

"He called in sick."

"I hope it isn't serious."

He winked. "Good fishing on the Atchafalaya today."

She laughed and found an empty seat midway. It was faster to ride than drive in the traffic and find a parking place in the Quarter. But today heat and humidity encapsulated the crowded streetcar like a natural sauna. Fumes from the traffic drifted through the open windows. But she enjoyed riding it—a big red flowerbox on wheels bursting with human blooms of all colors. Weary of intrigue, she lowered her yellow flag to half-mast.

Suddenly, an iron-strong hand grabbed the closing door. He squeezed his broad shoulder through and shoved till he forced it open. The stranger in sunglasses stepped aboard. Once again his opaque lenses aimed toward her.

14

THE STRANGER CLAIMED THE AISLE. NECK RIGID. JAW TIGHT. BLACK CANvas bag over his shoulder. People stepped aside. He advanced toward Lynn and took the seat directly behind her.

Her yellow flag turned red. She couldn't see him, but she could feel him, like rays of negative energy. The hackles rose on the back of her neck. She slumped down in the wooden seat, feigning invisibility.

You're not invisible, Lynn. Pretending to be isn't helpful.

True. She took a deep breath. Tried to calm herself. She stood to get off as they reached the next stop. He stood also. She sat back down. He moved into the aisle and gestured to a standing woman to take his seat, continuing to stand behind Lynn's seat.

She decided to ride the streetcar until at least one stop after he got off. To the end of the line and start back again if necessary. The old streetcar would reverse directions, with the rear as the front and the seat backs flipped to face forward again. At that point I'll know for sure, she thought. I'll call Cy Bill at the police station. No way will I endanger Galen. Or Bubba.

Endanger Bubba, Lynn?

I should have taken karate, she thought.

At Lee Circle, a tall woman boarded. She smiled at Lynn as she approached.

Lynn nodded. Should I know her? She had kind brown eyes and dark curly hair cut short. She wore a neat cream suit, gold earrings, and a mint scarf at her neck. Lynn tried to remember but didn't know which mental disc to pull up for a search. There were too many faces from too many places.

The woman passed Lynn's seat and stumbled. Lynn turned around to help. The woman grabbed for something to break the fall. Her hand bumped the stranger's face and knocked his sunglasses askew.

Immediately he straightened them. But Lynn saw! For an instant she'd looked again into icy gray eyes with an alarming capacity for cruelty. The mime!

Stunned, she found herself outside the scene, like watching a slow-motion movie. She watched herself bend down beside the woman. Watched herself carefully avoid looking at the mime. Watched herself pretend she didn't recognize him.

But she knew! And she feared he knew she knew!

The driver immediately stopped the streetcar. He glanced at Lynn in the rearview mirror. "Is she all right?"

"I'm OK," the woman answered. Lynn took her arm to help her up.

The mime, sunglasses secure, reached down to help also. He bumped against Lynn. "Excuse me," he said with a foreign accent. He nodded toward an empty seat. Together, they eased her into it.

The driver watched through the mirror. "Are you sure you're not hurt, ma'am?"

"I'm OK," she repeated. She looked at Lynn and managed a smile. "Just embarrassed."

As the streetcar started again, the mime moved silently to the door, his back to Lynn. She pulled her phone from the pocket of her blouse and waited for the next stop. She flipped it open as the door released. Pretending to make a call, she aimed the lens toward him, clicked and stored his right profile. She wanted to capture a frontal view of his face, but he stepped in front of the streetcar and hurriedly crossed St. Charles. Still pretending to make a call, she caught his left profile through the window.

For a moment she felt relieved that he was gone—but only for a moment. Those gray marble eyes hurled through her mind like a hurricane. She pondered his accent. German. But not quite. It was hard to peg in only two words. A tap on the shoulder startled her. She jumped reflexively.

"I'm sorry, Bishop Peterson," said the woman who'd fallen. "I didn't mean to frighten you."

Lynn smiled. "I was lost in thought."

"You may not remember, but we met when you came to my church. I'm Rosa DuBois, a member of Mt. Zion Church."

"It's good to see you again. I hope you really are all right."

"Just clumsy, I guess."

"Aren't we all! That was quite a tumble."

"It surely caused a commotion. One second I was walking down the aisle, and the next second I was flat on the floor." She paused. "That man was nice to help me."

Lynn would have chosen an entirely different adjective for him.

"But you know—" She raised her eyebrows, puzzled. "It sounds silly, but I'd almost swear he tripped me."

Lynn remembered feeling him bump against her and immediately put her hand in her pocket. Relieved, she felt Bubba's money and note. She checked the other one. Nothing! Elie's medal was missing.

15

Troubled, President Helena Benedict stood erect beside her dark cherry secretary in the private quarters of the White House. Confidential information seemed to rebound into heightened conflict and chaos. Am I growing paranoid? she wondered. Or is someone playing sinister background music in a *Phantom of the Opera* crescendo? Someone well-informed, someone close. She scanned the list of staff, advisors, Secret Service agents, Cabinet and Inner Circle members. One of these names could be at best her enemy, at worst a traitor to the country. Contrary to her trusting nature, she decided to pay very close attention to them individually and in meetings.

Feeling very much alone, she set the list down, withdrew a small key from the hidden compartment in the secretary and crossed the room to the old brown trunk at the foot of the bed. Its gold trim glistened in the late morning light. She kept it unlocked to avoid suspicion that a secret hid inside. She sifted through the trunk's mementos and lifted out the one significant item, a beautiful rectangular box inlaid with ebony and pearl in an alternating pattern of small squares. It had been one of the items in the ancient saddlebag her father, retired Senator Matthew Morgan Heffron, III, presented to her as an inauguration gift. When he died three weeks later, she emptied the saddlebag with its distinctive M for McGragor tooled on the flap and displayed it in the Oval Office where she and her father were sitting when he gave it to her. She'd moved its simple treasures, each one part of her family story, to this beautiful box that brought a tactile sense of his presence in his absence. Using the small key, she unlocked it and felt again the centering power of connection with her roots. The smell of old paper brought back her vivid memory of that day, easing her loneliness:

His eyes sweep the Oval Office. "During my four terms in the Senate, I sat in this room many times with many presidents." He focuses on the presidential desk. "My life goal is unachieved: to be elected to sit behind that desk. But now it is fulfilled in you, Madam President." His watery old eyes shine with pride. He opens the saddlebag and begins to tell her a story, displaying its precious contents one by one as he talks. He concludes with a family secret of defining-moment proportions. A secret that changes nothing. A secret that changes everything. A secret known only to him.

And now known only to her. A secret so buried that even presidential historians would never be able to uncover it.

She is proud of these unknown ancestors, proud that her heritage includes an Apache great-great-grandfather. Her father's story brings her strength during the tight spots—and they come daily in the presidency. It reminds her that serving boldly is more important than serving again, and gives her courage to make responsible decisions despite the risk of losing the lobbies' financial support—and the concomitant risk of losing a second term. She smiles as she remembers his view on polls: Essence explains the simplistic fallibility of polls. Statistics deal with percentages, and percentages miss essence. Not being linear, essence can't be measured. But it can be sensed, discerned, grasped. The power of polls is manipulative: they initiate a self-fulfilling prophecy. That day he gave her a brief but deep course in wisdom. Did he know it would be the last time he saw her?

She caressed the inlaid lid of the box, longing to reach out and touch her father. She needed his wisdom. Yet she knew what he would say: Words are mirrors. Listen to a person's language and the patterns of logic behind it. Look for the values and motives the spoken words expose. Watch the eyes, their blinks and movements, and the soul they reveal. He was a man too pragmatic to ignore the human soul—the essence of a person. She realized how difficult it would be to ferret out her enemy. Or enemies. Perhaps impossible. But she planned to walk into meetings with acute perception, practicing what her father had taught her. Listening. Watching. Seeking to glimpse the essential character of each one there. Beginning this afternoon with the Inner Circle.

She ran her hand across the monetarily worthless but essence-filled contents, then closed the box and locked it. She held it close for an instant, crossing her arms around it and hugging it against her heart, cherishing her father and the story that gave her courage.

16

LYNN HAD INTENDED TO GET HER CAR FROM HOME AND DRIVE TO HER office to make the eleven o'clock meeting. But feeling violated and heavy-hearted, she called her executive assistant and asked him to attend on her behalf. She left the streetcar at her stop and made her way through the traffic across the boulevard. She hurried down the cracked sidewalk that arched and sagged over hidden roots of ancient oaks. St. Charles Avenue no longer felt like a friendly place to be. Wariness wrapped around her like the humidity. She glanced from side to side and listened for the click of steps behind her.

She fumbled with the house key, dropped it twice, and finally unlocked the door. She punched in twelve-ten. *Lyndie.*

The streetcar scene replayed in her mind like a nightmare in daytime. When something was hard for her to handle, she usually took a long bath and soaked it away. But how do you soak away murder? And riding on a streetcar with the murderer?

She felt again in her pocket, hoping for a miracle. None came. She took pride in her ability to resolve problems—to mend broken systems and restore hope to broken souls. But she couldn't fix this. Now poor Mrs. Darwish would not get to have Elie's medal. Not get to hold it to her heart and feel his presence. Lynn's eyes teared. "I'm so sorry," she said aloud. Guilt's silence engulfed her.

You have to get it back, Lynn!

But how, Ivy? She ignored the beep that signaled phone messages. Not now. She felt enough weight on her shoulders. And messages always brought something else. She turned the kitchen radio on and heard happy Cajun music. A dirge seemed more appropriate. She debated whether to call the police about the medal and the mime. Robotically she iced a diet Dr. Pepper, added a stemmed maraschino cherry, and spread pimento cheese on whole wheat bread. And tell the police what?

Tell them I got my pocket picked?

Right, Lynn. You and a zillion other people.

Tell them the eyes of the stranger in sunglasses matched the mime's?

They'd roll their eyes and hang up—another paranoid-schizophrenic conspiracy theorist.

Tell them I have photos of his profile?

Pictures of one more tourist in a T-shirt? Big deal.

Tell them the stolen medal belonged to Elias Darwish, and Bubba Broussard took it from the crime scene? Lynn didn't need Ivy to know the outcome of that: FBI agents, whom Bubba considered as useful as a life jacket in a hot tub, would be all over him again.

Talk to Cy Bill about it?

Brilliant, Lynn. His first responsibility is to the law. If he takes you seriously, he'll probably have to report what you tell him.

Bottom line: Don't do anything to get Bubba in trouble. The Cajun music abruptly stopped.

> "Listen up, ya'll. We're going to patch in to a live NOPD news conference with Chief Martin Luther Armstrong about the murder of Elias Darwish, our Saint with a perfect record."

Lynn turned up the volume.

> "I am proud to announce that due to the tireless efforts of the NOPD during the last twenty-four hours, the murder of Elias Darwish has been solved." He paused, giving the words a chance for impact. "Yesterday I promised to provide the good citizens of New Orleans full information. Today I want to make the evidence public."

No mention of the FBI, Lynn noticed. This was still his city.

> "First, a piece of red fuzz found in the suspect's hair matches the mime's wig. Second, the ballistics report shows that the gun found at the scene with his fingerprints on it fired the bullet that killed our star kicker. Third, his fingerprints identify him as a man wanted by the federal government for another murder."

"They've caught you since you got off the streetcar, Mr. Mime! Or they're about to!" Cynicism caught up with her elation. "But you'll probably hire a slick lawyer and go free." Too often justice related more to a lawyer's guile than a defendant's guilt.

> "Unfortunately, we cannot seek a confession or take this case to trial. The mime who murdered one of our favorite sons was found dead at dawn. There were signs of a struggle, and he was shot with his own gun. The NOPD solved the heinous murder of Elias Darwish in record

> time. And justice has been served by a Higher Court."

Slowly his words sank in.

Reporters began asking questions. So did she. If the police found the mime dead at dawn, how could he have been on the streetcar half an hour ago? Who made a mistake? The police? Me? Could two different sets of eyes be exactly alike?

Pondering the chief's statement, she took her lunch outside and sat down at the glass table on the back veranda. A rainbow of flowers encircled the courtyard, but their color faded as rain clouds rolled in. Gray sky. Gray eyes. Cold marble eyes stared at her from gray bushes in every direction. Eyes of the mime. Eyes of the stranger on the streetcar. *The same.* The same. Lynn was sure about that.

Chief Armstrong had made a terrible mistake! Her mind whirled in circles like a paddle wheel. What if the mime set up his second victim to look like Elie's murderer? What if he planted evidence easy to find? What if the two killings added up to one double murder?

Perfect. The accused can't proclaim his innocence and the double murderer roams freely about town. Drinking coffee at a cafe. Riding the streetcar. Stealing a medal.

The diet Dr. Pepper trembled in her hand. An old cliché came to mind: Dead men don't talk.

17

THURSDAY AFTERNOON THE PATRIOT RUSHED INTO THE OVAL OFFICE, LAST as always, creating the impression that his schedule barely permitted another meeting, even with the President. He strode straight to her and shook hands, conscious of her small fingers in his long ones as she greeted him in her Katie Couric voice. His charming cover intact, he smiled cordially and gave a respectful nod, then moved quickly around the room to speak to each member of the Inner Circle. He called them all by name and added a personal word of appreciation, habitually mindful of cultivating business and political networks that crossed party lines. Duplicitous but necessary.

"Let us begin," said President Benedict. Her low-key way of opening the monthly "Inner Circle gathering" strained unsuccessfully for informality.

Oval Office informality—the pinnacle of oxymorons, he thought, seating himself in the dark leather chair directly across from her. He recalled past visits since 1990 to this room-above-all-rooms, ever the same even with change.

The President's three little words brought an abrupt shift in mood. All eyes turned to her. Sentences stopped midway. Coffee cups clinked against saucers. Postures straightened.

People leaned forward in their chairs. The Inner Circle—the chosen ones—sat proudly at the feet of the President like the twelve apostles at the feet of Jesus. The Patriot scanned the table. A widely acclaimed national historian sat to the President's right. Her task was to listen to members' ideas and draw historical parallels that pointed to successes and failures. Next were four international relations scholars whose areas of expertise included the Middle East, North Korea, China, and Russia. An environmental scientist sat to her left, followed by specialists in the fields of health care, education, poverty, the space program, plus a retired general with diplomatic skills. And himself, a financial magnate who offered insight regarding how potential policies could impact the corporate world—who also profited from the inside information that led to his being in the right place at the right time for his covert arms business.

The Inner Circle's makeup indicated that the President placed knowledge above party affiliation and political opinions. Worldviews within the circle clashed, but she apparently considered this to be an asset in making good decisions. Instead of stating her positions so the group would tell her what she wanted to hear, she expected each of them to share concerns in their areas of expertise, to be followed by a discussion based on penetrating questions. Her open style of leadership created options, and he couldn't predict the outcome. He found that troubling but masked his feelings.

Bored by the members' look-at-me-I'm-in-the-inner-circle egotism, he let his mind wander back to the President's call to the Secretary of Defense on a secure line. Was she, too, masking something? How well did she know Major Manetti?

And what about Bishop Peterson? Nothing unusual about a bishop giving an invocation for a dinner the Vice President attended in New Orleans last night. But why did he invite her to ride back to the airport with him? Relevant or coincidental? The Patriot did not believe in coincidences.

From behind his affable mask, he refocused on the meeting. Doris, the historian, made a point. He asked for clarification, showing interest and appreciation. He might need her someday.

He had quickly gained insight about former presidents, but Benedict was far more difficult to read. Sitting opposite her made it easy to seek personality clues in her demeanor. He watched her blue-green eyes, sometimes cautiously blank, sometimes sharply piercing. Always alert. He couldn't tell what she was thinking, another thing he didn't like about her. Yet he pretended admiration.

Her attire offered few hints to her personality: Clothes tailored with a feminine touch. Simple jewelry. Always dressed tastefully and camera-ready. There would be no photos of a sloppy President Helena Benedict! But he preferred a president with a tie.

Faking a genial smile and nodding appropriately while half-listening, he discreetly scanned the office for clues—pictures, mementos, citations of honor. But the only personal items in the room were in a display case standing unobtrusively against the back wall near her desk. One was an ancient saddlebag, its leather wrinkled and scuffed, its silver buckle worn and scratched—an unworthy item in this historic seat of power. He noted the M on the flap and thought of Manetti. Logic told him that was too big a leap. Next to the saddlebag was a sculpture of a mother and little girl, striking in its simplicity. He'd asked about it during his first visit to the Oval Office after she became president. Joy had lit her face as she looked at it, and she gave the longest reply he'd ever heard from her: It's an Allan Houser. For me, he demonstrates the power of art through suggestion and invites us to be partners in our interpretation. He was a National Medal of Arts winner. This is titled *The Shy One.* Her tone, like a caress, brought life to the cold bronze. Speaking rapidly, she'd added: Haozous, his birth name, was Anglicized to Houser because it was easier for the children in his Oklahoma school to pronounce. He was a descendant of the great Apache Chief Mangas Coloradas, and his father rode with Gerónimo. Though dead now, he remains my favorite sculptor. That ended her only self-revealing conversation with him.

Today's pointless meeting droned on. And on. It irritated him to waste energy pretending interest. Past presidents had shown him deference and treated him like an unofficial advisor. But not this President—an irksome shortcoming on her part. She treated him like everyone else, and the members saw themselves as his peers. Equality eroded his edge to shape committee decisions. His agitation increased as the minutes passed—minutes he could be spending to gain information about Major Manetti and Bishop Peterson and to prepare for his long flight to Frankfurt this evening. Here he sat, deprived of his due. Unacceptable! Infuriating!

Suddenly the President's eyes darted to him. "Is something troubling you, John?"

Caught! John Adams of BarLothiun realized he'd dropped his mask!

18

LYNN WENT THROUGH THE MOTIONS OF LIFE'S MINUTIAE THROUGHOUT THE afternoon. Words from Luke's gospel ran through her mind: Nothing is covered up that will not be uncovered, and nothing secret that will not become known. Lynn waited until 5:30 to call Francine Babineaux, giving her a chance to get home where she could speak freely. As an employee in the crime lab, she might know something. As a close friend, she might share it. After the customary small talk, Lynn asked her about the Darwish case.

"Just between you and me?"

"Always."

"To be fair, the evidence appears adequate."

"*Appears?*"

"Commuting over that twenty-five-mile bridge across Lake Pontchartrain gives me lots of time to ponder things."

"Things like?"

"Prematurely closing a case."

"You think that's what happened?"

"Perhaps."

"But they listen to you, Francine."

"Usually. But not on this one." Her voice dropped nearly to a whisper. "Somebody above—I don't know how far up—brought pressure to declare the murder solved."

"That isn't the reassurance I'd hoped for."

"They have their reasons, I suppose. The people of New Orleans need confidence that our star Saint can't be taken out and the perp roam the streets."

Perp? Short for perpetrator, Lynn supposed. But he *is* still roaming.

"Anyway," she added, sounding unconvinced, "they're calling the evidence sufficient."

"So it looks good. But the real murderer remains free?"

Francine whistled softly. "I don't like it put so directly. Let's just say I'm still troubled."

"About whether the mime killed Elias Darwish? Or whether the second victim is the mime?"

"The mime killed him, all right. There's no doubt about that." She paused for several moments, and Lynn didn't interrupt the silence. "Just between us—the evidence that the second man is the mime seems too obvious."

"Like it was planted?"

She sighed. "You got that right."

"Francine, did you happen to see the body—the one they're saying is the mime?"

"Yes. Why?"

Lynn recalled the mime's cold gray eyes when she walked past him in the Quarter. "What color were his eyes?"

"Brown as they come, *cher*."

19

IMMEDIATELY FOLLOWING THE INNER CIRCLE MEETING IN THE OVAL OFFICE, the Patriot rushed to his office, pushed the *fleur-de-lis* on the stand holding JFK's bust, removed the hidden items needed, loaded his briefcase and headed to his private jet for the jaunt to Frankfurt. He drove himself, as always. Too much of his life was concealed to have a chauffeur and, besides, *John Adams drives himself* was part of the legend that made him popular. It also protected his itinerary.

As his Challenger rose above the earth, he reflected on the near disaster of the Inner Circle meeting. To drop his mask was a perilous mistake, especially in the Oval Office. Turning crisis into opportunity, he'd made a quick recovery and explained that a comment had reminded him of the horrific Balkan crisis. He stated with compassion that war does dreadful things to people. It won him points from most of the Inner Circle. His cleverness pleased him. But as usual he'd been unable to read President Benedict. Her intelligence and depth of perception both surprised and troubled him.

He envied her flawless diction, a gift from simply growing up with her father, old Senator Heffron whose voice he remembered well. He contrasted that gift with his own long, grueling struggle to perfect his diction, finally erasing every trace of an accent. She was one of the privileged class born into life with pretty packaging. He, on the other hand, had been forced to claw through the refuse of their crumpled wrappings. Unlike the D.C. politicos who thwarted justice, he understood the little people because he could identify with them. Somehow the President seemed able to do that also—another surprise. He tended to underestimate her. Dangerous!

A story about President Truman had taught him the power of presidential friendship. When Truman faced the momentous historical dilemma of partitioning Palestine to grant a Jewish nation, he worried about the long-term effect on the U.S. of continuing to support Zionist policies. He refused to be influenced by pressure from Zionists on one side and oil interests on the Arab side. He also declined—and found offensive—a Zionist offer of cash. But where pressure and money failed, friendship succeeded. His friend Eddie Jacobson, a non-Zionist Jew, went to see him and shared his concerns about the plight of the Jews—and the Jewish state of Israel was born at midnight on Friday, May 14, 1948. Truman wrote later that Jacobson's contribution was of "decisive importance."

Never forgetting that story, John Adams began his own efforts as a young man assigned to a terrorist task force while Cheney was Secretary of Defense in the first Bush administration. From that time forward his cool logic had served him well. He'd worked in the CIA and NSA, befriended presidents as his wealth grew, first through his covert arms business and later, when he could afford it, while building his infrastructure business. His presidential friendships had resulted in influence and access, and their concomitant power—until Benedict. His efforts to befriend her were courteously received but disconcertingly unrewarded. But, he muttered, I'll continue to court her friendship. Deceitful but necessary.

He ate his four-course dinner in a leisurely manner as his plane droned through the sky. Particular about the finer things in life, he was served on white linens with china, crystal and sterling—including real knives. In denial of his past, or perhaps because of it, he expected gourmet meals with artistic presentations and fine wine even in the air. He appreciated his private jet more than any other possession. How humiliating it would be to fly commercial, to march through security chutes like suspected convicts guilty until proven innocent, forced to submit to pat-downs and the legalized nudity produced by full body scanners. He shook his head at the foolishness. For the truth was that he or anyone in his cadre of elites—or any serious terrorist—could figure out ways to get on board with what they needed despite the restrictions. He'd been at a State dinner once when uninvited publicity seekers had managed to get themselves inside the White House—presented, seated, and hand-to-hand with the President. But, he thought, the illusion of security gives lots of people jobs and helps the economy.

He flew frequently and appreciated the uninterrupted block of time on overnight flights. He looked at his watch and set it forward to Frankfurt's time zone. He would arrive in good time for his late morning meeting tomorrow. As he often did while flying east or west, he pondered how human beings had peacefully come to agreement on time zones around the globe. Perhaps one day righteous justice could be as easily mandated.

He glanced at his briefcase, tonight's work ready for him thanks to Lone Star. He was exactly the kind of Secret Service agent the Patriot had sought. Originally trained by the CIA, his superiors' orders took precedence over his conscience, and he accepted the fact that he held only one piece in the puzzle, and they had the whole picture. He trusted them to judge what was best for the country, bowing to an ingrained mantra: One-two. Left-right. Do-or-die. Don't reason why.

Lone Star was a tech prodigy and had been honored to be tapped for the deep-cover project called Genesis, so deep that it appeared not to exist. He was willing to be available as needed and keep his regular Secret Service schedule to avoid questions. He understood that a Genesis operative was not allowed to know the name of anyone else in the project nor speak of his assignments nor acknowledge—under any circumstances—the existence of Genesis. The code of silence was as strong as the Cosa Nostra's *omertà*. Lone Star believed in the project's noble purpose: to provide an additional layer of invisible protection for the President. He understood that this called for access to all of her communications, an essential prerequisite to keeping her out of harm's way. Proud to serve his country and his life already committed to taking a bullet for the President if necessary, he secured all the technological access Genesis required. The Patriot smiled, happy to put Lone Star's blind loyalty to use.

In truth, Genesis consisted of a mighty force of one: Lone Star. It wasn't to protect the President but to keep the Patriot in control. The ruse provided insight about presidential interests, opinions and connections, and advance information about potential arms needs. Lone Star was stupid to fall for it. Patriotism was to be commended; blind patriotism could serve the enemy.

He finished his all-American dessert of apple pie with ice cream and nodded for a second cup of coffee. He took a sip, opened his briefcase, and pulled out the files on Manetti and Peterson. As requested, Lone Star had obtained the Homeland Security and FBI information on Manetti and researched everything available, public and otherwise, on Peterson. Unethical but necessary. The extent of restricted information on her surprised him. He wondered if her visits to Moscow, Beijing, and Gaza had triggered it. Lone Star's reports revealed no personal connection between President Benedict and Lynn Peterson, easing his mind. But they indicted Major Marshall Mario Manetti.

The major was a longtime friend of the President. During her conversation with the Secretary of Defense, she had not misstated about his being a good Catholic, but she had illogically omitted their friendship. The Patriot frowned and entwined his long slender fingers like a man in prayer, contemplating his decision. Life was sacred. He did not take termination lightly, but communication channels beyond his access were unacceptable. His need for control was not an obsession but essential. Blocks impeded his Holy Vision of justice and therefore must be quashed. *Quashed.* The harmless-sounding word brought a smile.

He switched to Irish coffee and continued to ponder the matter. The President had used her secure line to call the Secretary of Defense. Why? She gave Manetti's Catholicism as the reason for selecting him, not their friendship. Why? She had avoided a direct call to Manetti. Again, why? Cool logic prevailed as he considered every possible angle. The only plausible reason was an attempt to create a clandestine means of contact. He may have underestimated Benedict, but she had also underestimated him. He'd discovered her attempt.

The President, not he, bore responsibility for the necessity of Manetti's termination. As with Darwish, he had no choice. Zero tolerance. Regrettable but necessary. He lifted his Irish coffee, breathed deeply of the aroma and took a sip, the whipped cream rich on his tongue.

20

AT 10:55 FRIDAY MORNING ZECHARIAH ZELLER CLOSED HIS PHONE AND hurried through Flughafen Frankfurt to meet the Patriot—whose sobriquet was dubious but not his power. True to form he'd said only the name of the place and had disconnected. The Patriot's pattern was consistent: always meeting at the Frankfurt airport, calling five minutes before the designated time to set the exact place, changing disguises like a chameleon, arriving first and sitting at a corner table with his back to the wall.

Zeller spotted him, the whipped cream already melting in his coffee glass. Today his hair was black with gray streaks, his eyes blue, and a salt-and-pepper goatee hid the cleft in his chin. Disguises altered the Patriot's appearance but not his intensity, not his inner makeup. No.

"Sit."

Zeller did so.

"You are free this week?"

He knew this was not a question but the preface to a directive. Another contract so soon surprised him, but he nodded, stifling a jet-lag yawn from his New Orleans flight to this stopover. He handed the Patriot a tie box wrapped in birthday paper. "As I recall, you like neckwear." Inside was Elias Darwish's medal. He knew better than to ask why he was directed to retrieve it. He also knew better than to show up without it.

"Thank you." Long, slender fingers lifted the glass of *Einspänner* in tribute. "You did well."

Silently Zeller disagreed. His perfect plan scrolled through his mind: Shoot target. Take advantage of crowd panic. Toss mime costume in litterbin. Retain scalp liner to avoid DNA. Save strands of wig to frame next victim. Rush forward. Pretend concern. Retrieve medal. Leave scene. But the perfect plan had failed. He'd not foreseen the presence of a Hercules who would kneel beside the target, notice that the bullet had broken his neck chain, see the medal on the street, and pick it up. No!

Zeller had no difficulty finding out the identity of Hercules—Bubba Broussard—and getting his address. It was easy to follow him to the café yesterday morning, watch him give the woman the medal, and pick it from her pocket on the streetcar. So easy. Easy but beneath him. He was a world-class marksman, not a petty thief. No. Now he hid his resentment behind opaque sunglasses.

The Patriot set his glass back on the table and handed across the *International Herald Tribune* folded to an article about the murder of the New Orleans Saints star kicker.

Zeller scanned it, feeling the thick cash envelope between the pages. Prompt and generous payment as always. He liked to read stories about his work and how the authorities "solved" the crime with the false clues he left behind to mislead them. The article said that Darwish's murderer had been found and had himself become a victim. Proof consisted of strands of the red wig discovered in his hair, matching fingerprints, and, most important, the gun that ballistics reports confirmed had killed Darwish. Investigation closed. Crime committed.

Crime solved. He enjoyed the challenge of solving the first crime with the second, but his disciplined facial muscles concealed his inner satisfaction.

"The timely . . . *silence*," the Patriot raised an eyebrow with his euphemistic reference to Darwish's termination, "is a lesson to others. Lamentable but necessary," he added softly.

Zeller had no clue to the Patriot's identity. Darwish had tried to discover it. And been "silenced." He did not intend to make the same mistake.

"I have learned something interesting about a major," the Patriot said like a gossiping cleric, as unsuspicious to onlookers as a tie box wrapped in birthday paper. Only the intensity in his eyes and the raised right eyebrow revealed the comment's significance.

Zeller listened intently, knowing that the Patriot was introducing the target for his new assignment. He sipped his *Mokka gespritzt*, waiting without impatience to hear the name.

"You may know Manetti, chief aide to the NATO commander in Naples." The Patriot paused, then issued the death warrant in words and in a tone that sounded like a simple party invitation. "He deserves the biggest surprise of his life." Again, the master of disguise raised his eyebrow. Zeller gave a slight nod, and the Patriot stood abruptly and left. He would be told nothing else. No. Their ongoing arrangement had been agreed upon during their first meeting three years ago: limited information about *who* and no strings about *how*—and a generous cash payment made in person at Flughafen Frankfurt upon successful completion.

As always Zeller would access everything known about the target. This background work was essential in order to keep himself safe and to retain his perfect record. Looking forward to the challenge, he slowly finished his *Mokka gespritzt* and headed toward the gate for his connecting flight back home.

With two hours to wait he stopped for a small *Mokka*, no brandy this time, and carried it to the computer station nearby.

His phone rang. No name. None needed. The familiar voice said, "Thank you for the birthday present. I omitted one detail. You are to leave a conspicuous calling card at the site where you conduct your business: St. Sava claims responsibility." That ended the call.

He could not sort out the Patriot's truths from his lies. But he knew for sure that he was not careless enough to omit details. St. Sava was a new ingredient. Interesting.

He took a sip of his *Mokka* and Googled *NATO base Naples*. Then clicked *Staff*. Found Manetti. Major Marshall Manetti. Googled his name. Marshall Mario Manetti: Graduate of St. Thomas Catholic High School in Boston, and the Naval Academy with honors; aide-de-camp to General Theodore Thornburg with NATO, stationed in Naples. Zeller had sufficient information to begin forming his plan. He checked his watch. Just enough time to take the first step before his flight. He found the number for Manetti's office and used the U.S. cell phone he'd taken to New Orleans. He'd listed it in the name of American Liberty Bank Corporation—impressive, familiar sounding, and nonexistent. When the secretary answered, he asked to speak to Major Manetti, counting on his slight Austrian-German accent to sound scholarly.

"He is not available," she answered, strictly business as expected.

"I am Dr. Stephen Schwartzenburg with the alumni association of St. Thomas Catholic High School in Boston. We are honoring the major for his fine service to our country. I want to give him the good news."

Her tone warmed. "I'll relay the message."

"It is important that I speak to him personally. How can I reach him?"

"I'm sorry, but I'm not at liberty to discuss his schedule."

"Oh," Zeller's voice reeked with disappointment. "I don't know what to do. I am in charge of planning, and we need to set a date. It will be a memorable event."

Less businesslike now, she said, "I could reach him and ask him to call you, Dr. Schwartzenburg."

"Thank you. My number is . . ." he started to offer, knowing it had already been recorded.

"I have it, sir." He heard the smile in her voice as she added, "Major Manetti is a fine man. He well deserves the honor."

Zeller hung up and waited with a smile on his own face. So easy.

As he stood in the boarding line for his flight home, his cell phone rang. *Ja!* He ignored it until after the voicemail, then listened to the caller's brief message.

> "Dr. Schwartzenburg, this is Marsh Manetti. Thank you for calling. St. Thomas High! Those were the days! I'm taking a brief trip and will be unreachable during flight. I'll try to contact you again later."

Zeller noted the phone number retained by his cell. During flight. To where? Tomorrow morning at home he and his computer, fondly called *Mutter* and loaded with Chinese software stolen from the CIA, would tap into passenger lists on departing flights from Naples and ultimately get Manetti's itinerary. Google had given him a good beginning, but *Mutter* had the capacity to obtain enough information about Manetti to predict how often he brushed his teeth and the kind of toothpaste he used. So easy.

21

On Friday evening Lynn set the table for a special shrimp dinner, their tradition on Cross-the-Pond Eve. She needed ample time to discuss with Galen her misadventure on the streetcar yesterday, and ample time was hard to find. Last night he'd come home late from hosting a visiting lecturer at Tulane. This morning she'd hurried off for an early breakfast meeting and spent the day in Type-A mode to finish up the loose ends for her absence. Preparing dinner together distracted them, and her story about the mime and medal required his full attention. Now, as she lit the candles, delayed tension boiled within her like Mount St. Helens ready to spew.

Galen seated her and prayed their thanks for food and blessings.

Her story tumbled forth before they finished the bisque. "So," she concluded, "Elie's murder isn't solved. The mime is alive."

"Chief Armstrong probably has information that Francine doesn't. We can trust him."

"You don't believe me!"

"The man on the streetcar scared you. That's understandable. Think what you've been through."

"But his eyes! Cruel eyes! Identical to the mime's. Same color. Size. Shape."

"Fear heightens imagination, Lynn."

"If I wanted to be analyzed, I'd go to a therapist!"

Cool the Mount St. Helens, Lynn! It isn't helpful.

This time Ivy was right. She took a deep breath and a new tack. "How do you explain the missing medal?"

Galen followed his exasperated sigh with an exasperating patient-father tone. "It could have fallen out of your pocket."

She felt discounted and deserted.

"I don't like to see you so frightened." He reached his hand across the table and covered hers, then smiled. "You're the brave one. Remember?"

"Don't patronize me!"

His smile vanished. A chilly silence hung in the air. He broke it first. "Would you like to call the police and report that Elie's medal is missing?"

"*Stolen*, Galen." She took another deep breath. "Reporting it might get Bubba in trouble. The police might say he removed evidence."

The mime is probably far from New Orleans by now anyway, Lynn.

Right again, Ivy. The acknowledgement brought a painful sense of hopelessness.

"There's no point in continuing to worry yourself. The medal's gone. The murder's solved."

"But it *isn't* solved!"

"Lynn, it's time to turn the page," he said firmly.

Mount St. Helens erupted. So much for a candlelight dinner! She tossed her napkin on the table. "I'm going to pack." She stomped up the stairs, perturbed that carpeting stole the sound effects.

Anger's energy helped wrestle her black L.L. Bean roll-aboard from the closet under the attic stairs. She was tempted to curl up and sulk in the secluded space it left. But there wasn't time. There was never time for a proper pout!

She jerked the hangers from her travel clothes: three mix-and-match skirts and jackets. Different weights and wrinkle-free. A versatile black dress, five space-saving blouses, a pair of slacks, quick-drying lingerie, inexpensive jewelry including Mardi Gras beads that could pass for pearls in the dark, a purse, and two pairs of black shoes—flats and heels. Done. Record time. Anger has its benefits.

She unzipped Big-Black, her old oversized leather tote she defined as a "small personal bag." A gift from Galen. We'll make up tonight, she thought, anticipation softening her mood. We always do. She tossed the leftovers into Big-Black. Travel-size toiletries and makeup, a couple of paperback books, travel toys like diagramless crosswords and cards to play gin rummy with Galen on the plane, small gifts, and emergency snacks. She added her cell phone and the full-capacity baby laptop adaptable to all electrical currents. E-tickets and passport. Last came Bubba's note and money for Mrs. Darwish.

But no medal. One more time she pointlessly checked the pocket in the skirt she'd worn yesterday. Just in case. But the medal fairy hadn't come. She felt miserable. I can't tell Bubba it was stolen. I don't want to heap that disappointment on him on top of everything else. For his sake, she told herself. But she lied. The truth was that she didn't want him to think badly of her. She decided to tell him when she returned—and if she was killed in the Balkans she wouldn't have to tell him at all.

One decision remained—the President's envelope for *Marsh with NATO*. She didn't want it found if her luggage was searched by security. She stowed the envelope in her metal-free waist wallet and hung it with her travel jacket.

Almost more than she could handle had happened in the past 57 hours. She sagged down on the bed and closed her eyes. *Maybe Galen is right about the streetcar. Maybe I was just scared. Maybe the two sets of eyes don't match.*

But they do!

She zipped the roll-aboard closed with a quick, loud *ZZZ*. Finished!

Tomorrow she would board a plane. Unfinished!

22

ZELLER STOOD AT THE WINDOW OF HIS THIRD-STORY VIENNA APARTMENT ON this sunny Saturday morning. He did not take this new assignment from the Patriot lightly. His profession required four parts: the research, the plan, the act, the escape. Of the four, the act itself took the least time. He always tried to foresee the unforeseeable and devise alternative strategies for success. But even with meticulous planning, he needed a thread of luck. He felt uneasy about unwinding too much of that thread in too short a time. Wednesday in New Orleans. Tomorrow here in his own city. A thread of luck could knot.

His coffee steamed and the smoke from his cigarette curled upward as he observed the oblivious people below. Children in uniforms going to school. Men and women in suits going to offices. Mentally, he used them for target practice. A feeling of power surged. How easy to cause chaos! One single shot. Then screams. Panic. Running. Survival at all costs. Compassion shoved aside along with any person in the way. Trampling others to save themselves. He'd seen it before. But parents would protect their children. And some husbands their wives. One simple pull of the trigger could end any life he chose. Or many lives, rapid fire. He smiled, smugly aware of his power to spread terror on the streets of Vienna—and proud of his discipline not to do so.

He poured a fresh cup of coffee, savoring the aroma, and said kind words to *Mutter* as they began to probe the virtual world for data about Major Marshall Mario Manetti. The War on Terror had simplified getting information. The more personal data stored by security agencies, the more facts he had at his fingertips, literally. All he and *Mutter* had to do was crack the codes. A wizard at this—since his life depended on the details—he scrolled through the supposedly secure military and financial data files on Manetti. *Mutter* thrived on revealing secrets, humming happily along. He also searched for flights departing yesterday afternoon from Naples and tapped into passenger lists. *Ja!* Manetti's itinerary flashed on the screen: Naples to Frankfurt on Friday afternoon. Frankfurt to Vienna on Sunday morning. Thank you, *Mutter!*

He noticed that the return to Naples wasn't scheduled. He walked mentally through alternative plans and weighed the options, then set the scene: Vienna, the city he knew best. Flughafen Wien, the most familiar airport in the world to him. Upon Manetti's arrival from Frankfurt. A perfect place and time for the biggest surprise of his life as the Patriot had euphemized. So easy.

He must not hurry the final details. No. First *Freund.* He opened the false panel in his closet and removed his high-powered sniper rifle and gun-cleaning kit. As he rubbed the barrel, he thought about the Patriot. Meticulous planning required him to understand the personality of the one who issued the contract. He considered whether he could best the Patriot mentally. A dangerous thought. The master of disguise was as rigid and unforgiving as the statue at Dr. Karl Lueger Platz. Like Lueger, the Patriot used every means at his disposal to obtain his goals, building his reputation on stories of mythical proportions. "Will he target me one day, *Freund*?" he whispered to his sniper rifle. "Not as long as he needs me. And he will always need the world's preeminent shooter."

Patting *Freund* he veered away from thoughts of Lueger and the Patriot, clearing his mind to focus totally on Manetti. He would not lose that focus. No. Not until the unlucky target was dead—one shot to the head. Zeller smiled again, tingling with anticipation and the thrill of the challenge. "Say your prayers, Major Marshall Manetti. This is your last night to do so."

23

LYNN FELT AS ANXIOUS AND WATCHFUL AS A FIRST-TIME FLYER WHEN SHE and Galen faced the security check before boarding the plane on Saturday. She fretted her way forward in the slow line, the President's envelope burning through her waist wallet like a teardrop of molten glass. Her hand acquired the tic of rubbing across it every few minutes. Finally she made it to the other side without a glitch—envelope undiscovered. She gathered up her roll-aboard, Big-Black, baby laptop, travel jacket and shoes and breathed an audible sigh of relief.

Not one to waste an opportunity to worry, her moment's reprieve turned into angst over getting the envelope to *Marsh with NATO* when they landed in Frankfurt. How would she find him before their Vienna connection departed? Make a sign with his name and hold it up like drivers waiting for unknown passengers?

Brilliant, Lynn!

As expected, she and Galen had made up last night, once again restoring their musical marriage—a loving duet of harmony, rhythm, and joy. At least for now. Lynn knew from both personal experience and counseling others that marriage is one of the most difficult relationships to sustain and enrich. It had taken her years to understand that when two strong people marry, agreement is not necessary but mutual respect is essential. *Both* of them wanted a musical marriage, and that in itself gave them hope and perseverance. On trips across the pond they did their best to sing a duet. They anticipated adventure but were also aware of the concomitant strain of adjusting to unfamiliar language and culture. They wanted to be at their best for each other and for those who would become part of their lives, broadening their global sense of family.

Once in the air they played gin on the tiny tray tables and ate the contents dubbed "dinner" served in divided cartons with plastic forks and knives, and Lynn slept through the movie. She awoke once and pondered the enigma of time in travel. From New Orleans to Vienna they would go through enough time zones to lose seven hours of their lives, regained on their return. What do you do with hours regained that once were lost? The same, the same. You fly. And fly. She went back to sleep and dreamed she was a soaring eagle, wings widespread, claws clutching a medal. And then she morphed into a girl in a blue dress running through the forest with her hand extended, holding an envelope, and calling out Marsh! Marsh with NATO!

24

On Sunday morning Major Marshall Manetti checked out of the Frankfurt hotel and was driven to the airport. The meeting yesterday had gone well. All the bases were covered. The offensive was necessary, but what could have been done to prevent the necessity? That question always troubled him. He returned the salute of the driver and made his way through the airport to the gate for the next flight to Vienna. As he waited, attentive to passengers in his subtle search for the Petersons, he mentally reviewed Friday morning's orders from General Thornburg—spoken, not written.

The general had stood behind his desk, hands on hips, scowling. "A request came from higher up," he said brusquely. He took a step backward and narrowed his eyes at Marsh. "Do you have connections at the State Department?"

"Not that I know of, sir." Higher than that.

"Well, they requested that you take care of a matter on your way back from tomorrow's meeting in Frankfurt." General Thornburg made no effort to cover his ire. "They want you to look after a bishop. *Discreetly.*"

Meaning *secretly*. "Yes, sir."

"Women bishops, for God's sake! State said she's a 'prominent' religious leader with 'skills and sensitivities' in multinational situations. The problem is she tends to put herself in harm's way. *And* instead of keeping her safely at home, her fool husband tags along like a tourist all agog!"

Marsh hid a smile. The general divided women into two separate groups. Civilian women were "the fair sex" to be protected at all costs. The women under his command were "female soldiers," and he'd trained himself to delete the *fe* before *male*. A soldier was a soldier.

General Thornburg jerked back the chair and sat down, waving his hand across the piles of paper on his desk. "The world is exploding all around us, and I can spare my chief aide to babysit a bishop!"

"Bad timing, sir."

"There is no good time. The post-Cold War spews icier danger than the Cold War. Iraq. Afghanistan. Pakistan. The Balkans. And eternally Israel and Palestine." He sighed. "We're bent on destroying ourselves."

"Would you like for me to find a way to impede obedience to the order, sir?" Marsh knew the answer.

The general laughed sardonically. "We have to appease the prissy politicians. Our world would be safer if they were the ones sent into battle instead of the ones sending other people's children off to fight."

Marsh could have mouthed what would come next.

"The bravest and the best." His tone came from a softer place, distant, deep. "That's why this job is so hard." He scanned the unwanted communication from the State Department, his gruff manner returning. "Go on to Frankfurt today as planned, and when you leave tomorrow morning you're to go to Vienna on their plane." He handed Marsh their flight schedule. "Google their photos. State didn't even bother to send them." The general glanced up at him. "Be sure you take good care of Bishop Peterson."

"Yes, sir."

"Find a *discreet* way to have them delayed in Vienna an extra twenty-four hours. You know what hits Tuesday night."

Marsh nodded, dreading it.

"Their flight to Macedonia would probably be safe, but somebody doesn't want to take any chances. State wants the matter handled at this level instead of through subordinates. It avoids the risk of questions or rumors that could spoil the NATO surprise offensive. Get back here as fast as you can."

"Yes, sir."

"I'll need you, Marsh." The informality was a rare show of affection, an indication that the general was gravely worried about the ripples from the NATO "surprise."

"You can count on me, sir. I'll wrap up the babysitting and be back before the fireworks start."

Now, as Marsh's mind came back to the present and his wait at the Frankfurt gate for his flight to Vienna, he boredly surveyed the passengers. None looked like a bishop. He caught himself in the stereotypical thought. And how does a bishop look, he asked himself, moving beyond his image of a man in a collar and black suit. He wondered if his church would ever allow women to be priests. Or priests to marry. He stepped across stereotypical borders. Any of these women could be a bishop. He pulled her Googled photo from his pocket, snapped it mentally, and returned it. He scanned the area again, then glanced at his watch. Not much longer.

He gazed out the airport window as a plane lifted from the runway and soared gracefully into the clear turbulence-free sky. In a month he would be on a plane that took him back home for his leave. He sighed, ready for a break from the world's hostilities. His thoughts turned toward the award he would receive from his high school. He felt honored. It would be fun to go back and see old friends.

25

Crossing the Atlantic distanced Lynn's body clock from the correct time zone, but it didn't distance her memory of those cold marble eyes. Nor lessen the weight of the President's envelope in her waist wallet. As their plane descended toward Flughafen Frankfurt, Lynn's angst and tic returned. But she'd be rid of the letter within the hour. A comforting thought. *If* she could find this Marsh with NATO. She scanned the crowd as soon as she entered the airport. Seeking one stranger in a mob of strangers. Searching each face. Pointless. She wouldn't know him if she saw him. Next time, Madam President, please enclose a full name or a photo!

Next time, Lynn?

They checked in for the Vienna flight. She handed her E-ticket and passport to the agent and pronounced her name stage-projection loud. But no Marsh stepped forward to introduce himself. Her eyes checked out all the waiting passengers minus women, children, teens, elderly men, and everyone not in uniform.

He might not be wearing one, Lynn.

She looked for straight posture, a short haircut, shined shoes.

That's a military stereotype. It might not fit him.

Then you find him, Ivy! Panic squeezed around her like an airless coffin. She felt for the waist wallet.

"You seem jittery," said Galen in a soothing tone. "Are you all right?"

She forced a smile and nodded. Act normal, she told herself. But what is normal when you're a courier for the President of the United States? The question itself isn't normal. I should have thrown the envelope back at Parker before he closed the limo door. Departure time ticked closer. Overwhelmed by the odds, she sat down to wait and prepared herself for defeat, the six-letter *D*-word she'd deleted from her vocabulary.

A man of medium height approached Galen and her. He had dark hair and eyes and a Tom Hanks smile. He wore the white summer uniform of a Navy officer.

Marsh with NATO! Please! Oh, please!

"You look like people from the States," he said.

"Is it that obvious?" His comment wounded the pride she took in her ability to blend in.

Galen offered his hand. "Galen Peterson."

"Major Marsh Manetti, US Navy. Serving with NATO."

Thank you! She restrained a sigh of relief and re-deleted the six-letter *D*-word. "I'm *Lynn Peterson*," she emphasized as they shook hands. He didn't react. Not a nod or knowing look. Not a twitch of a facial muscle or even a flicker in his eyes. He was either great at masks or had never heard of her. Regardless, she realized that she had never been so grateful for a stranger's hand in hers. "Thank you for serving our country." The words came sincerely, without thought. She meant them. But they weren't helpful.

He smiled. "I've been enough places in the world to know how lucky we are to be born in the States, ma'am."

"A gift by birth," Galen agreed.

Her mind swirled. Doesn't he know I have something important for him?

How could he know, Lynn? If the President had access to confidential communication with him, she wouldn't need you.

Lynn's relief to see him morphed into another attack of anxiety. Her fingers jerked to the waist wallet. How do I get it to him? Something short of "By the way, sir, here is a letter for you from President Benedict." Galen wouldn't believe that either. Just like he hadn't believed the mime was on the streetcar.

Whoa, Lynn! Don't rebait that hook!

"Where are you stationed, Major Manetti?" asked Galen.

"In Naples. I'm the assistant to the NATO commander in charge of strategy for the Balkans."

"Are you waiting for the flight to Vienna also?"

The major nodded. "What will you be doing there?"

His behavior bewildered Lynn. Apparently he knew nothing about the letter. Yet his idle little chat left the impression that he wanted to hang around them. Why?

Maybe he's genuinely interested, Lynn.

"My wife is giving a speech. She's a bishop," said Galen as Lynn simultaneously responded, "Attending a conference."

The major smiled at Lynn. "By that, I take it you are giving a speech at a conference."

"And meeting with a chaplain from our area. He's going to pick us up at the airport." Maybe if I give him enough information, something will click.

"All the chaplains do good work. I'm Catholic. Sometimes our wounds are spiritual wounds instead of physical ones. Sometimes," he added pensively, "they are both."

"After Vienna we're going to Skopje and then on a peace mission to Sarajevo. Are the Balkans safe?" she asked.

"Safety there depends on your purpose and timing. By the way, if anyone asks your purpose, you may want to say it is humanitarian aid. Both sides try to protect people with that aim. Fact-finders are more suspect." He shook his head. "As for timing, yours is not the best."

"Ours never is," said Galen with a wink at Lynn.

Galen's confident manner and his willingness to go difficult places with her soothed her turbulent sea of tension.

Time is running out. Think, Lynn!

She remembered *Balkan Ghosts* stuffed in Big-Black. That could work. She excused herself to find the restroom. Stood in line. Minutes passed as slow as hospital time. Next! She locked the door to a tiny stall. Noticed the filthy toilet. Unzipped her waist wallet with trembling fingers. Removed the envelope. She stared at it for a moment, awed by the potential import of a letter from the President of the United States.

Hurry, Lynn!

She pulled *Balkan Ghosts* and a small pad of sticky notes from Big-Black. Wrote: For Marsh with NATO. Folded the envelope in half. Added the sticky note. Hid it inside the book. Noted the pages: 50/51. Returned the book to Big-Black. Zipped her waist wallet. Unlocked the stall door. As an afterthought, she flushed the toilet.

Instead of dangling the bag nonchalantly from her shoulder as usual, she put the strap over her head and draped it across her chest. She clutched it nervously with both hands, aware that her compulsive behavior sent an invitation to purse snatchers. But she couldn't release her protect-it-at-all-costs grasp on Big-Black.

She neared the gate. The major appeared to be watching for her. Was there anxiety in his stance? He smiled and seemed to relax as she approached. Again his behavior bewildered her. Merely a new friend or a co-conspirator?

Boarding any moment, Lynn. Stop procrastinating.

She removed the book from Big-Black and made her pitch. "Major Manetti, I need as much information as possible about Skopje and Sarajevo before we go there. If you have a chance on the plane, would you be willing to scan some sections of *Balkan Ghosts*?" She offered it to him. Please don't say you've read it.

Galen frowned at her, and she knew he thought she was imposing. I know, she wanted to say, but there's a good reason—far beyond your imagination. "You'll find those sections in Part I. It deals with Macedonia and Bosnia-Herzegovina. With your experience in the area, it would be helpful to know whether you think Kaplan was on target."

"I'll be glad to," he said. "I like to read on planes."

She breathed a silent thank you. "I especially wonder about pages 50 and 51." Please don't open to those pages now.

He tucked the book under his arm.

Another silent thank you.

"I'll return it before we land. What are your seat numbers?"

Galen checked and told him.

"I'm in the row behind you." His eyes twinkled. "How's that for coincidence!"

The agent called them to board. Galen shook his hand. "I enjoyed talking with you, Major Manetti."

"And you." He turned to Lynn. "Good luck on your speech, Bishop Peterson."

Lynn smiled at him. "I hope you find something interesting in the book."

Ahhh! she thought. This clandestine nightmare is behind me.

PART II
The Rancher

Sunday, 10:37 A.M.

Vienna. City of intrigue and inspiration. Art and architecture. Parks and palaces. Culture, cathedrals, and prancing Lipizzaners. Place of death for Emperor Marcus Aurelius. Home to Sigmund Freud, father of psychoanalysis, and Karl Lueger, shaper of Hitler. Music capital of the world for more than two hundred years. The provincial capital of the German Reich for seven.

Vienna. Nestled between plains of the Danube basin and foothills of the Alps. Governed by rulers dethroned; the conquerors in turn dethroned. Struck by sieges, plagues, and religious strife.

Vienna. City of mystery and malevolence.

26

LYNN HAD BEEN SLYLY WATCHING MARSH WITH NATO IN HER PERIPHERAL vision throughout the flight to Vienna and knew he'd found the envelope and read the letter. She'd harnessed all the discipline she possessed to keep from turning back to him and asking about it. If she'd been seated beside him, she feared she would have tried to read it. She felt the plane's descent toward Flughafen Wien and a tap on her shoulder. He handed her *Balkan Ghosts*. His eyes met hers for a knowing moment, and he offered the slightest of nods. "Thank you, Bishop Peterson. Kaplan is on target."

"I appreciate your help with this more than I can say."

"My pleasure. You gave me an opportunity to be of service."

So, Lynn, both of you practice double-speak.

She fanned the pages to 50 and 51 to check for the letter. Gone! A note scribbled in small script on his boarding stub replaced the burdensome message. Hallelujah! Mission accomplished!

"What's his note about?" asked Galen, looking over her shoulder.

She'd already scanned it and read it aloud:

> The author is knowledgeable, insightful, and helpful. Some pages contain interesting surprises. Thank you.

Ah, Love, if I could only share the whole story with you! She relaxed and looked out the window. But the mystery of the request would always float around the edges of her curious mind.

The flight attendant welcomed them in three languages as they taxied to a stop. When the cabin signal dinged, the passengers jumped to their feet like Pavlov's dogs salivating to get off the plane—grabbed belongings, competed for space, stood single-file, and guarded their place. Lynn raised the handle of her roll-aboard and slipped Big-Black over her shoulder. Without the President's letter, her waist-wallet seemed ten pounds lighter, her tic of checking it cured. She glanced behind her expecting to say a word to Major Manetti, but he'd stepped back to assist a woman with her suitcase. Several people stood between them. He winked at her confidently and brushed his fingers nonchalantly across his breast pocket.

Ah, yes! Mission fully and successfully accomplished. She closed her eyes for a second. Thank you.

The restless line of passengers began inching down the aisle. They deplaned on a portable stair ramp in the airfield. So much for a roll-aboard! As Lynn carried it down the narrow metal steps, she realized once again how misleading the ratio of weight to size can be—like a large balloon and a small paperweight.

A man in camouflage fatigues, lean and smiling, stood at the bottom of the ramp and reached up for Lynn's suitcase. "Bishop Peterson?" he shouted over the noise of the plane. "I'm Dick Osborne. Welcome to Vienna." The chaplain wore his blue cap low across his brow, the brim touching the rims of his glasses. His multi-pocketed jacket with rolled-up sleeves hung over pants tucked into laced leggings that covered the tops of his black military boots.

Lynn extended her hand. "Thanks for meeting us." She introduced Galen above the roar.

"Dr. Peterson," Dick shook his hand and yelled, "You're a historian as I recall."

Galen nodded as the pilot cut the engine. "Thank you for meeting us, Chaplain Osborne."

"Dick. Please call me Dick. My pleasure, sir." He turned to Lynn. "Bishop, thank you for taking time to see me. It means a lot."

She smiled at him. "I understand you just returned from the base at Zagreb, Dick."

His eyes clouded. "It's tough there."

"I want to hear about it over lunch."

"Are you here on leave?" asked Galen.

"Just a brief reprieve—a Partnership for Peace meeting. As you know, the Balkans need all the help they can get."

Fumes filled Lynn's lungs as they walked on the paint-outlined path to the terminal. She glanced back at the plane.

Marsh with NATO exited the door, his Tom Hanks smile and military bearing intact. He stood at the top of the ramp, a notable figure in his crisp white uniform.

A single shot rang out.

Passengers stumbled on the ramp and fell in a heap. Lynn glimpsed a white uniform sprawled across the landing. The man it clothed angled askew down the steps. Unmoving.

27

IT'S MAJOR MANETTI!" LYNN SHRIEKED.

"Quick!" Dick propelled her toward a Jeep parked in a reserved VIP space.

She tried to jerk free. "We have to help!"

"There could be more shooting!" Galen exclaimed.

"But it was *Marsh with NATO!*"

The two men shoved her into the back and jumped in the front. Dick raced toward the exit before officials had time to close everything down.

"We don't know whether Major Manetti was shot, Lynn."

Shot.

"He probably just fell with the others, Bishop."

A siren blared. "There's the ambulance," said Dick. He swerved to get out of its way.

When they cleared the airport, Lynn leaned forward and placed her hand on the chaplain's shoulder. "Dick, I *must* get to the hospital." She spoke in her nonnegotiable tone. Rarely used, never retracted, always meaning exactly that: *nonnegotiable.* "Please wait for the ambulance and follow it."

Dick looked back at her. "Is the major a friend, Bishop?"

"A friend of . . . of a friend of mine. We talked together in Frankfurt." And, her mind screamed so loud she was afraid they'd hear, he has the President's letter!

"If he was injured, he'll get the best care possible." Dick found a place where he could pull the Jeep off.

Galen turned and put his hand gently over hers. "You've had a shock," he said soothingly. "We all have."

"A terrible way to welcome you!" said the chaplain. "I'm sorry."

They were silent until the siren wailed again. Dick placed some VIP credentials on the dash. As soon as the ambulance passed them, he thrust a whirling red light through the window onto the top of the car and floored the pedal. A skillful driver, he wove his way through the traffic right behind it. He sped through an intersection just as the light turned red. It threw Lynn's mind back in time to another speeding car, another red light. Her throat tightened. She felt light-headed. Shrank down in the seat. She felt herself falling, the familiar swirling waters sucking her under. Down into the irresponsible, irreversible, irrevocable crash three years ago.

> Precious Lyndie jumps in a red Mustang with a friend. She waves goodbye as they pull away laughing. It is Sunday evening, and they head to the church for youth group. They reach the corner. A drunk driver flies through the red light. He crashes full speed against the passenger door. The machete drops. And precious Lyndie—sweet and beautiful, bright and joyful, filled with goodness and hope—never regains consciousness.

And neither did part of Lynn.

She felt Galen's strong hand on hers. She struggled within to wrench herself upward from the dark waters whirling around her, over her, drowning her. He began to chatter, so unlike himself. She hung onto his deep, soothing tone more than his words. His voice reached down, a single sunbeam in her darkness. It penetrated her mind and touched her soul, gradually strengthening her. She opened her eyes and saw his loving look upon her, knowing he had read the signs and was calling her back. Slowly surfacing, she took a deep breath and tucked Lyndie safely back in her heart.

"Are you all right, Lynn?" he asked gently.

She nodded. But she knew she would never truly be all right. And neither would he. We don't fully recover from some losses. We just try to get through the rest of our lives the best way we can.

They reached the hospital just after the ambulance. Dick parked in a reserved space. "Let's go."

He opened her door, and she walked with trepidation toward the *Krandenhaus* doors. The sun beamed down with the gift of light and beauty that denied reality's storm. She entered the hospital with a sense of foreboding. That's normal, she reminded herself. Hospitals evoke anxiety. Antiseptic smells. Hushed voices. Hurried steps. And a permeating sense of foreboding. Especially when an unknown language is spoken.

Using the authority of his chaplaincy, Dick talked with a nurse who spoke English and agreed to keep him informed.

Lynn paced. Seconds took minutes to pass.

Settle down, Lynn. There's nothing you can do right now.

She prayed fervently for Marsh to be all right. Please. Oh, please!

The nurse who'd spoken with Dick scooted back a canvas curtain hung on rings and looked at him. He stepped forward and spoke softly to her. She mumbled something and shook her head. He returned to them with heavy steps. "I'm sorry." He put a steadying arm around Lynn. "Major Manetti was dead on arrival."

28

Dead on arrival. The words of finality fell into time and space. Lynn barely knew him, yet she felt she'd lost an old friend. The President's letter had stayed in the shadows of her mind since Wednesday night's limo ride, waiting for release to Marsh with NATO. In the few sentences they'd spoken this morning, she'd seen his competence and sensed his integrity. No wonder President Benedict trusts him.

Trusted him, she corrected. Major Manetti was dead. The loss gripped her heart. The last scene of him alive flashed in her mind and held like a snapshot: his wink as he brushed his fingers across his breast pocket when they stood in the aisle to deplane. The President's letter delivered! Now undelivered. She groped for light in the midnight gloom of a sky without stars.

A voice on the speaker system said words that Lynn couldn't understand, but the tone was like *Code Red! Code Red!*

The nurse returned to Dick. "A bus was bombed!" She pointed beyond the door. "A block away. Can you help us? We'll tend to injuries. You tend to fear. And families. *Ja?*"

"*Ja.*" Dick, experienced in the MASH unit at the Zagreb base, looked at Galen. "They'll need our help carrying stretchers. It'll free the medics, Dr. Peterson."

"Doctor?" asked the nurse hopefully. "*Der Mediziner*?"

Galen shook his head. "Sorry. Ph.D. in history. But strong arms."

"I'll stay in here," said Lynn, then pointed to herself and added to the nurse, "*Bischof.* Help care for the families." Galen and Dick hurried out. Lynn watched the staff move with choreographed haste. She kept her eye on the canvas curtain the nurse had scooted back. A man in scrubs rolled out a gurney at full speed. A sheet covered the body head to toe. He quickly relegated it to an out-of-the-way cubicle down the hall and hurried back to prepare space for the injured.

Medics rushed. Patients groaned. Superiors shouted orders. Unnoticed in the confusion, Lynn walked down the hall with a forced air of poise and purpose. She ducked into the cubicle and stood beside the gurney. To touch the sheet, to lift it, to uncover the face would turn this impersonal John Doe into a specific person, a new friend. She wanted to bolt.

Not an option. The bedlam beyond kept eyes on the injured and off the cubicle. But for how long? Slowly she lifted the sheet and lowered it to his shoulders. Her stomach lurched. Tears stung her eyes. She stared at the wound to Major Manetti's head. Horrified. A vibrant life violated. One minute here. The next, gone forever. Like Elie. Like Lyndie.

Get the letter, Lynn.

The medics hadn't bothered to remove his clothes. Dead on arrival. She forced herself to lower the sheet to mid-chest where she could see his pocket. The cubicle began to spin. Not real. TV scene. TV prop. Just a show. Just pretend. She kept the chant running through her mind. Not real. She watched her hand hover over the body. TV scene. A hand that belonged to someone else. TV prop. She saw it reach into the breast pocket of the uniform. Just a show. And take hold of the envelope. Just pretend. And pull it out.

But it wasn't pretend. The body was real. Major Manetti. A good Catholic. And no priest had prayed for him.

So Lynn did. She put her hand over his. His lifeless hand with a wedding band. A hand that would never move again, never salute an officer or shake another's hand, never rest around his wife's waist or on his child's head. She closed her eyes and prayed the Lord's Prayer. Then she whispered the Twenty-third Psalm.

With blinding tears she crammed the President's letter into Big-Black. She bowed her head respectfully to Marsh with NATO, re-covered him with the sheet and crept out of the cubicle on tiptoe. Head down. Heart heavy. And went down the hall to tend fears and families.

29

John Adams usually played golf on Sunday mornings, but not today. Anxiously he checked his watch, figured the time difference and ran his thumb across the *fleur-de-lis* in JFK's stand. He fingered the secure phone and paced around his office while waiting for Zeller's call. Mentally he reviewed their meeting in Frankfurt, satisfied. The elite marksman never failed.

He pulled Darwish's medal from his pocket. His fingers tingled as it drew him to old memories. Memories of Jerusalem. He sat down at his desk and stared at the engraved symbol. He'd recognized it when he opened Zeller's "birthday present" in the privacy of his jet. He'd known without knowing that Darwish had been a member of the Society of St. Sava. Now he held proof. He brushed his thumb across the medal and felt the weight of a dreaded portent. But he must do his duty and dispose of it properly. Honor demanded it despite the risk. Unreasonable but necessary.

The exhausting round-trip Frankfurt journey had drawn dark circles under his eyes. Meeting with Zeller. Getting Darwish's medal. Assigning the Manetti contract. This morning the *Juggler* seemed a more appropriate sobriquet than the *Patriot*. He had more balls in the air than prudent: two identities to execute, covert and overt businesses to run, the Inner Circle to influence, a President to lure into his debt. And his beloved wife and adored children to care for. He glanced at their happy picture and smiled despite his burdens.

Moving to the window, he parted the drapes and squinted into the rising sun, then looked down at the city that empowered him, a city often driven by fear and chaos. A verse from Psalm 73 came to mind: You place them on a slippery slope and drive them down into chaos. But from the ashes would rise his Holy Vision of justice. In the meantime chaos and fear wrought damage to cities and countries. But they were good for business, both illegitimate arms sales and legitimate rebuilding after the conflict. Good business meant more money. More money resulted in more power and influence to shape his version of justice.

He checked the time again, impatient for Zeller's call, envisioning the disturbance that would be caused by Manetti's termination. Potentially it could affect NATO. But his death would be a small disturbance compared to what was arranged for tomorrow afternoon. He'd had nothing to do with the bombing of the Vienna bus today, already an international news story. But its timing was fortuitous. It would increase the impact of his special surprise for the President of Austria. What better opportunity to spread the contagion of chaos than a gathering of delegates from around the world? He would be a fool not to take advantage of it.

These were times of crisis, and he was good at translating crisis into opportunity. Thus, BarLothiun's success. Rebuilding infrastructures after natural and human disasters had made him one of the wealthiest men in the country. Since he held his company privately, he didn't have to appease stockholders quarterly. His wise long-term decisions kept BarLothiun's coffers overflowing, and he didn't have to share the profits. He could lavish them on generous employee salaries and benefits.

People were proud and grateful to work for BarLothiun, and he kept it that way. His beloved but polarized country seemed bent on destroying itself from the inside, and he did what he could: he gave more money away. And more money bought more influence, more power, more control. But that old truism didn't work with President Benedict. He was not sure what or who pulled her strings—if she had any. But not money. Nor him. He found himself respecting her for not being for sale but also resenting her for it. She complicated his life. He needed to gain her friendship and loyalty to ensure his power. Not for himself. Never for himself. Always for the pursuit of righteousness and the fulfillment of God's plan for justice.

The secure phone rang. He clasped it in his long, slender fingers and listened. Another success for Zeller, as expected. The ace was a stranger to failure. As he returned the phone to JFK, a frown replaced his smile. This was not a time to dance, but a time to mourn for Manetti's family and their loss of husband and father. Unfortunate but necessary. He reminded himself that he was clear of any blame. Guilt fell squarely on the shoulders of the President.

The Manetti problem was cared for, but the Peterson factor continued to nag at him despite the lack of incriminating evidence. Bishop Lynn Peterson traveled in international circles, a perfect opportunity for a presidential conduit. Was she involved?

All of these worrisome problems because of President Benedict. Vice President Parker, like former presidents, was a good friend and understood what that meant. He would be a better leader for the country. Why not target Benedict and solve all his problems?

The thought shocked him.

It scared him.

But it didn't release him.

30

AT THE HOSPITAL LYNN PRAYED WITH THE INJURED WHO WANTED TO PRAY and listened to family members who wanted to talk. After an hour, she found herself exhausted from the emotional trauma of Marsh's death and retrieving the President's letter and not knowing what to do with it and trying to be a channel of God's love for the injured and their families and the night on the plane and jet lag. She turned down a hall that led to a quieter wing of the hospital. She leaned against the wall and closed her eyes. She began to breathe deeply in this silent space. In a moment or two she felt someone watching her.

Across the hall through the door directly opposite her a lone teenage boy sat on a table. Both legs were missing, and his left hand clutched the edge of the table for balance. She'd learned from Dick that some of the wounded NATO soldiers fighting in the Balkans were transferred here when they needed therapy and longer care than the Zagreb MASH unit could provide. He'd obviously been deserted in the chaos of the tragedy, and he was probably one of those soldiers. She wondered if a landmine had cost him his legs.

His youth struck her. Maybe eighteen, but she guessed sixteen. *Lyndie.* She started to lower her eyes to give him privacy, but he looked straight at her from deep blue wells of sadness. She smiled and took a step toward his door. "Where are you from?"

He just stared at her.

"English?" she asked, hoping he spoke it. Or at least understood that nearly universal word.

"*Nyet*," he said.

Nyet. He said the word gently, but Russian was her favorite language for expressing an adamant *No!* What better sound for defiance than *NYET!* Landmines: *NYET!* She longed to comfort him, knew nothing could. What is the word for *son*? Think! It came to her: *syn.* Сын in the Cyrillic alphabet. The letters came as quickly to her mind as the sounds. "*Dobryi dyen, syn*," she said in her style of mixing transliteration and phonetics. "Good afternoon, son."

Hearing the simple greeting in his own tongue brought a surprised smile to his face. "Добрый денв," he said, repeating her greeting.

She wondered if anyone in the hospital spoke his language. There must be so many words of reassurance he needed to hear as he stared at the space where his legs used to be, so many things he wanted to say. Hesitantly she entered the room and introduced herself. "My name is Lynn. *Moya familiya* Lynn."

He smiled and pointed to himself. "Sasha."

Grateful for the courtesies she'd learned in Russian, she told him she was very pleased to meet him. "*Ochen' priyatno*, Sasha." She meant it.

Again he politely repeated her greeting. "Очень приятно." He searched her face. Timidly he opened his right fist. A cross lay in his palm.

She noticed that it wasn't the Russian Orthodox style with double-slanted crossbars. Instead, it had a single straight crossbar and was on a round silver disc. She wondered if her presence in the hall had interrupted a prayer, probably one of desperation. She gestured toward herself. "*Yepiskop.*" She couldn't remember whether the word for bishop had an alternative feminine ending, but it didn't matter at the moment.

"Елйскол?"

She nodded, realizing that since the Russian Orthodox Church was the predominant faith in his homeland, a woman bishop probably seemed . . .

Unorthodox, Lynn?

She felt a strong urge to offer to pray for Sasha and bless him. She hesitated, then formed praying hands. "*Da?*"

Untroubled by her gender, he bowed his head expectantly. She placed both hands on the top of his head and offered a prayer of blessing in English. She longed to be able to bless him in Russian.

When she finished, there were tears in the boy's eyes and a sense of peace on his face. Prayers and blessings are multilingual. "Спаснбо," he said quietly, thanking her.

Just as *nyet* was an expressive word for *no*, so *spasebo* was a beautiful word for *thank you.* She sighed, not wanting to move on, but it was time to say goodbye. "*Do svidaniya*, Sasha."

"До свидания," he repeated.

She restrained herself from giving him a hug, sensing that right now he might confuse it with pity. He needed confidence that he was still a man. She placed both palms together and bowed her head respectfully to him, Russian style, then turned away before her own tears welled up. She summoned again the pretense of a TV show so the horror of war wouldn't seep through her defenses and force her to face torn flesh and broken hearts and missing limbs and sickened souls. She knew that Sasha would be with her for the rest of her life. Landmines, she thought again, *NYET!*

Just as she stepped through the door, she heard something drop, and Sasha called to her with heart-rending desperation. She moved quickly back to the table. He pointed downward, and she realized he'd dropped his cross. It lay on the floor upside down, revealing the other side of the silver disc. As she bent to pick it up, her hand froze. In the center stood two crescents in a mottled greenish-bluish gemstone. They overlapped vertically like connected waning moons. Like Elie's medal! Could it be Elie's? A medal stolen in New Orleans on Thursday and found in the hands of a wounded Russian in Vienna on Sunday? With a cross welded onto the other side? Impossible.

She glanced up at Sasha. She had hesitated too long. He could tell she found something familiar about it. He looked frightened. He put his index finger to his lips and locked his eyes on hers as though concentrating all his power of being, merging their souls for a moment, willing her to silence. She recognized this mysterious magnetic force of intercommunion because she had initiated it herself in a few rare and desperate situations. She nodded and mimicked his finger-to-lips gesture, a promise of silence that they shared this secret together, and she would keep it.

She picked up his cross and felt its cold metal against her fingers like an echo of Elie's medal. She placed it gently in his palm and for a moment held her hand over his. A secret links us, she thought, but she didn't know how to say it. At least she knew how to say farewell. "*Proshchat'sya*, Sasha." She smiled warmly, her mind framing the Cyrillic word, Прощаите.

Laden with questions, Lynn plodded to the hospital entry. Was Elie's medal a symbol of some kind? Did Sasha realize she recognized it? Is that what frightened him? Did it link Sasha and Elie? She wanted to go back and ask him, but she couldn't cross the language barrier. And she couldn't seek a translator because of the fear in his eyes when he thought she recognized the symbol. She would never know. She would have to settle for turning the page.

Sun shone through the hospital windows, but darkness engulfed her. She needed time alone to center herself. But there was none. Instead of a calm center from which she could reflect God's love to others, a tornado hurled within her. Two gunshots. A heart wound and a head wound. On opposite sides of the sea. Both in her presence. Her mind flashed images like blinking neon lights. Elie's laugh then blood on his T-shirt. The major's wink then his face on a gurney. And a Russian boy without legs.

Russian! That's what triggered a flash of memory when she first saw Elie's medal! The overlapping crescents were made of Амазонéт, or amazonite, the most beautiful gemstone in her Russian collection. Bluer than malachite. Greener than turquoise. Mined on the Siberian border in the Ural Mountains. A medal and a cross with Russian stones designed in the same symbol. She felt sure the unique symbol connected Elie and Sasha. But how?

And now she, too, was connected with Sasha through a secret. Eerie chills snaked up her spine.

31

ZELLER AMBLED ALONG THROUGH THE STREETS OF VIENNA TOWARD DR. Karl Lueger Platz, reflecting on the morning. He commended himself for outsmarting airport security. Games have rules, but rules *are* games. People with nothing to hide follow them; the rest maneuver around them. He had timed his arrival at Flughafen Wien to coincide with the early rush of departing flights. He checked his bag containing his rifle and typical travel clothes. Got through security with a fake boarding pass. Entered a restroom stall. Took off his inconspicuous gray suit worn over a baggage handlers' uniform, turned off the water flow to the toilet and stashed his suit in a plastic bag in the tank. Donned fake ID tags and put an out-of-order sign on the stall door. Went to the baggage loading area, blended in with the other handlers and retrieved his suitcase. Returned to the restroom stall, changed back into his suit, made his way to the chosen site, and waited for Manetti's plane to land with plenty of time to settle himself and focus totally on his task. So easy.

After the single shot, he took apart his rifle, put it back in the suitcase, effortlessly and efficiently escaped from his firing position. This time he blended in among the dazed, panic-stricken crowd, one more person with a bag. He made himself invisible with his inconspicuous gray suit, a slouch, and a vacant stare. He left through the nearest exit before an official procedure could be implemented. Once again, so easy.

But he must not grow overconfident. He reviewed his escape. Had he covered his tracks? Absolutely. He never left evidence unless intentionally planted. Yet in a dangerous profession many things can go wrong. The Manetti success could still go wrong. He fought a strong impulse to look over his shoulder. No. Suspicious looks would result in looking suspicious.

It began to mist as he entered Dr. Karl Lueger Platz. He ignored the dampness. This morning he'd been robbed of his customary exhilaration after a perfect shot. He deserved a high after a success, had earned it. He quelled his rising anger. Anger affected thought processes. It was dangerous. Like overconfidence. Mentally he reran the landing scene in slow motion:

> My plan is perfect. I am well positioned. The plane lands. I lift my rifle. I telescope each deplaning figure. I wait for the target. A familiar face comes into focus. She lifts her suitcase to carry it down the ramp. The tall man behind her reaches out to take it. She shakes her head. I keep her in my scope. I remember! The woman with Hercules in New Orleans! The one I took the medal from on the streetcar! Seeing her almost unsteadies me. Steady! *Steady!*

He reran the scene again and reached the same disturbing conclusion. Unquestionably she was the woman from New Orleans. He prided himself on never forgetting a face—or the name attached to it. His perfect memory matched his perfect aim. An essential skill for both assassins and politicians.

Honor was the major difference between the two professions. Politicians did not keep their promises, whereas his word was gold.

The woman's presence stole away his post-hit high, a theft inviting consequences. She had seen his face close up on the streetcar, his eyes bare of sunglasses for an instant. Eyes are distinctly individual and memorable. She could recognize him if she saw him again—and she was on his turf in Vienna. He considered what he knew about her from his observation at the café. She was naïve, a window without curtains. So naïve that she put something valuable in her skirt pocket, had no suspicion that the woman on the streetcar was tripped and did not even notice when her pocket was picked. Apprehension lessened, and he felt relieved. He could reject her as a target, at least for now. He declined contracts on women. In the beginning he had accepted one, his first and his last. Her face in *Freund's* telescopic lens kept blurring into his mother's face. Never again! No. His code of honor was a three-point star: He would not shoot anyone in the back—unless absolutely necessary. He would not terminate a woman—unless the contract paid enough to retire. Nor would he terminate another ace—not without a critical reason. He took pride in his elite profession. If Manetti had been a shooter, he would still be alive.

He stood in the mist, staring up at Lueger's statue. The small woman from New Orleans and the tall man behind her remained in the shadows of his mind. But he would not let them return to the forefront. No. Not unless they crossed his path again.

32

WHEN THE CHAOS CALMED AT THE HOSPITAL, DICK ASKED LYNN IF THEY still had time for a late lunch. She wanted to go over her speech again before the banquet, but she knew he needed to talk. She could tell by the strength he'd shown at the hospital that he was a rock for the troops. But even the strong need times when they can lean on a rock instead of be one. "Of course we do," she said. "You're an exceptional chaplain, and we've been looking forward to lunch together."

He took them to a small, quiet place. Lynn tried but couldn't eat. Elie's shooting, Marsh's gaping head, Sasha's missing legs, the bombing victims. All the violence whirled through her mind. And then there was the discovery of another medal like Elie's. She toyed with her soup and forced herself to focus on Dick. He began to talk about hardships in the Balkans. The troops live with danger and demoralization. The chaplains have a difficult job. The MASH staff an impossible one. Casualties mount daily. Chaos is the norm. Galen joined her in being a rock for Dick today. Galen genuinely cared for people. He loved to talk about history, but he also knew when to listen. Gratitude for him welled up within her.

A light mist fell as they returned to the car. Dick seemed embarrassed as he opened the door for her and climbed into the driver's seat. "I'm sorry to let all this spill out." With a sigh he added softly, "I guess I needed a pastor."

She reached forward and patted his shoulder lightly. "That's why I'm here, Dick. You have to be strong for the troops. You don't have to be strong for us."

But the rock returned. Their conversation was light as he drove them to the hotel. They talked about the picturesque city that rested against the skyline like an old painting. Window boxes of red geraniums dotted the ancient buildings, drops of mist sparkling on their blooms. Beautiful Vienna!

When they came to the inner city ring, Dick pointed out Dr. Karl Lueger Platz and his statue.

"I read that Vienna has more statues of Lueger than Mozart," said Lynn.

"He was Hitler's mentor in demagogy," said Galen. "Unfortunately, he wasn't the first or the last to use prejudice for political sway."

Lynn smiled to herself. How Galen loved history! And how he loved to share his knowledge of it! That was one of the things she loved about him. Another was being able to draw on his strength. They had different strong points and that was good. They could count on each other.

She noticed a lone man in the mist, an intimidating figure even at a distance. He was looking up at Lueger's statue, his back to her. Broad-shouldered in his trench coat, he stood as rigid as a mime. As they drove past, he turned away from the statue and stepped double-time through the *platz*. He had a frown and thin lips above a square jaw. His opaque sunglasses drew her attention, markedly out of place in the gray mist. He blurred into her image of Sunglasses in New Orleans. It couldn't be!

She pulled her phone from Big-Black and glanced quickly at the profile pictures she'd taken on the streetcar. Could it be?

Galen looked back at her. "Are you checking phone service?"

"We have it, Love," she said, telling a truth without answering his question.

You're getting so slick, Lynn.

Not a compliment. She put the cell away without mentioning the resemblance of the man in the mist to the man on the streetcar. No point in shelling that shrimp again. But her fingers automatically moved to her waist wallet, tic recurring. She felt for the letter to "Marsh with NATO." Still there.

Dick planned to take them to the airport for their flight to Skopje, so they were spared a final goodbye when they reached the hotel. "See you Tuesday afternoon," he said.

"Good," said Lynn. "Thanks for everything today."

Galen added his appreciation, and they rolled their luggage into a hotel lobby alive with the rush of bellmen and the laughing hubbub of friendly delegates. At the moment, however, being tired trumped being social, and they hurried toward the rapidly filling elevator. Lynn stepped back from the door to wait for the next one, but felt Galen's hand in the middle of her back pushing her forward. The doors closed. People pressed close while the small, ancient elevator groaned its ascent.

Perhaps because of exhaustion. Or grief. Or man-in-the-mist anxiety. Or reprisal for being prodded onto an elevator. Whatever the reason, Lynn blatantly peered at everyone behind her. Over her left shoulder. Over her right shoulder. Then she stage-whispered to Galen, "Which one is the undercover agent?"

An immediate hush fell—except for Galen's exasperated sigh.

Perfect! They assumed the tall man in the front was upset because she'd revealed a clandestine presence. But her delight was short-lived. Disappointed in herself, she grew up once more. Why do I do things like that? *As long as you both shall live* must be a burdensome vow for Galen at times.

Definitely.

She shushed Ivy and defended herself. He won't push me on a crowded elevator again. Not soon, anyway. Sometimes we just have to make things memorable.

33

President Helena Benedict arrived early in the Oval Office. She liked a head start on the day before interruptions. But before she closed the door, her secretary put through a call. She listened numbly. She continued to clutch the small, black source of horrible news long after the goodbyes. Beyond her window, pastels of pinks and violets painted the promise of sunlight in the dawn sky, a promise broken by the midnight darkness of her spirit. She finally put down the phone, still reeling from the shock of her friend's death. A sense of loss gripped her like a vise that choked off air.

She sat down at the desk to write a personal letter of condolence to Mrs. Manetti. Her heart grieved for the family. She wondered how many condolences had been written at this historic desk. Too many. She reread the heartfelt note and again lifted the old Mont Blanc pen used for years by her father. Her short dark hair fell across her cheeks as she bent to sign it. A letter for a life.

Or a life because of a letter? Fear of responsibility clotted her veins. Perhaps the reason for death had nothing to do with her. Perhaps the timing was coincidental. But deep within, where the subconscious rings true, she knew that she might as well have pulled the trigger. She had singled out Marsh. She had attempted to have a covert letter delivered to him. Her lack of prescience was no defense.

She scraped her soul from the floor and forced her tears to dam behind her eyes. *Remember the Alamo*, her father would have said. She could almost hear his voice. For him, and therefore for her, it referred to a family behavior code for standing alone: when we face overwhelming odds and no one else will come to help, we remember our roots and honor our family by standing our ground and doing what we can—without whining. For the rest of the day she went through the motions duty required, wore an emotionless mask, maintained a façade of presidential demeanor. *Remember the Alamo!*

34

GALEN UNLOCKED THE DOOR TO THEIR HOTEL ROOM. FLORAL DUVETS COVered the side-by-side twin beds that dominated the small space. Large, inviting pillows beckoned them. Lynn wanted to curl up in the fluff and sleep for three days. But there wasn't time. She had to go over her keynote address before the banquet. She realized that Galen must be equally weary. "You could skip the banquet, Love, and get some rest," she told him, partly to make up for her elevator stunt.

Tenderness replaced exasperation. "Miss my favorite speaker? No way."

Steadfast Galen. They didn't talk about all that had happened since landing this morning. They were too spent to face it all again. Besides, there wasn't time. There was never time.

She showered off the long flight and horrible day. The water brought her to the source. To stilled waves. And the deep well. And the Living Water. She centered herself and silenced the tornado within her. She slipped into her short, silk travel kimono and draped a towel around her hair. Galen had lifted her roll-aboard to the bed. She took out lingerie and heels and shook out her black dress. She paused for a moment and watched him slide an oval gold cuff link into his shirtsleeve, twisting it to get his initials right side up. She smiled.

"What?" he asked.

"You dress as sharp on this side of the pond as the other."

He raised questioning eyebrows. "What does the ocean have to do with it? Besides," he winked at her, "a bishop's spouse has to look 'sharp' when the bishop is giving the keynote at a worldwide conference. Rule 4526 in the unwritten code."

Oh, yes! How she loved him! She donned the strand of Mardi Gras beads, confident that the dim banquet light would transform them into a string of pearls, and distance would do the same while she stood at the better-lit dais. We see what we expect to see.

They walked down the two flights of stairs to the ballroom—no mention of the elevator. As they entered the banquet hall, the aroma reminded Lynn how long it had been since she'd eaten a real meal. They nodded to Bishop Booker T. W. Phillips and his wife, Sylvia. Lynn loved them both. Two decades older, he was her unofficial mentor in the episcopacy, and Sylvia was the best friend anyone could have. The women hugged. The men shook hands.

Booker stood almost as tall as Galen. A bit of gray sprinkled his black hair and mustache. The lines in his face etched the character of one who walks the faith talk.

Lynn asked about their four sons: Cato, Plato, Prince, and Quamony, named for the courageous Revolutionary War veterans of African descent generally omitted from textbook history. To her, their names summed up the story of Booker and Sylvia's patriotism and pride.

"Did you fly in today?" asked Galen.

"Yesterday," said Sylvia in her Maya Angelou voice. She was aging gracefully, a striking woman with thoughtful dark eyes, a habitual smile, and a beautiful spirit.

"I wish you well tonight, Lynn," said Booker.

"Thank you. Speaking to this inordinately diverse group is no small challenge."

He smiled. "Simply getting around the title sounds like a challenge."

"*Psychoanalysis, Meditation, and Spiritual Practice.* I didn't pick it. I was assigned it."

"What title would you give it?" he asked.

"*Faith and Feelings*," she said without forethought. "No," she reflected, wanting to take her mentor seriously. "I'd call it *Journey Toward Transformation*."

He nodded. "That's what we're about, Lynn. Growing deeper, reaching broader, going higher. I'm eager to hear what you have to say."

"Please hold me in prayer, Booker." She paused and stated a deep private truth. "Knowing you're doing that will give me courage."

At that moment Bishop Jeff James and his wife, Tiffany, joined them. Lynn winced internally. She'd failed to discover an appreciation of Jeff. He had a tendency to hang mirrors where windows should be, appearing to wear his life rather than live it. She glanced from Booker to Jeff. One, a man of integrity and purpose. The other, a man of expediency and pretense.

Sylvia would have the capacity to think gracious thoughts about people like Jeff, Lynn.

Right, Ivy. All kinds of people. All kinds of bishops. Why am I so hard on him? Being judgmental of him made her feel small.

Jeff eyed her necklace in the dim light. "I hope you have the good judgment not to wear those pearls on the street, Lynn. They're an invitation to trouble."

We see what we expect to see. But not always. The man in the mist entangled himself in her thoughts like Spanish moss. Cold gray eyes stared at her from a streetcar. A red stain grew on an old friend's T-shirt. Red drops spattered on a new friend's uniform.

Turn the page, Lynn.

She tried, but the winds of fear blew it open again.

Galen took her hand. She squeezed it, knowing that he was aware of how hard she'd prepared for tonight's address and how exhausted she was from lack of sleep and today's strain. Again she realized how grateful she was for him and his loving support. A gentleman by habit, he offered his arm. She took it and leaned into him, borrowing his strength and recentering herself as they made their way to the head table.

35

While Lynn was being introduced, she centered herself and prayed to get her ego and vanity out of the way, to focus on the people before her, and that her words might dance into their minds and hearts. She stepped to the podium, paused a moment, and a sense of peace descended. She looked over the faces, connecting, one with the Spirit and the people.

The standing ovation when she concluded surprised her; it was a rarity for bishops. She glanced at her dual-time watch. She'd bounced out of bed Saturday morning at six o'clock and hadn't been in one since. She was operating on sheer will power. But it was another hour before she could leave the ballroom. Nearly every bishop and spouse in the room came forward to greet and commend her. Their comments tended toward appreciation that she'd invited them to consider ways to transform their own life journeys and given them ideas about paths to do so. Like the busy cobbler's neglecting his own holey soles, busy bishops could sometimes neglect their own holy souls.

The ballroom emptied, and Galen, who'd waited in the background, bowed to her and proclaimed with a grin: "Let it be known that on this Sunday night in Vienna, Austria, Bishop Lynn Prejean Peterson—beautiful and brilliant wife of Galen Peterson—reached the pinnacle of oratorical perfection, warming the audience with her *prolegomena* and showing no pusillanimity in her forthrightness." He kissed her. "Clarity. Depth. Humor. Even a bit of history. I am so proud of you."

She knew that he would never criticize her after something important like this, but neither would he lie. His affirmation always meant more to her than anyone else's. "Thank you, Love." His arm around her, they made their way up the two flights of stairs, each step taking her closer to their lovely little room and the floral duvets and a night's sleep in a real bed!

Elevator phobia trumps exhaustion, Lynn?

It's not a phobia, Ivy! Her fingers brushed her waist wallet. First, the letter. Then, bed. The day blurred through her mind, from the night on the plane to the shooting, to the hospital bomb to retrieving the letter, to being a pastor to the chaplain to giving the banquet keynote. She hadn't had time to decide what to do with the letter, although it had hovered unceasingly in her mind. She maneuvered to be last in the bathroom, hoping Galen was asleep by the time she finished her nightly regime.

She removed the boomerang message from her waist wallet and eased herself onto the bed. Sadness seeped into her soul like mold as she held it once again in her hands and thought about Marsh with NATO lying on the gurney. Lifeless. She stared at the unsealed envelope. He had appeared confident when he winked at her after the plane landed. She held the letter reverently for a moment, willing it to transmit to her his thoughts, conclusions, plans. The moment ended as emptily as it began.

How had the bullet changed the future? What did the President have in mind? What am I supposed to do with it now? She fingered the envelope indecisively, arguing with herself one way and then the other, like a priest swinging incense from side to side. It made sense to get in touch with President Benedict. But it wasn't exactly like calling up her friend Francine Babineaux at the crime lab. Frivolous words came to her exhausted mind: "Hello, Helena. How's the first gentleman? Y'all doin' fine?" The

President has gone to great lengths to keep our contact secret, she thought, and her staff wouldn't take seriously a request for her to return a call. Perhaps I should try the Vice President and ask him what to do. Same problem. Besides, how can I be sure he was privy to what was in the envelope he gave me? He might not have known that it was about Major Manetti. If he did, wouldn't he have simplified the process merely by asking me to deliver the message to Marsh? So my options are down to one: Read the message myself, without permission.

Stewing about permission is one way to continue to procrastinate, Lynn. You're good at that.

So . . . read it. The thought hiked her heartbeat. What if it's top secret? Or vague? Or misleading? But what really scared her was the tiny possibility that it would ask for something that she could actually do.

Oh sure, Lynn! You're another Major Manetti.

Unanswered questions marched toward her like foot soldiers to a drumbeat: Why was Major Manetti shot? Was it random? Was he targeted? Did someone know the President had a special assignment for him? Not on my watch, she thought. I've kept it with me at all times. And nobody else knew unless the Vice President had opened it. A scary thought.

Two people killed within a week, each by a single shot. In two different countries halfway around the world. Countries where she just happened to be. They couldn't be connected. Yet she felt like dodging bullets.

Enough, Lynn! Open the letter or tear it up!

She started to rip it into pieces. Wiser. Simpler. Maybe safer. But curiosity won. As always. She inhaled and slowly put her right thumb and forefinger into the envelope. Tentatively touched the single piece of paper. Hesitantly pulled it out. Cautiously unfolded it. And then she exhaled. No letterhead. No addressee. No signature. Not all caps like the one to her but again handwritten in a carefully drawn, unnatural style.

> To Ranch Foreman:
> Troublesome events on the Ponderosa. Suspect a pattern. Difficult to connect the dots. Fear ranch hand involved. Don't know who. Maybe more than one. Need your help. Vini McGragor will phone for you Wed. A.M. at 10. Have call put through. Secure line mandatory.

Four words were added at the bottom, apparently as a hurried afterthought.

> Start with St. Sava.

The note made no sense—and yet it made perfect sense. Lynn understood the ranch metaphor. She could empathize with President Benedict's having reason to mistrust someone close to her and not knowing who. On a tiny scale Lynn had experienced that when she was a rookie bishop. But to be *President* and have a traitor close by when the stakes are so high! Lynn shuddered. She stared at the last line as though it would suddenly transform into some kind of sense. Start with St. Sava. She'd never heard of St. Sava—except for the saint. And she doubted that Manetti was supposed to go to church and pray to him. But it was the code name that stunned her. It rose from the page with a haunting familiarity. Vini McGragor. Was it coincidence? Could the President know of her? How?

She reread the letter, discouraged. The President should have given her a Plan B. Now she'd have to come up with her own plan—and that was beyond her knowledge and experience. But not beyond her commitment. She must communicate personally with the President of the United States. She simply had to figure out a way to do it.

Simply, Lynn?

36

ON MONDAY MORNING A GROGGY LYNN OPENED HER EYES AND TRIED TO remember where she was. Ah, Vienna! A beam of sunlight filtered through the lace curtains of the hotel room. Intricate shadows fell in a pattern on the wood floor, duplicating the lace. She glanced at the dual-time travel clock. Her first mistake of the day—midnight in New Orleans, seven here. The conference began at nine. She reached over and tenderly touched Galen, who sat on the edge of the bed staring at his slippers, trying to wake up.

Drawn by the sun that overcame yesterday's darkness, she went to the window and pulled the curtains apart. They framed a dazzling morning sky, cloudless except for drifting wisps arcing behind jet planes. "It would be lovely to take a quick walk and watch the city wake up."

"Let's go." He abandoned meticulous appearance for running togs. She skipped makeup, trying to beat him dressed. But donning the waist wallet with the President's letter slowed her down. The President's letter. Before, she'd at least known its destination. Now she didn't know what to do or where to turn, sure only that being its courier made her responsible for it. The burden bent her with anxiety. They avoided the elevator and took the two flights of stairs to the ballroom level and another to the lobby. Not a phobia, Ivy, just good exercise.

The charming area around the hotel invited a stroll, but time ruled. Lynn set a power-walk pace for herself to keep up with Galen's long legs. The scent of flowers in small gardens and second-story window boxes wafted through the morning air. Workers swept sidewalks in front of stores. Some washed doors and windows. The water splashed on the old, uneven walkway and ran in crooked lines toward freedom. Lynn and Galen followed the ancient way of the fortress moat along the Graben toward Kärntner Straußе. Shops in ornate buildings from far-off centuries spanned both sides of the street. The Pestsäule stood in the center, an old pillar that still mourned the devastating plague in the seventeenth century.

"Do you know what today's plague is, Love?"

"No," Galen grinned, "but I bet you're going to tell me."

"A malaise of the spirit."

He sobered. "And just as contagious."

She looked at her dual-time watch. "Elie's funeral is at St. Mark's this morning at ten. Five, actually, Vienna time." *Elie.*

He took her hand. "I wish we could be there."

"Me too. But we'll be there in spirit. Maybe we can say a prayer while it's going on."

"I brought a CD of the Olympia Brass Band. Afterwards we could kick up our heels a little with our own New Orleans second line."

She smiled. "I wonder what the Viennese would think of dancing in the street in a second line. I love New Orleans! I already miss it."

Galen pointed to the date on the old plague pillar. "Built in 1687. On our side of the globe that year, we had the story of the Charter Oak. England had consolidated the colonies into the Dominion of New England. The governor demanded the

Connecticut charter, but Captain William Wadsworth prevailed. He hid it in a hollow oak tree."

She enjoyed hearing him connect historical timeframes. "New Englanders can be as stubborn as a rose stem clinging to a bush." She looked with appreciation up and down the ancient street. "These old monuments remind me how young our nation is."

"Perhaps that explains the adolescent arrogance of some politicians."

"Some bishops too." She meant it as a joke. Sort of.

"Are spouses exempt?"

"I wish, Love!" They hurried on to St. Stephen's Cathedral and stopped, fascinated by the multicolored roof-tile mosaic that formed the coat-of-arms. "I think I saw this roof from the airplane window but couldn't make out what it was."

Galen gestured toward the Stephensturm nearby. "Vienna's major landmark. One of the greatest achievements in Gothic architecture. I'd bet an entire fortune of one euro that President Nausner will mention it this afternoon."

She craned her neck to follow the lines of the 450-foot tower. Suddenly she felt an uneasy déjà vu sensation of being watched, as at Café du Monde. She thought of the man wearing sunglasses in the mist at Lueger's statue, and her fingers brushed her waist wallet. She looked around warily. An eerie thought prowled through the shadows of her mind: seeing the mime's cold gray eyes here in Vienna—or not seeing them as they watched her standing here. She felt centipedes crawl on her skin and shuddered.

"Are you cold?" asked Galen.

"No. But I think it's time to get on back," she said as she power-paced away. This is ridiculous, she told herself. Be logical.

Logic has its limits, Lynn.

37

ZELLER STOOD AT HIS APARTMENT WINDOW AND TOOK A SIP OF COFFEE. In the distance a man whose height made him notable stared up at the Stephensturm. He stood at least a third of a meter taller than the woman beside him. An image tugged at Zeller's mind. Deciding to get a close-up view, he smashed his cigarette stub in the ashtray and removed the false panel in the wall. He opened his rifle case, took out the scope, and returned to the window. The woman from New Orleans! Again! And the tall man who had followed her off Manetti's plane. Her husband, he assumed. He remembered noticing her wedding ring on the streetcar in New Orleans. She did not seem the type to go gallivanting around the world with someone besides her husband.

He watched the couple for a few moments before they turned and left at a quick pace. Both their pace and lack of a camera distinguished them from the ambling tourists. He stored the man's face in his mental file beside hers. Never to be forgotten.

After pouring another cup of coffee, he sat down at the table to read Vienna's *Österreich Journal.* Most people read newspapers for pleasure. He read them for research. Broad information and small details ensured a contract completed with his success and survival. As he flipped to the second page, the woman gazed at him. Stunned, he read the caption: Bishop Lynn Peterson opens International Conference of Bishops with keynote address. He stared at her picture, a backdrop for his startling thought: I picked the pocket of a bishop!

A *woman* bishop? Perhaps only men are bona fide, he reasoned, cautious about getting on the wrong side of any god that might exist. It was not superstition. No. But he needed all the luck he could get.

He also needed every piece of background information *Mutter* could give him. He patted his computer. *Mutter* and *Freund*. What other friends did he need!

He began a thorough search. Frau Peterson was indeed a bishop, one with many credits. Yet he could not get his mind around her title. He assumed that a bishop's profession was made up of extreme fundamentalists. Ergo easy targets for manipulators. Ergo unwitting allies of the corrupt. Ergo a dangerous group. Simply convince them that you speak for their god and you can get them to silence their doubts or even support your aim: Spread hate. Steal land. Take lives *en masse*. It seemed to him that whatever their professed religion, people could excuse any act if they based it on the belief that it is for their god. Not so with his elite profession. Aces didn't *worship* gods; they *were* gods, holding the power to bring death or permit life at their will. His thoughts trailed again to *Frau* Peterson and her kind face on the streetcar. He had not seen the traits of a demagogue in her. No. Besides, he didn't like bishops. She would remain Frau Peterson to him.

Her husband was Galen Lincoln Peterson. *Mutter* found him: Ph.D. in history, professor at Tulane University in New Orleans. His record, like hers, included many outstanding credits. He read carefully through all the details. Thank you,

Mutter. Now he knew everything he needed to about this tall man who had appeared twice in his life and might be his enemy.

The international conference explained Frau Peterson's presence in Vienna. But what about Herr Peterson? Was he simply her traveling companion, or did he have his own agenda? Could he have been on Manetti's plane because of a connection with him? Did they work together on something that ran counter to the Patriot's interests? If so, one of these days the Patriot would raise one eyebrow and speak Peterson's name to Zeller with a gossiping tone, contracting *the biggest surprise of his life.* Like Darwish and Manetti. But he would not share these suspicions of a Manetti-Peterson partnership with the Patriot. No. He took a sip of coffee. My aim is for hire, not my mind.

Galen Peterson's presence near his home agitated him. Was he observing the apartment instead of admiring the Stephensturm? Did he see me watching out the window? Is that why they left abruptly? Is he after me? If Peterson knows where I live, maybe I need to change locations. No! You terminate insects! You don't let them drive you away!

He warned himself not to become paranoid and shoved his dangerous anger back into his mental cooler. Perhaps everything related to Galen Lincoln Peterson was happenstance. Yet caution required him not to risk discovery. *Freund* and I will not act yet.

Time will tell, *Mutter.* Time will tell.

38

AFTER THE BISHOPS' MEETING AND LUNCHEON LYNN, AGITATED, RUSHED into the hotel room.

"What's the matter?" asked Galen.

"We spent the morning listening to reports from all around the world. Most of them troubling. Something is not right, but I can't put my finger on it." She glanced at her watch and abruptly changed the subject, along with her blouse. "We have to hurry. President Nausner's aide wants two bishops and spouses from each continent to be first in the greeting line at the reception."

"I take it you were selected for North America?"

"And Booker, of course. Government cars will take us to Schönbrunn Palace ahead of the buses. We're to meet in the lobby in ten minutes." She attached her clerical collar to her shirt of traditional episcopal purple and glanced at Galen. He wore his gray suit, a red tie, and silver cuff links. She smiled at him. "You look sharp."

"Thought I'd move upscale from running togs."

"We'll need our passports and the invitation. The Austrian government ran checks on everyone, and we received security passes this morning."

He grinned. "I hope none of the bishops failed."

"It's the spouses they'd better worry about, Love."

He smoothed his shirt and checked the points of his handkerchief. "I'm looking forward to President Nausner's reception this afternoon—one of the perks of being married to my esteemed wife."

"I'm glad Will invited us to dinner tonight. It'll be fun to see them again."

"Ambassador Whitcomb," he said, trying out Will's new title. "It's comforting to know someone with integrity has that position."

"Do you think it will change him? Power can do disappointing things to people."

"Like bishops?"

"For some of us, all the time." She added pensively, "For all of us, some of the time."

He put his arms around her. "What saves you from power's seductive force is that you don't have a need for external power."

He'd never said that to her before. The compliment touched her. She reached up and ran her palms down his beloved face. Gratitude for the gift of their marriage welled up like a river overflowing its banks. Tears came to her eyes. The world always felt safer and gentler with Galen's arms around her. She savored the moment. And like all moments, it passed and another one rolled in to take its place.

They went to the lobby via the stairs and joined the Phillipses while waiting for the car. "Booker, what did you think about the bishops' reports?" Lynn asked, skipping small talk.

"A world conference is complex because of different languages and cultures."

"I know," she agreed. "Generally I don't pay much attention to isolated incidents. But hearing all of those reports together puts our global situation in a different perspective."

Booker looked thoughtful for a moment. "I see what you mean. They have a cumulative impact."

Sylvia joined in. "Conferences like this help people feel the pulse of the Earth."

Galen nodded. "And an opportunity to direct history, at least in a small way."

"As I listened, I wondered if we are spinning subtly toward global chaos." Lynn heard Vice President Parker's words in the limo echo in her mind: Heightened chaos and conflict. Breaches of trust at high levels. Her hand automatically touched her waist wallet, the tic returning with her anxiety. The boomerang envelope for Marsh with NATO was safe. For now. She must let President Benedict know she'd retrieved it. But how?

39

THE PATRIOT FOCUSED ON THE SIX TV CHANNELS ON THE LARGE SCREENS on his office wall. At any moment he expected breaking news about the bomb he'd had planted in Schönbrunn Palace. He envisioned the rush of reporters in a glutted field, competing for the most sensational story. As always, some would run slipshod over ethics. Some would play the blame game. Some would use a religious spin, pitting faith against faith. He could count on them to spread fear and chaos like little tin soldiers, their strings pulled by the master puppeteer. I'm always the puppeteer, he thought smugly, never the puppet.

He checked his watch, disappointed, and pushed the TV remote to clear the wall screens. He could not be late to an advisory meeting on the economy at the White House. He had valuable experience and strong opinions in that area and wanted to use them to benefit his beloved country. Perhaps the bomb news would break at the session, and he could observe President Benedict's reaction.

After Thursday's fiasco at the Inner Circle, John Adams brought his full charm to the table. He had to admire the President's uncanny capacity to listen carefully, attentive to word choice and its revelations about the speaker. Always cautious about his language, he was exceptionally so in her presence. She seemed to hear all the way down to the soul. He couldn't afford that! Neither could he afford a repetition of dropping his mask, so he was doubly cautious to keep his face and eyes guarded.

He faked an interested smile when others shared their ideas, nodding appropriately while half-listening. His mind wandered to the Internet craze of first-gentleman jokes. They went from unfunny to unkind. As much as he disliked the President, he considered publicly trashing anyone in the presidential family to be disrespectful to the office and the country. In truth, Miles Benedict deserved better. John Adams had to give him that.

At any moment he expected the dramatic delivery of a message to President Benedict about a bomb in Schönbrunn Palace. She would unfold it. Read it. Share it aloud. Her words would jolt the group. He would feign shock and consternation. Spurious but necessary.

40

SCHÖNBRUNN PALACE GLOWED IN THE SUN. THE MAGNIFICENT 1400-ROOM structure evoked simultaneous comments about its size from Galen and Booker and its beauty from Lynn and Sylvia. As Lynn expected and dreaded, security agents stood in place. All comers guilty until proven innocent. It seemed a pointless inconvenience to Lynn—the good folk were harmless and the bad ones stayed a step ahead of detection systems. She approached nervously, President Benedict's letter to Manetti screaming its presence.

Unexpectedly, an agent escorted them past the metal detectors and bag-search tables, sparing them the demeaning process of being wanded like criminals. The agents dealt with people instead of possessions. They efficiently matched the name on invitation, passport, and security pass while glancing up pleasantly to check the likeness of photo to face. The agent whom Lynn drew had no problem identifying her with her horrible passport picture. Disappointing.

An official introduced himself as Franz Schober and led the twelve selected representatives and spouses into the Great Gallery, a stunning room. He lined them up alphabetically by continent and asked them to take that formation to greet the

President. Lynn and Galen were placed between Europe and South America, just ahead of the Phillipses. For Lynn, protocol fell into the air with a Shakespearean ring of much ado about nothing, but as a guest in another country, she always honored the rules.

A string quartet played Mozart in the background as bishops and spouses arrived from the buses and began filling the room. Gold-trimmed white walls and sconces had heard centuries of secrets and kept them all. White floor-length cloths covered round tables with large colorful bouquets in the center. Plates of cut fruit and crystal glasses of sparkling white grape juice surrounded the flowers. Paper napkins monogrammed in gold were swirled in small clusters around the edge of the tables. An attendant stood at each one, dressed in the traditional black and white of waiters. Lynn admired the beautiful Gregorio Guglielmi frescoes painted on the ceiling in homage to Maria Theresa. She pointed them out to Galen as they waited for President Nausner's arrival.

Franz Schober returned to the Great Gallery through the door the President would enter. He gained control of the room in easy fashion. With courteous authority, he cleared the designated place near the door for the continental representatives and efficiently managed to get all the others to form a large circle along the walls. No small feat, as getting a group of bishops and spouses obediently organized was, in the accurate words of the cliché, like herding cats. Lynn glanced fondly around the room. Bishops in their purple shirts. Spouses standing beside them. She cared deeply for most of them. Disliked only one—Jeff James, who had, typically, jockeyed his way to be first in line after the continental representatives.

The President of Austria would be entering at any minute. The absence of Suits with earphones struck Lynn. The bishops were a safe group. But what if someone came pretending to be a bishop? All of us know some of the bishops, she thought, but no one knows all of them. She scanned the room again and leaned toward Galen. "Where is security?" she whispered.

"You can't 'bish' the Austrian Secret Service, Lynn." He grinned and winked.

The mime appeared on her mental screen, out of place in this elegant room.

The door opened, and President Nausner entered the Great Gallery. Voices hushed and eyes turned. He wore a smile and a tailored charcoal suit with a burgundy tie. Mrs. Nausner followed him. Elegant in a lavender tea dress of silk, she reminded Lynn of a beautiful iris in bloom. Lynn noticed that the attendant at the nearest table came subtly to attention, poised for action. She looked at him, *really* seeing him. He filled out the common uniform of black and white with an uncommon physique, more like a weight-lifter than a waiter. She guessed his neck at size seventeen. Watchful eyes belied his passive face. She glanced at the table attendants around the room—not all Size-Seventeens but all watchful. That answered her question about security. Several unnotable table attendants instead of a few notable Suits. Perhaps this was another difference between an old civilization and an adolescent one.

Unlike the typical reception line in which all the people moved toward the immobile person of prominence, the President moved toward the immobile people. Much more efficient, thought Lynn. Rather than be stuck with someone who wouldn't move on, or resort to a pull-the-person-forward-handshake some clergy practiced on Sunday mornings, he could graciously control how long he talked with each person. The two couples from Africa were first. He shook their hands and called them by name without glancing at their tags. He said something personal to each one and moved on to Asia, Austria, Europe. It impressed Lynn that he'd taken the time to be blue-booked on the twelve representatives and spouses and had bothered to digest the information, a gracious gesture of hospitality.

Or pragmatic public relations, Lynn.

Give him a break, Ivy!

"Bishop Peterson," said the President, shaking her hand. "You have been in Austria before. It is good to have you back."

"Your beautiful country and this city are special to us," she replied sincerely.

He smiled. "Then you have good taste in both culture and geography." He turned to Galen. "Dr. Peterson, I hope that if you ever write about Austria your words will be favorable."

"How could they be otherwise, President Nausner? You moved past Karl Lueger long ago."

"Thank you both for your warm hospitality to all of us," said Lynn.

"It is a pleasure. Religious leaders have influence that can be helpful . . ." He paused.

"Or destructive," Lynn finished with a smile.

"Your own influence, Bishop Peterson, falls into the former category. I appreciate your international work for peace and the poor." President and Mrs. Nausner moved on to Booker and Sylvia. When they finished greeting the continental representatives, they continued on around the room, welcoming every person in the Great Gallery.

After the reception, they were escorted to a stateroom for President Nausner's address. Lynn scanned the spacious room. Emerald green drapes trimmed the tall windows. The sun shone through them, partnering with the two-tiered chandeliers to light the cobalt blue walls. Austria's coat of arms hung on the wall above the dais. The eagle, retained as the country's symbol for more than a thousand years, brought her comfort. Galen pulled out his BlackBerry to take notes.

The President spoke pridefully of the Stephensturm, as Galen had predicted. He shifted to the neighboring Balkans and with a sense of urgency reminded the group of that area's impact on world history: Igniting World War I when a Serb assassinated Archduke Franz Ferdinand in 1914. Sending a spark flying toward World War II when Croatian Ustashe agents murdered King Alexander. Producing the first terrorists of the twentieth century by getting men from the Skopje, Belgrade, and Sofia slums to swear allegiance to IMRO—taking their oath over an Orthodox Bible and a gun.

Lynn looked at Galen, who was loving every historical word.

The President spoke eloquently of world peace, then concluded his address with two related points. First, citing yesterday's bus bombing as an example, he made a compelling statement against political and religious leaders who foment conflict and violence under the guise of religion—a contradiction of faith, he insisted, in all religions. Second, he built a persuasive argument that bishops must take responsibility for calling religious extremists to accountability. "If *you* don't," he asked, "*who* will?"

The entire global body rose for a standing ovation just as Franz Schober joined the President at the podium, whispered briefly, and took his arm to lead him off the platform. President Nausner offered a gracious bow of his head to the audience and smiled warmly. Immediately he turned to leave, flanked by two Size-Seventeens, no longer dressed as waiters.

Something had caused the abrupt departure. But apparently nothing that mattered. What does matter, thought Lynn, is what is happening at St. Mark's. She reached for Galen's hand and tapped her dual-time watch—ten in the morning in New Orleans. While the bishops and spouses were ushered toward the doorway in an orderly fashion, she and Galen remained in their seats and prayed for Elie's friends gathered at his jazz funeral in the Quarter.

41

AN OVERFLOW CROWD OF PEOPLE STANDS UNDER A CLOUDLESS blue canopy outside St. Mark's Church in the French Quarter in New Orleans. They wait with hushed respect for the service to end and the procession to begin. The doors click open, and sunlight glints on the casket carried by Bubba Broussard and five other Saints. The bells of St. Francis Cathedral peal in honor of Elias Darwish.

Bubba clutches the cold metal handles, his heart hurting as they carry Elie's body up Rampart Street to the hearse. The mucky smell of the river mingles with the sweet scent of flowers in the wreath on the casket. A tugboat horn wails its sadness, for the earth is a lesser place. A light breeze cools Bubba's face and his eyes blur as he helps place his friend in the hearse. But he is not alone. For this is a jazz funeral.

The grand marshals and the Olympia Brass Band lead the people up Rampart. Bubba and all the Saints parade somberly behind the band. Cy Bill is on Ebony, both decked out in black, the silver trim polished. Chief Armstrong in full dress solemnly joins the procession.

Along with Francine Babineaux from the crime lab and Fay Foster from the bishop's office. Yoo-Sei from Café du Monde and Rosa DuBois from Mt. Zion Church. And Bubba knows Bishop Lynn and Galen are present in spirit. Pete Fountain, the Neville Brothers, members of the Marsalis family, and other New Orleans musicians join the first line in tribute to Elie. The people walk along to the soulful lament of the slow, mournful hymns that haunt the procession up Rampart and past Louis Armstrong Park toward the cemetery. As they turn on Basin Street, Fats Domino waves from a chair, too ill to join the line, but his voice can be heard as "A Closer Walk with Thee" is played in a woeful dirge. Hundreds of feet march in the street, the first line, mourning the death of Elias Darwish.

The hearse moves on to the cemetery, and Elie is laid to rest.

Their goodbyes said, the mood begins to change. The moment comes. The moment of long tradition. The moment when they cut the body loose and the music shifts in tone and beat. From death to resurrection. The people whose white handkerchiefs dried their eyes in the church now wave them as they dance in joy. Clarinets and saxes, trumpets and trombones, tubas and drums play a rollicking rendition of "When the Saints Go Marching In." It reverberates through the Quarter. Fans join in and well-wishers and onlookers, stepping high like the Saints and twirling fringed umbrellas. Thousands of feet dance in the street, the second line, celebrating the life of Elias Darwish.

Bubba has tears in his eyes but a smile on his face. He can almost feel Elie dancing, too, on his nimble feet. The sniper shot him, but he won't have the last word. Bubba sees a vision as clear and true as jazz itself, a vision of Elie living on from generation to generation through the stories that fans tell their children:

> As we get ready to watch this game, kids, I want to tell you a story. There was once a Saints kicker named Elias Darwish—*a great kicker.* He had a magic foot, and *I* saw him play.

> As we get ready to watch this game, kids, I want to tell you a story. There was once a Saints kicker named Elias Darwish *the greatest kicker in the country*. He had a magic foot, and *my daddy* saw him play.

> As we get ready to watch this game, kids, I want to tell you a story. There was once a Saints kicker named Elias Darwish—*the greatest kicker of all time.* He had a magic foot, and *my grand-daddy* saw him play.

Yes, the sniper shot Elie. But the people won't ever let him die. Bubba is sure of that.

42

As the meeting in the Oval Office continued, John Adams made excellent contributions to the discussion of the economy. BarLothiun gave him good experience, and he was pleased to share it for the sake of his country. He kept his composure intact despite his agitation regarding the lack of news about the Schönbrunn Palace bomb.

His sense of justice ruled out the loss of innocent lives. Death wasn't his objective at the palace. Since the 9/11 tragedy, bombs didn't have to explode to create a news frenzy that spiked fear. The palace bomb merely had to be found. He'd given his bomb specialist, Frank Fillmore, a directive with a twist: build a bomb that can't detonate but whose flaw must appear to be accidental, then get it inside Schönbrunn Palace. He had total confidence in Fillmore's ability to build it as instructed and figure out how to breach security. The guards were apt to consider bishops a safe group and soften their procedures. He was also confident that President Nausner's personal security team, perpetually on high alert, would discover it. Natural consequences would follow: The rapid removal of President Nausner. The frantic announcement. The terrified audience ordered to evacuate. Afterward the bishops would simultaneously carry their stories back to their various worldwide homelands, like a scattergun spreading personal stories that put a face on terror.

The Peterson factor continued to bother him, and he trusted his instincts. She had both opportunity and cover as a bishop. Opportunity did not prove action. But lack of proof of action did not prove inaction. Zero tolerance. The major was dead. Should the bishop follow?

No rash decisions! He needed more information. Life is precious.

He peeked at his watch and did the time-zone math. The news should have broken long before now. He itched to excuse himself and contact Fillmore, an itch that had to remain unscratched. Had the bomb specialist failed? Impossible! But something had gone wrong.

And he thought he knew what. The impact of a violent act or threat is not ultimately determined by the act itself but the reaction. A leader's response diminishes or intensifies fear and instability. He would bet a sum equal to BarLothiun that Fillmore successfully planted the faulty bomb and the security team found it. But President Nausner had frozen its impact by keeping the whole episode out of the news. The Patriot had gained nothing. All of that planning, risk, effort, money for nothing. *Nothing!*

Unacceptable! Beneath his charming mask he seethed for revenge.

43

ON MONDAY EVENING, FOLLOWING THE SCHÖNBRUNN PALACE RECEPTION, Ambassador Will Whitcomb stood at the open door of his home, the personification of hospitality. His hair matched the silver rims of glasses that framed hazel eyes without guile. He wore a navy blazer, gray pants, blue oxford shirt with a button-down collar, and a striped tie. The bishops also wore ties—it was not a color-purple evening. Will and Galen greeted each other warmly, their college camaraderie unbroken by the years. Anne, who held a Ph.D. in Korean studies, stood at Will's side. A petite woman, she wore an elegant black dress with a single diamond pendant at her throat. Her ash blonde hair was swept upward in a French braid. Most striking to Lynn was Anne's diligence to look for the good in others.

Anne and Lynn greeted each other with a silent hug, needing no words. But the moment stung Lynn. Their last hug had been at Lyndie's service three years ago. Lyndie's service.

Don't go there, Lynn.

"Can you remain after dinner?" Will invited softly. "We could catch up."

They nodded and moved on so the Whitcombs could continue to greet the line of guests. They crossed the foyer over colorful peacocks woven into the luxurious oriental carpet and entered a spacious room with dark paneled walls. People mingled with one another, greeting old friends and meeting new ones. Sparkling goblets and fancy hors d'oeuvres eased the social need for something to hold. Conversation filled the area like lively music in surround sound, bass to soprano.

Jeff James held court in the corner. His gaze circled the room like a searchlight scoping the social sea. He rode Roman-style around the arena on twin horses of arrogance and criticism, content to let opinion rush in to fill the void of wisdom. Only his wife, Tiffany, appeared to listen, her eyes fixed on him in an adoring gaze.

He's toxic to me, thought Lynn.

Because he personifies the pompous, self-aggrandizing stereotype of bishops, Lynn?

Probably so, Ivy. It hurts us all. Yet Lynn had sympathy for him. He reminded her of a little three-year-old who tugs at a coattail for attention and approval. As we all do at times, she admitted. Self-importance is an equal-opportunity dysfunction.

Anne led everyone into the dining room. Large windows ran along the back wall, draped in pale yellow to match the carpet. White votive candles marched down the Battenberg tablecloth with pastel petals scattered among them. A colorful bouquet graced the center of the long table, and crisp white napkins folded into bishops' miters stood at each place, a gesture typical of Anne. Place cards in calligraphy showed Jeff James directly across from Lynn. Thanks a lot, Anne.

Running for God's prosecutor are you, Lynn?

Ouch! Time to judge him less and like him more.

After Will said grace, the four-course dinner began with cold prawns in a zesty cocktail sauce. Jeff tried to dominate the table, but Will deftly broadened the monologue when Jeff paused for breath. "Bishop Phillips, what did you think of President Nausner's address?"

"He received a standing ovation, Mr. Ambassador. Rare for our group." Booker's smiling eyes darted to Lynn. "Except, of course, when Bishop Peterson speaks."

She brushed off the compliment with a smile and a shrug. "Last night everyone just needed an excuse to stretch after sitting so long."

Praise for the President's address and the reception and comments about the international conference lasted through the second course of delicately seasoned asparagus soup. The aroma of a special Viennese chicken dish on well-presented plates slowed the conversation.

"This is a perfect dinner, Anne," said Sylvia. Everyone raised a glass, and Booker offered a toast.

Jeff cleared his throat. "Speaking of perfection, I wonder if John Wesley knew how close he was to Zen and Taoism when he stressed the process of going on to perfection instead of stressing perfection itself."

Way to go Jeff, thought Lynn. Always trying to impress us.

Judge him less and like him more. Was that it, Lynn?

Ouch again.

"I appreciate the common ties of the great religions," said Booker. "As Bishop Peterson stated last night, we do not grasp God. We merely glimpse God. It is good to be open to others' glimpses."

Sylvia nodded. "Lynn reminded us how many things influence our glimpses. Like culture."

"Formal education and informal instruction," added Jeff.

"Don't forget our values," said Tiffany.

Other words popped up around the table.

"Customs and traditions."

"Our family."

"Our opportunities."

Our losses, thought Lynn. She hadn't included that one last night. She felt Chris Nyangoma's eyes upon her and glanced at him. He was here as Bishop Ntaryamir's representative, and she hadn't met him until tonight. He looked bored.

"It takes time to become aware of the power of these influences," said Jeff. His bravado in check, he sounded almost wistful. "And even longer to free ourselves from those that fetter us."

His sincerity rang the doorbell of appreciation for Lynn. Maybe there's hope for me yet, Ivy. Her mind wandered to the President's letter. As an ambassador, Will might have personal access to her. Lynn was glad they were remaining after dinner and wondered how to approach him. More than fellowship was at stake.

44

After the long jazz funeral ended and things settled down into what passed for normal in New Orleans, Bubba and Cy Bill took a walk by the river. The wind danced with the waves, and sunbeams kissed the ripples. Bubba glanced from the water to his friend and saw the frown on his brow, the worry behind his eyes. Was it the loss of Elie? Or something else? "What's the trouble, Cy Bill?"

"I'll take that as an offer to listen." He hesitated. "I need to get something off my chest."

"Ol' Bubba is a safe haven." He ambled along beside Cy Bill, waiting silently, as Lynn and Galen would.

Cy Bill watched the waves for a few moments. When he spoke, it was like the whisper of the pine trees. "Chief Armstrong was pressured to close Elie's case. They cut off the investigation too soon."

"The man they found dead—he isn't the sniper?"

"The chief is a politician and understands that the city economy depends on tourism. It's growing but still isn't what it was before Katrina. A Saint's murder makes national news and tourists won't come unless they feel secure. The case needed to be solved."

Anger shot through Bubba. "He stopped the investigation of Elie's murder because of *tourism*?"

"That's what puzzles me. He will please and appease up to a point. But—"

"I thought the chief stands for justice."

"Always. And Francine Babineaux got his attention. She suggested that the surface clues add up all right, but they make things too simple and leave some questions unanswered."

"I'm with Francine, Cy Bill. A man smart enough to shoot him and get away isn't going to be careless enough to get himself killed the same night."

"At first the chief was proud of that quick result, but now he isn't as sure as he was. He asked me to work on the case covertly."

"*Covertly!* I can't see him getting the trembles when someone puts a little pressure on him."

"There are only two forces I can think of powerful enough to send him underground. A vicious Mafia threat intended to cower him—but the chief doesn't cower. So it must be an entity more powerful than the FBI."

Bubba thought about the careful search of his condo while the FBI detained him. Nothing displaced. But someone had been there. Like Lynn said, you can just feel that kind of invasion. Maybe it wasn't the FBI as he'd thought. "What would motivate your mysterious *entity*?"

"That's what I'm trying to figure out. Francine agreed to help me."

"You can count on me too, Cy Bill. I'll do anything you ask."

"Thanks."

"I may even try a little sleuthing on my own."

"You stick to linebacking, Bubba," said the former quarterback. "I'll carry the ball."

45

LYNN AND GALEN SLOUCHED COMFORTABLY IN THE DEN. THE MEN SAT IN mocha leather chairs, the women on the settee upholstered in a complementary plaid. The cozy room invited conversation rather than inhibited it. Lynn noticed she felt nervous about asking Will to be a communication channel to the President. Contrarily she felt tempted in this comfortable setting with these three trustworthy people to unload the whole story from envelope in the limo to retrieval at the hospital. But as long as the secret stayed with her—and only her—it couldn't ripple and end up where it shouldn't. Her silence was necessary to protect the President.

Right, Lynn. The President of the United States of America needs your protection! A little case of vanity, is it?

Ouch. Ivy was good at delivering ouches. But Lynn chose to keep her promise to Vice President Parker.

Anne lifted the Wedgwood teapot from the silver tray. The amber tea poured from spout to cup like a small fountain replaying the ancient melody of liquid meeting porcelain.

"The golden elixir," said Lynn, its fragrance carrying her mind from anxiety to the beauty of the mundane. "According to tradition, the golden elixir was first presented to Lao Tse, the founder of Taoism, at the gate of Han Pass—five centuries before Christ."

"Surnamed the Long-Eared," added Galen.

Anne wrapped her fingers around her cup. "If we're playing Wikipedia, Okakura Kakuzo called tea 'the cup of humanity.'" She looked at Galen, her eyes amused. "Cited in *The Book of Tea*, Dr. Peterson, written over a century ago."

He smiled and raised his cup to her.

"Tea taught me my primary lesson as an ambassador." Will grinned at their puzzled faces. "Marco Polo records that a Chinese minister of finance was deposed in 1285 for augmenting the tea taxes. Half a millennium later in Boston, as we learned in elementary school, England also levied a heavy tea tax. It cost them the Colonies and we gained a country. People get riled over their golden elixir! Lesson: Don't mess with the basics."

They savored the richness of friendship. Drinking tea and dancing with words. Filling in the spaces that time apart had left blank.

Now or never. "Will, I have a favor to ask."

"Anything, Lynn."

"We flew from Frankfurt to Vienna on the same plane as Major Manetti." The expressions of both Will and Anne registered recognition of the name. "We had a good conversation with him." Her voice cracked. Friends did that to her. They reached inside her veneer and offered a safe landing for her feelings. She cleared her throat and let the tears trickle down her cheeks, pretending that if she didn't acknowledge them they'd be invisible. "One of the topics was the President."

Galen frowned. "I don't remember that."

"Maybe it was when you were in the restroom."

Oops, Lynn! First, vanity. Now, fabrication.

Hush, Ivy! "He spoke very highly of her." Well, not exactly. But since the President trusted him so much, surely he would have if given the opportunity. "Those would have been some of his last words. It's silly, but I would really like to send a note to her sharing that."

"It isn't silly, Lynn. All of us like to hear we're appreciated—even presidents. Angry letters abound. People are far more apt to take the positive for granted and act on the negative."

"I'm a nobody, and she'd never get it."

Will grinned. "Are you taking the long way round to ask if I would send it?"

"Is it appropriate for me to email it to you and you forward it to her?"

"You're my friend, Lynn. I'll be glad to."

"Thank you, Will," she said, relieved to get this cared for.

"Thank you, Lynn," Sylvia interjected. "President Benedict needs all the positive feedback she can get."

Will went down another track. "I saw you both talking with Chris Nyangoma. What did you think of him?"

Galen frowned. "Trusting that he is not a mendacious man, I wanted to ascertain the situation in Burundi and the reason Bishop Ntaryamir wasn't permitted to leave. But he simply said the country is in chaos again and changed the subject."

Chaos. That word again, like the reverberating *bong* of a grandfather clock at midnight.

"All Chris knows about Burundi is how to pronounce it," laughed Will. "Late this afternoon protection was mandated for tonight. He was it."

"Protection from bishops." Anne smiled. "That's understandable."

"Not from the bishops. From their spouses," Will corrected with a grin. A staffer brought a message into the den and handed it to him. He read it with features as immobile as Abe's at the Lincoln Memorial. "I'm sorry. I must take this phone call."

Anne poured another round of tea. "I miss the four of us being together like this." She looked closely at Lynn, her eyes filled with kindness. "You look good."

"Do I hear relief?"

"Oh, Lynn . . . I don't think I could walk in your shoes . . . I mean . . ."

"Lyndie is with me in a different way now, but I'll always feel her presence." The quicksand threatened, and she changed the subject. "It was a lovely dinner party."

Will returned, his demeanor somber. "That was President Nausner." He sagged into the leather chair. "Originally I resented the mandate of protection tonight, but now I understand." He hesitated. "I don't want to alarm you."

Alarming words, Lynn.

Right, Ivy.

He leaned forward in his chair and spoke softly, inviting confidentiality. The other three mirrored his posture. "This must be kept between us."

Galen's intense dark eyes deepened. "Both Lynn and I hold *everything* in confidence, Will. Information shared with us is the *teller's* to tell—not *ours*."

"I know," said Will. "That's why I'm entrusting you with this. The President told me a black briefcase identical to his—complete with his initials in gold—was found at Schönbrunn Palace this afternoon." He paused and swallowed, collecting himself. "It contained a bomb." After letting the words settle, he added, "It was supposed to blow up during the President's address. Franz Schober discovered it."

Lynn distanced herself from the surreal image and crept into her safe haven deep inside.

Galen's eyes darkened, his irises moving back and forth in a journey from horror to gratitude. "Something seemed to be amiss at the end of the address, but no *bomb* was mentioned!"

"And it won't be. That's why this is absolutely confidential. President Nausner has an unwritten policy he calls a 'strategy of silence.' He is adamant that publicity abets terrorism. Even when a bomb does no damage, news of the attempt itself spreads fear."

Lynn thought back to the afternoon. They hadn't created chaos by whisking the President away without a word or evacuating the audience or calling in the Austrian equivalent of the FBI and CIA, the local police and Green Beret. "They handled a bomb threat without creating anxiety!"

"No publicity. No panic. No reward for the perpetrator," Will said.

"Think about the terrorists who planned this. Can't you see them turning on the news? Watching. Waiting. And *nothing!*" Lynn loved it.

"How did someone get a bomb into the palace?" asked practical Anne.

"Bishops and spouses tend to be trusted." Will glanced at Galen with a grin. "Despite present company."

"Trusted and also trusting." Lynn thought of Chris Nyangoma and their lack of suspicion that he was anything other than a bishop's representative.

"What's interesting is that President Nausner said the bomb turned out to be faulty. Even if they hadn't found it, it wouldn't have gone off."

The oddity struck Lynn. "I don't understand, Will. How could a terrorist be skilled enough to get a bomb inside the palace but so unskilled that it was faulty?"

"That, Lynn, is the ultimate question."

The ensuing silence was interrupted by the mantle clock's eleven chimes. Galen set his teacup on the tray. "I don't want this evening to end, but we leave for the Balkans tomorrow and still have to pack."

"I wish you would reconsider your fact-finding mission. This is not the time."

"You would go, Mr. Ambassador," said Lynn. "The concern that this is not the time makes it *exactly* the right time."

"If I were saying that, I suppose I would consider it a logical argument. But hearing it, it sounds like insanity."

"We'll be perfectly safe, my friend," said Galen.

"Perfectly safe!" Anne shook her head.

Will looked at them, hazel eyes concerned, smile gone. "Be alert. Err on the side of caution. A surprising number of people work against peace in the Balkans." He paused and added in a grave tone. "There are some rumors about a terrorist organization called St. Sava."

Lynn tried not to react. Start with St. Sava. The President's final words in her message to Major Manetti.

"I tended to discount them."

"Why is that?" asked Lynn, trying to sound casual.

"The CIA doesn't think it exists. They believe it's merely an ancient myth."

She was puzzled. Does President Benedict know something the CIA doesn't? Or is the CIA covering up St. Sava? Neither option seemed helpful.

"Austrian security found where Manetti's sniper hid at the airport yesterday morning. He left behind only one piece of evidence: a note kept out of the news. It said that St. Sava claims responsibility."

"Puzzling." Galen rose. "But we'll have to ponder it tomorrow."

Lynn remained seated. "What do you think about St. Sava now, Will?" She'd just made her first attempt—feeble as it was—to comply with President Benedict's request of Major Manetti. Start with St. Sava. She felt she was dancing with danger at a masked ball, unable to distinguish friend from enemy. But sitting it out was not an option.

"I'm not sure what to think." He took their hands. "What I am sure of is that I don't want you special people to end up a terrorist target."

Lynn hugged Anne and him. "I'll email you a note for the President. My deepest thanks, Will."

46

BEFORE REPACKING LATE MONDAY NIGHT, LYNN TURNED ON HER BABY LAPtop to write an email to President Benedict. *An email to President Benedict*—the irrational reality stunned her. She saw a message from Bubba and read it first. He described Elie's jazz funeral. What a celebration! She would always regret not being there. She gave herself a few moments of silent gratitude that his life had touched hers. He would live on in her memory.

She moved on to the rest of Bubba's email. His last sentence puzzled her:

> Elie's case is officially closed, but thanks to the persuasion of our friend at the lab an end run is in the works. I pledged to help your favorite cop.
> Stay safe in the Balkans,
> Bubba

Chief Armstrong had to be responsible for this maneuver. Evidently Francine Babineaux had convinced him to take a closer look. Way to go! But why an *unofficial* green light? So unofficial that he was wary of using his department detectives and had turned to trustworthy Cy Bill Bergeron. She wished she could help.

You can, Lynn. You're withholding information—like not telling Cy Bill that the mime is still alive.

Ouch. She wanted to. She should have told Bubba immediately that Elie's medal was stolen. She started to rationalize. Stopped herself. Refused to dig up those clams again. Hurriedly she replied:

> The sniper is alive. I saw him. More later.

When would later come? But right now the priority was her email for the President. She typed the first three words quickly:

> Dear Madam President,
>
> Thank you for leading our country with courage and honor. I greatly admire you.
>
> So did Major Marshall Manetti. He was grateful for an opportunity to serve his Commander-in-Chief. We became acquainted at the Frankfurt airport while waiting for our plane to Vienna. Perhaps you are aware that a sniper killed him when we landed. During that fateful flight, the major spent the final moments of his life reading a little item on ranching. After the tragedy, a chaplain friend, my husband, and I followed the ambulance to the hospital. Major Manetti was pronounced dead on arrival.
>
> Immediately afterward a bomb exploded on a nearby bus, and all the medical staff frantically treated the injured. Under the circumstances the major was left unattended in an alcove. I stood beside him and prayed. Being so close, I noticed that the item on ranching was in his pocket.
>
> I have the impression that you shared a common interest in ranching, and he was a

> friend of yours. Because of that, I thought you might like to have something special to both of you, so I saved it. If he was indeed the friend to you that he seemed to be, I offer my condolences. One minute a man is alive and reading, and the next minute the machete falls. An officer as competent and committed as Major Manetti is irreplaceable. The world goes on, but not without a void.
>
> If I can be of assistance to you in any way, I would be honored to do so.
>
> Respectfully yours,
> Lynn Peterson

She reread the cryptic email. Too cryptic. But she didn't have time to perfect it. She put in Will's email address and hit Send. Done! Little black letters forming little black words forming little black sentences—all virtual. Like communication itself.

For the last time she removed from her waist wallet the innocuous ranch message President Benedict had written to Major Manetti—concrete evidence that her imagination hadn't sent her on a trip into fantasyland. No sane person would link it to the President of the United States. Nor even believe Lynn if she suggested the absurdity. She was tempted to save it as presidential memorabilia. But mostly she wanted rid of it. Rid of its burden. Rid of any possibility of a situation necessitating an explanation. Even to Galen. She wadded up the plain envelope and tossed it in the wastebasket. Then she tore off the strip at the close of the letter: Start with St. Sava. It left her with such an eerie feeling that she didn't like holding it. She tore it into the tiniest pieces she could, then ripped the rest of the letter into tatters and flushed it down the toilet. Free at last! From the written message, yes. But not from its words. They remained indelibly printed in her mind.

You are in w-a-a-a-y over your head, Lynn.

47

THE TUESDAY MORNING AGENDA FOR THE INTERNATIONAL CONFERENCE OF Bishops called for a break at ten o'clock. Lynn used it to go to the quiet of her room and call Mihail Martinovski in Skopje, the pastor in charge of the Macedonian leg of her trip. Galen, free from the boredom of meetings, was spending the morning touring Vienna and delving into its history. She unlocked the door and walked in on the maid, startling them both. Recovering, Lynn smiled at her. A thin and tallish woman, she smiled back shyly and moved to the bed to smooth the floral duvet. She wore an immaculate gray dress and starched white pinafore apron with matching cap.

Lynn sat down at the desk with paper and pen for notes and punched the numbers. "This is Bishop Peterson for Pastor Martinovski." As she waited for him, she watched the maid straighten the towels and smiled at her.

"Good morning, Bishop Peterson. It is good to hear from you."

"And a good morning to you also, Mihail."

"Are you still coming?"

"We will arrive this evening."

"I am very glad." His voice sounded genuinely pleased.

"Do you remember that we go from Skopje to Sarajevo on Friday?"

The maid glanced up.

"Yes." He paused. "Are you worried about the danger?"

"We know that there is a no-travel advisement. But sometimes the State Department exaggerates. What do *you* think about the situation in Sarajevo?"

The maid puffed the pillows, lingering.

"It is fairly safe, I think."

"*Fairly safe* is good enough."

"We want you to stay with us while you are here."

"That is very kind. We would enjoy being with you and Elena, but the hotel is arranged. Maybe next time."

"I will meet you at the airport."

"Thank you, Mihail. We appreciate that. We'll see you after we go through customs."

The maid glanced up.

When she ended the call, the maid pulled at her apron and spoke timidly in broken English. "Sarajevo? You go?"

Lynn nodded.

She pulled back a strand of brown hair that had fallen loose from her stiff cap. "*Ja se zovem* Natalia." She pointed to her name badge. "Natalia."

Lynn recognized the Serbo-Croatian words, surprised they weren't German. "*Dobro jutro*," she greeted Natalia in her language—thanks to Elie. *Elie.*

The familiar greeting seemed to stun Natalia, then please her.

Lynn continued, pointing to herself, "*Ja se zovem* Lynn."

"*Govorite li . . .*"

"No. *Ne*," Lynn interrupted, shaking her head. "Speak few words," she said slowly, indicating a tiny space with her thumb and index finger.

"*Možete li mi pomoći molim Vas?*"

Lynn only caught "please" and shook her head again. "*Ne razumem.*"

Natalia made the phone gesture with thumb to ear. "You say *Bishop* Peterson?"

She nodded. "*Da.*"

"You help?" Natalia touched the small gold Orthodox cross around her neck.

"If I can."

"*Majka* . . . Mama. Mama in Sarajevo. I give *novac* . . . money."

Lynn decided to double her tip.

"No *pošta! Krasti* . . . steal!"

"*Da,*" Lynn agreed, remembering Elie's concern regarding his mother getting the money he sent because of stolen mail.

"You take." A conclusion, not a question.

"Take where? *Gdje?*"

Natalia stretched out her left palm and made writing motions with her right forefinger like addressing an envelope, then mimed putting in money, licking the flap, and sealing it. "I bring." Bobbing her head, she added, "Easy place. You find."

Lynn nodded and smiled. "OK."

"*Hvala Vam mnogo.*"

Lynn gestured around the clean room. "*Hvala.*" She followed Natalia to the door. "See you later. *Dovidjenja.*" That depleted her repertoire.

Natalia bobbed her head again, picked up a canvas tote that Lynn assumed contained cleaning supplies, and went on her way.

Lynn walked with her to the door. Before closing it, she glanced down the hall. Something seemed different about Natalia. It was the way she walked. She had exchanged a timid-maid bearing for an air of Hillary Clinton confidence. Puzzled, she silently closed the door and scanned their room.

The packed suitcases still stood zipped and against the wall. She shrugged off her suspicion, attributing it to an imagination as out of control as a racehorse with broken reins. She locked the door behind her to return to the meeting.

Why was the door closed while the maid worked in your room, Lynn? Yesterday morning weren't all the maids finished before now? Did you see any others between here and the meeting room?

48

JOHN ADAMS ROSE AT HIS USUAL FIVE-THIRTY, EAGER TO GET TO HIS OFFICE for a few hours of uninterrupted work. He took a shower, still seething over yesterday's bomb debacle. He wasn't used to being thwarted.

He stood under the warm water and calmed himself. His conversation with Frank Fillmore last night had confirmed his theory. Fillmore had delivered. Nausner had applied the strategy of silence. Fillmore was the only elite who had no recognizable conscience. His concern about this assignment had been the twist. Why build a bomb and make it faulty? But whys were unacceptable. The Patriot kept him heeled like a dog on a leash through a generous retainer that bought his loyalty and assured his availability. He used extreme caution in dealing with all of his elites, but especially Fillmore.

One reason he'd had the bomb planted was to profit from people's fear. It served God's purposes for money to be in his hands—the one God had chosen to define and implement justice. But he also wanted to teach President Benedict a lesson. Distasteful but necessary. She seemed unaware that the Secret Service exists precisely *because* of presidential vulnerability. The discovery of a bomb at the feet of another country's president would knock a hole in her innate confidence, and he'd intended to rush in with his *Triple S* maneuver: sensitive, solicitous, and supportive. The cover-up, and that's exactly what it was, meant that Benedict still rode the wings of invulnerability. His Vienna teaching-moment had been a costly failure. He grew angry again. A pointless reaction he realized as the water massaged his tense shoulder muscles.

Dawn broke in a cloudless sky as he rushed to his office, the traffic already humming. He liked the feel of the steering wheel in his common, thus invisible, black Ford. He always bought cars made in the USA to further his patriotic image. As he drove, he reran last night's second phone call. Acting on his instincts, he'd decided to initiate a personal investigation of Lynn Peterson. He'd contacted his Balkan connection, the investigative genius in his cadre of elites. As sharp as Zeller and nearly as committed as Lone Star. The right man in the right place. He sighed and a frown followed. All of this because of President Benedict.

Her Inner Circle benefited him but also discouraged him. Thoughts rolled through his mind about the plague of pretense within it. No one dared acknowledge the real problem: anti-American Americanism. The grand beginnings of the Great Democracy had eroded into pretense. He had watched statesmanship drown in the stormy sea of fogged facts, sound bites, and photo ops. Propaganda shaped perspective, hype shaded honesty, and revenge stole reason. Too many elected and appointed officials showed a woeful lack of vision. They sacrificed their ideals and honor, selling themselves to flag-tattering causes—trading the eagle for the golden calf of reelection. President Benedict had inherited the situation, not caused it. He had to give her that.

The politicos had learned the power of words. They hired think tanks and focus groups to promote self-interest instead of American interests. Brilliant linguists and hardball marketers filtered facts through nuance and euphemism, contriving spins that worked despite slapping logic in the face. They could reshape public perspective in inconceivable ways akin to snipping off American beauty roses and renaming them thorn bushes. Bombardment changed gullible citizens' ideas and vocabulary. The power of language! The power of deception!

He parked and took the stairs to his office. Yes, deception was the name of the game. With more pride than shame, he admitted that no politico could beat him at it. At least he didn't ask anyone to vote for him. And his Holy Vision of justice was righteous, not self-serving. President Nausner's strategy of silence might slow him, but it couldn't stop him!

49

After Lynn's luncheon meeting and Galen's sandwich at a small café near the Stephensturm, they met in the room to get their luggage. A small rectangular package about the size of a check box, wrapped in plain brown paper and tied with string, lay on the floral duvet. "What's that?" asked Galen, picking it up. He looked at the note tucked on top beneath the strings. "It's from Natalia."

"I offered to take an envelope for her to Sarajevo. Evidently the envelope she mimed had become a wrapped package." She moved beside Galen and read the note:

> To Bishop
> Ples tak to Fr. Nish. Orthdx prest, Sarajevo.
> He give mama.
> Thank U.
> Natalia

Lynn remembered the difference in bearing between the meek maid in the room and the confident woman walking down the hall. Airport security frowned on taking aboard something received from someone else. She debated unwrapping it.

"Bless her heart," said Galen. "I'm glad we can help her." He pulled out a large euro bill and set it on the dresser for a tip before stuffing the package in a corner of his suitcase.

No suspicion from him. She, too, was weary of suspicion. Standing on tiptoe, she put her hands tenderly on his face. "I love you, Galen Peterson. You are a kind and honorable man. I'm blessed to be your wife."

"And you, my darling Lynn, are a blessing."

Chaplain Dick Osborne was right on time to return them to Flughafen Wien. They found long lines moving at a snail's pace through airport security. "We could expect this," said Dick. "A hidden sniper can't shoot a high-profile NATO aide right here and things go on as before. And the bus bombing probably compounded it. Believe it or not, Vienna is usually safe."

Lynn and Galen glanced at each other, both thinking about the likelihood of an additional nondescript directive from President Nausner's security after the successful planting of an unsuccessful bomb at his reception. But they could never mention that.

Officials opened each suitcase, briefcase, tote bag, package and purse, searching them like voyeurs pawing through lingerie drawers. "They'd never get the contents back inside this thing," Dick grinned, referring to Lynn's roll-aboard he carried.

Why tote when you can roll? she wondered with an inner smile—a guy thing.

"NASA should hire her to pack their spaceships," joked Galen. "She sets the Guinness world record for packing the most weight per cubic inch."

Dick grinned. "I'll write a reference, Bishop Peterson." He scanned the zealous agents and lines of passengers and left levity behind. "This won't do." Avoiding the security checkpoint, he led them through a special door reserved for ranking military personnel and VIPs. He called the guard by name, returned the salute, and walked them to their gate. As he set Lynn's roll-aboard down, his eyes grew somber, his voice grave. "I'll pray for you while you're in the Balkans."

Lynn nodded appreciatively. "And I for you. Prayer really does make a difference, you know." She shook his hand, then hugged him. Sasha came to mind, young and legless Sasha. She didn't doubt that he could live a meaningful life, but neither did she shrink the size of the challenge he would have to face. "Thank you for all you do for the soldiers."

"I'm glad you took the time to contact me." His voice softened. "And to listen. Both of you." He turned quickly away.

Lynn saw his shoulders sag for an instant, then straighten into military bearing. Discipline, faith, and humor would get him through. "We'll keep in touch," she called, meaning it. He was now a member of their large global family.

While they waited for their plane to Skopje, Galen read a book about Lincoln. Lynn didn't know what to do—if anything—until she heard back from the President. She felt paralyzed as she stared out the dirty terminal window. *Terminal.* A thoughtless term for a place where planes departed. Departed. She lost interest in the wordplay and noticed that Galen had closed his book.

"Lynn, I've been thinking about Skopje and what we'll find. One of Paul's visions comes to mind—when the man pleads with him: 'Come over to Macedonia and help us.' Acts 16:9."

She had learned long ago to trust his photographic memory. He stored the Scriptures on his mental hard drive alongside historical facts and the name of every person he'd ever met. "I wonder how much help we can be to them," she said pensively. And how much help, if any, I can be to President Benedict. Surely Will had forwarded her email. Lynn wondered if she had it by now. Maybe she'd even read it. Would she respond? What would she say? She reminded herself that a response could take days. But on the other hand . . . "I saw a wireless area nearby, Love. I think I'll go check email."

"I'll come get you if we start boarding."

"Optimist! Half the passengers are probably still in the security line." She found an empty chair within wireless range and pulled out the Baby from Big-Black. One message. From: Will Whitcomb. Subject: Forwarded Letter. She felt the rise in her adrenaline.

> Lynn:
>
> I forwarded your note and have already received a response. The "friendship" appears to be exaggerated and a common interest in ranching a figment of imagination. You and I are aware of the human tendency to stretch things in order to feel important. A mere greeting or handshake from a prominent person can enlarge to a boastful story of a close friendship. Your kindness and good intentions, however, were appreciated.
>
> Will

She reread the puzzling email, more confused now than before she received it. Will's guarded language surprised her. The President's immediate response surprised her. The lack of direct communication surprised her. She was left to assumptions about why.

Maybe the President did write the notes to Marsh and me, and now regrets it. Maybe she's lost trust in me. Or maybe Marsh's murder alarmed her and she's protecting me by these disclaimers.

Oh, sure, Lynn! Your safety is the number one national priority!

If Marsh with NATO was not the President's friend and if the bit about ranching has no significance to her, what on God's precious earth is going on? Suppose the President didn't write the letter to Marsh nor the note to me requesting delivery. Who did? Suppose the Vice President misled me in the limo. Did he set me up? Did he set Marsh up through me?

Whoa, Lynn! Don't go there!

Another thought prowled at the edges of her mind. Suppose the email was intercepted and the reply isn't from her and she still doesn't know I have her letter.

Nothing made sense, because one thing was clear: For whatever reason, the President lied in her email to Will. *Or* the Vice President lied in the limo. *Or* someone has obtained access to, and control of, President Benedict's communications. The implications sent fear zigzagging through Lynn like a lightning bolt.

50

BUBBA'S GAZE FOLLOWED THE PADDLEBOAT ON THE BIG MUDDY, FRAMED by the office window. The sun turned the wheel-rippled waves into splinters of light. His eyes roved to the nameplate on the walnut desk, Boudreau Guidry Tietje, Attorney-at-Law, and then settled on the man who sat behind it engaged in a monologue. He was in his fifties, with receding hair and a broad smile, his worries written in wrinkled calligraphy across his face. He wore a dark, tailored suit and a custom white shirt with *BGT* embroidered on the French cuffs. A gaudy crawfish tie bedecked his neck as incongruous as nude-show neon lights at the symphony.

"As you know, I'm the executor for the estate of Elias Darwish."

Bubba nodded. The secretary had told him that when she called to set up this appointment.

"His mother is his heir. But settling a foreign estate is going to take a while—that's for sure."

Bubba wished he'd given Lynn more than five hundred dollars for Mrs. Darwish. Boudreau Guidry Tietje, Attorney-at-Law, did not appear to be motivated by efficiency and economy.

"Elias was as protective of his mother as a mama gator protecting her baby. Persuasive too. He convinced me to sign a contract setting a ceiling on my fees and expenses as executor. But it's a generous contract—that's for sure."

Neither Elie's insistence on a contract nor his generosity surprised Bubba.

Boudreau placed his hand on a shoebox in the center of his desk, the lid sealed with duct tape. "Elias brought this to me the day before he was killed."

The timing startled Bubba. "Last Tuesday? Was Elie expecting . . . trouble?"

"You know Elie. He was casual, as always. He said the contents weren't worth renting a safe deposit box, but they had sentimental value. Workers were coming to renovate his condo and he was afraid it might get lost."

The renovation was news to Bubba.

"Workers'll do that—that's for sure," said Boudreau. "Strew everything like a rainstorm scatters pine needles. Anyway, I told him I'd keep it here in my safe until he returned. He thanked me and then jokingly said, 'Give it to Bubba Broussard if something happens to me.' He was always joking." Boudreau glanced out the window at the river, losing his flamboyance. "Not anymore."

No, thought Bubba. No more serious talks. No more jokes. He would miss both.

"It was such a casual remark that if he'd said any name but yours, Bubba, I probably wouldn't even have remembered it." He picked up the shoebox and gave it to him.

Bubba held it with reverence. Elie had touched it, taped it, thought of him. Boudreau eyed the shoebox, curious—"that's for sure." But Bubba wanted to open it in private. He stood and extended his hand across the desk. "Thank you. I hope your meeting with the crawfish farmers goes well."

The lawyer looked surprised, then glanced down at his tie and laughed. "The tie stands out like a sucked thumb on a dirty baby."

The secretary opened the door. "The crawfish farmers are here."

Bubba threw his legs over the door of his silver customized Corvette and looked at the empty passenger seat. "Oh God! I miss the best friend I ever had!" The meeting with Elie's lawyer brought another reminder that death terminated everything but memories. He put the shoebox in the empty seat and headed for the Superdome. It was the place he felt closest to his friend. It was closed when he arrived, but a security guard let him in. He could always get in anywhere in New Orleans. He loved this city. And this place, he thought, walking out on the field, shoebox in hand, memories vivid. He sat down at the fifty-yard line, feeling Elie's presence and seeing again that magic foot kick field goals from this very spot—sometimes even farther from the goal. He pulled the duct tape from around the shoebox and slowly removed the lid, not knowing what to expect. He smiled at what he saw. Sentimental value, indeed—a stack of photos. They'd had many good times together. Victory celebrations. Football signings. Benefits. Parties. He sat there a long time. Looking at each picture. Remembering. Reliving. With gratitude he realized how vividly the mind stores memories—sights, sounds, smells. All there. But no new ones with Elie. Never again. He would give anything for them to have been anywhere but Jackson Square last Wednesday morning.

In a few of the photos they wore their Saints uniforms. In some there were groups of people. He and Elie were in all of them. Except one. He held a picture of an older woman standing beside a wall shelf that held framed pictures too small to make out. He wondered if Elie had included it by mistake. She must be his mother. He turned it over to see.

Instead of a name there was a small white sticky-note in Elie's handwriting: "Clean out that locker, Bubba!" He chuckled, fondly remembering the silly joke between them—our lockers are so messy we'd make our mamas ashamed. A thought about Elie's personality broke the laugh: his tendency to say in a joking way the things he felt most serious about. His words echoed: "No one could find anything in your locker, Bubba! If I had something important, I wouldn't put it in a safe deposit box. I'd just hide it in your locker." He'd said it jokingly a couple of weeks ago. "Give it to Bubba Broussard if something happens to me," he'd told his attorney, also jokingly, the day before he was killed. Bubba shuffled through the stack of photos again. Something in that stack had to be significant enough for Elie to deliver it to his attorney for safekeeping and to concoct a story about condo renovation. All the photos were four-by-six. All in color. All included the two of them. All but one—a three-by-five, black-and-white picture of an elderly woman. It just didn't fit, like finding the Queen Mother added to the face cards in a poker game. And it was the only photo with a note on the back. "Clean out that locker, Bubba!"

He gathered up the photos and headed to his locker.

51

THE AGENT ANNOUNCED THE FLIGHT TO SKOPJE, AND THE BOARDING LINE moved slowly forward. He methodically matched Lynn's name on her ticket to her passport and her photo to her face. He glanced down at the roll-aboard, scanned it, froze for a moment, and looked up, glowering. Fear shot through her. But there couldn't be a problem—she didn't have the President's letter anymore.

With a suspicious glint in his eye he scrutinized her passport again. Then he eyed Galen's suitcase and didn't bother with his passport. He muttered words she didn't understand and thrust a whistle between his lips. It reverberated shrilly against the concrete and steel of the airport.

Terror seized Lynn. A security guard advanced on them. "I don't understand," she told him. "*Ich verstehe nicht.*" But she did understand, all too well. Somehow they knew she'd given a secret letter to Major Manetti and then stolen it back.

The guard didn't bother to explain. His face and body language declared "no nonsense"! He marched them back to the security checkpoint that Dick had avoided earlier. With great flare that entertained the bored passengers, No-Nonsense deposited them at the end of the line. He pointed to their bags. "No security stickers!" he said in heavily accented English.

"Security stickers?" Relief washed over Lynn. "Security stickers!" she repeated with the titter of a teenager.

Galen was anything but elated. He had spent his life as the quarterback, whatever the playing field. He pointed to an empty security station and rose to his full height. "Take us there," he ordered in his most authoritative manner, "and get someone *immediately* to do the security check!"

No-Nonsense glared at him like he hoped Galen would bolt so he'd have an excuse to shoot.

"We *cannot* miss that plane!" Galen's tone was close to the edge. Lynn knew that partly he was concerned about her itinerary, but mostly he rebelled against being ordered around.

"The U. S. Empire might rule the world. But when I am on duty, it does not rule this airport!"

Lynn decided to try a softer strategic approach. "Please, sir, we don't have security stickers because we were escorted directly through the private entry."

No-Nonsense looked skeptical.

"I'm sure you know that Major Marshall Manetti was . . ." she swallowed, finding it hard to say the word, ". . . killed by a sniper Sunday."

He nodded.

"You probably know that Major Manetti was the chief aide to the NATO general in charge of Balkan strategy."

He looked surprised but nodded again as though he knew everything of significance.

"It is a terrible loss," she said. "More complicated than I can explain." You wouldn't believe!

No-Nonsense scrutinized her eyes and face.

"We flew to Vienna with him Sunday."

He leaned forward slightly, totally attentive.

"You see, my husband has a high position and is known for his international work." With studied innuendo, she added, "If you know what I mean."

He took new measure of Galen's authority. For a moment Lynn thought he was going to salute.

"We exchanged vital information with the major." Poor Galen thinks I'm exaggerating. "And it is essential that we get to Skopje tonight." A blatant non sequitur, but maybe it would work.

"I understand." He drew to attention and hoisted her suitcase, escorting them back to the gate in double time, clearing the crowd like a tank. The boarding door had closed. He zeroed in on the agent who'd called security. Lynn couldn't understand his ensuing diatribe, but it vanquished everyone at the counter, reopened the boarding door, and halted the pilot's preparation for takeoff. Satisfied, No-Nonsense escorted them onto the plane.

"*Vielen Dank*," Lynn said, meaning her thanks. He nodded, clicked his heels, and marched off the plane. With a relieved sigh she settled into her seat. "For a few minutes, Love, it looked like you and the security guard were about to play *High Noon*. And you didn't have a gun."

"That man doesn't need a gun! His words alone left a bloodbath at the boarding counter." Galen paused, eyeing her. "Speaking of words, I'm going to have to start watching yours more carefully. You told him the truth—mostly—and managed to leave a completely false impression."

Lynn felt no pride in this new skill she'd developed as a courier. Deep inside she wondered if it was leading her down a path toward becoming less than she was.

52

Bubba Broussard entered the locker room to an eerie silence. The contrast to the normal motion, muscle, and mockery unsettled him. The stillness shouted Elie's absence. His locker stood open and empty. The police—or someone more menacing—had already cleaned it out, seeking clues, he supposed, but it seemed invasive. The dead are helpless, their privacy no longer honored.

Clean out that locker, Bubba! He opened his, beside Elie's, and began taking everything out, examining one item at a time. Clutter encircled his feet by the time he reached the bottom. Bubba grinned. "OK, Elie. You get the last laugh. My locker's clean."

A lone white sock remained, tucked in the back corner. He picked it up to toss in the throwaway pile and felt something in it. Even in the silence he looked over each shoulder to be sure he was alone and kept the sock in the locker protected from view as he stuck his hand inside. His fingers touched a small, hard object. He pulled out a USB flash drive.

Bubba rubbed his thumb across it and carried on a mental monologue aimed at Elie. Why didn't you just tell me about this? Why didn't you just stick it in the shoebox? You had to have some reason. Regardless of the why, the what was clear: Its secrecy was imperative to Elie. I'll honor that secrecy with my life, bro.

Paranoia persuaded him to keep his own computer clean. He'd already had one stealth visitor. He looked at his watch, stunned by how late it was. He didn't have time to take the flash drive to the library computers at Tulane before the Saints' private tribute to Elie. Missing it was unthinkable. Afterward the library would be closed. He'd go to Tulane first thing in the morning before shooting the TV ad for United Way. He started to put the flash drive in his pocket but decided to leave it in the locker where Elie had chosen to hide it. He put it back exactly as he'd found it and piled everything on top. He had no idea how long it had been there, but it had been safe so far.

Safe so far. He hesitated. Surely it would be safe one more night. He slammed his locker door and headed for the team's tribute to Elie.

53

THE FLIGHT FROM VIENNA TO SKOPJE, UNFORTUNATELY, WAS MEMORABLE. The adventure—or misadventure—began soon after No-Nonsense deplaned. The attendant, a large-boned woman with masculine features, charged toward them like El Toro. "Seatbelts!" she ordered. Her gaze darted to Big-Black, obviously measuring its size as Lynn shoved her "small personal item" under the seat. A budding starlet with a captive audience, she dramatically shook her head and gave a disdainful there's-always-one roll of her eyes.

Lynn wondered if her embarrassment and humiliation had something to do with the rules being on El Toro's side. It's self-defeating to alienate a flight attendant, so Lynn smiled at her—a gesture evidently interpreted as the swirl of a matador's cape.

"Mr. and Mrs. Peterson, your extravagant lack of consideration is *not* helpful. First you delayed our departure. Then you had yourselves escorted on board by a security guard who left the wounded in his wake."

She excelled in the capacity to make Lynn feel small. And to do it in fluent English.

Before El Toro could continue the goring, takeoff was announced. Nostrils flaring and head down, cheated of pawing the ground, she wheeled and charged to her seat.

Seatbelt, Lynn was tempted to call. She and Galen looked at each other, astonished. "Well, Love, that was entertaining!"

"I hope you have a couple of parachutes in your 'purse.' She may make us jump."

As the plane rose into the air, the feeling of being watched returned to Lynn. Well, she thought, no wonder. El Toro played to the passengers at our expense. Everyone in the area is looking at us.

The man across the aisle from Galen leaned toward them and initiated conversation. His eyes belied his open pose. Lynn thought of a crouching tiger waiting to pounce. She trusted Galen's sense of judgment. He didn't need help. Her well of emotional reserves was close to the bottom, and she turned toward the window. The tiger will get nothing from me.

Lynn rued the reality that there was not time for deeper reflection on Vienna before preparing for Skopje. And the same would be true when she left Skopje for Sarajevo. There was never time to reflect on the last place and anticipate the next place. They just hustled themselves from one setting to another with research in between. She gazed out the window, watching the sunset colors dance with the distant horizon. Soaring through the darkening sky five miles above the stench of recent realities playing out on the planet, she moved at last into the center of herself. Peaceful. Resting. Feeling her heart beat to the rhythm of the universe. Breathing slowly and deeply. Speeding through space, profoundly still. Refilling the well.

A tap from behind startled her. She peered down at the broad fingers of the large hand on her shoulder and turned around toward its owner, who sat directly behind Galen.

"Excuse me. Little English." The passenger spoke hesitantly in a thick accent that Lynn recognized as Russian. His firm jaw and direct eyes left her with the impression of a straightforward man who got to the bottom of things. "Mrs. Peterson?"

She nodded, unsurprised since El Toro had broadcast their last name.

"Bishop Lynn Peterson?"

Now *that* surprised her! She couldn't recall her first name or title being used on the plane or while waiting at the gate. She nodded but decided to withhold both her warmth and limited words in his language until she had a better feel for the situation.

"Viktor," he said, putting his hand on his chest. "I see your . . ." He framed a picture with his thumbs and forefingers and said slowly, laboriously, "You write . . . little Russian book."

Ah! Lynn fell in love with anyone who recognized her face from a book cover instead of a passport photo. The "little book" was about her denomination's work in Russia. "Yes, sir," she acknowledged with a smile. "*Da, gospodin.*"

It was his turn to be surprised. "You speak Russian?"

She shook her head. "*Nyet.*"

"Your book . . . good book."

She refrained from leaping over the seat and kissing him on each cheek, Russian style. "Thank you, Viktor. *Spasebo.*"

Struggling for the words, he said, "It . . . catch Russian . . . spirit."

She basked in his compliment.

Cool the vanity, Lynn.

Then a maelstrom of questions swirled through her mind. How did he know my full name? Did he really recognize me from my picture in the little Russian book? How did he learn about it?

It wasn't exactly an international best seller, Lynn.

He didn't Google me. This plane doesn't have wireless. And he couldn't have known I'd be on the plane. She smiled to herself, realizing that what she wanted to believe actually made the most sense: Viktor was a nice man who had discovered her book, read it, and liked it, just as he had said.

Suddenly the plane banked to the left and interrupted Galen's conversation with the man across the aisle. He turned to Lynn. "Do you suppose we're returning to Vienna?"

Hijacked, she thought, then joked because she was scared. "Just avoiding a black hole, Love."

"The lady likes hyperbole." His grin looked less spontaneous than contrived to console. The plane lurched. Dipped. Seemed to go into freefall. The wings caught the air again. The engines roared with a mighty thrust of power. The plane rose in a sharp climb, then leveled and flew steadily through the night sky.

"Well, Love, that was entertaining!" She realized they were clinging to each other.

A voice from the cockpit filled the plane, first in German-accented English. "This is the captain speaking. Vienna Air Traffic Control failed to provide a flight plan that took into account heavy military action in the Balkans. As a precaution to ensure your safety, we have been diverted and issued a new flight plan. Our arrival time in Skopje will be later than scheduled. The crew apologizes for the Vienna ATC. Thank you for your understanding." With an edge of levity, he added, "My friends, we would volunteer to participate in this noble NATO cause, but all we could drop is luggage."

Lynn glanced out the dark window, grateful she couldn't see fireworks.

PART III
The Tragedy

Tuesday, 8:33 P.M.

Skopje. City of myths and mysticism. Where poets speak in bitter hyperbole, and ethnic versions of history are disparate paintings of the same landscape. Where in ancient days Alexander the Great set out to conquer the world and in current days Goce Delchev, guerilla-terrorist who founded IMRO, lies buried under a fir tree at the Church of Sveti Spas.

Skopje. Capital of Macedonia. A place of changing borders and unchanging strategy. Recycling savagery from ruler to ruler. Provoking religious hatred to dispel the threat of a people united. Igniting wars because of unresolved issues.

Skopje. City with a new dream rising from the darkness like a bright moon at midnight.

54

THE PLANE LANDED SAFELY AT SKOPJE'S ALEXANDER THE GREAT AIRPORT AT 8:33 on Tuesday night. The moment Lynn stepped off, her mind reverted to the shot she'd heard when she had disembarked at Flughafen Wien two days ago. She heard it again. Felt the same fear. Saw Marsh sprawled on the ramp in his white uniform.

Galen put a gentle hand on her shoulder. "You're shaking, Lynn."

"The sniper . . ."

He bent down and whispered tenderly. "It's OK. That was *there*. It's over."

She doubted it would ever be over for her.

All passengers deplaned safely—it was getting admitted to Macedonia that proved a nightmare. President Basil Dimitrovski well understood that both factions in the Balkan conflict used the age-old ploy of evoking revenge to gain support, and one strategy was to commit a terrorist act that would look like the other side did it. Loose airport security at a busy airport was an open invitation. Not on his watch!

The passengers snaked toward security, slowed by scanners, metal detectors, and agents who searched both luggage and people. Lynn scanned the crowd. The man who'd sat across the aisle from Galen and engaged him in lengthy conversation stood third behind them in line, El Toro now on his arm.

Aha, Lynn! A little hanky-panky?

As they crept forward, Lynn reviewed their itinerary. "Mihail Martinovski is meeting us at the airport and taking us to the hotel," she told Galen.

"I remember meeting him in Oslo when President Dimitrovski received the World Peace Award. 'In commendation for his creativity, consistency, and courage,'" cited Galen.

The myriad details stored on Galen's mental hard drive amazed Lynn. "We're scheduled for coffee with the President tomorrow morning."

"Good! He's a remarkable man, the only Balkan leader able to keep his country out of the conflict. No minor miracle."

"*And*," Lynn added proudly, "he's in our denomination. Mihail is his pastor."

Watch the brag, Lynn.

"I'm afraid our delay is keeping Mihail waiting far too long." Galen's voice rang with impatience.

"Since there's nothing we can do, Love, we just have to let things unfold." She knew her words would bounce off him like raindrops on an umbrella. He focused on getting things folded rather than letting them unfold. A do-it man instead of a to-do-list man.

"We should have taken a cab to the hotel."

"I disagree, Galen. It's as important to accept hospitality as to offer it."

He grinned. "I'm bored, Lynn, and pulling your string. You're right about Mihail's hospitality."

"I really like him," she said, restraining all the other words that came to mind about pulling someone's string.

When they reached the head of the line, the security agent took everything out of her roll-aboard, piece by piece. He thoroughly and methodically unfolded each garment. Unzipped each pocket. Opened the toiletry bag. Checked her compact and lipstick tube. She expected him to tell her to open her mouth so he could inspect the mint in her mouth. By the time Mr. Thorough-&-Methodical finished, she had no secrets from him or anyone nearby.

T&M looked at the pile of things he'd removed, his eyes measuring it against the size of her suitcase. He shrugged, gestured for her to repack, and turned her over to a woman agent. She opened everything in Big-Black, including two envelopes—one containing their itinerary, and one the note to Mrs. Darwish from Bubba. She patted Lynn down, felt the waist wallet, and asked to search it. Lynn had included Bubba's money with her own—not enough combined to be suspicious for a traveler from the States. No note from the President. Lynn smiled, feeling like a pro.

But this was not Galen's day for positive experiences with security agents. The trouble started when T&M's gloved hand lifted Natalia's wrapped box. For the first time he spoke, using careful English, "What is this?"

"You may open it," said Galen with his customary air of authority.

T&M's glance over the rims of his glasses stated that permission was not needed.

Galen reached for the package to show him what Natalia had written on the brown wrapping paper: To Father Nish from Natalia.

"*No!* Hands back!"

With difficulty Galen swallowed words and obeyed.

"What is it?" he repeated.

"A little money," said Galen. "The hotel maid in Vienna asked us to take it to her priest in Sarajevo. He'll give it to her family."

"She doesn't trust the post," Lynn added, a corroborative witness.

"How did you get a wrapped package through Vienna security?"

Galen and Lynn looked at each other. To confess that she misled No-Nonsense seemed incriminating.

"*Austrians!*" T&M muttered with cultural contempt. He untied the string on the package, neither careful nor careless, thoroughly and methodically doing his duty. As he unwrapped it, the paper crackled like convicting evidence before a jury. When he removed the lid from the check-size box, he whistled softly.

Lynn felt scared.

"Do you expect me to believe that a hotel maid earns this much money? And entrusted it to a stranger?" He turned the box upside down. An inch-thick wad of pretty pink bills tumbled to the table, each worth 500 euros. "You insult me!"

Lynn and Galen gaped at the stack as T&M fanned through the bills.

"I don't understand." Galen's tone of authority had vanished.

"Perhaps not." The agent's eyes narrowed. "But perhaps you do."

Everyone in line behind them watched this center-ring circus performance. Viktor called to her in his limited, Russian-accented English. "You . . . need help?"

She shrugged, palms up, then shook her head. There was nothing he could do. Besides, T&M might lump Russians right there with *Austrians!*

T&M reached into the box and pulled out a piece of blue paper at the bottom.

Lynn stared at it and gripped the table. The paper held a simple drawing in ink. It depicted two vertically overlapping crescent moons that were enclosed in a circle. The symbol! Elie's medal. Sasha's cross. And now Natalia's box. She felt T&M looking at her, his eyes dissecting her behavior.

She recovered and tried to hide her recognition. "Interesting little drawing," she said meekly.

Those were the last words she spoke standing beside Galen. A nod from the agent brought two uniformed guards, who separated them despite capable Galen's best effort to keep them together. With a firm grip the guards escorted Lynn and Galen to different rooms for interrogation. Interrogation! Images of Abu Ghraib flashed vividly.

Galen glanced back at her and smiled. A brave front, but she saw the fear in his eyes. That was when terror struck her.

55

Lynn sat alone in a small room with two hard chairs. Right now Galen was being interrogated. It was the scariest word she could think of for someone in a foreign country. She would be next. Her stomach churned. Fear pounded in her heart. Breath grew short.

Get a grip, Lynn!

She struggled to think. Thoughts shattered and scattered like fragments of a smashed kaleidoscope. She slowed her breathing. Deepened it. Closed her eyes. Calmed herself with the ancient Jesus Prayer, slowly praying "Lord Jesus Christ" while inhaling, and "Have mercy on me" while exhaling. Breath. *Ruah.* Spirit.

The laptop! She took a quick mental inventory of anything personal or incriminating. The email to President Benedict and Will's response! She took the laptop from Big-Black. Pulled up the web mail file. Thank you for speed. Clicked *Sent Items. President. Delete.* Pulled up *Deleted Items.* Hit *Delete* again. Repeated the process for *Received Items.* Clicked *Whitcomb. Delete. Delete deletions.*

The door jerked open.

With three quick moves she exited the email file, clicked on the Solitaire shortcut and opened a game.

"STOP!" The officer grabbed her laptop so fast she feared he'd drop it. The fury in his face matched the anger in his voice.

She tasted fear, a bitter bile in the back of her throat.

He glared at the screen. Blinked. A deck of cards greeted him, lined up in a tidy row, ready for play. He stared at them for a few moments, his anger subsiding. He looked from the screen to Lynn. He actually smiled.

She smiled back, and they both laughed. His laughter came from surprise. Hers from the release of sheer terror. Then tears began to roll down her cheeks. Tears for Major Manetti. For young Sasha with no legs. For Galen in another room—undergoing what? Tears of stress and weariness. Silent, uncontrollable tears.

The officer sat down in the second straight-backed chair and watched her for a while. "If you have done nothing wrong, you have nothing to fear." His accent indicated British-taught English. Lynn saw compassion in his eyes. "The same is true for your husband."

Trying to keep her voice from shaking, she said, "Sir, Pastor Mihail Martinovski has a church here in Skopje. He is meeting us."

"I know of him."

"I am concerned about his long wait. He may be worried." She could feel the tears still overflowing. Her voice was timorous but steady. "Could someone tell him we have been delayed?"

He pondered the request an inordinate length of time. "I do not see how that can cause any harm." He rose. "I will tell him myself."

"Our names are . . ."

He smiled as to a child. "I have your name, Lynn Prejean Peterson."

"Of course," she stammered. "This is new to me."

He handed her the laptop. "Playing solitaire is misleading. I think you should put this away."

"Yes, sir."

Time dragged on after he left. Lynn sat unmoving. Worrying about Galen. Waiting and wondering. Worrying about Galen. Feeling watched. Worrying about Galen. She tried again to center herself, this time in vain. She feared she'd lost the center for good.

The door opened, and the officer reappeared. "I am sorry, Bishop Peterson," he apologized. "I wish you had told me."

Told him what?

"I did not introduce myself earlier. I am Agent Nedelkovski. Please come." He held the door open, a gentleman for a lady, and bowed like a squire. She could imagine him doffing a plumed hat. The situation had clearly changed.

She saw Galen, already in the hall, Natalia's box in hand. He appeared fine. Thank you. They rushed to each other. No one stopped them.

Agent Nedelkovski escorted them through customs directly to Mihail. He waited, smiling and patient, a replica of St. Francis at peace within despite the turbulent world without. Obviously the good pastor had done something on their behalf. Nedelkovski spoke to Mihail in words she couldn't understand, but she understood the respect in his voice.

Before departing, he turned to them and spoke with the same respectful tone. "Good night, Bishop Peterson, Dr. Peterson. I sincerely hope the rest of your stay in Skopje is better than the beginning."

Mihail ushered them toward his car to take them to Hotel Aleksandar. Lynn took a deep breath of freedom's air and gazed up at the clear Skopje sky. "Look! A swing moon!"

"That's what she always calls it," Galen explained, putting his arm around her.

"The same one all around the world," she marveled.

"It's beautiful," said Mihail. "A message of light and oneness for all God's people."

She touched his arm. "I don't know what you did, Pastor Martinovski, but thank you."

"You have our deepest appreciation," Galen added.

Mihail chuckled. "To be truthful, Agent Nedelkovski discounted my opinion of you. So I telephoned President Dimitrovski. He remembers you from Oslo, Bishop Peterson, and speaks highly of you. He said he's looking forward to coffee with us in the morning. He personally made a telephone call on your behalf." Again he chuckled. "Nedelkovski did not discount *his* opinion. Here in Macedonia, only God ranks above him!"

56

BUBBA WAS THE LAST TO LEAVE THE TEAM'S PRIVATE TRIBUTE TO ELIE. HE swung his leg over his 'Vette and noted the crescent moon above. Normally he would enjoy driving beneath it, but not tonight. His friend's death left a hole in his life, and the flash drive consumed him. His cell phone rang, and he recognized the voice of Boudreau Guidry Tietje, attorney-at-law.

After dancing around the Southern niceties, his voice dropped to a whisper. "I'm calling to warn you."

The nervous tone jarred Bubba more than the words. He knew scared when he heard it, and this man was terrified.

"Tonight two gunmen barged into my office. They threatened my *life*."

The Mafia came to mind.

"They knew I was Elias Darwish's attorney."

"Call the police. Speak directly to Cy Bill Bergeron."

"They demanded all my information. They were specifically interested in whether he had a safe deposit box. I told them he didn't. Then they asked if he had given me anything to give to anyone else."

"You told them about me?" Bubba tried to keep alarm out of his voice.

"Not exactly."

That means yes.

"I said I follow my clients' instructions, and everything went to his mother as requested."

"Good for you. So the work is on its way?"

"I told the gunmen that everything *went* to her. I didn't say I'd *sent* it."

Lawyer legalese. But the wily man had shown courage in misleading them.

"So they don't know about the shoebox?"

"They were holding *guns* on me! They forced me to let them examine his file. They said they'd just as soon kill me and locate it by themselves. It's filed under *D*—as easy to find as old Andy's statue at Jackson Square." He paused.

Bubba waited for the words he knew were coming.

"I'm sorry, Bubba. They saw your name. You'll be next—that's for sure."

57

LYNN AWOKE AND LAY QUIETLY IN BED IN THEIR ROOM AT HOTEL Aleksandar, a room similar to the one in Vienna. She checked the clock: four-thirty. She wanted to roll over and go back to sleep, but she had work to do. Quietly she took *Balkan Ghosts* into the bathroom and turned on the light for a crash course on Macedonia. She padded the back of the tub with bath towels and leaned against them. What she read chilled her. For more than a century, the "Macedonia Question" had repeatedly flared and led to war. Each nation that had ever ruled in any part of Macedonia still felt entitled to the country, and zealous patriots from those countries considered its reclamation a matter of national pride. A nation a bit smaller than Maryland had repeatedly shifted world history!

Her own world had also shifted. Thoughts of Elie, the major, and the mind-bending mystery of President Benedict's response cycled through her mind. Start with St. Sava. She checked the index and found two references. Both referred to Serbia's patron saint, also written *Sabbas.* Born Rastno, he was the youngest son of Stefan Nemanja, king of Serbia. His father ruled a highly civilized state and could sign his name at a time in history when the Holy Roman Emperor in Germany had to use a thumbprint. She recalled another St. Sabbas seven centuries earlier, who founded Mar Saba near the Dead Sea and was over all the Palestinian houses. She scanned the rest of Kaplan's information. Too weary to concentrate further, she put down the book and went back to bed.

But she lay awake, rerunning Will's puzzling email. Why didn't he simply forward the President's response? Lynn didn't doubt for a moment his integrity, which brought her back to her original tilt-a-whirl. Since that fateful ride with the Vice President, she'd begun to doubt his honesty, or worse, the President's honesty—or the security and control of White House communications. Accepting that envelope had proved a curse. It had caused her to be less than truthful with Galen, turned her fluffy little world awry and evoked a new level of inner terror. All she really wanted to do was make measures of music in the song of life. Instead, she was embroiled in measures of malice in a world of conspiracy.

58

BUBBA FELT THE DIFFERENCE IN HIS CONDO THE MOMENT HE ENTERED. He glanced around warily. Nothing disturbed. Poised for action, he left the door slightly ajar and listened.

Two men stepped from the bedroom, guns drawn.

Bubba sized up the opposition. The shorter one's jowls and stance mirrored a pit bull. The taller one's face was a mass of wide, chubby wrinkles, reminding Bubba of his sister's obedient Chinese shar-pei. Game time. He donned his warm TV interview smile. "Whatever you folks want might as well be discussed in a friendly fashion over a beer."

They glanced at each other. "This ain't no social call!" snarled Pit Bull.

Bubba eyed their guns. "I see you boys brought your toys."

"Look, Bubba, we don't want no trouble with a Saint," Shar-Pei replied.

"You're Saints fans?"

Shar-Pei's wrinkles wiggled their way into a smile. "We like to bet on the Saints when we think y'all will win."

Bubba tried a diversion. "The odds were better when Elias Darwish was alive. You should've thought of that before you killed him."

They both looked shocked—the real thing. "They caught his killer," said Pit Bull. "Where you been?"

"We ain't in the Saint-killing business." Shar-Pei lowered his gun. "We might bribe a Saint, but we ain't going to shoot one."

Bubba smiled approval. "Cabrioni's boys are smarter than that."

Shar-Pei nodded. "No cops and no Saints."

"That's the code." Pit Bull spoke the word *code* as reverently as a priest offering the Holy Cup. But he didn't holster his gun.

"The shoebox is on the table." Bubba gestured. "Right there."

"He left you *shoes*?" asked Shar-Pei.

"Some photos."

"For blackmail?" Pit Bull's personal interest increased mightily. "Keep him guarded while I take a look." He removed the photos and flipped through them. Then he flung them back on the table.

Shar-Pei took a turn. "Just a bunch of pictures of you and Darwish."

"Are you trying to insult us?" Pit Bull aimed his gun and steadied it with both hands.

Shar-Pei scowled. "A man doesn't leave some stupid pictures with his *lawyer*! What do you take us for!"

A couple of clowns play-acting Mafia goons in a B movie, thought Bubba.

"Don't force me to make an exception to the code!" barked Pit Bull.

He needed to be careful. They were the New Orleans version of the real thing. Unpredictable and dangerous. He shifted to his persuasive shoe-ad style. "That's all he gave me. Maybe as a tough kicker he wanted to hide his sentimental side. The three of us know how that is."

They pondered the idea but remained skeptical. Shar-Pei spoke. "You got to give us the rest of it, Bubba."

Pit Bull lowered his aim. "First it'll be the knees. That'll kill your career."

Cy Bill shoved the door open. "*Police!*"

Three guns aimed. Bubba stood in the crossfire. He called the play. It wouldn't hurt to have these guys in his debt. "Not to worry, officer. My good friends here were just leaving."

Cy Bill's eyes stayed on them. "Explain the guns."

"These gentlemen are just feeling protective after what happened to our kicker."

"That's right," said Shar-Pei, holstering his gun.

Pit Bull followed suit. "He's safe now that you're here, officer."

"You have my word as a Saint," said Bubba, his right hand raised, "that those pictures are what Elias Darwish left me." Legalese: Distort perception by telling only part of the truth. "You boys can take the photos if you want to. After your boss has a look, get them back to me, and I can probably arrange some fifty-yard-line seats. Down close." Appeased and relieved, they thanked him as they left.

Cy Bill holstered his gun and parked himself in a chair. "I'm glad ol' Boudreau warned you, Bubba."

"Let's talk unofficially, Cy Bill." He waited for a nod. Bubba told him about the note and flash drive. "I think it would be wise to make a *confidential* backup copy for you. As a friend—not a cop." Again he waited for a nod. "As backup."

"I'll keep it in the safest place in New Orleans—the police station. Unofficially, of course."

"By the way, thanks for coming."

"Well," Cy Bill grinned, "I'm making this YouTube video, and riding in on Ebony with six-shooters drawn was a dramatic way to begin it."

59

Working till nearly midnight in his office, the Patriot had one more task. He called his Balkan connection. As always he spoke with a French accent, tenoring his bass voice and offering no apology for waking him before six—the man was well paid. He asked about the Peterson results.

The elite's investigative ingenuity and success merited a bonus. He had managed to get himself on the Petersons' flight and was now in the hotel room next to theirs. The informative narrative included the bishop's actions, contacts, and conversations on the plane and at the Skopje airport. The Patriot listened intently to the minute details. Time-consuming but necessary.

Finally the monologue reached its conclusion. "The man is a historian, interested in the past, not the present, and certainly not the future. The woman is a naïve bishop. No more. No less."

"Do you guarantee that, *monsieur*?"

"When they leave their room, I will take advantage of their absence. She carries a laptop. I'll check it."

"Excellent." The Patriot had almost as much confidence in his Balkan connection as in himself.

"If I find anything that alters this report, I'll contact you. The usual way." With a chuckle he added, "I think the bishop actually believes that the power of love can change the world."

Compassion—ineffective but harmless. "I appreciate your thoroughness," he said, putting a smile in his voice. "*Au revoir.*" The Patriot ran his thumb across the *fleur-de-lis*. The panel dropped, and he returned the phone to JFK, whose sculpture guarded the secret storage compartment. Still smiling, he commended himself for using caution before targeting an innocent. "There are so few of us these days," he muttered. The Statue of Liberty had once welcomed him as a young man to an idealistic America, a land of honor and dreams, where individualism danced with the common good, and patriotism partnered with reason. He longed to restore the days before polarization tainted the country. Yet BarLothiun had profited from the demise of the old ways. John Adams knew how to walk beside all peoples. Sometimes disturbing but always necessary.

As his thoughts turned to the President, he wondered if he was becoming obsessed. He quickly dismissed the idea. His initial thought about her . . . *exit* . . . had shocked him, too frightening to pursue. Yet it still hovered in the shadows of his mind.

60

LYNN HEARD THE ALARM CLOCK. HER HAND GROPED FOR THE *OFF* BUTton, her eyes still closed. It wasn't set. But it rang on. Where am I? Possibilities sifted through grogginess. New Orleans. Vienna. Skopje! Five memories fired like bullets in rapid succession: the Major's death/the President's letter/her denial/the Elie-Sasha-Natalia symbol/isolation for interrogation. She felt battle fatigue.

But for the moment she was safe, tucked in a cozy bed at the Hotel Aleksandar. It's Wednesday, she recalled. And then she remembered what she wanted to forget: Elie was killed a week ago today.

The ringing stopped. "Hello," said Galen's half-awake, sluggish voice. "Thank you." He clicked the phone down. "Our eight-thirty wake-up call."

"Eight-thirty! They're joking." She opened her eyes and willed them to focus on the clock. Eight-thirty. It was in on the joke. Yesterday's exhaustion and her sleepless night contaminated her muscles and seeped into her bones. Her eyelids shut again, closing the drapes on the new day, settling into oblivion's comfort.

Galen's words drifted through the fog. "I have good news and bad news."

She didn't muster the energy to open her eyes. "Good news first, Love," she mumbled, planning to be asleep before he got to the bad news.

"President Dimitrovski invited us for coffee this morning. Remember?"

"And the bad news?"

"President Dimitrovski invited us for coffee this morning." He put his arms around her and with a hug lifted her into a sitting position. "Mihail will pick us up in an hour. We have to get up."

She opened one eye. Get up. Unpack. Dress. Her eye closed.

"I suppose we could make apologies, Lynn. With all that's happened, he would understand."

That opened her eyes. "Brilliant, Galen!" This time her eyelids pulled off the first feat: staying open. Muscles pulled off the second: dangling legs off the bed. Before her toes hit the floor, she prayed as always. But this morning instead of lifting up her long list of names individually and enjoying the image of each face, she abbreviated the process and prayed for The List. An unworthy shortcut. My loss, she confessed, trusting God's grace to encompass shortcuts.

"You're a trooper, Lynn."

"No. Just curious. I don't like missed opportunities."

"It *is* an honor that the President invited us."

The President. Her mind triggered to Will's weird email. Maybe the President had sent it to mislead him and would send another directly to her. She set the Baby on the dresser and started to open it.

"Email will keep, Lynn. We're short on time."

"Right." She had to let it go. Nothing at the moment was as important as their meeting with President Dimitrovski. She showered quickly and put on her blue suit.

Galen picked up Natalia's checkbook-sized box. "This little package was a source of unintended consequences." He wrote "To Father Nish from Natalia" across the lid in blue ink, remembering the words tossed away with the brown paper at the airport. The euros and drawing were still inside. "We can't leave all this money lying around the hotel room. Let's take it with us." He looked at Lynn. "Is there room in your purse?"

"Barely. I don't want to lug Big-Black. Inappropriate for coffee with the President of Macedonia. Besides, they might suspect me of sneaking in a bomb."

"Granting Natalia's favor caused us almost as much trouble as a bomb." He handed it to her. "This courier business is perilous! It leads to the unpredictable."

You wouldn't believe!

61

PRESIDENT BASIL DIMITROVSKI, ALMOST GALEN'S HEIGHT, SAT TALL IN THE cushioned wrought-iron chair in the small garden outside his private office. Birds sang violin and cello parts while a cascading fountain sang an aria, splashing and sparkling in the sun. Flowers scented the air. The server set a tray on the wrought-iron coffee table. Four small, pretty jam jars stood beside teaspoons and glasses of ice water.

"*Tursko Kafe*," explained Mihail. "You are getting a taste of one of our traditions." He pointed to the jam jars. "That is *slatko*."

President Dimitrovski added to Milhail's cultural information. "It is sour cherry, my favorite," he said. "First, we will have *ozguldum kafe*—the welcome coffee. The second coffee follows, the *muabet kafe* of long conversation, and then the *sikter kafe*, the farewell coffee."

Lynn realized his graciousness to offer them so much time. She anticipated a delightful morning. "We are grateful for your kind invitation and your time, Mr. President."

He peered at her with eyes darker than Galen's but equally piercing. "We could retain *President* and *Bishop*. However, titles would distance us and limit the potential outcome of our time together."

"I respect you and your office," she explained.

"You may call me by my Christian name with equal respect." His face folded easily into a smile. "Perhaps you will permit me to do the same."

The issue, settled for the President, left Lynn unsettled. *Basil* would stick in her throat.

He lifted his cup. "I welcome you as friends." Lynn, Galen, and Mihail did likewise.

"We celebrate your friendship," Galen said, avoiding calling him by name.

Lynn noticed the seal on the tray—a golden sunrise over a royal blue mountain with wavy waters at the base, the sides bordered by wheat and poppy plants. "Is that your coat-of-arms?" she asked, also omitting his name.

"So it is, Lynn. It portrays the sun rising above Shar Mountain and Ohrid Lake. It represents the sun of freedom rising over Macedonia."

"We waited many years to be free," added Mihail wistfully.

"When you received the World Peace Award, we sang your national anthem. First in Macedonian," Lynn carefully pronounced the *c* like a *k* as a native would, "and then in English. I remember words about freedom and liberty."

"Today above Macedonia," sang the President in resounding bass. Mihail's tenor joined in. "The new sun of liberty is born." He looked into the distance, his face and eyes smiling. "That night in Oslo was a happy one for me."

"For all of us," said Mihail. "You brought pride to our whole country."

"I don't forget for one moment that it is the Macedonian people who deserve the peace award. President Jimmy Carter made a memorable statement in his inaugural address." As an aside he added, "I like to read biographies of U.S. presidents." He straightened his posture and orated: "'You have given me a great responsibility—to stay close to you, to be worthy of you, and to exemplify what you are.' I remember his words because they express my feelings also."

President Dimitrovski's passion, the power of his presence, and the strong Turkish brew awakened Lynn totally. The flavors of coffee and *slatko* enhanced each other. She savored these moments in his garden.

"Macedonia is lucky to have you," said Galen. "So is the world. No leader tops you in efforts toward international peace."

"Do not tempt me with arrogance, Galen. Arrogant leaders do not engender the common good; they endanger it. I recall a story about Franklin Roosevelt. After watching the stars for a while with a White House visitor, he said, 'I think we feel small enough now to go in and go to bed.' I glance up at the stars each night and remind myself of his statement."

Lynn thought this man had arrogance completely under control.

"You travel internationally more than most. I want to know what you think about an observation I have made."

"I hope we can be helpful," said Lynn, eager to hear his comment.

"Everyday I read the newspapers from around the world. I have been observing a gradual shift toward global chaos, as subtle and real as the shift toward global warming."

She sat forward, startled. "I attended the Bishops' International Conference in Vienna this week and observed the same phenomenon when their area reports were given."

"That isn't what I wanted to hear. I was hoping you would tell me I'm seeing something that isn't there."

"But that wouldn't be like you," said Mihail. "You have a gift for observing scattered pieces and putting them together in an enlightened way. It may be the gift of seers."

"Even my pastor tempts me with arrogance! I know Mihail plays chess. Do you?"

The abrupt non sequitur brought an enthusiastic "yes" from Galen and a faint nod from Lynn, who knew the rules but not the strategy.

"In chess it is not the capability of any single piece that defines it, whether pawn or queen—or bishop," he added with a smile. "What matters is the relationship of all the pieces to each other. It is a game of *ou tout se tient*."

"Where everything holds together," Lynn translated from French.

"Exactly. I see the current global situation like a chess game. Everything depends on everything else. It is no longer the *power* of any single nation that defines it. What matters today is the *relationship* of each nation to every other nation. Everything holds together."

"Or nothing does," said Lynn.

"We are in a new day, but governments still behave in the old way."

"Not ours under your regime," said Mihail proudly.

"Albanians, Bulgarians, Greeks, Gypsies, Serbians, and Turks all call Macedonia home. A pattern of ethnic and religious division has persisted here for centuries. The atrocities remained no matter who was in charge. The persecutors and victims merely exchanged places. My dream is to lead this diverse country away from letting witless history repeat itself."

"As we taste the power of unity that you are bringing," said Mihail, "we will not be so easily divided again."

"That is why unity is a threat to those who seek power rather than the common good; they gain by repeating divisive history." President Dimitrovski spoke through a veil of sadness. "And that is why they see me as their enemy."

"You lift us up," insisted Mihail. "The people love you."

"And you, my dear friend, are naïve."

62

THE BALKAN CONNECTION DID NOT GO BACK TO SLEEP AFTER THE PATRIOT'S inconsiderately early phone call. It was imperative to remain connected. For one thing he liked their agreement: assignments made by untraceable phone, payments routed through circuitous bank wires, money received as agreed. He let the voice sink into his memory. Male. Neither young nor old. Loud nor soft. Void of inflection. Strained from bass to tenor. Probably a fake French accent. A voice distinguishable only by its assertion of power and authority. God help anyone who gets in the way of the Patriot!

Last night had been productive. He'd waited unseen for the Petersons to clear security at the airport. Had his cab follow their car to the Hotel Aleksandar. Stood behind a pillar at the edge of the dimly lit lobby within earshot while they registered. Room 323.

After they pulled their luggage into the elevator, he checked the floor plan layout hanging on the wall and chose the clerk he'd observed to be the least rigid. She also happened to be the youngest and prettiest. Aiming to get the room next to theirs, he smiled warmly at her. "I have a special request if it isn't too much trouble," he said in English with a U.S. accent and a salesman's charm. "May I have room 321?"

"I am not sure that specific room is available, sir," she said in careful English.

"I hope so. That's my lucky number. I was born on *3-21*, the twenty-first day of March. I have *3* children, *2* boys and *1* girl. And I've gone from number *3* in my company to number *2*. If things go well tomorrow, I'll be number *1*. I need all the luck I can get."

She smiled at him. "Room 321 is vacant, sir. Your luck has already begun."

This morning he'd overheard the Petersons' wake-up call and listened through the wall to their conversation. The invitation to coffee didn't surprise him. President Basil Dimitrovski was good at building connections. Maybe as good as I am, he thought. He heard them leave and glanced at his watch. Timing was everything.

The Patriot expected thoroughness and would get it. He freed the lock and opened the door into their room. He scanned it quickly, noting again their limited luggage. Neither suitcase was locked. No point, as seasoned travelers knew. Luggage locks were a joke to thieves. All locks, actually. He didn't find the small box that caused such a stir last night. Disappointing.

The small laptop was on the dresser. A picture of a beautiful girl in her mid-teens rested beside it. He saw the mother-daughter resemblance and assumed the photograph was Lynn Peterson's one travel non-necessity. Probably, therefore, a necessity of the heart.

He looked at his watch again and quickly opened the laptop. A tiny tangle of dark hair fell to the dresser. She must have used this mirror when she brushed her hair. He turned on the computer and found what he'd expected—a memorized password. Busy people like conveniences. He glanced at the screen. A shortcut marked *Someday* pricked his curiosity, and he took a second to open the file. It contained few words: *Novel* and *Secrets*. In a smaller font was a question in brackets: [*Secrets do what?*] She probably didn't know much about secrets. But he did. Mentally he answered the question for her: Secrets within secrets compose and discompose my life.

Another convenient memorized password gave him access to her email. The empty *Sent* and *Deleted* files as well as a single message in the *Inbox* pointed to an efficient, organized person who handled email as it arrived and cleared it out. Or it pointed to someone with something to hide. Her? He chuckled to himself. He noted a new message from Bubba Broussard. Subject: blank. The name seemed vaguely familiar, but he couldn't remember why. If it were important, he would remember, so he didn't spend time opening it. He avoided arousing suspicion of computer invasion, but he was tempted to do so as a favor—the suspicion might give her an idea for a lead sentence: Secrets are stolen. He grinned, catching his reflection in the mirror. Ah, yes. Man of many secrets and accents. Yesterday's Russian on the plane, admirer of little Russian book. Last night's businessman from the States, getting the room next to this one. Viktor Machek closed the computer.

63

PRESIDENT DIMITROVSKI AND HIS GUESTS HAD FINISHED THE SECOND COFfee, the *muabet kafe* of long conversation, and were beginning the *sikter kafe*, the farewell coffee. The sun had begun its farewell, too, as clouds began drifting in. He asked Lynn about her connection with President Benedict.

She swallowed hard and recovered. "I met her once when she was campaigning. You know, just a quick handshake in the crowd of people."

He looked surprised. "I am sorry to hear that. Mihail is God's special gift to my presidency."

Mihail lowered his eyes and bowed his head in genuine humility.

"He gives me fresh views uncontaminated by vested interests, is prophetic when necessary, and isn't swayed by what he thinks I want to hear. Every president needs a Mihail Martinovski!"

She smiled warmly at Mihail. "I hope our President has someone like you."

"I have met with her." President Dimitrovski's eyes crinkled into a smile. "She is one of the few world leaders who shares my appreciation of President Theodore Roosevelt's words. Again he orated the quote: "'To announce that there must be no criticism of the President, or that we are to stand by the President, right or wrong, . . .'"

"'. . . is not only unpatriotic and servile,'" Galen joined in, "but is morally treasonable to the American public."

"Ah! We are truly brothers!" President Dimitrovski reached across the table toward Galen, who met his hand in the middle and held it in both of his, admiration filling his eyes. "I consider Roosevelt's statement to be one of borderless accuracy and boundless time."

Mihail agreed with the President. "Wedding disagreement to a lack of patriotism is a most unpatriotic marriage!"

"I am not surprised that our president also honors those words," said Lynn. "She is an excellent president who offers openness and values justice like Lincoln."

"Justice can cause problems." President Dimitrovski spoke as one who knew firsthand.

"Even so, you have always had the courage to put that word into action." Mihail also spoke as someone who knew firsthand.

"I hope she has good people around her. I wish you would befriend her, Lynn. All of us need someone we trust. President Grant understood one of the biggest problems that a president faces, which may come as a surprise. He spoke of mistakes in the selection of the assistants appointed to aid in carrying out the various duties of administering the government. Some appointees prove less than helpful. Generally benignly," his eyes flashed steel as he added, "but sometimes deliberately."

Lynn thought about President Benedict. Her note to the major showed her growing suspicions about some of the people around her.

And Major Manetti was assassinated, Lynn.

She wondered again if his death was related to the President's attempt to contact him. A scary question intruded: Where does that leave me?

President Dimitrovski's secretary, Dimka, came into the garden and spoke softly to him. He looked surprised. "Dimka tells me that you met Viktor Machek on the plane yesterday."

"He sat behind us," said Lynn. "Or someone named Viktor did. I didn't catch his last name."

He replied briefly to Dimka, and she nodded and left. "He is concerned about you," the President explained. "He saw the difficulties you were having last night and considered the situation important enough to notify my office in case you need help. In fact, he thought it was so important that he came personally. And here he is." With that, Dimka arrived with Viktor, and the server arrived with another cup of coffee.

Lynn smiled warmly at her new best friend who liked her Russian book. He smiled back.

"Come. Please sit. You obviously know Bishop Peterson and Dr. Peterson. May I present Pastor Martinovski." He gestured from Mihail to Viktor. "This is Viktor Machek."

Lynn noted the President's shift to titles in Viktor's presence. *Lynn* had sounded so much warmer. She also noticed that his last name did not have the Russian ending. It wasn't Machekov. She recognized Machek as a Croat name.

"Mr. Machek is multilingual, knowledgeable about international matters, and has been helpful to me at times," said the President. "Dr. Peterson is a highly respected historian, and Bishop Peterson's international accomplishments through the church are outstanding."

Viktor gave a respectful Russian bow to Lynn. "She is also an excellent writer."

Vanity would not allow her to lower her eyes in humility like Mihail. She loved the compliment, especially in front of the President. Vanity blocked for an instant the blatant difference in his language. His broken English had disappeared overnight. Unwelcome second thoughts emerged about her new best friend.

As though reading her mind, Viktor said, "My grasp of English is probably a surprise. I apologize for deceiving you. To speak English fluently can complicate life in the Balkans."

Neither affirming nor negating his statement, President Dimitrovski moved on. "I am curious about the package that caused so much trouble last night."

"We brought it." Lynn retrieved the box. "Galen was afraid to leave the money in our room."

He picked it up and read the inscription in blue ink: "To Father Nish from Natalia."

"That's my writing," said Galen. "We are going to get it to him when we go to Sarajevo. If we can find him," he added.

"Consider it done. I'll see that it is delivered and save you more problems." The President opened the box. He merely glanced at the pink euros but picked up the blue piece of paper, scrutinizing it.

Lynn saw the flicker of recognition in Viktor's eyes. "What does it mean?" she asked.

"Do you know anything about this sketch?" asked the President.

Galen shrugged. "Nothing at all."

Lynn debated how much to volunteer.

The President turned to her. "Bishop Peterson?"

She chose honesty. He deserved it.

When did you reduce honesty to a choice, Lynn?

She hushed Ivy. "I've seen that symbol three times." She noted Galen's surprise.

"Three times?" Viktor failed in his effort to sound casual.

"First in New Orleans on a friend's medal," she replied.

"It was on Elias's medal?" Galen was stunned.

"Who?" asked the President.

"Elias Darwish," Galen replied. "A kicker for the New Orleans Saints football team."

"From Sarajevo," Lynn added.

"I remember now. CNN International reported his murder last week." His dark eyes lasered into hers. He sat tall, his very presence presidential. "You are *sure* this symbol was on his medal?"

She felt intimidated. "Yes, Mr. President."

"I am sorry. Please forgive my brusqueness." He visibly relaxed his posture and took a sip of coffee, allowing time and his amiable smile to ease the tension.

Viktor asked cordially, "When did you see Elias Darwish's medal, Bishop Peterson?"

She decided not to involve Bubba. "After he was shot. I planned to bring it to his mother in Sarajevo."

"I have to go to Sarajevo," Viktor said. "I can take it to her."

Did her new best friend seem a little too interested in the medal? No, she decided. He was just being nice.

"The war would make the task very difficult for you," he continued. "Perhaps impossible."

"Definitely impossible," she replied. "It was stolen."

"When was the second time you saw the symbol?" asked the President.

"In Vienna. A Russian soldier in the hospital there has one." Galen's eyes questioned her, and she explained. "I saw it while you and Dick were helping the injured from the bus bomb. It was on the back of his cross, Mr. President," she continued. "He dropped it on the floor, and he couldn't pick it up because . . ." The image of the young paraplegic sitting on the bed struck her full force again. She blinked back tears. "He lost both legs. And he's so young. Only a boy, really."

The President shut his eyes for a moment, then spoke with quiet despair. "War is declared by old men in safe places who send the young to be killed and maimed. I pray that at the end of my term I may repeat the words of President Eisenhower, that my country 'never lost a soldier or a foot of ground in my administration. We kept the peace.'"

"I have a dream for the world," said Lynn softly, somewhat shyly. "That someday we'll view coercion as impoverished imagination, and we'll begin to put as much energy and resources into discovering creative solutions as we now put into forced ones."

"Your dream honors the young wounded from all nations. Don't let it die." The President glanced again at the sketch. "And last night was your third time to see this symbol?" When she nodded, he said lightly, "You seem to attract it."

"What does it mean?" she asked again. In the ensuing silence tension thickened like a Louisiana fog. She stared down at the symbol that had come into her life through Elie and Natalia from Sarajevo and Sasha from Russia. Suddenly the two crescents leapt up from the paper. One above the other. Slightly overlapping. She *saw* it! Not crescents! Cyrillic letters! The letter *C* for the *S* sound! *CC!* Start with St. Sava.

"*St. Sava!*" she exclaimed.

64

AFTER THE MIDNIGHT CALL TO HIS BALKAN CONNECTION, THE PATRIOT relaxed. Viktor Machek would do a good job in Skopje. He decided to remain in his office suite and sleep on the comfortable Murphy bed in the library. When not in use, the bed sprang into vertical position and hid in a large mahogany cabinet with double doors. Bookshelves lined the wall on both sides, and the cozy room smelled of lemon oil and leather-bound books. His beloved family understood that his work occasionally demanded an all-nighter. Actually, he rather liked the solitude here. He could let down the guard that his dual life necessitated.

The sun was not up yet, but he sat at his desk and pondered the President's lack of due respect and appreciation of him. She was like an agitating allergy to him. A self-defeating response, he realized. The pragmatism of wisdom called him to be cognizant of her strengths as well as her weaknesses. They shared in common the uncommon traits of superior intelligence, charismatic persuasiveness, and to-the-death commitment. She was alarmingly astute and a quick learner. She was a master at keeping the trust of the American people—as though her own trust in them evoked their trust in her. Despite the mud-slinging politicos and deans of deceptive language, her approval ratings continued to climb.

Resentment roiled inside him over the presidency. He stood superior to anyone who'd run in recent decades. This great democracy had his absolute loyalty, his total allegiance. He could be the greatest president in American history. That, however, would never be. A *woman* could be President of the United States, but the Constitution denied *him* the opportunity! He was an adopted son, not a natural-born citizen. He had an impulse to spit on the flag by his desk. Immediately ashamed, he stood, put his hand over his heart and repledged his allegiance. With liberty and justice for all. Yes, justice! The most beautiful word in any language. A wonderful word of Life.

Life. He thought of Elias Darwish. The Patriot unlocked his desk drawer and took out the silver box. The desk lamp caught it, and the silver reflected back the light. With a deep sigh he slowly removed the lid and lifted the medal to his palm. The amazonite gleamed in the lamplight. Darwish had been killed a week ago today. He had delayed long enough. It was time to do his duty. Unpalatable but necessary.

65

ST. SAVA. LYNN HAD DECIPHERED THE SYMBOL! *ALOUD!* HER WORDS sucked up the cacophony of the universe and obliterated it into deadly silence. Only the dread in President Dimitrovski's eyes spoke.

He recovered first. "You look frightened, Lynn. You needn't be." His reassuring smile failed to reassure her.

Viktor began to chuckle. "Oh, Lynn Peterson, now I see why you are a good writer. Good writers need big imaginations! St. Sava!" He chuckled again.

The President looked at his watch and stood. They rose as he did. "Thank you for coming."

With a Russian-style bow of his head, Viktor hurried away.

"We appreciate your taking care of Natalia's package," said Galen, leaving it on the coffee table.

"My pleasure."

"Thank you for a memorable morning," said Lynn. "I can't express how grateful I am. Macedonia is very fortunate to be in your hands."

"I pray so. I understand from Mihail that you leave on Friday." When she nodded, he eyed her and then Galen in the way he had of commanding complete attention. "Please trust me."

"We trust you completely," said Galen.

"Then you will do what I ask." His gracious smile remained, but his tone gave a presidential order. "Mihail will take you back to the hotel to check out." He looked at Mihail. "Is that all right?"

"Of course."

"Also, Mihail, please leave their Macedonia itinerary and cell phone numbers with Dimka." He turned back to Galen and Lynn. "Since you know Agent Nedelkovski from last night, I'll arrange for him to pick you up from your last engagement today and take you to a safe place to stay."

Why? Lynn wanted to ask but felt it wouldn't be appropriate to question him.

"You will keep your schedule. I'm not concerned about your meetings with peace committees held in churches," he said, "but when you are not with them, I prefer to err on the side of caution in looking after your safety."

Galen looked surprised. "We will be fine."

"I hope so. But many people saw the security circus last night at the airport. I am concerned that you may be linked to that symbol. And," he smiled at Lynn, "you astutely figured out what it represents. Unfortunately, I'm not the only one who heard you. Those words are best left unspoken."

Was he talking about Viktor? About the server? His secretary? Lynn chose to disregard his concern. The alternative was too frightening.

"If I were not flying out of the country this afternoon, I would invite you to stay with us." He grinned. "In our version of the Lincoln Bedroom. My wife would enjoy getting to know you."

"Perhaps Gonka and I will have an opportunity to meet another time." Calling the President's *spouse* by her first name did not stick in Lynn's throat. "I would like that."

"Before we part I have a favor to ask, Lynn." His mood shifted, and so did the atmosphere. It became heavy like the gray clouds gathering in the distance. "Would you pray for me each day?" His somber eyes turned a common request into a troubled plea.

66

ZECHARIAH ZELLER FINISHED HIS LUNCH OF BRATWURST AND BEER. HE TOOK his habitual place at his window and gazed at the Vienna skyline in the high-noon sunlight. One hand held a cup of coffee, the other a cigarette. His eyes roved to the perpetual crowd of tourists below. He glanced at the Stephensturm and thought about Galen Peterson's troublesome presence. He counted up using his fingers: Manetti's flight on Sunday morning. The Stephensturm on Monday morning. And the Stephensturm again yesterday noon. Three days in a row, and yesterday he was alone and packing a camera. Zeller considered whether Peterson was a tourist snapping pictures of landmarks or a spy capturing his apartment, a zoom lens aimed at his window. Evidence mounted toward the latter. Zeller's address was known to no one, his most protected secret. He intended to keep it that way.

Peterson hadn't returned today. Apparently he'd completed his task. Zeller moved from the window and greeted *Mutter*. All the data on Peterson appeared legitimate—a necessity for a secret agent. A dull history professor interested only in the past. What a cover!

Time has told us, *Mutter*. Time has told us.

Frau Peterson—he still refused to think of the kind-eyed woman as *Bishop* Peterson—was simply trying to serve her god while her hypocritical husband covered up his clandestine work, dragged her into danger, and probably pretended to serve her god. What god did he *really* serve? Zeller envisioned him sending her to that Hercules at the café and making her get the medal for him. Anger sneaked into the edges of his mind. The poor woman would be better off as a widow than married to Peterson. His forefinger pulled an imaginary trigger. No! Anger is dangerous. Planning is necessary. He stowed away his imaginary gun. Temporarily.

He tapped into Peterson's flight itinerary. So easy. The U.S. to Vienna through Frankfurt last Sunday. Vienna to Skopje yesterday evening. Skopje to Sarajevo on Friday. Perfect. He knew Sarajevo well. Things would be smooth and simple, always important but especially so for pro bono work. With no pay, he wanted no risks. No complications. He reconsidered baiting the Patriot's interest and drawing a fee. That would not be wise. No.

As a bishop Frau Peterson would probably be adequately cared for. But that was merely a guess. He wanted her to live comfortably and would keep an eye on her situation from a distance.

Already he tingled with the excitement of the challenge. The irony pleased him. The Petersons' presence had cheated him of a well-deserved high when he shot Manetti. Now Peterson would atone. He opened the false panel and took out his gun-cleaning kit from the back of the closet shelf, the yellowed rag smelling of oil. Tenderly he removed his best friend from its hiding place. "*Freund*, we have another job Friday," he said aloud. "This one is for us."

He pulled out his last cigarette, scrunched the pack up in a ball, and lobbed it into the trash. His upper lip rose, showing his teeth in a rottweiler snarl. Live two more nights, Galen Lincoln Peterson, Ph.D.

67

MIHAIL WAITED IN THE CAR IN FRONT OF THE HOTEL. LYNN AND GALEN hurried to their room. Grabbed their stuff. Lynn jammed everything back in her suitcase. Almost everything. No time to make it all fit. She clutched a pillow. Shook the case free. Crammed the overflow into it.

Galen frowned at her.

"We'll bring it back later, Love. Want to share?"

"Thanks."

She caressed Lyndie's smiling photo on the dresser. Added it to Big-Black. Reached for the laptop. Felt silly about leaving a tangle of hair on it this morning. She started to brush it off. Gone! She stooped eye-level. Peered closely. Frantically rubbed her fingers across the top. Nothing!

When she spotted the tangle, her stomach pitched. It lay behind the laptop, where it had fallen onto the dresser when somebody opened the cover. "Galen! Someone broke in!"

"*What!*" He circled the small room looking carefully for something amiss.

Lynn felt violated. She raised the computer lid. Pushed *Power*. Opened email quickly offline. It showed a new email from Bubba, unopened.

"Nothing seems to be missing, Lynn. What makes you think someone broke in?" He noticed what she was doing. "We don't have time for email now. Mihail is waiting."

"We never have time." She opened it anyway. Scanned it. Anticipated a saner world across the pond where her friend was merely dealing with straightforward murder and cover-up:

> Bishop Lynn,
>
> I have information indicating our friend knew he was in danger. I wish he had told me. Maybe I could have prevented what happened.
> I don't suppose you have had time to find his mother yet and give her the jewelry and my note.
> I ate a beignet for you at Café du Monde. Yoo-Sei sends greetings. I hope you two can endure going without New Orleans food!
> Stay safe in the Balkans.
>
> Bubba

"You're becoming obsessed, Lynn!"

"If so, Love, you're becoming obsessed with my obsession!" She quickly replied to Bubba:

> You couldn't have prevented what happened. Don't do that to yourself.
> More later.

Galen responded to Lynn's barb with a loud *zzzippp* of his suitcase.

Not to be outdone on marital-disharmony sound-effects, she *ZZZIPPP*ed her own suitcase louder, plopped Big-Black over her shoulder, and beat him out the door.

68

PRESIDENT HELENA BENEDICT CONFRONTED THE ONGOING PAIN OF MARSH'S death by wandering down a mental trail of wonderings. She wondered if the Vice President read the messages before giving the envelope to Lynn Peterson. Surely not. Surely she could trust him. Besides, he didn't know who "Marsh" was or about her request to the NATO general.

She wondered if speaking to the Secretary of Defense to request protection for Bishop Peterson because of the Balkan air strike and suggesting Major Manetti for the task had been a fatal error. Surely not. The request was not suspicious because of the bishop's prominent international work, and she'd carefully justified the reason for choosing the major. Surely she could trust the Secretary of Defense. Besides, he didn't know about her covert attempt to deliver Marsh a message.

She wondered if Defense used her name when they contacted the NATO general to make the request. Surely not. But even if so the general's military background demanded respect for authority including loyalty and obedience to his Commander-in-Chief—regardless of gender. Surely she could trust the general.

The Vice President, the Secretary of Defense, the NATO general. They played repetitively in her mind like three-beat measures of a waltz growing faster and louder. Yet if her intuition was correct about the only three men involved—and she'd learned to trust her intuition—the final inconceivable source of information became conceivable: her secure phone was insecure. If the phone, then probably email also, and certainly the Oval Office. Her eyes circled the room suddenly grown cold and unfriendly. She controlled the shudder that rose from the core of her being. The traitor was far more powerful, far more knowledgeable, far more dangerous than she had suspected.

President Benedict reflected on Lynn Peterson's actions. She had shown intelligence in delivering the message to Marsh and courage in recovering it. The inexperienced courier had done well to write a cryptic email and find a way to bypass the White House correspondence staff, reaching the President's office directly. A feat meriting congratulations.

She congratulated herself also. She had done well to select Lynn Peterson. After what had happened to Marsh, she'd distanced herself from Lynn to protect her, communicating with her indirectly through Ambassador Whitcomb. Disassociating herself from a close friendship with Marsh must have been very confusing to Lynn. But she did not want another death on her hands, and she feared an electronic voyeur. She'd never intended to place either Marsh or Lynn in harm's way. Another wave of guilt splashed over her.

Defense sent her a follow-up report regarding Bishop Peterson's safety. In the wake of the major's death, she had not been delayed in Vienna as planned. But her plane had landed safely in Skopje. Defense, actually General Thornburg's staff, had checked the restricted flight plans for passenger planes Tuesday evening because of the NATO action, and had issued a revised one for Bishop Peterson's errant plane. Potential danger averted. Barely. Defense did not know how Vienna Air Traffic Control had mistakenly sent a passenger plane into a no-fly zone.

President Benedict felt a sense of urgency to act. She hurried from the Oval Office to her bedroom in the private quarters and opened the old brown trunk. She clutched the box that contained the items from the saddlebag her father had given her and rummaged through the contents for the cell phone. She could almost feel his fingers brush hers just as they had that afternoon of his last visit. His words rang through her mind. Someday you may need a totally private phone not connected to your office or your name. This one has Swiss encryption technology, its security guaranteed. It is registered to your great-grandmother Vini McGragor and has an eight-year untraceable pre-paid contract. He smiled. You will, of course, serve two terms.

"Someone may not want me in power even through the first term," she responded in a whisper. Remembering his story that day about her great-grandmother evoked her own courage and determination. "Whoever it is underestimates me!"

He'd extracted from her a promise to keep a charged battery ready for use as long as she served as President. At the time she'd found her frail old father's cloak-and-dagger protection humorously overdramatic, yet endearing. Now, she thanked him silently. She slotted in the charged battery, attached the miniature hands-free set, changed into her walking clothes and put the phone in her pocket. She tucked her hair up under a roll-brimmed straw hat, put on large Jackie Kennedy Onassis-style sunglasses, and announced she was going to talk to Lincoln. She did this early in the mornings when she wanted to think. The Secret Service had become used to it and adjusted to the caprice with respectful compliance. This idiosyncrasy served her well today—the Lincoln Memorial was not bugged. This morning Honest Abe looked out at the people under a clear dome of azure flecked with birds in flight. *Honest Abe.* She hoped that in another century or two her historical tag would be as noble. She intended to conduct herself as President in a manner that left a legacy not only of courage but also honesty and integrity, with a dash of humility.

Her hand in her pocket, she began to thumb the memorized string of numbers. She wanted to have a personal phone conversation with Lynn Peterson, and she trusted President Basil Dimitrovski to arrange it.

69

LYNN AND GALEN FINISHED LUNCH WITH THE LEADERS OF MIHAIL'S CHURCH. The aroma of cooked apples with cinnamon wafted around the table. His secretary entered quietly, her floral skirt adding color to the room. She spoke softly to Mihail. He nodded and turned to Lynn. "You are wanted on the phone. I am sorry, but no name was given. She will take you to the office."

Lynn thanked her and followed, wondering if it was Fay Foster from the office and whether something had happened to one of the Louisiana clergy. Then she thought of Bubba. "Hello?" she said uncertainly.

A pleasant voice responded, "One moment please."

"Lynn?"

She recognized the speaker's voice, astonished. "Yes, . . ." she started to add "Mr. President" but realized he had withheld his name for a reason.

"This is Basil."

"Thank you for this morning." Lynn said what was on her heart: "I'm very sorry I spoke . . ." The secretary was listening. Paranoia won. ". . . a disturbing name."

"St. Sava," the President repeated with a troubled sigh. "Things are not always what they appear to be." He sounded rushed. "I am flying to Bosnia for a conference in Mostar. I will return by noon tomorrow. Please be in my office at one o'clock." The *please* tempered only slightly the presidential order. "You will receive an important telephone call on my secure line."

She swallowed, struck by the ominous *secure line.*

"A car will be arranged."

"Thank . . ." He hung up. ". . . you," Lynn finished to a dead line. Puzzled, she moved the phone from her ear and peered at it a moment as though it could alleviate her curiosity. She thanked the secretary again and returned to the luncheon.

"Who?" asked Galen.

They were at the head table with Mihail, somewhat distanced from the other people, so she replied softly, for Galen's ears only, "President Dimitrovski. No *muabet kafe* of long conversation this time."

"And?" he asked, cutting his volume to hers.

"I'll be receiving an," she fingered quotation marks, "*important* telephone call tomorrow on his," again, quotation marks, "*secure line.*" Saying those two words seemed even more ominous than hearing them.

"From?"

"He didn't say, Love. He's flying to Mostar. He was in a hurry."

"What time?"

"One o'clock. He'll be back by noon." Lynn looked anxiously at her watch. It would be a long twenty-three hours.

70

A RUMBLE OF THUNDER ANNOUNCED RAIN, A STORM THAT FIT THE PATRIOT'S ongoing mood this morning. Lone Star's daily 8:00 A.M. report first stunned him, then infuriated him. Lone Star had been on duty when President Benedict took an early morning walk at the Lincoln Memorial and thought he saw her lips moving. He'd managed a close observation that indicated a tiny, hands-free bud beneath the wide brim of her hat. The conversation eluded the monitors. The Patriot wanted to yank her presidential picture from his wall and hurl it out the window. He settled for a menacing stare and a morning handful of chocolate-covered peanuts.

Somehow she had obtained a clean phone with encryption technology, one neither provided nor sanctioned by the U.S. government—a feat as impossible as skating on the moon. Yet she'd done it. And Lone Star could not obtain access. She was smart—he had to give her that. The trusting President had grown slippery. He was not worried personally. John Adams's reputation was built on trustworthiness. He would likely be the last person in D.C. she would mistrust. In the first place, he was too good at predicting trouble spots both nationally and internationally—a skill abetted by his initiating some of them. Second, his BarLothiun mop-up contracts afterward were appreciated as economically and responsibly fulfilled. He knew how to act surprised by news he'd already learned through his arms sales. He excelled in these games but grew weary of them.

The President's clandestine call required him to peer carefully into the cracks and crevices he might have overlooked earlier and to reconsider her potential contacts, another wearisome task. Repetitious but necessary.

Why does one little phone call matter, John Adams wondered. The Patriot knew why. The call that is the most secret is the most significant. She had slipped through his invisible net, and he felt defied, demeaned, even defiled. Oh, yes! One little call mattered!

He'd expected passivity and appreciation from President Helena Benedict. Instead she'd forced him into a power struggle, and he didn't intend to lose. The word was not in his vocabulary. But he resented the energy that winning took, energy he wanted to spend on building a kingdom of righteous justice. He didn't need an errant president! Neither did the country.

Nor did he need an errant Frank Fillmore. "Terrorize and paralyze" was Fillmore's mantra. From the beginning he had tracked the maverick elite, keeping tabs on his location and other jobs he accepted. Now Fillmore was in Skopje and had, in fact, flown on the same plane as Viktor Machek. Fate had defied the Patriot's immutable rule to keep elites separated. They didn't know each other, but he didn't like it. Machek was on the plane to investigate the Petersons. He didn't know why Fillmore went to Skopje, but he felt uneasy. Perhaps it was better not to know the reason.

71

THE MORNING SUN HAD MADE IT TO THE BIG EASY AND BEAT DOWN on Bubba as he hopped into his silver 'Vette's red leather seat and headed to the Superdome. He gave the steering wheel a couple of fond pats and glanced at the clock on the matching red dash. Wind whooshed through the convertible, sucking up the humidity and cooling his shaved scalp. Days like this reminded him why he lived here instead of up North where a man wasted a good part of each year just buttoning and unbuttoning his overcoat.

He thought of Elie as he opened the locker room door. One week since your death, bro. And no progress on who did it. But maybe that is about to change.

Last night's visit from Pit Bull and Shar-Pei had left him with an unaccustomed sense of wariness. His eyes zeroed in on every inch of the locker room before entering. It stood empty, as quiet and mournful as yesterday, still permeated with the scent of male athletes. Once again he pawed through his locker. Last night's goons didn't limit break-ins to condos. Locker rooms would be a snap. He dug faster for the flash drive.

Found it! Right where he'd left it—where Elie had left it—still in the white sock. Relieved, he pulled it out and palmed it like a thief. Dropped it into his sports bag. Tossed some gym clothes on top. The closer he drew to learning what the flash drive would reveal, the greater his sense of urgency. He drove too fast to the Tulane library. A Saint could always talk his way out of a ticket.

As Bubba entered the library, a young woman waved to him. "I'd be right pleased to help you find something, Bubba Broussard."

This morning wasn't a good time to be recognized, but he smiled at her and glanced inconspicuously at her name badge. "Today all I need is a computer. Thank you for offering, Miss Jean." She beamed when he said her name—each person's favorite word. Unless, came the sinister thought, they're hiding behind an alias.

His eyes circled the room for trouble—only a few people at the library this early, all concentrating on their own work. To screen out onlookers he chose a back corner and plugged in the flash drive. The little device took on a power of its own as he realized it might have cost Elie his life. His tension mounted as the letters appeared on the screen. It listed only two files: *BUBBA* and *PROJECT.* He scanned the room again. Muscles taut with suspense, he opened *BUBBA.*

> If you're reading this, I'm dead. I knew you would figure out the note. Tell NO ONE about this flash drive.

I've already messed up that play, Elie. But Cy Bill is on our team.

> There are people willing to kill for it. DO NOT let it fall into the wrong hands.

> Keep it safe until the right person comes to you. He will identify himself with the symbol below.

Elie had scanned in the symbol on his medal.

He opened the *PROJECT* file, unconsciously leaning in toward the screen. Eager. Impatient. Apprehensive about what he'd find. Hoping it would solve the enigma of Elie's death. The document emerged. His fist clenched and he almost slammed it into the screen.

He stared at an obscure tangle of undecipherable, incomprehensible Cyrillic letters. He couldn't read it and he didn't dare risk getting it translated. If Lynn were here, she'd be able to read the letters and make out the sounds. But that wouldn't really help. Knowing the alphabet of a language but not the words was like knowing a team's jersey numbers but not the plays they could form together.

He decided to try *Google Translate*. He looked laboriously for the Cyrillic symbols to match the first three words in Elie's document. The translation for each came out as gibberish. Not only Cyrillic, code in Cyrillic. He sat there with no more information than before. Frustration led to anger. He felt angry at the inanimate flash drive. Angry at the people who'd caused Elie's death. Angry at the violation against the Saints. And angry at Elie for living so dangerously and not asking for help *before* it was too late.

Yes. Angry at Elie. Immediately, guilt about his anger set in like gangrene. Grief is a process, he reminded himself, a painful process. Anger is part of it. Take it one step at a time. Over and over and over again.

With a heavy-hearted sigh he copied both files to his own flash drive. You wouldn't like this, Elie, but if Cy Bill has a copy, he can carry on if something happens to me. *If something happens.* That could scare a man. But the big *something* would happen someday anyway. So what's the big deal?

Bubba deleted all his input and also clicked on *Empty the Recycle Bin*, leaving the computer as innocent as he'd found it. He wasn't quite paranoid enough to crash the hard drive. In high-alert mode he tucked the original and the copy into his pocket, sorely aware that all traces of Elie's data would disappear if anything happened to him before he got to Cy Bill. On his way out he forced a nonchalant nod to the student librarian. "Good day, Miss Jean."

Her smile reflected all that was good in the world. A stark contrast to the evil of Elie's death.

72

THROUGHOUT THE REST OF THE LUNCHEON MEETING AT MIHAIL'S CHURCH, part of Lynn's mind remained on the mysterious one o'clock call coming in on President Dimitrovski's secure line tomorrow.

You know who is calling, Lynn.

Who but President Benedict would bother with a secure line? Still bewildered by her confusing response via Will, Lynn hoped without much hope that was who it was. As the courier and retriever of the note, she felt responsible and wanted to assist the president.

If the note actually came from her, Lynn.

Even if it didn't, Ivy, she needs to know what I was asked to do supposedly on her behalf.

The meeting ended with some time to spare before the next one, and Lynn took the opportunity to check email. She wanted to catch up on whatever Fay had forwarded to her and also to respond more fully to Bubba. First Bubba. Awash in guilt over Elie's medal, she reread his email.

She had let both him and Mrs. Darwish down. The medal would have been precious to her. Lynn knew firsthand the value of a symbol of a child's presence when faced with the forever-absence of the beloved one. She puzzled over Bubba's choice of the euphemism *jewelry* for the medal. We're both using code.

She recalled Viktor's eagerness this morning to pounce on Elie's medal when he thought she had it. She was almost relieved it had been stolen. She rued saying *St. Sava* when she recognized the symbol as Cyrillic letters. She'd never heard of St. Sava until she read President Benedict's note to Marsh. Even Will was under the impression that the CIA had no proof of its existence. Yet saying those two words had made a profound impact on President Dimitrovski and Viktor, changing the atmosphere in the garden and landing Galen and her in a safe house tonight. Did Elie's medal mean he was connected with St. Sava? What about Sasha? And what role did Natalia play? This puzzle had too many edge pieces missing. President Dimitrovski's words from his phone call a while ago rang in her ears as clearly as though he were speaking them again: Things are not always what they appear to be.

She longed to tell Galen the whole story from limo envelope to delivery to stealing it back to presidential denial. She needed his insight. Again Vice President Parker's voice echoed from the limo: Totally confidential. Maybe he said that because he didn't want the President to know what he was doing.

Don't go there, Lynn.

At least she could tell Bubba about Elie's medal. Confession time. Way past confession time. She tried to distance herself from his disappointment as she began her confession:

> Bubba,
>
> I won't go into why now, but I don't have the jewelry. So very, very sorry. Sniper stole it. Have cell phone photos

Whoa! She wanted Bubba and Cy Bill to know about those profile photos, but the memory of his cruel eyes gave her pause. More than just pause. She was trembling. His eyes zoom-lensed on her mental screen. They seemed to follow her everywhere. New Orleans. Frankfurt. Vienna. She shook off the irrational horror, but still feared writing in an email that she had his photo. As soon as she could get the software and load it on the Baby, she would send her photos to him. She deleted "Have cell phone photos" and continued:

> The jewelry is not unique to our friend. Have discovered the symbol's meaning.

She felt a tremor of fear for Bubba.

> Stay alert. Watch yourself.

Because of her two bad laptop experiences since landing in Skopje—last night when Agent Nedelkovski grabbed it but only saw solitaire on the screen, and this morning when someone broke into their room and opened her email—she added:

> Imperative to guard words in emails to me.
> Stay safe in the Quarter.
>
> Lynn

She clicked *Send.* Deleted both his and her emails. Deleted the recycle bin copies.

Her message required too much reading between the lines. Communication with Bubba had been reduced to enigmatic notes and immediate deletions. She thought back to that fateful morning last week when she sat at Café du Monde going over her lecture for the bishops' conference. She didn't feel like the same person. She had lost her innocence.

73

As his entourage rolled onto the airfield, President Dimitrovski admired the white presidential plane, a Beechcraft Super King Air 200 with sleek blue trim outlined by a red strip on the nose, tail, and wings. He heard the pilots start the twin-engine turboprop. It would take about two hours to fly over the mountains to Mostar. "Where is our passenger?" he asked, agitated by his absence. "What is his name, Branko?"

"Frank Fillmore." Branko opened the door for the President as they stopped beside the plane. Four other officials also prepared to board. "If I may say so, sir, I don't like a stranger traveling on your plane."

The President smiled at his most loyal—and favorite—bodyguard. "It is difficult for staff to refuse the CIA and MI5. Anything in threes takes on mythological power."

"I am not afraid of them, sir!"

"Neither am I, Branko. Unfortunately that puts us in a very small minority." He smiled at the dependable young man, moved by the fact that he would die for him without hesitation.

Shifting from Macedonian to English, Branko said, "The request to travel with you was impudent, impertinent, and ill-mannered."

The President smiled again, aware that Branko fervently studied the English dictionary and enjoyed practicing new words. He must have reached the letter *I*, he thought fondly.

"The *President's plane* is not public transportation."

"Ah! It is Macedonian pride, then, that troubles you." His loyal bodyguard deserved to hear the truth. "A call was received this morning that Fillmore is needed in Mostar for an emergency. We are the quickest transport. A staffer granted permission as a favor."

Branko's lack of approval showed clearly on his face. "Did he check the source to be sure?"

"That is protocol."

He tried another tack. "Look at the cloudbank in the northwest, sir. We cannot wait for Fillmore."

President Dimitrovski noted both the cloudbank and Branko's persistence. "Agreed."

With a relieved smile he suggested, "We can board immediately, sir. The rest of your delegation is here, and the pilots made the plane secure upon their arrival."

As they moved toward the plane, a man exited the boarding door, waving feebly and teetering down the ramp. "Mr. President," he greeted weakly. "I am Frank Fillmore."

"We were not aware that you were already on board."

"I arrived early, sir. It's a booger to keep someone waiting." He reached the ground but still held onto the rail.

"So it is."

"I have suddenly taken a bit ill." He reeled and began to retch.

"More than a bit, I'd say."

"I am sorry, sir," he apologized. "A spot of food poisoning, I think. Portabella mushrooms, perhaps. Even the thought of them is sickening." He retched again.

"Obviously, you aren't able to go to Mostar. My driver can take you to a doctor."

"That is unnecessary, sir. Just a bed and a bucket will do."

President Dimitrovski turned to Branko. "Please ask the driver to take Mr. Fillmore back to his hotel."

"Yes, sir."

Fillmore crawled heavily into the backseat and mouthed a feeble thank-you.

The President watched the car turn around to leave the airfield. "I was preoccupied and didn't notice earlier, Branko, but I don't recall seeing today's driver before."

"You haven't, sir. He's new. His credentials are impeccable."

President Dimitrovski smiled to himself. Branko had definitely reached the letter *I* in his well-worn dictionary. He walked up the ramp and paused at the top to turn around. His eyes swept across the skyline of the city he loved. He glanced up appreciatively at the beautiful mountains on the horizon and then toward the darkening cloudbank above them. He turned back toward the plane and placed his hand for a moment on the painted coat-of-arms beside the boarding door—the wheat and poppy plants, the wavy waters and blue mountain, the sun of freedom rising above them all. The words of the national anthem came to his mind again: "Today above Macedonia the new sun of liberty is born." How he loved his country! May we continue to live in peace, he murmured to himself, a prayer without ceasing.

He stepped inside the plane and felt an unease he didn't understand. The King Air B-200 started down the runway, and he glanced at his watch. Departure, 14:48. Three minutes late.

Through the window he could see his car carrying Frank Fillmore fade into the distance. But he could not see the flight-steward-turned-driver, hired because of outstanding references, credentials, and resume—all false—remove the chauffeur's hat, hair falling to her shoulders. El Toro looked back at her "ailing" passenger and smiled in complicity.

74

JOHN ADAMS STOOD AT HIS OFFICE WINDOW, HANDS BEHIND HIS BACK, staring blankly through the drizzle toward the Pentagon. He needed to concentrate on BarLothiun contracts, but his thoughts ping-ponged between President Benedict's phone contact and Frank Fillmore's curious presence in Skopje.

Inside information pointed to factions displeased with President Dimitrovski. His ability to keep Macedonia out of the Balkan war worked against two groups: those whose purpose was based on profit and also those whose purpose was based on principle. President Dimitrovski's enemies included people who considered peace to be contrary to their self-interests, political adversaries he'd beaten in his election, and blocs that wanted Macedonia to fight on their side. Logic leapt to a contract between Fillmore and one of the factions that wanted Dimitrovski overthrown. Shaken by the possibility, he turned away from the window and walked thoughtfully to his credenza to retrieve his phone from JFK. He had met President Basil Dimitrovski, who was the kind of president for whom faith and justice were more than expedient words to gain political capital. He expected his elites to serve justice by protecting the Dimitrovskis of the world, those rare leaders worthy of their office. The kind of president I would make, he thought, unlike Benedict.

He had contacts on his payroll in most of the capitols in the world. They gave him current information on their countries, invaluable for initiating timely BarLothiun contracts as well as getting a heads-up for arms sales opportunities. Devious but necessary. Underpaid custodians were his best informants. A tax-free cash stipend was a way he could help the little people, a form of justice. Secretaries were careless about the phone messages they tossed in the trash and loose about leaving communication logs lying around. Custodians had keys to their offices. Clerks like Radmila, his contact in Skopje, were second best. A granny-type woman who'd been on staff for decades, she could gain access to any information he wanted.

The Patriot followed the usual procedure to reach her. It took her less than ten minutes to find a secure place to talk to him. They spoke in Kwanyama, a relatively uncommon African language that his global contacts received a bonus for learning—except Africans, who were offered the same bonus for learning Lakota, an American Indian language spoken by fewer than ten thousand people.

Radmila was very efficient, but there was little news that mattered and no trouble he could logically link to Fillmore. Before ending the call, he courteously asked about President Dimitrovski. She was loyal to the President—a prerequisite for his global contacts. Disloyal people would also be disloyal to him. However, his contacts' loyalty stopped short of confessing their financially rewarding arrangement to pass on information.

Radmila responded with affection in her voice. "He is well. He left about an hour ago to fly to a conference in Mostar. A CIA agent is flying with him. He needed emergency transport."

CIA agents didn't need *emergency transport*. "Say more."

"He showed his credentials and was approved. No one dares question the CIA."

John Adams felt a reflux of acrid foreboding. "Who was it?"

"Someone else handled that."

A dead end. For a second he felt relieved.

"But it seemed a strange request," she continued thoughtfully, "so I remembered the name. Frank Fillmore."

Trepidation riveted him. He gripped the phone. His mind raced. Six months ago he'd arranged false CIA credentials for Fillmore, who considered one identity for a period of time less risky than simultaneous aliases. His assignment had been to free a journalist abroad whom the U.S. government had shown an enormous capacity to ignore. Justice called for her release, and her gratitude put her in the Patriot's pocket, a great asset. Now Fillmore, always for sale, had reused those credentials and perhaps built a bomb to kill President Dimitrovski—but his survive-at-all-costs mentality would stop short of throwing in his own life. "So Fillmore flew with him?"

"No. He became ill just before takeoff. The President's driver took him back to his hotel."

Oh, Jahweh-Christ-Allah! He must alert Air Traffic Control. "Thank you," he said, intending to end the conversation.

"The President called today," Radmila added.

"Dimitrovski?"

"No. Benedict."

"When?"

"At one."

He translated it to seven this morning in D.C. *That* was the Lincoln Memorial call.

"She set up a telephone appointment for tomorrow afternoon."

So her call was merely to another president, not a secret liaison. He felt reassured and a bit paranoid.

"The President contacted—"

"Benedict?"

"No. Dimitrovski. He contacted another person to participate in the call. She must be important. He phoned her himself."

"Do you know who?"

"An American. She and her husband had coffee with him this morning."

"Who?" he asked again.

It seemed a very long time before Radmila answered. He could almost hear her thinking. "I remember now. Bishop Lynn Peterson."

75

A STORM BLEW IN FROM THE EBONY BANK OF CLOUDS IN THE NORTH-western sky as Lynn and Galen finished the day's schedule. Agent Nedelkovski and a driver picked them up as President Dimitrovski had requested, and began the circuitous route to a safe house. The very idea of a safe house made her feel unsafe, and the armed escort for security brought anything but a feeling of security. She wanted to know where they were going, but the tense atmosphere did not invite questions.

Galen sat rigidly beside her, concentrating, probably on their route. She saw anxiety in his eyes. They were used to being in strangers' hands—but those were church people. These men were trained to expect the worst from people.

The storm worsened by the minute while the driver circled blocks, made sudden turns, reversed directions. She wondered if they were being followed. Or if they were being taken *into* danger instead of out of it.

Stop it, Lynn!

This time she listened to intrusive Ivy. If President Dimitrovski trusted Agent Nedelkovski, then so would she.

Just think of him as Ol' Ned.

He was too fit to be thought of as *old*, but *Ned* would work.

Finally the car came to a stop near a house set amidst trees. Lynn couldn't see it clearly because of the heavy rainstorm. It ran in rivulets down the driveway, etching a myriad of mud puddles like oversized honeycomb. She gripped the door handle to get out.

"Remain in the car!" Nedelkovski commanded. He drew his gun and scanned 360 degrees, then unlocked the door to the house. Gun held steady with both hands, he shoved the door open with his foot and stepped cautiously inside.

Silence.

Ned returned and opened her door. She tasted sulfur as a bolt of lightning raced in a zigzag path across the sky. They ran into the house, drenched by the rain. He gave them a moment to scan the room, then smiled. "President Dimitrovski asked me to give you a message: 'Welcome to the Lincoln bedroom.'"

Galen and Lynn laughed, releasing tension, tension that the President would have assumed they would feel as they entered a safe house. She asked what she'd been wondering. "Was someone following us?"

"No one can follow our drivers," he replied proudly.

Lynn's eyes roved over their surroundings, the simplicity inviting. Sparse furniture—old but comfortable. Two olive wingback chairs opposite a tweedy tobacco sofa. Wooden table with four unmatched chairs. Small kitchen off to the side. Stairs that probably led to the bedrooms. Cozy, but she verged on imploding with anxiety when she noted the bars on the windows in this isolated place.

"There is tea in the kitchen if you would like to make it," suggested Ned. "I'll check upstairs."

"Are we prisoners or guests, Love?" she whispered to Galen softly.

He put his arm around her reassuringly. "President Dimitrovski is overcautious."

She went into the kitchen, found a jar of tea on the open shelf, and put water in the kettle. Thunder played tympani while gales of wind bent the trees and wailed down the safe-house chimney. Sheets of rain pounded the roof and splattered the window panes. The musty odor of wet leaves mingled with the aroma of tea leaves. As she waited for the water to boil, she thought of the novel she hoped to write someday. Agent Nedelkovski and the driver would be holding them hostage, surreptitiously working for the bad guys instead of President Dimitrovski. Maybe hired by St. Sava. It was not a comforting scenario, especially accompanied by the sound effects.

Ned and Galen walked into the kitchen as the agent said, "Tonight I'll place one guard outside and another inside."

Safely guarded or under guard, Lynn?

Either way, she'd be glad for the company. Thick trees hide more than just four-footed animals, and thunder covers more than bird chirps.

"I apologize for any inconvenience."

"We are the ones who should apologize," said Galen. "Our stay has become troublesome for you. We would be quite content to stay at our hotel."

"You are important people to President Dimitrovski. I am honored to have responsibility for your safety."

"Thank you, Agent Nedelkovski." Lynn smiled at him. "I know we are in good hands."

He returned her smile with a twinkle in his eye. "It is safe for you to play solitaire here."

She laughed, feeling more at ease, and poured three cups of tea that they carried into the main area.

"I understand you met Viktor Machek," he said, that same twinkle in his eye. "Many tales are told about him."

And, thought Lynn, he tells many tales. Like being Russian and pretending to admire my book. Ouch.

"What is your favorite tale?" asked Galen.

"I'll tell you one just as it was told to me." He cleared his throat and began:

> Four men with Uzis captured Machek. They strapped his wrists together in the front and walked him deep in the woods to a place of interrogation, a guard leading and the others following their prisoner. One moment all was calm. The next a hurricane hit!
>
> Machek leaped at Number One in front of him. Looped his strapped wrists over One's head. Locked his arms against his sides. Grabbed hold of the Uzi. Held his finger on the trigger. Pivoted so he and One faced the others, Number One in human-shield position.
>
> It happened too fast for them to react.
>
> "Throw down your guns!" Machek ordered.
>
> Number Two balked. A mistake! Machek pulled the trigger. Shot the gun from Two's hands.
>
> "Throw down your guns!" he ordered again.
>
> Number Three hesitated. Another mistake! Another bloody hand!
>
> Number Four complied.
>
> "Now drop your weapons belts!"
>
> Number Four rebelled. Charged him. Machek heaved the butt of the Uzi backward into One's belly. He gagged and tripped. Machek hung on to the Uzi. Jerked his arms

> over One's head. Slammed him into Four. Spun. Landed a knockout kick. It put Four on the ground with a broken jaw.
>
> Machek grabbed a knife from a weapons belt. Put the handle in his mouth. Raised his hands above the blade. Slashed the wrist straps. Freed his hands.
>
> One lunged. Machek dodged. Spun and kicked. Broke One's nose and knocked him out.
>
> Machek took nylon cords from the weapons belts. Rolled each guard face down. Tied their hands—bloody or not—behind them. Bent their right knee backwards. Tied their right foot to their hands. Four guards deactivated in seconds! Like a cowboy wrestling steers in an American movie.
>
> Machek brushed off the knees of his pants and walked off a free man again.

Ned paused.

"That's a remarkable story," said Lynn, wondering how much it had been exaggerated.

"And it's true. I know because I'm the one who found the four." He paused dramatically. "All of them enemies of Macedonia. Machek did us a favor." He smiled. "What's interesting is that they spoke of him with admiration, almost awe. They got some battle scars, but he could have killed them and didn't." He wrapped the words in his own admiration.

Better to have Viktor as a friend than an enemy, Lynn.

Three sharp staccato rings alerted Ned. "Excuse me. I must answer."

Lynn didn't understand the words he spoke into the phone, but she did understand his silence. His face paled in the universal language of tragedy. Dazed, he rushed to the door.

"Agent Nedelkovski, wait!" she called. "Can we help?"

"Pray for a miracle." He jerked open the door. Rain poured in.

"What happened?" Galen asked.

He glanced back at them, unable to control the quaver in his voice. "It's President Dimitrovski. SFOR Air Traffic Control lost his plane from radar at 16:01." Automatically, he glanced at his watch. "Ten minutes ago."

76

GENERAL THORNBURG STOOD BEHIND HIS DESK CHAIR AT NATO HEADquarters in Naples. His aide entered and handed him a communiqué:

> SFOR Air Traffic Control reports that the plane carrying President Basil Dimitrovski of Macedonia was lost from radar control at 1601 hours in the region of Stolac, BiH. ATC recordings of pilot's words indicate a crash.

The news hit him like a preemptive strike. He slammed his fist into the back of the chair and glowered at his aide. "What is this!"

"I am sorry, sir."

The general watched him shrink and tried to control his rage. "I know—don't kill the messenger. You're dismissed." What he wouldn't give to discuss this with Marsh. Grief surfaced, and abruptly he shut it down.

The eighteen hours of fireworks that began Tuesday at 1800 hours had gone well. No NATO casualties and, as far as he knew, not a single civilian casualty. But now this! The news alarmed him primarily because the loss of President

Dimitrovski's leadership would be a gigantic step backward from international peace, perhaps an irreversible one. The general knew that he must predict all the possible repercussions and plan accordingly. A strategic nightmare. One more step in the march toward chaos.

He thought again about Major Manetti. The unusual request from the State Department for Major Marshall Manetti to protect some fool bishop and her husband who doesn't have enough sense to keep her out of harm's way. Followed by the major's assassination. The best soldier I've ever known. The best man. The best friend. Who was behind it? Someone at State? A prissy politician who requested the favor? Why? Again he tried to shut down his grief. Then a bomb was planted at the Austrian President's reception, though not made public. And now President Dimitrovski's plane is missing—meaning it crashed on a stormy day in the mountains. Or something more sinister. He wondered whether some of these disasters were connected.

He decided to design his own strategy. If there were connections, he'd find them. Shifting to combat stance, he picked up the phone and ordered a plane and four aides to go to Stolac, Bosnia-Herzegovina, immediately. To their surprise, he boarded the plane himself. He personally would get to the bottom of this. He owed it to Marsh.

77

GALEN LOOKED AT HIS WATCH AND TURNED ON THE TV. "IT'S 4:16. AIR Traffic Control lost sight of the President's plane fifteen minutes ago."

Each roll of thunder seemed to reverberate the words. Lynn stared at the screen, rigid and silent, fervently praying for the plane to reappear.

At 4:30, BBC aired breaking news:

> The plane carrying Macedonian President Basil Dimitrovski is missing.

"Missing," repeated Lynn. "Not crashed. There's still hope."

> The Bosnian Civil Aviation Administration reports that radar lost the plane at 16:01 about 30 kilometers south of Mostar in the mountainous region of Stolac. Radio contact is broken. A crash is feared. We will continue to bring you updates.

While Lynn worried about the President, Galen painted the big picture. "His death could send ripples through the Balkans like another tsunami across the earth."

And it would break the hearts of Gonka and their children, Lynn thought. She forced herself to step beyond stunned paralysis and trudged upstairs, her ears attuned to TV for the next update. She noted the packing mess from their hurried hotel exit, and while raindrops kerplunked rapidly on the slate roof, she piddled away the time by straightening the clutter. A methodical and mindless task. Something she could control. Everything tucked into its bit of space. No surprises. No sadness.

But also an illusion. In the real world a giant soul like Basil Dimitrovski was threatened, a man of peace among warmongers. She thought of her own small existence. A woman who could not even keep her own child alive. She ceased her idle movements, centered herself, and prayed for him.

She heard the TV show interrupted for a news bulletin and ran down the stairs.

The somber-voiced reporter spoke:

> Bosnia and Herzegovina—BiH—officials have confirmed that President Basil Dimitrovski of Macedonia has been killed in a plane crash. There are no survivors. The Macedonian delegation accompanying the President on the King Air B-200 was en route to an economic conference in Mostar.

They showed a photograph of President Dimitrovski.

> A rescue team found the crash site and the plane's remains in the region of Bitunje village in Berkovici municipality. The Civil Aviation Administration has established an investigating team, but bad weather is expected to be the cause.

Lynn heard raindrops hit the window panes like tears of the Loving Creator.

> Tomorrow will be a National Day of Mourning in Macedonia.

"The planet is a lesser place tonight than it was this morning," said Galen, taking her hand as she sat beside him on the sofa. "President Dimitrovski's life controverts the old image of pulling a hand from a bucket of water and it makes no difference."

She agreed. "The waters part like the Red Sea around the space he leaves." A few minutes later they heard church bells pealing in the distance. Galen rose and began to pace. Lynn watched him. Action for him, she thought. Tears for me. We handle grief in our own way. "Poor Gonka and the children," she said, vividly recalling the moment she'd learned of Lyndie's death. She also remembered the morning she laid all the pieces of her broken heart before God, hoping that someday, somehow, God would put them back together and make her whole again. Be with his family, her heart prayed as tears rolled down her cheeks. The loving care of their church would support them. How, she wondered, do people bear their loss if they have no faith community and pastor's presence? She sat immobile for a long time, a deep sadness spilling over the levee and flooding her soul.

78

John Adams hunched over his desk. President Dimitrovski, killed in the plane crash. He'd done nothing to stop it, and the consequence was unalterable. Shame crept into an empty crevice of his guarded heart. He relived those fateful moments of his decision: I thumb the first three numbers to call Air Traffic Control and ask them to warn the pilot. I see the worldwide headlines: JOHN ADAMS SAVES LIFE OF MACEDONIAN PRESIDENT. Then I freeze. How will I explain my knowledge? I can call anonymously on my secure line. But what if an investigation of Fillmore's false CIA credentials leads back to me? Fillmore will do anything to save himself. What if he incriminates me for previous directives? Or cuts a deal by accusing me of ordering the assassination? The charge won't stick, but the accusation itself will tarnish my image. And what if an investigation ultimately links the Patriot and John Adams? Elias Darwish is dead for nothing. Logic wins: Intervention is not prudent. Besides, any blood will be on Fillmore's hands, not mine. It isn't my country and it isn't my problem. Onerous but necessary. I put down the phone, relinquishing my power to prevent disaster.

And now the President was dead and Fillmore was safe. He wondered who had contracted Fillmore. I'll find out, he swore, ignoring the darkest part of his heart that knew the other reason he hadn't finished his call to Air Traffic Control: A crash would accomplish the objective of the failed Schönbrunn Palace bomb—bringing fear and chaos, demonstrating that presidents are not invulnerable, and prompting POTUS to stop discounting one who can give her wise counsel—like John Adams. Deep down where he didn't want to go, he felt vindicated.

Radmila's second piece of information—that President Benedict had arranged to include Lynn Peterson in a call with President Dimitrovski—unlocked the liaison conundrum. How had he missed it? Selecting Lynn Peterson was brilliant—he had to give Benedict that. She had international connections and the capacity to make contacts. She had links to high places and a broad range of associations with all classes of people. He realized that part of the reason for his mistake was that she was a female bishop. His traditional stereotype of women had blinded him. Another reason was that Viktor Machek, his trusted Balkan connection, had cleared her. Did his investigative elite fall victim to the same stereotype?

He strung together the evidence that indicted her. First, tomorrow's call, though he doubted that it would occur in light of this afternoon's disaster. Additionally, two of President Benedict's emails: Lynn Peterson's forwarded one, via Ambassador Whitcomb, regarding a conversation with Manetti that appeared merely complimentary and innocent; and the President's response to the Ambassador, interestingly not directed to Lynn Peterson, but notable because of her swift reply and another false denial of her friendship with the major. To let Peterson go free for the same action that cost Manetti his life would show partiality. Partiality defamed justice.

Darwish, Manetti, and now Lynn Peterson. Too many too soon, thought John Adams.

But the Patriot shrugged. The bottom line, as always, was zero tolerance. Besides, the bishop was guilty of involving herself in governmental affairs—mixing church and state! Nothing galled the Patriot more than an affront to the Constitution.

He reviewed her travel itinerary obtained by Lone Star. The Petersons would arrive in Sarajevo around noon on Friday. He couldn't risk using Zeller again and giving him too many pieces of the puzzle. Despite his loss of respect for Fillmore, he needed him one more time. He was in Skopje and could easily get to Sarajevo. The Patriot retrieved his secure phone and left Fillmore a brief encrypted message:

> Be at the Sarajevo Airport by noon Friday. Wait there for instructions. Come prepared for target practice.
> You have been busy with a weighty Macedonian matter.

The last line was more than a veiled threat to remove potential reluctance. It was a declaration of knowledge. He owned Frank Fillmore now!

With a heavy sigh he swiveled his chair toward the bust of JFK, opened the hidden panel, and replaced the secure phone he'd failed to use to save President Dimitrovski—God rest his good soul.

But it was time to move on. Justice, and only justice, you shall pursue. Retaining the power to do justice sometimes mandated death. Onerous but honorable. President Benedict, kiss your liaison goodbye!

79

LYNN LOOKED AT HER WATCH AND REALIZED THEY SHOULD BE HUNGRY. "Let's see if there's anything to eat in the kitchen, Love." Food, the often-sought filler of voids. Their exploration of the kitchen resulted in a round loaf of bread, a chunk of cheese, and a sealed carton with a picture of reddish soup on the front. Tomato, she assumed. She took a saucepan down from the open shelf, lit the back burners, and refilled the teakettle—more methodical and mindless tasks. Galen found a couple of bowls and spoons and rinsed out their tea mugs. They ate in front of the TV, staring blankly at the screen. The next BBC update came shortly after 7:30. In the background was a picture of the President boarding his plane, taken from files for a different trip. They listened, stunned:

> The earlier Search and Rescue Team report about finding Macedonian President Basil Dimitrovski's crashed plane and bodies—with no survivors—was inaccurate. At 19:30, an SFOR spokesman denied that the plane had been found. The plane carrying Macedonian

> President Basil Dimitrovski and his delegation has not—repeat, has *not*—been located.

BBC cut to a video of the spokesman's announcement:

> SFOR Search and Rescue teams searching for the plane and the President's remains found no evidence of the crash at the site announced earlier by BiH officials. They have stopped the investigation in that location.

The next video showed the spokesman for President Dimitrovski's cabinet:

> There is no official report of the fate of President Basil Dimitrovski and his associates.

The reporter added:

> SFOR has moved the search to other areas on Versnik Mountain. The aerial search is expected to be suspended within the hour because of nightfall and bad weather conditions. Foot patrols will continue, but they are hindered by fog and landmines.

Lynn and Galen absorbed the news in numb silence. Galen spoke first. "A rescue team found the crash site and the plane's remains in the region of Bitunje," quoted Galen from the earlier report, "and now there's *no evidence of the crash* at that site!"

Lynn embraced hopefulness. "But if the President's plane has not been found after all, maybe he's alive!"

"You're crawling into a cave of denial. The plane fell off the radar screen."

"Maybe there are survivors."

"There would have been radio contact."

"Maybe the radio shattered, Love."

"Perhaps you noticed that tomorrow's National Day of Mourning was not canceled."

She gave up. Not on hoping, but on getting Galen to hope with her. Now Gonka Dimitrovska would be hopeful that her husband was alive. May it be so! Lynn wanted to bring her comfort and knew that no one could. She remembered the spacious, grace-filled sea that had kept her own little sailboat afloat despite the storms when Lyndie died. She knew the true Comforter would be with Gonka and help her bear whatever had to be borne.

The absurdity of the earlier report troubled Lynn less than the delay it caused in a broad search. How could a team report its discovery of plane debris and dead bodies that were nonexistent? What a horrible mistake!

A mistake, Lynn?

80

IT WAS GENERAL THORNBURG WHO STOOD AT FULL COMMAND PRESENCE in Stolac. "I WANT YOU . . ." In three words, he took control of the bedlam in the improvised headquarters at Stolac. The room went silent. All motion ceased.

"No, I COMMAND YOU to establish communication with every VILLAGE, every HAMLET, every Gypsy CAMPSITE within a fifty-kilometer radius from here. I EXPECT you to be ORGANIZED, EFFICIENT, and THOROUGH. And I don't care about the weather and the dark! Do you UNDERSTAND me?"

His fierce eyes circled the room, deliberately intimidating, confident that no one would dare disobey him. "This is your procedure: The circle will be divided into four sections like a clock. Due north is 1200 hours. Each of my four aides will be responsible for a section." They stood at attention.

"MANZANARES, take 1200 to 300 hours."

"Yes, sir." He saluted.

"CARVER, 300 to 600. KAWASAKI, 600 to 900. AWAD, 900 to 1200."

The aides acknowledged their orders in turn, saluted, and remained at attention.

Again the general's eyes circled the room. His voice took on a persuasive tone. "The people in this room who know these mountains are the key." His translator stopped spitting his commands and took on a similar tone. "You know the terrain. Your expertise in communicating with the locals is essential. They will trust you." The general swept the room, making eye contact with each man who looked like he knew the area. "YOU are tonight's heroes." He paused. The silence held. The energy in the room began to build. He could feel it. "Move to the officer in charge of the geographic area you know best. NOW!"

When the division was complete, General Thornburg gave two final orders before leaving the room: "Avoid areas known for landmines. You are to report to me by 2300 hours. GO!"

81

Lynn and Galen lay restlessly awake in a strange bed in a now unprotected safe house in an isolated area, their minds muddled by the found/unfound crash-site reports. A thought whispered unrelentingly through her mind: *Was it on purpose?* "Love," she whispered in the dark, "do you think the false report could have been deliberate?"

"Why?"

"I don't know. But it delayed searching for the real site." She thought he would charge her with being a conspiracist. But he didn't. He didn't respond at all. She found his silence more discomfiting than the expected accusation. She began to tremble. "I feel we're rowing a little pirogue in the dark on mile-high tidal waves."

"The storm will end. They always do," he added softly. "You taught me that, my darling Lynn." He saved that phrase for anniversaries and deep moments when words were inadequate. He wrapped her in his strong arms. Held her. Kissed her hair.

She huddled in his refuge, a still cove safe from the world's stormy seas. Gratitude for him welled up in her heart, leaving no empty space where fear could crouch. Wrapped in the solace and ecstasy of each other's arms, they staved off the nightmare of reality.

It was midnight when Lynn awoke with a start. The memory of the President's plane descended like an avalanche on a lone skier. The storm had abated, replaced by an eye-of-the-storm eeriness in this remote and unguarded safe house. Careful not to awaken Galen, she reached for her blue silk robe beside the bed. Her toes brushed across the floor for unseen slippers. She felt her way to the bedroom door, puzzled that no light beamed from the lamp she'd left on downstairs. Feeling the wall along the way, she padded through the hall to the staircase. She gripped the banister, each foot groping in the dark for the next step.

As she neared the bottom, she had an eerie sensation of another presence. She paused. Remembered seeing Galen lock the door and hearing Major Nedelkovski say, "No one can follow our drivers." She repressed her fear.

She took the last step, then closed her eyes and opened them again, desperate to adjust to the darkness. Shadowy shapes loomed. Black against blacker. She felt for a light switch on the wall but couldn't find one. Her breath came loud in the noiseless night. She held it. Her heart beat like a kettledrum. Picturing the room, she extended her arms to keep from bumping into something and crept forward in cautious silence toward the lamp she remembered on a table. The sense of another presence, like the keen awareness of unseen bats in a dim, dank cave, grew stronger. The sniper's eyes revisited her in full-screen memory. She suppressed a shiver.

A powerful hand jammed across her mouth. A Rambo arm pinned her back against the man's chest. His chin pressed down on the top of her head. Terror sparked a scream.

His hand muffled the sound. His palm crushed her nose. Blocked her breath. His mouth bent to her ear. "You must not scream!"

She recognized the voice. Viktor! The Russian/non-Russian. Who'd crashed the President's coffee. Who'd heard her utter *St. Sava*. Who'd rushed away immediately. Terrified, she hunkered down in the chain mail of silence.

82

As Bubba drove his silver 'Vette to his favorite bookstore in the Quarter, he reran Lynn's email. When he'd first read it this afternoon, he'd felt angry with her for not telling him immediately about the stolen medal. He thought about it as he drove. She'd blame herself for it. She cared more for people than anyone he knew and wouldn't forgive herself for not getting Elie's medal to his mother. And she'd beat up on herself something fierce for letting him down. She probably hadn't told him sooner because she dreaded disappointing him. "I shouldn't have laid that on her," he said into the wind. But he hadn't realized what he was asking. He didn't know then what he knew now.

The tone of her email bothered him far more than her delay in telling him. "Stay alert. Watch yourself. Imperative to guard words in emails." She wasn't a fearful person and didn't talk that way. But what really disturbed him was that she hadn't risked putting in an email the meaning of the symbol.

He parked and made a call on his cell as he walked toward the bookstore. "Cy Bill? Bubba here."

"I've already taken care of your little package, Bubba. Safe and unofficial. For your eyes only. No need to get into the *unless* part."

Unless something happens to me, Bubba finished mentally. "I need to talk to you."

"Do you want to grab a sandwich and call it dinner?"

"I'd suggest the Acme Oyster House, but we need some privacy. How about a bench at the Moonwalk? I'll pick up a couple of muffalettas."

"I can be there in half an hour."

Bubba pocketed his cell as he entered the bookstore and looked for a book on the Cyrillic alphabet and the languages that used it. He found one and looked forward to the challenge. He liked to learn new things. Maybe, like Lynn, he, too, would soon be able to read Elie's name in Cyrillic.

His mind went back to Lynn's email. He wasn't scared for himself but he was for them. Something had scared her, and she didn't scare easy. No telling what they faced in the Balkans. The unsafest place on the planet right now. Worrying about them was like wringing his hands on the sidelines. He made a decision: here comes Broussard, an army-of-one. First he called Fay Foster at the bishop's office to check out their itinerary.

"They're in Macedonia, Bubba. In Skopje."

"Where the President's plane crashed!"

"Is missing," she corrected. "I guess in the Balkans, they see things like a crashed plane and dead passengers that turn out not to be there! Maybe it's their version of the Easter resurrection story!" She paused for breath. "I tell you what, Bubba, I'll be so glad when the bishop and Dr. Peterson get back home!"

"Me too. Do you know when they go to Sarajevo?"

"Tomorrow morning."

"Thank you."

"Take care, Bubba."

He started to call Bishop Lynn's cell and remembered the time difference. Seven hours, he thought. He looked at the world clock on his phone. A bit past midnight. They'd be asleep. Soundly, he hoped. And safely.

He picked up the muffalettas and joined Cy Bill. They sat on a bench facing the river. Sunlight caught the water like rippling diamonds, and the sky celebrated the day in a sweep of blazing color. Bubba handed Cy Bill the email from Lynn. He read it through twice before speaking. "Do you think she's right about the sniper?"

"I'd bet a deep-sea fishing trip in the Gulf that he's alive and stole that medal. She knew the mime did the shooting before Chief Armstrong made the announcement. I was at their house that night."

"Why didn't she report the stolen medal?"

"Maybe she was afraid she'd be asked how she got it. That would lead straight to me."

"How did you get it?"

"Are you off duty?"

"Absolutely, bro."

"I removed it from the crime scene."

Cy Bill's eyebrows went up.

"The chain broke. I didn't want it to get lost." He swallowed and shoved the words out around the lump in his throat. "I wanted to give it back to him as soon as he . . . regained consciousness." Cy Bill looked away to give Bubba time to collect himself. Bubba dropped a mask over his grief and grinned. "Last I heard, dead men can't steal medals."

"I know she's reliable. But I've been doing my best on this investigation. If the sniper is alive, why haven't we found something? Anything. It's like he disappeared."

"Well, he didn't disappear. That . . ." Furious, Bubba said, "Even *I* can't think of words bad enough for him. And he's still walking around on God's good earth," he ranted. "Stealing things and scaring folks." For the first time in his life Bubba understood how someone could kill another human being.

"We need to talk to her."

"I'm planning to call them around midnight. Morning for them. I'll call you about the conversation after I run in the morning."

"Don't you generally run at six along the levee?"

"So?"

"So routines are predictable. They are helpful to people who want to harm us. You might want to vary it, Bubba."

He recalled Elie's warning. There are people willing to kill for it. The attorney's warning. And Lynn's. Now Cy Bill's. An epidemic of warnings.

83

I apologize for scaring you." Viktor Machek lightened the pressure of his palm against Lynn's mouth. "Don't scream. I won't hurt you. If ill-wishers are nearby, I want surprise on my side." He released his hand to turn on the lamp. The sudden light blinded her. He removed his night goggles.

She saw his briefcase by the sofa and remembered that the palace bomb was in a briefcase with President Nausner's initials. Panic seized her.

"Let's sit down." He gestured to the sofa.

She stepped to the wingback chair instead, farther from the briefcase. He took the chair's twin close by. Too close.

"You are a remarkable woman. I underestimated you in the beginning. Connecting Natalia's symbol with St. Sava was amazing. You note details and fit them together like working a jigsaw puzzle in a nanosecond."

She had succumbed to his flattery before. No more. His navy blazer fell open and she saw a shoulder holster against his blue shirt, the black gun handle visible.

He followed her eyes. "I would never hurt you, Lynn Peterson."

Right, Lynn! That's why he carries a pistol in his holster and probably a bomb in his briefcase.

Lynn heard noise from the stairs and turned. Galen jumped the banister. Rushed at Viktor.

Viktor drew. Aimed. "Halt!"

Galen crouched for a flying tackle.

"*No!*" Lynn shouted. "The pistol!"

"I mean you no harm!" Viktor held the weapon steady in a two-handed aim.

Galen paused, still poised to lunge.

"If I planned to shoot you, you'd be dead now." Slowly Viktor lowered the gun and gestured toward the sofa. "Please sit down."

"First, give me the gun."

"You're unarmed! And you dare to demand my weapon!" A twinkle replaced the invincibility in his eyes. "I need to change my image of bishops' spouses."

"Most people do," Galen replied with icy calm.

"Lynn Peterson, your husband is David and Daniel rolled into one."

A good description, she thought, admiring her hero in maroon pajamas.

"*Give me the gun!*" Galen's raw power introduced her to a side of him she didn't know.

A smile played at the corners of Viktor's mouth. He removed the ammunition clip and handed him the gun.

Immediately Galen stepped back beyond reach and pointed it toward the floor. "I remember what my father taught me as a boy: Every gun is loaded."

"A careful man."

"This semi-automatic, for example, retains one bullet when the magazine is removed."

Viktor looked surprised. "I underestimated you. Book knowledge or experience?"

"I don't plan to aim this gun at you, Viktor Machek. But let's be clear. If the need arises, I will." Galen spoke with authoritative calm, his fierce eyes as backup. "And I will make the single bullet count."

Lynn felt his resolve crackle in the air. A flicker in Viktor's eyes told her he did also. She knew Galen had spent a good part of his childhood target-practicing with his father. She'd seen his medals. But he hadn't handled a gun since his father died.

The two men locked eyes. Tension packed into the room like too much air in a balloon. "No one holds me captive," Viktor replied, the words measured and menacing. He eyed Galen in his own let's-be-clear statement: I don't need a gun to protect myself.

Four men with Uzis had proved that. Lynn wanted desperately to ease the tension. "Viktor," she said his name softly in a tone as calm and soothing as she could muster and then offered him a face-saving compliment, "Agent Nedelkovski told us about your brilliant capture of four men with Uzis who were wanted by the State." An image from the first *True Grit* came to mind: John Wayne wearing a black eye patch and holding the reins in his teeth, both guns blasting, his horse thundering toward the gunmen. Still trying to dial down the tension, she said lightly in the same gentle tone, "You're another Rooster Cogburn, Viktor."

A grin turned up the corners of his mouth, reshaping his care-worn face. "I know that movie."

She grinned back, admitting to herself that she liked Viktor.

But tonight he scared you to death, Lynn! And he may be the one who broke into your hotel room and read your email this morning.

Ivy made sense. Was uncanny Viktor playing a good-writer game with her on the plane? Was he on that plane because they were? He'd stayed close behind them in the airport security line and would have seen Natalia's stash of euros and the symbol with them. Did he also follow them to the Hotel Aleksandar? He'd managed to get himself invited to join them for coffee in President Dimitrovski's garden and had interrogated her about the symbol. That still rankled her. "I'm curious, Viktor. Why did you search our hotel room and open my computer?"

The question stunned Galen. He almost dropped the gun. For an instant Viktor was also taken aback. His eyes moved from side to side like a clock pendulum as he reran a mental scene. Recognition dawned in his eyes. He raised one eyebrow. "The bit of hair! You deliberately placed it on your computer."

She was surprised that he'd noticed the hair and even more surprised that he didn't deny the break-in.

He began to chuckle. "Rooster Cogburn meets Baby Sister!" Lynn and Galen joined him in the runaway laughter of tension release. Finally, Viktor said, "I came here to protect you."

"In a safe house?" Galen's suspicion was not subtle.

"A safe house with no security tonight."

"Agent Nedelkovski sent you."

"No." He gave Galen a searing look. "Agent Nedelkovski and his team have more important things to do than guard you in this time of national tragedy. I followed your driver here."

And you've been hiding out, spying on us since we got here, Lynn thought but didn't say.

What would you expect of Viktor the Voyeur, Lynn?

He seemed to have access to information on lots of fronts. She took a leap and shifted the conversation's focus. "I'm deeply concerned about President Dimitrovski. I don't understand how officials could find a crash site with no survivors and later simply wave the report away as a mistake."

"*Mistake!*" Fury distorted Viktor's face. "Almost immediately they report the crash site—the wrong one! Then just before dark—when it's too late for further searches—the report is retracted! *Excuse us!*" he mocked. "A minor mistake has been made. There were no bodies at the crash site after all. In fact, there was no plane!" His voice rose. "It was not a *mistake* but a *diversion.* It protected the real site from discovery this afternoon and all night tonight, allowing ample time to alter evidence!"

That wasn't the road she wanted to go down. But what else makes sense, she wondered with a shudder.

Viktor clenched his fists, barely controlling his rage. "St. Sava has obtained evidence that the President's plane was sabotaged."

84

GENERAL THORNBURG, UNABLE TO SLEEP, LOOKED OUT THE DARK WINDOW onto slumbering Stolac. The long night of reports from his aides left him unsettled. Awad's group had hit pay dirt in small Huskovici. And dirt, he judged, was exactly what it was.

The villagers, interviewed individually, had been eager to talk. Their alarming stories, even allowing for exaggeration, contained too many similarities to be false. At about 1600 hours they heard a loud noise coming in close over the mountains. Afraid they might be under attack, they kept their eyes on the sky. A white plane trimmed in blue and red hurtled through the clouds like a bird with a broken wing. The plane dipped into the tree line, and they couldn't see it any longer. General Thornburg saw the scene in his mind as he stared into the darkness.

The crash echoed across the mountain and the villagers wanted to help. Immediately they sent out their best five men, mountain-born and bred, to make the slow, rough climb through the storm to the site of the crash.

It was the later helicopter the villagers mentioned that drew the general's curiosity. No, his fury. They saw it fly over and land at the crash site. The five Huskovici men were close enough to hear the victims groaning. But suddenly armed Stabilisation Force (SFOR) soldiers stopped them at gunpoint and ordered them to return to the village. They said it was a matter of national security. Later the people of Huskovici heard a blast and saw a cloud of smoke above the treeline where the plane had gone down. The general remembered the exact words Awad shared from the interview report of one villager: *Black smoke rose into the sky like a bad omen.*

A bad omen indeed. The general looked at his watch—0200 hours. He turned down the bed covers and began the familiar process of willing himself into a state of sleep, a pre-battle discipline that had served him well in the trenches. He needed to be at his best when he rose in a few hours.

At first dawn a helicopter would take him to the location of the crash described by the five Huskovici men—a site half as far from Mostar as the false one first named. He wanted to examine the site himself. So many inconsistencies in the public reports of the "facts" pointed to pernicious incompetence or to deliberate misrepresentation. And the latter pointed to sabotage. He trusted the Huskovici men's account. Should he be greeted by some gun-happy SFOR soldiers—fake or real—let them just *try* to turn him away! He hadn't become *General* Thornburg by running from a fight.

Afterward, he would go to Huskovici and personally interview the five villagers who'd wanted to help the victims. He knew he intimidated people. Tomorrow was too important to let that happen. He needed the men to feel at ease with him, to feel free to share whatever tumbled into their minds, to feel unafraid. He thought of Marsh, who had a knack for helping people feel comfortable. What a loss! Professionally and personally. He sighed as he thought about his friend's gentle courtesy—a character trait that only a fool would confuse with weakness. He could learn from Marsh and would try to keep him in mind while interviewing the villagers.

It was not his business to interfere with official spins on the death of the president of any country except his own. "But," he muttered aloud in the dark, "it's my business to know the truth."

85

THE FIRST RAYS OF DAWN CREPT THROUGH THE CRACK BETWEEN THE CURtains in the bedroom window. Lynn oriented herself. Thursday. Day eight, ABC—After Becoming Courier. The calendar of her old world stopped with Tuesday, BEM—Before Elie's Murder. The great divide. She put on her blue silk robe and padded downstairs to make coffee. The aroma greeted her before she reached the kitchen. Viktor had already done it. She accepted the cup he handed her and sipped the strong brew. "Thank you, Rooster," she said genially.

He skipped the preliminaries. "You mentioned my uninvited visit to your hotel room. You deserve an explanation." His eyes met hers steadily. "You and your husband may be in danger."

That woke her up.

"Elias Darwish was trying to discover the identity of a man who calls himself the Patriot. We don't know whether he succeeded or was getting too close. We think the Patriot had him killed. It is imperative that I find the data Darwish left."

Questions swam through Lynn's mind like spawning salmon. Who is *we?* Why is the *we* concerned about someone called the Patriot? She recalled Bubba's email: I have information indicating our friend knew he was in danger.

Where did Bubba get that information? How much did he know? What if he has the data Viktor wants? When could she let him know that it might put him in danger? But she kept her face as blank as an empty canvas. Viktor was likable, but she didn't trust him.

"The Patriot may also have been connected with yesterday's sabotage of President Dimitrovski's plane."

Galen walked into the kitchen and heard the accusation. "What is the evidence?" he asked, pouring himself a cup of coffee.

Lynn wanted to cast her call-in vote for a wild conspiracy theory on Viktor's part. But it was just crazy enough to hold more truth than fiction.

"Let me tell you about the Patriot. You both travel the globe. Surely you've noticed an apparent increase in scattered disruptions throughout the world. Europe, South America, the Middle East, Africa, even the United States."

Galen nodded.

"These little eddies of chaos appear unrelated, but they are too well executed for all of them to be coincidences."

Lynn glanced at Galen, remembering their conversations about the same thing.

"The Patriot is present on many fronts. That indicates an access to privileged information, not just from one country but apparently worldwide. This access gives him great power."

"I don't see what this has to do with us," said Galen.

Viktor eyed Lynn. "You have connections around the world, and as a bishop you are above suspicion. A perfect conduit. And that is exactly what makes you suspicious to someone as paranoid as the Patriot."

"That's absurd! Lynn's not a conduit!"

Ouch!

"We suspect that the Patriot has hacked into President Benedict's communication channels. If so, any links he can't monitor are holes in his dike—and the Patriot is a man who plugs holes."

"Again, what does that have to do with us?" asked Galen.

Viktor looked each one of them in the eye for a long moment. Despite everything he'd said that stung Lynn to the core, she managed to hold his gaze. When he spoke, he used a matter-of-fact tone, scary to her because of its authentic ring.

"The Patriot hired me to investigate you." He looked at Lynn. "Why would he consider you a threat unless he suspected a secret connection between you and the President of the United States?"

Galen slammed down his coffee cup. "Get off it, Viktor! Lynn has no connection with President Benedict!"

Lynn regretted Galen's response. She feared his intensity might cast suspicions on himself.

Viktor ignored Galen and gave her a long look. "No connection? Having the same religious affiliation could be viewed as an important one. But whether you actually have a connection does not matter. What matters is whether the Patriot thinks you do."

What have you done, Lynn? You should never have accepted that letter in the limo.

"I investigated you as he requested. Including breaking in to the privacy of your room. I apologize for that. However, my top priority is to remain connected to the Patriot long enough to learn his identity."

Oh, sure, Lynn!

"I reported to him that you are a naïve and harmless bishop and her equally naive and harmless husband." His eyes wrinkled into a smile as he finally included Galen in his level gaze.

"As I think about my gun in your hand, Galen, perhaps I made a mistake."

Lynn didn't smile. "Your report is accurate in that we try not to bring harm to anyone—to any sentient being, as the Dalai Lama would say. But we are certainly not *naïve*."

"My report diverted him, but I can't guarantee for how long. You will be in harm's way again. Perhaps you already are."

Galen calmly shook his head in dismissal. "The Patriot, as you call him, seems to be going to more trouble than we're worth."

"Hear me, Galen," he said forcefully, his eyes intense. "He is the most dangerous man I know. One of the things that makes him so is his belief that his noble cause justifies ignoble acts."

"He's not alone in that," said Galen.

"Our world is a very small one now. One person can do irreparable damage not just to a part of it but to all of it. If not directly, then through the ripple effects. We must stop the Patriot, and we need Elias Darwish's information to do so. Tell me about Bubba Broussard."

Caught off-guard by his sudden shift, Lynn did a double-take.

"To be frank, I looked at your email addresses and noticed his name and Darwish's. Both are Saints. Were they good friends?" He scrutinized her for a reaction.

She hid behind her well-worn bishop's mask, her mind whirling. Elie would have trusted Bubba. He was the logical link.

Galen came to her rescue. "I assume all the Saints are friends to some degree," he said casually.

"How did you get the medal, Lynn?"

"A Saint who saw one of my TV interviews learned that I was going to Sarajevo and asked me to take it to Mrs. Darwish."

"Who?" He eyed Lynn, seeking facts behind the façade. "How did he get it?"

She stared back. His invasive stare burned her courage to a stub, but she held fast. No reaction. No response.

"It's time for you to leave my wife alone, Machek," said Galen.

"Fair enough."

"You keep talking about *we* must stop the Patriot. Who is the *we*?" Galen asked.

It was Viktor's turn not to respond.

Lynn remembered President Benedict's words in the note: *Start with St. Sava.* I'll try to, Madam President. "You mentioned St. Sava last night. Please tell us what you were talking about."

"It's a long story. Right now we only have time for the conclusion. People have become paranoid about terrorist cells. Despite what you may be tempted to think, St. Sava is not a terrorist organization. It is an ancient secret society based on benevolence."

Right, Lynn! And the CIA stands for Compassionate Idealistic Altruism!

86

ZELLER'S ALARM WOKE HIM TO A MOZART MINUET AT 6:00 A.M. STILL obsessed with Galen Peterson's appearances in his life, he did only two things before sitting down with *Mutter:* made a pot of coffee and lit a cigarette. He turned on the computer and began. Details. Always details. The Macedonian President's plane crash might disrupt airline schedules or change Peterson's itinerary. He searched BosnaAir: Skopje to Sarajevo, Friday, 11:00 A.M. Flight still scheduled. It took only a few minutes to tap into the passenger list. So easy. Two Petersons. No changes.

He glanced out the window and saw only a few thin clouds. A good day for flying. Another search provided Vienna-to-Sarajevo flights this afternoon with one at 3:01 P.M. Perfect.

A full flight. Not so perfect. He ran through the passenger list and selected an Arab name. "Terrorist Arabs!" he muttered. With little effort he broke through the firewall, deleted the name, and replaced it with his alias of the day. He printed his e-ticket. It pleased him to think of the Arab showing up with an invalid ticket and officials viewing it as forged because their computers couldn't lie. Thanks, *Mutter.*

Zeller took pride in his computer expertise. He had the power to wreak havoc. Tamper with financial records, embezzle funds, spread viruses. But as a man of honor he wouldn't do that. No.

He reexamined his pistol and rifle. He had prepared them with precision. Anticipating tomorrow brought an adrenaline rush. To shoot or not to shoot. That was the question. He was totally prepared for the former. Would thoroughly consider the latter. He patted *Freund* tenderly, his most faithful of friends. His only friend besides *Mutter*, he admitted, requiring noble honesty of himself. He returned the pistol to its case and packed it and his rifle in a large navy duffle bag, worn and unnotable. Having to ship them through always worried him, but he'd never had any trouble. Sometimes he chose to discard the last half of his round-trip ticket and rent a car to return. He preferred to keep control in his own able hands.

He wondered how the few hours in Sarajevo would conclude. Once again he was about to write the final chapter in someone else's story. Unless his thread of luck knotted. Was Peterson worth the risk? No. But privacy and freedom were. He would never live his life on the run. And he would never let them take him. If necessary, his last bullet would be for himself. Again he patted *Freund*. The dance of death had begun.

87

Lynn heard her cell phone ring and excused herself from Galen and Viktor. Blue slippers flopping, she ran upstairs to the nightstand where she'd left it. The last voice she'd heard on a phone was President Dimitrovski's. Silenced forever. She glanced at the alarm clock. Seven. The search and rescue helicopters would soon be back at work. Dread hung around her like thick fog. "Hello."

"I don't know what time the sun rises in Macedonia, Bishop Lynn. I hope I didn't call too early."

"Bubba!" She'd never been so grateful to hear that deep, reassuring voice! "Not to worry. I've been up a long time." The time difference hit her. "It's midnight there!"

"The night is young." His tone changed; enough banter. "Are you all right?"

She hesitated too long before her habitual, "Always. How are you?"

"Can you talk?"

"Yes." She closed the bedroom door, glad to be free of Viktor's eyes and ears. Bugs came to mind. Now *that* is paranoid! "Are you on a cell phone also?" she asked as a reminder of how easily their conversation could be overheard. She wished she hadn't used his name. She wouldn't do it again. "I am *so sorry* about the jewelry." Tears came to her eyes.

He quoted back what she had emailed to him: "You couldn't have prevented what happened. Don't do that to yourself."

She caught the boomerang. Grace and forgiveness. "Thank you."

"I talked to a guy who likes black horses. He wants to know if you are *sure* who stole it."

"Absolutely!"

"By the way, I learned the Cyrillic alphabet tonight. Now I could recognize the inscription, just like you did."

She wanted to ask him why that was so important. Not on a cell phone. "Good for you."

"I'd sure like to know what the design stands for."

She heard his plea. But again not on a cell phone. "When I return, we'll go to Café du Monde and have a leisurely talk. Did you hear about the President of Macedonia?"

"A little. You know how it is here. If a country isn't big or rich, it's just a minor one."

"He was not a minor man." She silently thanked Bubba for letting go of the symbol's meaning. Aloud she said, "I'm glad you phoned. I'm concerned about you."

"Maybe you should look in the mirror."

"Please hear me, Bubba. A man I have no reason to trust links you to our friend. He suspects that you have some important information and he wants it."

Bubba hesitated a couple of beats. "And if I did?"

"All I know about him for sure is that he's tough enough even unarmed to trounce four men with Uzis. He's downstairs now."

"What kind of crowd are you running with?"

Images scrolled across her mind. The sniper. The nut who planted the bomb in Schönbrunn Palace. Viktor the voyeur.

A megalomaniac who had us investigated and may be behind Elie's murder. "Pretend I'm the quarterback and listen a minute. Don't underestimate the danger."

Bubba chuckled. "You've been reading too much Tom Clancy. I can handle it."

His dismissal exasperated her. "They don't play by the rules."

"I can handle that too."

Fear was simply not in his vocabulary. "Aren't the Saints taking a break?"

"For another week. We're taking some time to put ourselves back together after Elie's . . . passing."

"Why don't you get out of New Orleans for a while to be on the safe side?"

"You're sounding like my mother. I didn't call to talk about me. I want to know about you—without a rote response."

She debated her answer and told the truth. "There have been some scary moments." His silence lasted so long she began to think they'd been cut off.

"Where are you staying?" he asked when he finally spoke again.

"In Skopje."

"Where exactly?"

She dreaded answering. "In a safe house."

"A safe house!"

"We leave for Sarajevo tomorrow morning. Maybe things will get back to normal." In Sarajevo? She almost laughed.

"It sounds like you're the one who needs to stay clear of the bad guys!"

"Good guys. Bad guys. All their uniforms look alike. I can't sort them out."

"I'm going to take your advice about getting out of New Orleans."

"That's good news!"

"Those thugs scaring you better back off. An army-of-one is on the way."

"What . . ."

"See you tomorrow in Sarajevo!"

88

LYNN DRESSED QUICKLY IN A SKIRT AND JACKET, AVOIDING FLASH AND flaunt that might separate her from others. She added a blue-green scarf that matched her eyes and headed back downstairs. Viktor and Galen were still drinking coffee. The gun was on the table. "Who called?" asked Galen.

"It was Fay, Love," she replied lightly.

Quick thinking, Lynn. Lies come easier and easier.

"She was up late," said suspicious Viktor.

"The time difference is hard for her," Lynn said truthfully.

"I talked to Mihail," said Galen. "Viktor can take us to a café to meet him for breakfast."

"I couldn't see Baby Sister trudging through the mud toward the church bells we heard last night and begging a stranger for a ride."

Lynn smiled at Viktor. "Thank you, Rooster."

But he apparently was through with that game and said abruptly, "Galen and I were talking about Elias Darwish's death and also what happened to the medal. Can you tell me more about it?"

She had no reason or desire to protect the mime/sniper/thief. Let Viktor and him do battle with each other. Just leave Bubba out of it. "The mime—the sniper—stole it."

Viktor frowned and looked at Galen. "I thought you said the sniper who shot Darwish was killed the same night."

"That's right."

"It was made to look that way," explained Lynn. "But the next morning he rode my streetcar and picked my pocket. I recognized his eyes." The scene dropped around her again. Fear rose like a river, and pent-up words washed over the sandbank of caution. "I think I saw him again in Vienna the day we arrived." She added softly, "The day Major Manetti was shot—with a single bullet like Elias Darwish." Caution warned her not to use Elie's nickname and appear close to him. She trusted the instinct.

"You didn't tell me you thought you saw him!" said an astonished Galen.

She let her eyes say it all: *You wouldn't have believed me!*

"Could you identify him?" asked Viktor, setting the briefcase on the table beside the gun. The lock clicked.

Lynn jumped and closed her eyes. Several seconds passed.

"Are you expecting a bomb?" Viktor chuckled. "Too James Bondish."

"We were too close to a planted bomb recently," said Galen. "It isn't funny."

Viktor opened the harmless briefcase and pulled out a thick file folder. "Please take a look at these photographs. They are some of the world's assassins."

"I have a couple of cell phone photos."

"*What?*" said Galen.

"I took them when he got off the streetcar, but I could only get his profile." She pulled her phone from her pocket and showed Viktor the two photos. Galen looked also. She began flipping through his stack of pictures. She'd almost reached the end when familiar cold eyes stared at her. Her hand recoiled from the photo. The folder fell to the floor.

Viktor picked it up. "I'm sorry. I didn't realize it would frighten you." He and Galen compared the small cell phone images to the profile shots.

"It's a match, Lynn!" said Galen. "I owe you an apology beyond words. Flowers at least. Maybe diamonds."

Lynn touched his hand. "Actually, Love, I preferred your version: the mime is dead, and I have a big imagination. It's far less scary."

Viktor looked at the name on the back of the photo. "Zechariah Zeller. Many a.k.a.'s. World class sniper."

Putting a name on the face made him more real, more terrifying. Lynn tried to stop trembling.

Viktor scanned the rest of the information. "You probably did see him in Vienna." He eyed Lynn and then Galen. "I want to emphasize that your lives will be in danger until I learn the Patriot's identity. And I can't do that without the information that cost Elias Darwish his life. If I don't get it, he died in vain!" He paused, the words punching Lynn like a boxer's blows.

"Stop badgering us for information," said Galen, voice steady, eyes calm. "We don't have any."

He sounded believable, thought Lynn, because that's what he believed.

Like maybe he's been manipulated by his wife, Lynn? Are you proud of that?

"You are unraveling threads in a clandestine net—threads that could end up strangling you." Viktor rose. "I'll be back with the car." He removed the slicker he'd hung on the hook last night and opened the door to a beautiful sunny day. Atonement for yesterday's storm.

Galen watched him walk toward some trees that evidently hid the car. "I don't like not knowing where we are and how to get ourselves where we need to go."

She saw no point in adding to that bottle of beetles. "My stuff is already packed, Love," she said, sitting down in the wingback chair to wait for Viktor.

Galen moved quickly and within ten minutes was dressed in khaki pants, blue shirt, and navy blazer, and was carrying the roll-aboard cases downstairs. "I think we got everything."

"Viktor hasn't returned yet, Love," she said.

"I wonder if he made up the Patriot story."

Lynn thought about it. "Maybe so. It justified his break-in at our hotel room."

"And it pressured us to help him get that information he's obsessed with."

"The call this morning was really from Bubba, not Fay. He's going to meet us tomorrow in Sarajevo."

"That's a surprise!"

"We can go see Mrs. Darwish together, first thing tomorrow afternoon."

"Do you know whether he has what Viktor wants?"

"He didn't say, but reading between the lines, I think he might."

"If he does, I wonder if he'll bring it."

"I warned him to be careful."

"But he might feel that he can keep it safe if it's with him." Galen paused, his eyes thoughtful. "I wonder how far Viktor would go to get it."

"I'm afraid to guess, Love. I'm also afraid that Bubba might just see this as a game. He may not realize what he's up against."

Do you, Lynn?

Viktor sat in the car listening carefully to the conversation picked up clearly on the bugs he'd planted downstairs during the night. So he'd been right about Broussard. He'd also been right about the Petersons being the link to finding him. Elie must have trusted him like a brother. And now Broussard was on his way to Sarajevo. Good news at last! He decided quickly on a plan, wondering himself just how far he would go to get that information.

89

General Thornburg walked amid the shattered pieces of the presidential plane that were scattered across the rocky terrain like the charred remains of the victims. So dark a deed should have eclipsed the sun, but its rays beamed down on the crash site like a spotlight on evil. The general, respectful of the death around him during his inspection, noted a small, pocket-sized notepad off to the side under the low branches of a bush. He knelt to examine it and saw the pilot's name on the front. He had used it to record flight information. In his mind the general saw the pilot keeping it handy in a shirt pocket and pulling it out to make a needed note.

He stood again, pondering the notepad's distance from the nearest remains. Why was it over here? *Uncharred.* Had the pilot been able to crawl away from the plane? Had something happened before he died that caused him to remove it from his pocket and shove it aside, hidden under the bush? Had he hoped that someone would find it later and ask this very question? Would he be alive if the village five had reached him first? The general recalled that they had reported hearing groans. He looked full circle around the crash site at the remains of the passengers. Their condition was such that even a groan would have been beyond their capabilities.

Other questions plagued him also. Why was the pilot flying so low unless the villagers were right about a damaged wing? But if so, how? The plane would have been thoroughly checked before takeoff. What caused the damage? Perhaps the real question was not *what* but *who.* And why was the wrong site given since SFOR soldiers—if that's who they really were—found the crash quickly enough to turn back the villagers? The questions themselves pointed to an answer darker than the storm clouds blamed by officials.

He trudged back toward the helicopter, heavy-hearted. "Only fifteen kilometers from Mostar, President Dimitrovski," he muttered. "You almost made it." Distressing thoughts crowded his mind like rocks crowded the terrain. He stepped carefully, watching the ground to avoid stumbling. As he passed a clump of leafless bushes, he noticed part of the aircraft's crunched blue and white tail, its red stripe and small flower visible—unblackened. He noticed something small protruding between two pieces of the wreckage. He stooped to examine it and retrieved a small checkbook-sized box. *To Father Nish from Natalia* was written across the lid in blue ink. General Thornburg picked up the box and opened it. He frowned when he saw the wad of pink euro bills. A piece of paper was on top. He unfolded it and saw the sketch of a symbol, one few people could identify. "St. Sava!" he muttered. He put the lid back on and decided to keep it. If officials found this much cash, it might distract from their investigation. President Dimitrovski deserved better. Besides, he'd heard of Father Nish. He dropped the box into the pocket of his camouflage vest.

The general had asked Awad and the translator to wait with his helicopter pilot. One person tracking up evidence at the crash site was enough. As he approached, the three men tried to hide their impatience but failed. He glanced at his watch—800 hours. He scanned this place of death for the last time and asked the pilot to radio the crash site's correct location. He turned to Awad. "The villagers will remember you. A familiar face will be helpful."

His aide nodded. "Things went well last night. Once they understood that they were safe, they were eager to tell their stories."

General Thornburg looked at the helicopter pilot. "Next stop, Huskovici."

90

THE RIDE WITH VIKTOR TO MEET MIHAIL FOR BREAKFAST WAS LIKE NONE Lynn had ever experienced. Even though the plane crash had not been officially confirmed, President Dimitrovski's death pressed upon the city. Viktor crept slowly through the traffic, weaving around the sea of pedestrians. Macedonian state radio played classical music in his honor. Mourners stood outside the Parliament Building, the largest crowds ever gathered in Skopje. People swarmed in from everywhere in the country, joining together in their sorrow. In her mind she listened again to the President's vibrant voice joyfully bursting forth in Macedonia's national anthem. Now the people would have to sing about "the new sun of liberty" without him. No, Lynn corrected herself, not without him but on his behalf. In time they will sing it zealously! But for now they gathered in silence. With tearful eyes they lit candles. Hundreds and hundreds of candles. President Dimitrovski could die, but the light of peace and hope he had planted in their hearts would live on.

Viktor let Galen and Lynn off at the café and drove on. They sat in silence at a round table for three, waiting for Pastor Mihail Maritnovski and thinking their own thoughts until Mihail arrived, his face bleak. He looked bone-weary and had aged a decade since Tuesday night. She would listen to his worries, not cast her own upon him.

They ordered breakfast, yogurt and fruit for Lynn. Mihail talked about the day's packed itinerary. The repercussions of the assumed plane crash were devastating for many reasons, and he had prepared a brief liturgy for each meeting today, should they receive the expected bad news. The time of liturgy would honor President Dimitrovski and comfort the people. The day's schedule cared for, he delved into what was really on his mind and talked about his personal feelings. Lynn and Galen simply listened, giving him a safe haven from having to be strong for others. He shared his heart, exposing his agony over the loss of his dear friend. His primary concern was ministering to the President's family, who were enduring a battering-ram kind of torture: plane crash—site found—bodies discovered—no survivors. Then the haunting reversal: no bodies—no plane—no crash site. Then he seemed to shake himself out of his worries and loss, straightening in his chair and locking away his personal grief again.

Mihail's focus shifted, and he shared his concerns for his fragile country's stability. He could not imagine the impact of the esteemed President's death. Four national leaders had accompanied him, and their deaths would compound the difficulties. He lowered his eyes, toying with his fork, his voice as gray as his mood.

"Filling the vacancies will turn into a wrestling match," he said with despair. "Sometimes the best men and women are defeated by those unbound by honesty and honor. You know how it is. My hope in the good was restored when we, the people, were able to elect Basil."

It was the first time Lynn had heard Mihail use his friend's first name.

He looked up wearily at them. "Why is it that the best often lose to the loudest, most aggressive, and least ethical persons?" His phone rang before either of them could attempt an answer.

Mihail listened for a few moments and the brief conversation ended. He slumped, no longer buoyed by the slim hope for the impossible. He looked weighted down to the breaking point by what he already knew but had hoped to be spared from facing. "It has not been announced yet," he said, the words barely forming in his throat, "but at eight o'clock this morning, the crash site was located near the village of Huskovici. The President's plane is charred by fire. There are no survivors."

91

NO INTIMIDATION. KEEPING MARSH IN MIND, GENERAL THORNBURG chanted this mantra to himself throughout his interviews with the Huskovici villagers. First he called the five men the village sent to help after the plane crash. He kept them together so they would feel more comfortable. It proved fruitful because their comments jogged each other's memories about details. Their words projected an IMAX movie on the screen of his mind. He saw their struggle through the storm to get to the victims. He heard their confusion when they were stopped by uniformed men with guns and ordered back to the village. He felt their anger when they later heard a blast and saw the smoke rising into the sky.

The smallest of the five seemed to be the leader, a wiry man, young and energetic. The general excused the others but asked him to remain. "Tell me the whole story again, Milosh. Start at the beginning. I am interested in every detail."

Milosh glanced at the translator, unsure.

"It is safe," stated the general with compelling authority.

Milosh stared out the window toward the distant treeline and spoke rapidly, getting rid of the words that might in turn get rid of the guilt he felt for being powerless to help the victims: "We picked our way toward the site."

He glanced at the general, his eyes troubled. "We tried to hurry. But the terrain is rugged, and the storm made it more difficult. We are always slowed by landmines. We have to be careful."

"Very careful," said General Thornburg as images of maimed children filled his mind. He detested landmines. "The coward's weapon!"

Milosh nodded vehement agreement. "Finally we reached the treeline. We were so close that we could hear people groan." He paused thoughtfully. "Three, I think. One sounded like a woman."

His voice caught. "When I heard their suffering, I moved toward them as fast as I could. All of us did. We came to a chasm. On the other side I could see part of a plane wing. We had to climb down and back up again to get across. All the time I could hear the groans. The terrible groans." He paused again, reliving it, as though they echoed in his mind. Perhaps they always would.

General Thornburg lived it with him.

Milosh continued. "I heard the second plane before I saw it. Its noise drowned out all the other sounds. I hoped it was a rescue plane, not a war plane. We never know about the planes." He looked away from the treeline toward the general.

"These are hard times," the general said, encouraging him as Marsh would have.

Milosh gazed once more into the distance. "A helicopter in camouflage colors flew overhead. I saw it dip to land. We kept going so we could help. Three SFOR soldiers suddenly appeared. They wore camouflage uniforms with French insignias. This is what I don't understand."

He glanced furtively at the translator and back again at the general, frowning. General Thornburg nodded encouragement.

Milosh lowered his eyes. "They aimed their guns at us. We explained that we wanted to help, but they refused to let us pass. It sounds weak . . ." He hesitated.

"Nothing you say shows weakness. It is all very important."

"I thought they might kill us."

"If you tried to advance?" asked the general.

Milosh raised his eyes and shook his head. "No. Even if we turned to go."

General Thornburg nodded. "Sometimes our inner warnings keep us alive."

"They argued among themselves. Loud. Explosive. Then one—the leader, I think—shouted at us to return to our homes. He spoke our language, but with a heavy accent. He warned us fiercely not to report anything." Milosh's lips curled into a sneer as he mimicked: "'It's a matter of national security.' *Whose* national security?" He fell silent, then shrugged. "We came back to Huskovici."

The story was over. "Are you sure that is all, Milosh?"

The younger man hesitated. Once again his eyes darted cautiously toward the translator.

"There is more?"

Milosh released a heavy sigh. "That is all that we saw. But," he looked timidly at the general. "I could not get out of my mind what had happened. Their actions made no sense. Later that day I realized something I had not noticed at the time."

The long pause tried General Thornburg's patience. He remembered Marsh's interrogation style and urged gently, "Go on, please."

"The soldiers wore French insignias but did not argue in that language."

"You speak French?"

Milosh nodded. "*Oui, monsieur.* I did not recognize the language they spoke, but it was not French."

The general's mind had been running various plots. Peacemakers make many enemies because war serves self-interests: financial ones for arms dealers and weapons manufacturers, psychological ones for bullies and the power-hungry and the arrogant, political ones for manipulative leaders who use fear to gain votes. A key question was whether President Dimitrovski's death was plotted inside or outside Macedonia. "Milosh, would you recognize the Macedonian language?"

Milosh shook his head. "I know Bosanski, of course. Serbian, Croation, French. But not Macedonian." His shoulders sank. "I am sorry."

"To speak four languages is something to be proud of," General Thornburg replied, thinking that Marsh would have said something like that. "Macedonian is only spoken by about two million people." He felt a bit of pride in himself as he saw Milosh sit up straight and lift his chin. He decided it was time to take the interview in for a landing. "I understand some of the villagers heard a blast later and saw smoke."

"All of us did. We heard it. We saw it. We smelled the smoke."

Exactly as he had feared.

"The smoke puffed into the sky like a mushroom cloud."

"Tell me again, Milosh. I want to be sure I understand. When the President's plane came over, something was wrong with the wing."

"That is correct."

"But there was no explosion when it crash-landed? No smoke at that time?"

"No explosion. No smoke."

"That came later?"

"Much later. After the soldiers sent us away." Milosh looked down at his hands, finished. He'd told the story in full, the story of what had happened that should not have happened.

General Thornburg thanked him, feeling most unthankful himself. President Dimitrovski had been killed—and not by the storm as officials claimed. Someone had deliberately taken the world a giant step toward instability. And the United States government needed to know the details. The problem was that since Marsh's death he had no trust in anyone—on either side of the pond.

92

During breakfast Lynn encouraged Mihail to spend his day with the President's family instead of accompanying them for the area church meetings. Gratefully he concurred and arranged for Andrej, a layperson from the Strumica church, to drive them and lead the brief liturgy at the meetings. Andrej was pleasant and helpful, understandably subdued on this Day of National Mourning. The outpouring of grief was as tumultuous as yesterday's storm. Hearts were heavy, and it was good to be with others.

But Lynn was distracted during the first morning meeting. She didn't know what to do about the phone call scheduled on President Dimitrovski's secure line at one o'clock. She shuddered at the insensitivity of barging in on this horrendous day. She also worried about simply not showing up. Yet, if President Benedict had scheduled the call—a big IF—her caring image precluded the coldness of expecting business to be done as usual in President Dimitrovski's office today. Lynn settled for the default decision of not deciding.

They were on their way to their second meeting when her cell phone rang. "Hello." Uncomfortable that the conversation in the car ceased, she felt cautious about words.

Look at yourself, Lynn! You don't trust a nice man like Andrej, highly regarded by Mihail. And you don't even trust Galen with the whole truth.

"Bishop Peterson?"

"Yes."

"This is President Dimitrovski's secretary."

Lynn could hear exhaustion and grief in her voice. "I remember you, Dimka."

"There are so many messages! I cannot keep up."

"This is a painful time, especially for those of you who worked so closely with him."

Silence. When she spoke again, her voice wavered. "It is very difficult."

"My prayers are with you, Dimka." She wished she could transmit her care by phone as easily as her words.

"Thank you. With God's help, I will get through it."

"Yes." Lynn's one-word affirmation said it all. She heard a voice in the background.

"Excuse me one moment, please." Muffled words sounded as though Dimka had placed her hand over the phone. "Thank you for your offer, Radmila. But I will care for these messages." There was silence except for the click of heels distancing themselves. "I am sorry, Bishop. Radmila has been here forever. She is always good about offering to help." She sighed, and Lynn wondered if this Radmila was a little too helpful. "I know you and Dr. Peterson were important to the President because he invited you for *Tursko Kafe*. He loved to do that. But only with people he . . ." her voice cracked. ". . . he valued as friends." She cleared her throat and shut down her emotions, returning to the business at hand. "A message came here for you, and I want to be sure you get it."

"How kind of you, Dimka." She caressed her name in lieu of the hug she would have offered had they been together.

"It has to do with Vini McGragor."

Lynn's breath caught. President Benedict's note to Marsh had used the codename *Vini McGragor.* Don't react, she told herself.

"It came at 8:30 this morning."

Lynn translated the time—2:30 A.M. for the President. She must have instructed someone to wake her if conclusive information was received about the plane crash.

"I remember that the message canceled a one o'clock call today. But there is also something about Friday. That's . . . tomorrow afternoon," Dimka added.

Lynn understood how grief muddles time. "Thank you, Dimka." She fought impatience to get to the point and asked gently, "What is it?"

"I have it right here."

Lynn waited for the words, registered the feel of the hard phone against her ear, noted the colors of cars in the traffic, smelled fumes from the old truck ahead, heard the sound of a horn somewhere behind. Alert. Anxious. Remembering to be on guard.

"It is brief: 'Vini McGragor will call your cell phone Friday, 1:00 P.M.'"

93

Unsettled by the phone conversation with Lynn, Bubba had slept little all night. He'd heard desperation in her voice. He volleyed pro-ball epithets for those scaring his friends. But it didn't decrease his rage. A killer tackle would be very cathartic. The bishop was a courageous woman, fearless in taking on the powerful on behalf of the powerless, and behind Galen's scholarly reserve was a quiet force emitting a sonar warning not to mess with his wife. Bubba wondered what had happened that had made Lynn afraid for them. The Petersons were his friends, and he intended to be there for them. His game plan took shape before his feet hit the floor.

He phoned his sister who, like him, rose at dawn. The best travel agent in the city, she assured him she'd take care of everything and he'd be on a flight to Sarajevo tonight. He loved New Orleans. The Big Easy meant it was easy to get what you needed, no matter how big. A smile here, a call there, sometimes a little financial gift of appreciation. This friendly way of *doin' bidness* suited him.

"I'll do it for you," said his sister. "But the *Balkans*? You've been hit one too many times!" They laughed together. They often did. He loved his sister. "Be careful, little brother."

"Not to worry." He threw on his togs and walked to the levee for his morning run. It would save time to drive, but he didn't like putting his sweat-dripping body in his shiny silver car.

After a shower and shave, he folded himself accordion style into his 'Vette and drove to the office of Boudreau Guidry Tietje, attorney-at-law. "I'm heading for Sarajevo," he told him. "I'm going to visit Mrs. Darwish. I'll probably arrive before the things you sent her."

"That's for sure—it's all still here."

As expected. "Would you like for me to take it?"

"Bubba, that would be a super blessing, like pulling a Maine lobster out of the bayou. I've been afraid those goons will come back and catch me with that stuff. And I'm even more afraid they'll catch me mailing it since I . . . left the impression it was already gone."

"How much 'stuff' is there?"

"It'll fit in a briefcase."

"How about you just getting on it? I bet you even have a spare briefcase."

"I don't know if I have time just now."

"I bet you can find it. You wouldn't want to contribute to the delinquency of a Saint—I need to answer that security question truthfully about no one giving me something I haven't seen." He added some body language that said, Boudreau Guidry Tietje, Esquire, time out is over. "Don't forget to include Mrs. Darwish's address."

On his way to his sister's office to pick up his flight packet, the full briefcase in hand, he thought about Elie's mother. He looked forward to meeting her, disappointed that he couldn't give her Elie's medal but glad he could take her the briefcase. It felt right to go there and offer his condolences in person.

As the wind blew across his shaved head while he drove the 'Vette, he made a mental list of what he needed to take. Tickets and passport. The briefcase. A few clothes. And Elie's flash drive. He didn't know anything about the gibberish on it. But he did know that he'd never go anyplace without it—and he'd never admit, under any circumstances, he had it on him.

As he pulled into a parking space in front of his sister's office, he called Cy Bill and gave him a brief rundown on his call to Lynn. "All of you are so scared for me, I decided I better go to the Balkans where it's safe."

Cy Bill offered one piece of advice: "Watch your back, bro!"

94

MIHAIL CALLED LYNN BETWEEN HER AFTERNOON SESSIONS. "HOW ARE THE meetings going?"

"Very well, Mihail. The question is how are Gonka and the children?"

"Gonka is devastated but coping." He muffled a deep sigh. "The funeral is difficult to plan. Not only must protocol be followed, but some people want to use this occasion to promote themselves. The politically ambitious are already competing to take his place." His voice notched up in anger. "As though someone *can* take his place!"

"I'm glad Gonka has you for support, Mihail. Please tell her that we have been holding her and the children in our prayers at each meeting today. Thank you for the liturgy you prepared. It has been very helpful."

"Good. Agent Nedelkovski," his voice became businesslike as though he was shifting to the purpose of his call, "asked me to give you and Galen a message. First he deeply apologizes for neglecting you."

"We understand!"

"He thought you would. He knows Andrej is driving you and is glad you are in his hands today. Andrej works for Agent Nedelkovski for special security details."

"I noticed that he seems watchful of our surroundings."

"Agent Nedelkovski said Viktor Machek offered to drive you back to the safe house and stay tonight since you have no security. Machek told him that the President had given him the location."

Another lie from Viktor—not surprising. She remembered his explanation last night: I followed your driver here. She didn't want to alarm Mihail, however. He had enough pecans to shell. She realized that he had called Viktor "Machek," the first time she'd ever heard him refer to anyone simply by the last name with no title. She read disrespect into it. Perhaps unfairly. But perhaps not. Maybe he resented Viktor's intrusion into their coffee together in the President's garden. Or didn't approve of his rude interrogation. Or didn't trust his abrupt departure after she identified the St. Sava symbol. Or maybe she was taking leaps into fantasy.

"He will come for you following the dinner meeting. He has to leave very early in the morning. Agent Nedelkovski trusted me with the safe house address, and I will take you to the airport tomorrow." Mihail paused. "Bishop Peterson, please call me at any time tonight if you become concerned. About *anything*. Whatever the time."

"Thank you, Mihail, but there is no need for worry."

"I will keep my cell phone on and nearby."

"Galen and I will continue to pray for you and the President's family."

That night in the safe house Galen fixed coffee for Lynn, Viktor, and himself, all of them bruised by grief. They kept their conversation cordial, their voices gentle. Viktor held his cup with both hands, gazing silently into it as the clock struck nine. Then he raised his eyes to Lynn. "You asked about St. Sava, and there wasn't time this morning. I will tell you the story now." His tone was reverent. "It began here in Macedonia over a thousand years ago, when the Orthodox Christians suffered from religious and political oppression. Ten young men came together to form a secret brotherhood to help them. They called it the Society of St. Sava."

"Why St. Sava?" asked Galen.

"He was their patron saint."

"Which one?" When Viktor hesitated, Lynn orated in the tone she'd learned from listening to Galen's history sketches. "The first St. Sabbas—or Sava in Slavic—was a Cappadocian who fled to Palestine in the fifth century and founded the Mar Saba monastery in a mountainous desert between Jerusalem and the Dead Sea. It's still active."

What a show-off you are, Lynn!

Undeterred by Ivy, she continued. "Seven centuries later, another St. Sava founded the Serbian Orthodox Church, promoted education, and built many churches. He was a diplomatic statesman as well as a skillful archbishop, and he wove together Serbian religion and nationalism." So, Viktor Machek, she thought smugly, don't expect lies to cut it! We're not interested in another of your tales!

"Once again I underestimated you, Baby Sister."

She didn't confess that the only other saints she knew much about were the New Orleans Saints.

"To answer your question, the Society's patron saint was the first St. Sava. The second one joined the Society before becoming a monk."

He's full of it, Lynn.

"Eventually the Orthodox Christians moved from oppressed victims to oppressing victors." He looked at her. "Power corrupts, even in the church."

"We can't disagree with that observation," Galen replied.

"St. Sava, under oath to use its power on behalf of the powerless, began assisting all persecuted Christians. Catholic and Protestant as well as Orthodox. Over the centuries, St. Sava cells have protected various religious branches from each other—different ones at different times."

St. Sava cells, Lynn. Is he talking about equal opportunity terrorism?

"During Hitler's reign, St. Sava recognized the plight of the Jews and reached out to non-Christians for the first time. More members of the brotherhood were killed helping Jews escape than in any other endeavor in its history."

Lynn strained to discredit the story. But she found nothing in his demeanor that gave her reason. No averting his eyes. No twitch. No stammer.

He deceived you on the plane, too, Lynn. Remember his Russian act?

"Since then St. Sava has aided the oppressed in all three Abrahamic faiths—Jews and Muslims as well as Christians."

"All the children of Abraham." Lynn began to wish his tale were true.

"Children that sometimes fight like jealous, malicious sibling rivals!" said Viktor.

"Like humanity," Galen commented.

"St. Sava jumps from side to side as dynamics change. For example, just as it once assisted Jews oppressed by Nazi military forces, a few decades ago it began assisting oppressed Palestinian Christians." He paused, and his eyes grew distant. "St. Sava works to transform oppressive forces and to foster reconciliation. Always behind the scenes. Always shrouded in mystery. Over the centuries St. Sava cells have scattered and are now worldwide."

Bigger is better, Lynn. Terror, terror everywhere.

"Based on the past, a future shift is predictable. Eventually St. Sava will likely assist the victimized in all world religions, not just the Abrahamic family."

"The guerillas of God," said Galen in a neutral voice.

Viktor searched his face. "The God-of-Many-Names."

Lynn felt he was inviting them to dance, viewing himself as their teacher. But she eyed his steps with skepticism. "If St. Sava is a secret society, why are you telling us all this?"

"You have put your foot in it—I think that is the American colloquialism. It is more problematic for you to make guesses about St. Sava than to know the truth."

He's seeking ambassadors, Lynn.

"There is one more thing. You mentioned guerillas of God, Galen. IMRO began with young men swearing their allegiance to it over a Bible and a gun. The members of St. Sava swear their allegiance over a Bible, nothing else. St. Sava does not engage in violence. The ancient society has concluded, from its long view of history, that change born of violence does not bring stability and security. Violence begets violence."

Galen nodded. "That's another observation I can't disagree with."

Lynn began to wonder if he was about to sign up. She recalled President Benedict's ever-present words: Start with St. Sava. How did she know about this secret organization?

Through the CIA, Lynn?

Doubtful. Will had said the CIA discounts rumors about it, considering it to be just an ancient myth. But perhaps President Benedict knew about it through the NSA. Or another secret agency buried deep in the unknown.

"You appear to be skeptical, Baby Sister."

"It's a lot to digest, Rooster." She smiled noncommittally.

"Think about Elie and the St. Sava medal so precious to him. What better recommendation could St. Sava have?"

Despite everything that had happened to spin her world backwards, she placed firm confidence in Elie's impeccable character. He would not—*could* not—participate in something connected with terrorism. Suddenly she realized that Viktor had called him *Elie*. "Are you saying you knew him?"

Silence settled heavily around them. The smell of the musty carpet drifted through the room. Bells chimed faintly in the distance. Viktor's eyes met hers, his tie picking up their copper brown. A tear threatened in the corner. He raised his brows and quickly blinked it away, regaining self-control. When he spoke, it was barely above a whisper. "I knew Elie well." Pain filled his voice. "I was his mentor in St. Sava."

PART IV
The Funeral

Friday, 11:13 A.M.

Sarajevo. City of the sacred and the secular. Home to Jews exiled from Spain, to Muslims and a hundred mosques, to Roman Catholics, Eastern Orthodox, Christian Protestants.

Sarajevo. City of slaughter and suspicion. Where fireworks that celebrated independence from Yugoslavia exploded into the red glare of warfare. Where Serb leader Slobodan Milošević enflamed ethnic and religious enmity. Where people who lived together peacefully and worked together proudly on the Olympics turned enemies to one another and now lie dead together, thousands upon thousands. Where little ones struggled with lost limbs from landmines and lost sight from shrapnel and lost parents from massacres. Where rows and rows of white tombstones rise above the white snow against a gray-white sky.

Sarejevo. City of secrets and survival.

95

AT 11:13 A.M. ON FRIDAY, GALEN AND LYNN BOARDED THE PLANE TO Sarajevo, their hearts heavy. Yesterday's National Day of Mourning for President Basil Dimitrovski was merely the beginning of the people's grief. The flight attendant held back tears with a forced smile. A somber silence replaced passengers' customary chitchat and laughter.

A montage of shadows edged Lynn's mind, the largest cast by Viktor. Last night's murmured words repeated in surround sound: I knew Elie well; I was his mentor in St. Sava. I knew Elie well; I was his mentor in St. Sava. The distinctive medal engraved with Elie's name convinced her that he had belonged to the ancient society, and his membership was enough to convince her that it was committed to good. But was Viktor actually part of it? Was he actually Elie's mentor? Did he actually want to get the man responsible for Elie's death? Or was he doing all of this to get the information he so desperately wanted? The questions played racquetball in her head.

A man in full military dress boarded the plane. Lynn glimpsed his array of medals with colorful ribbons and noted the dangling of his empty left sleeve. She winced. His eyes-down head-bent posture of shame said it all. Despite the symbols of courage that decorated his uniform, his self-esteem had been amputated with his arm. Another hero and victim of war.

He brought Lynn's war-zone memories to center stage. The curfews and long waits at checkpoints. The dusty convoys and soldiers in camouflage. The sounds of gunfire by day and bombers by night. Buildings scarred with bullet holes like an epidemic of chicken pox. Homes gutted like three-walled dollhouses awaiting furniture. Death certificates of family members posted on apartment house doors, lined up like marching cadets. The maimed and dying blown off the TV screen into the real world of human suffering. And everywhere, dead-eyed men and dull-eyed children trying to repress longings and recover from lies.

Yet no place else had shown Lynn so vividly the strength of the human spirit to engage in courageous normalcy while struggling for survival. Past images zoomed in from Sarajevo and Travnik, Zenica and Gorni Vakuf. An old woman knitting in the sunshine at a refugee collective, a rooster running loose in the rubble. Teenagers in the War Child Project gathering for a dance class. Two boys playing ping-pong at a table improvised from a slate slab balanced on concrete, a log subbing for a net. Refugee children playing tag on a small patch of ground free from debris, their laughter rising in counterpoint to the sounds of shelling.

As the plane flew northwest, Lynn thought about President Dimitrovski's flight two days ago and realized that he, too, had looked down on these green mountains and blue rivers before his plane veered toward Mostar. Galen is right, she thought. The globe is lesser without him. He helped keep us safe and hopeful. He showed us human goodness.

His death and the war-zone scenes embedded in her memory brought tears that spilled in rivulets down her cheeks. The threat of déjà vu crawled under her skin as she faced another

Balkan peace mission. Sasha came to mind, sitting legless in a Vienna hospital, a new victim in a new Balkan war. She thought of the decorated one-armed soldier seated nearby and could not begin to imagine all the violence and grief he had experienced. She wondered which moment of chaos had stolen his arm. Comparatively he was luckier than Sasha, older and still claiming both legs. But she knew too well that comparative is irrelevant in the pain of personal loss.

Galen put his hand on hers. "To quote Julian of Norwich: 'All shall be well and all shall be well, and all manner of thing shall be well.'" A heavy sigh exposed his doubts.

And echoed hers. The manner of the day about to unfold filled her with trepidation. She closed her eyes, pulling the curtains of denial over her fear. All shall be well. Perhaps in the sanctuary of my soul, she thought, but not in the rattlesnake den awaiting my stumble.

Lynn looked out the window and watched the plane kiss a puff of cloud. The beauty below belied the plight of this place, broken before and breaking again. She recognized Maglic Mountain to the south, Bosnia's highest peak. Light danced with the waves of the Miljacka River. Cherry and walnut trees hugged the sky. Sweet chestnuts and willows outlined the valley in defiance of horror. Vrelo Bosne, the river that named the country, wound haughtily at will. Nature goes her way, ignoring human games.

96

HIS STOLAC MISSION COMPLETED, GENERAL THORNBURG PLACED HIS Huskovici papers in his portfolio and scanned the makeshift investigation space before closing the door behind him. His mind, however, was still on last night's conversion call—*his* conversion. The decision to place it had been one of the most difficult he'd ever made, requiring him to break the military code he valued.

Duty had required him to report the Huskovici stories about President Dimitrovski's plane crash. His dilemma was to whom. He'd automatically followed military protocol throughout his career. But Marsh's death shook his trust. The general's conscience pelted him again. He would never be able to forgive himself for giving Marsh the order to babysit a bishop—an order that became a death warrant. The nagging possibility of a setup shook him to the core. Only State and Defense had known the major was on that plane.

When a man has a duty to perform and can't trust procedure, what does he do? He'd struggled for an answer throughout yesterday afternoon and evening. His final loyalty was to the Commander-in-Chief. It always had been. Even Marsh's death did not change that. He *must* trust the President of the United States. A woman, God help us!

It came down to whether he was willing to risk the consequences for breaking the military chain of command. Last night at 10:03 P.M. in Stolac, 4:03 P.M. in D.C., he reached for his phone and called the White House directly. Getting through to President Benedict was the immediate challenge. This was the time for intimidation and no one could best him at it! He stood with authority and went into command voice.

Ultimately, not even professional White House staff could force him to retreat, and they finally summoned President Benedict. The general smiled and recalled Ecclesiastes—at least that's where he thought it was—"a time to weep and a time to laugh." There was also a time to cultivate villagers, and a time to intimidate staffers. The latter better suited his nature.

When the President came on the line, he had difficulty leaping the gulf between a female voice and the Commander-in-Chief. He'd never before spoken to a woman with a higher rank than his. But by the time the conversation ended, she had earned her stripes—and he'd been converted.

Now, as he reflected on the call, every word recalled verbatim, he marveled at their dialogue. Yes, *dialogue.* Like the kind of conversation he and Marsh often had. When he told her about the Huskovici stories, she listened without interrupting him. When he finished, she asked pertinent questions. She exhibited no incompetence. No fear of admitting unknown areas. No confusion after an explanation was given. No misrepresentation. No pretense of superiority. No pressure toward a favored point of view. He felt ashamed of his surprise.

Instead, she'd shown respect for his authority and clearly expected him to honor hers by being honest, even when they disagreed—especially when they disagreed. He felt relieved that she was unconcerned about protocol and chain of command. She actually appreciated his coming directly to her and invited him to do so at any time, a genuine invitation since she gave him her secretary's direct line.

But what stood out to him above all else was her expression of sympathy over the loss of Marsh, and her sharing that he'd been a personal friend of hers. General Thornburg had heard in her voice the same guilt he felt over that death. He began to wonder if State's specific request for the major's assistance had originally come from her. If so, he wondered how the wrong person learned about their connection and why it had led to death.

Perhaps she was in danger also. He considered the horrific thought and found no supporting evidence. It was probably born of the fact that President Dimitrovski lay dead near Huskovici. He filed the thought under post-911 paranoia, then decided to leave the drawer open.

As he boarded the plane to depart Stolac, he realized that President Benedict had led him on a journey. It had begun with "hello" from a *woman-God-help-us*. And had ended with "goodbye" from the kind of Commander-in-Chief he'd previously only dreamed of.

97

HELLO, MOTHER."

"Adam! My Adam!" Rachel Darwish stared disbelieving at the figure standing in the hall outside her apartment door. Adam Ristich, her firstborn son! She reached out to touch him, fearing this was merely a morning version of her nightly dream. She put her arms around him, and he did not fade away. Real flesh enfolded her. She clung to him. "Here you are. After thirty-three years!" The younger son dead, the phantom son returned. Her tears dampened his tie.

Fearing he would escape and she might never see him again, she clasped his hand and brought him in, then closed the door without releasing him. She gestured him toward one of the two chairs in the small room and sat opposite him, ready to spring should he dart. Their knees almost touched, and he let her hold both of his hands. For an instant she tightened her grasp, reassuring herself of his presence. The warmth of joy spilled into the cold crevice created by Elias's death.

Her eyes feasted on Adam, home at last. He mirrored his father's looks so completely that it could have been Iliya sitting there. His face carried her back in time, down the path of youth when she met his father. Memory beheld a strong and handsome man, brave, well traveled, and ten years her senior. Though an Orthodox Christian from Macedonia, he was the guest of honor at a lavish party given by family friends of her faith. He'd helped them escape from the Nazis, and they'd moved to Jerusalem when the State of Israel was born. They had stayed in touch with him over the years, frequently inviting him to come for a visit. He finally accepted. Smitten immediately by him, she soon married Iliya Ristich. Now, joy filled her heart as she sat with Adam, their only child.

He silently scrutinized her. She looked into his eyes, disturbed by the hardness she found there, the one striking difference from his father. Taking a deep breath, she forced herself to say what had troubled her heart for three decades. "You could not forgive me for remarrying after your father died."

Adam spoke for the first time, sharply correcting her. "*Died?* Was killed, you mean. On my sixteenth birthday."

"Yes," she said softly as scenes from the past tumbled together in her mind. A member of the ancient Society of St. Sava, Iliya as a young man had repeatedly risked his life to assist Jews suffering under Hitler during the Second World War, and, years later, he'd taken those same risks to assist Palestinian Christians suffering under the Israeli Zionists. His final St. Sava mission in Bethlehem cost him his life. "Irony snaps at life with shark's teeth," she said pensively.

He lowered his eyes. "So it does." Then he looked up again; a hint of a smile played at his lips. She found his abrupt changes in expression confusing. "Your second marriage was a long time ago, Mother."

That husband also lies dead, she thought, somewhere among the masses of murdered Muslims.

"It was a long time ago. I have forgiven you for that."

"But you could not forgive me for having another son."

His silence confirmed her guess.

They had been speaking in the Macedonian of his childhood, taught him by his father. In her excitement she had forgotten to use the English she'd so carefully learned, thinking it might be more comfortable for him should he ever return. She rose and proudly spoke in the language of his adopted country, "I will prepare tea, please." She smiled when she saw the surprise on his face. Holding one of his hands, she drew him with her to the tiny kitchen, partly because she loved looking at him, partly so he wouldn't disappear. "If I had known you were coming, please, I would have cooked the foods you like." Glancing at her bare shelves, she added softly, "If possible. Many foods are scarce because of this difficult conflict."

"There is always a *difficult conflict* in the Balkans." He spat the words. "If you doubt me, look at history."

She was content with the silence that followed his outburst, content with his presence, with his watching her prepare their tea.

He broke the silence with a question. "Have you received anything that belonged to your second son since his death?"

She heard the forced casualness in his voice and answered in the English he'd chosen. "No."

"Will all of his things come to you?" His eyes probed into hers, as though this was his most important question.

"His *things*? I care nothing for them, please. I long for *him*."

"You have one son, Mother," he said, reverting to Macedonian. "The other is dead."

She sighed. "Your brother."

"*I have no brother!*"

His tone chilled her. "And no sister Milcah?"

"They are not my father's children!"

"You have never seen them."

"And I never will!"

She heard his bitterness and felt sad for him. "My Adam," she said tenderly.

They returned to their chairs, and she poured tea in his cup. Their years of separation wafted between them like the delicate scent of their tea. "My Adam," she said again. "The namesake of my father. He loved you dearly."

"And I him." His eyes softened.

"It broke his heart that you did not return home to Jerusalem after you took your father's medal to his parents in Macedonia."

"The St. Sava medal."

"You knew that's what it was?"

"Grandfather Ristich told me when I gave it to him. He showed me his own medal, identical except for the first name on the back. He told me in sworn confidence about the Society of St. Sava and urged me to join also. He hoped for three generations of family membership."

"Did you join?"

"I considered it."

"Do you know that Elias was a member?"

"That came to my attention."

She heard icy bitterness in his tone. During this mournful week she had experienced moments of wondering if Elias's participation in St. Sava had caused his death as it had her first husband's. In those moments bitterness haunted her own heart.

"I declined St. Sava for two reasons. First, my dream took me to the United States."

"Like Elias."

"I am nothing like him!"

Perhaps you should be a bit more like him, she thought, troubled by his arrogance. Immediately she felt guilty for comparing them.

"Second, St. Sava is rooted in Christianity. I appreciate the Scriptures, but I am suspicious of religions. The Abrahamic branches do nothing but fight. They obstruct justice."

"It was different when I was a child in Biram, my Adam. We all lived peacefully together as neighbors. Everyone got along. Things did not change until later, when the Zionists immigrated. After Biram was destroyed, my family moved to Jerusalem. The change broke the heart of my father. But," she felt warmed by connection, "your name honors him. He believed strongly that all three Abrahamic faiths share the same deep roots, that only the blossoms differ."

"You embody a unique bond with all three, Mother—born to Jewish parents, married to a Christian, taking a Muslim for your second husband. You are one bloom with the potential beauty of all three faiths." He spoke affectionately.

She basked in the love that flashed in his eyes. "Tell me about yourself," she said refilling their tea. "I want to hear about each year, each triumph, each hurt. I want to know all about your family. I want you to tell me stories about my grandchildren." The word came from a great distance accompanied by a lonely ache because she did not know them, had never even seen them. "I *do* have grandchildren?"

He nodded. "Two."

Her heart filled with joy.

"My daughter looks very much like you."

Pride swelled, and she thought she might burst with pleasure.

"Do you want to move to America? You could share in my life."

She hesitated.

"You know who I was, Mother, but not who I am."

His offer tempted her. Yet his land was far away, its ways strange. She felt too old to move to someplace so different. But perhaps a visit. Yes! If he invited her to stay in his home for a few weeks, she would return with him.

"What keeps you here, Mother?"

"This is the land of my memories. It is the land where I loved deeply and was deeply loved in return. Sarajevo and Jerusalem and dead Biram. They are home, Adam. No place else."

"But I am your son."

"My beloved son."

"Yet you will not move," he said with finality.

She held back a gasp at the great relief she saw in his eyes and tried to hide the pain that sliced into her soul. There would be no invitation to visit.

"I brought you a gift."

"The gift of your presence is gift enough, my Adam."

He presented her with a package that looked small in his long, slender El Greco fingers. It was wrapped in shiny paper of bright purple. Glossy gold ribbon was tied around it and looped into a bow larger than the box. "I remember that purple is your favorite color, Mother. Please wait until I've gone to open it."

"You cannot stay?"

His silence answered for him.

"At least the night?"

He lowered his eyes.

"Surely you will have lunch with me?"

"I have important business. I must be on my way. Disappointing but necessary." He handed her his business card. "This is my address."

"*This* is your name—*John Adams*?"

98

RACHEL DARWISH STARED AT HER SON'S BUSINESS CARD. *JOHN ADAMS.* No vestige of his past remained in her son, not even his birth name.

"Different but necessary. *John Adams* is patriotic," he explained. "He was the second President of the United States. *Ristich* would not serve my purposes there. I kept part of my name, however, as a reminder of Grandfather Adam. Besides, *Adams* comes toward the beginning of the alphabet, oftentimes a business advantage. People are too impatient to look through to the *R*s."

She ran her fingers across the embossed English words and stared at the impressive ecru card with a gold BarLothiun logo. It matched the elegance of his brown tailored suit and shiny brown shoes, his starched white shirt and expensive tie. "BarLothiun. I have heard of it," she said, recovering from the sudden awareness that the son who stood before her was a total stranger. "You are a man with a successful career. Far away, but successful. Your father and grandfathers would be proud of you."

When she looked up from the card, he stood at the door. "Write to me, Mother, if you change your mind about moving." With that, he was gone.

Rachel felt her soul would dissolve. His presence had catapulted her from the chasm of grief to the peak of elation. As he closed the door behind him without even a kiss, she felt herself free-falling through space. Down . . . down . . . down into a dry well of despair. She thought she had already borne all the pain she could. Now her heart broke in a new way. For what stole this beloved son from her was not his death but his life.

She hurried through the hall of the apartment building to the outer door and threw it open. "Adam! My Adam!" He drove away without looking back. She shuffled stiffly down the street after his vanishing car, waving her arms and calling his name again and again. Adam! My Adam! In her right hand she still clutched the unopened gift.

99

THE FLIGHT STEWARD WELCOMED THE PASSENGERS TO SARAJEVO'S BUTMIR Airport. Lynn deplaned and checked her watch. Twelve-fifty. Ten minutes until the one o'clock call from "Vini McGragor." Light poured in through the terminal's multi-storied glass wall, and she recalled a line from a Serbian poem: The "blind man is not hindered by eyes." Sunlight shone down like a plea to the people to *see*, to reject the blindness that allows the darkness of revenge to fester and explode.

She and Galen found a waiting area and began to watch for Bubba's plane. A nearby TV announced a Mostar press conference about President Dimitrovski's plane crash. Chatter ceased. Surprised, Lynn noticed the man who'd sat across the aisle from Galen on the plane Tuesday night, reminding her of a crouched tiger eager to pounce. "Love, isn't he the one who carried on a long conversation with you on the plane to Skopje?"

"You have a good memory. He's Frank Fillmore."

She also remembered that he had been near them in the security line—El Toro on his arm. Now he emanated an air of invisibility, his gray suit and gray tie fading into the gray seat. He appeared too deeply engrossed in the press conference to notice them, and she decided to ignore him. Perhaps it was mutual.

The Macedonian and Bosnian officials involved in the press conference reiterated that the bodies of the President and eight others had been found. That was the tasteful and respectful place to stop, but they went on to report painful details about one body being carbonized, another unburnt, and five bodies found in parts. Sickened, she turned away and looked at Galen. "A beloved President's death is bad news enough. We don't need vivid gore."

"Neither do the victims' loved ones." he replied.

When asked about the cause, the officials somberly blamed the weather. Sabotage clawed at her grief. Her cell phone rang. She glanced at her watch. Precisely one o'clock. "Hello," she said with forced calm, donning her mask.

A woman spoke. "Names are unwise."

Lynn recognized the voice, stunned by actually hearing the President of the United States speaking to her, even though she'd expected the call. She must guard her words on her unsecure cell phone. The President was taking a risk.

"There are still troublesome events on the ranch and beyond."

The ranch image written to Marsh! Lynn retained her mask and casual tone. "I know."

"I will attend my colleague's funeral."

Lynn was sure she meant President Dimitrovski.

"Please be there."

"Yes . . ." Lynn stifled the spontaneous "Madam President" and concentrated on posed nonchalance. The connection went dead. She did not know when the funeral would be or how they would get there. What she did know was that *nothing* could keep her from attending.

She felt that all-too-familiar sense of being watched and caught the gaze of a man who wore an air of timidity that contrasted with his well-tailored brown suit. He quickly averted his eyes. His face seemed vaguely familiar. Perhaps he was someone she knew distantly, maybe through the media. A celebrity or a politician. She thought of John Adams, but he radiated confidence. Besides, this man had gray hair and wore glasses, and a goatee dominated his face. He stood within earshot, a pasted smile on his face. Something about him raised her yellow flag.

"OK, Fay," Lynn said lightly into the dead phone for the benefit of any eavesdropper, especially the one with the pasted-on smile. "Thank you for letting me know." She remembered the time difference. A flat earth with a stationary sun would make life simpler for fakers. "Yes, this is a good time to reach us, but awfully early for you . . . Not to worry. We are doing fine." She punched *End*, withholding a sigh of relief. Trusting her yellow flag, she angled the phone's camera lens discreetly toward Pasted-on-Smile as she returned it to Big-Black and thumbed *Camera/Capture/Save* without looking. Not even Galen noticed.

Are you building a rogue's gallery, Lynn?

"What did Fay call about?" asked Galen.

"It was just some information for me, Love. I can take care of it later."

Congratulations, Lynn! You've mastered the primary skill of politics: manipulate perception through distorting the truth without actually lying.

And that's the good guys, Lynn thought. The others flat-out lie without blinking an eye—practiced, persuasive, and unperturbed.

An alliterative tirade, Lynn. But this is not the time.

She puzzled over Pasted-on-Smile's identity but still couldn't place him.

"Hey there!" a James Earl Jones voice shouted above the airport noise. Bubba raced a crooked path through the crowd toward them.

She rushed to meet him. "It's great to see you!" She and Galen didn't have time for many friendships, but the ones they had were deep and lasting—the kind where you'll always be there for one another. He lifted her from the floor in a line-backer hug that made her think of the movie *The Blind Side*—Bubba had her back. She grinned, hoping Pasted-on-Smile saw them but he had disappeared. So had Frank Fillmore.

They made their way to the exit and stood in the long taxi line outside. The Sarajevo itinerary didn't begin until six o'clock. First things first: Mrs. Darwish. Lynn both looked forward to seeing her this afternoon and dreaded it, smothered by the heavy pall of death. As they climbed into a taxi, she saw Frank Fillmore still waiting in line. Strange, she thought, he left before we did.

100

ZECHARIAH ZELLER HAD SPENT THE PREVIOUS HOUR HUNCHED INVISIBLY ON a bar stool, his sunglasses hiding his focus. As his beer stein emptied and his cigarette smoke rose, he viewed the passengers through the wall mirror facing the counter. So easy.

One man had been waiting at the airport for half an hour, noticeable for the very reason that he was nondescript. Zeller had watched him amble along apparently without purpose, wearing an unnotable gray suit and gray tie, skilled at appearing invisible. Too skilled. He dubbed him *Herr Invisible*—a man trained by the CIA or another nation's counterpart. He'd bet on it.

Another man had hurried into the airport about fifteen minutes later, then tried to blend in with the crowd. It didn't work. He'd evidently pocketed his tie and unbuttoned his shirt collar, but his perfectly tailored brown suit and shined leather shoes stood out. Something about him seemed familiar, but Zeller couldn't zero in on what it was. The painted-on smile reminded him of a politician. He observed that his eyes returned to *Herr Invisible* too often for coincidence.

Zeller noticed that his flight of interest had landed and began to watch its passengers stream by. A one-armed, medal-decorated soldier rushed by, leaving Zeller with the uncomfortable reminder of vulnerability. Losing an arm would end his career. But he wouldn't let that happen. No.

When he recognized Galen Lincoln Peterson, his trigger finger itched. The target kept Frau Peterson by his side as he hurried to the TV set. For a man playing dual roles, survival could depend on current information. Yet Peterson puzzled him. He did not appear cautious or take in his surroundings with a sweeping look or seem unduly aware of the people around him. Zeller found himself wondering if the Petersons' pattern of showing up in his life could be coincidental. A dangerous thought. He must not underestimate his opponent. No. Peterson was a skillful operative who used his pretty wife for his cover and sometimes dragged her into dangerous realms. Zeller tasted disgust and wanted to spit.

Through his mirror on the world he glanced again at the man in the brown suit. He seemed part of a familiar tableau but unrecognizable. Like the Patriot. The thought jolted him. It couldn't be. No. The Patriot emanated authority. As he observed the situation, he realized the man was covertly watching the Petersons, a frozen smile on his face. This game of espionage was proving more interesting than Zeller had expected. It crossed his mind that this man might also be after Peterson. Have at it, he thought. Save me the trouble.

Zeller saw Frau Peterson answer her cell phone. He noted a stunned nanosecond on her face. A glance at the man in the brown suit told him that he had noticed it also and was casually moving closer to her. Probably to get within hearing distance. Frau Peterson's total concentration belied her casual expression. Suddenly her demeanor lightened. Something about that call didn't ring true. No.

Zeller watched in the bar mirror as the man in the suit exited the terminal, still visible through the glass wall. He frowned. Why come to a terminal, wait around, and then leave without flying or meeting someone? He watched him punch in numbers on his cell phone, then step around the corner away from the front wall of glass. Simultaneously Zeller noticed Herr Invisible flip up the cover of his cell to receive a call. But logic fell on the side of coincidental separate calls rather than a connected one.

The loud arrival of Broussard from New Orleans brought another taste of disgust. The oversized brute had been a nuisance from the beginning, complicating things by taking Darwish's medal in the first place and then giving it to Frau Peterson at the café. Broussard was to blame for the whole thing—including the necessity for retrieval on the St. Charles streetcar. Obviously the man couldn't leave Frau Peterson alone. He shouldn't hoist her into the air, but she was too small to stop him and probably too kind to reprimand him. Or perhaps she was afraid of him. His frown deepened. His trigger finger twitched. But she did not appear afraid. No.

When the Petersons and Broussard started toward the door, Zeller faded unnoticed into the crowd. He retrieved his rental car and moved his navy duffle bag from the trunk to the front seat for ready access to his rifle, still disassembled. He maneuvered the car close enough to see the Peterson-Broussard taxi, confident that they were unaware of his presence. So easy. He gave the duffle bag a fond pat. "Ah, *Freund*, I will enjoy the challenge of the chase."

101

Frank Fillmore stood unhurried in the car rental line at the airport. His eyes had locked with Lynn Peterson's as her cab drove away. Whither thou goest, I will go, lady! On the plane to Skopje three days ago he'd learned a lot about her husband, a regular man despite being married to a bishop. He'd also observed her out of curiosity. An alert woman. But a dangerous one? Preposterous! Yet a contract was a contract. The target didn't matter.

The entire scenario of the Patriot's directive irritated him. First, the last-minute information ran contrary to his best interests and also the Patriot's usual insistence on thoroughness. He didn't even know the target's name until half an hour ago! There wasn't time to plan the place. He'd had to bribe a taxi driver to maneuver into position to pick up the target and stick with her, keeping him informed of the troublesome trio's plans by cell phone.

Second, the choice of weapon irked him. A gun instead of a bomb. With a bomb you set it up and get out of there! You have to stick around when you use a gun.

Third, the directive itself puzzled him. Always before the Patriot had avoided knowledge of details about implementation. Only the bottom line interested him: do not fail! But in today's directive he'd insisted on knowing in advance the site chosen for execution. He had no interest in working for a micromanager. Yet the Patriot paid top dollar.

Fourth, his major irritation stemmed from debasement. The target is beneath me, he thought. Lynn Peterson is unworthy of execution by Frank Fillmore, the man who brought down the plane of the President of Macedonia! The memory of the sabotage and its success kicked into his system like straight bourbon from a flask. He gloated over an impossible challenge well handled: Everything was done perfectly. Clever Frank Fillmore found a way to get on the plane and plant the small device under the seat nearest to the right wing. Then brilliantly got off the plane without suspicion, simply by retching in front of the President. Better to retch than to bow. Frank Fillmore bows to no one!

Irritated or not, he would obey the Lynn Peterson directive. The Patriot had tightened his leash with the words: You have been busy with a weighty matter. How did he know about the bomb on Dimitrovski's plane? Or who had placed it there? Simple. The Patriot knew everything.

Fillmore accepted the keys and a map of Sarajevo from the car rental agent. He slipped into the driver's seat and paused to familiarize himself with the streets of the city. When the taxi driver phoned, he'd be prepared. "Enjoy yourself, lady," he muttered beneath his breath. "It's your last meal before your execution."

102

THE TAXI DRIVER GLANCED AT BROUSSARD BESIDE HIM AND AT THE PETERSONS through the rearview mirror. "Are you hungry? I know a good café on the way to your hotel. If I tell him you are my friends, he will not overcharge you." He chuckled.

"Sounds good to me," said Bubba. "I left New Orleans a long time ago."

Galen and Bubba talked to the jovial driver on the way to the café, but Lynn paid little attention. She was more interested in President Benedict's few words on the phone. She felt relief, freed from guesses—the President had indeed written the message for Marsh and the Vice President could be trusted. Lynn didn't have time this afternoon, as usual, to tell Galen the whole story. But she would tonight. Her heaviness lightened as she anticipated release. The Vice President's voice echoed from the limo: Totally confidential. Sorry, sir, but it's time to bring Galen inside that wall. Way past time.

The driver stopped in front of a charming sidewalk café with blue and green plaid tablecloths and matching chair cushions. It was not a fancy place, but the aroma erased any doubt about good food. Nature's thermostat was set perfectly for eating outdoors. The driver introduced them to the owner. "He does not speak English. Trust him to decide for you. He will serve you well."

"Thank you," said Lynn to both of them.

"Enjoy your lunch. I will come back and take you to your hotel."

As he pulled away, Galen grinned. "Our driver didn't want to risk losing us—or at least our tip."

The café radio, tuned to RTVBH, was playing the old recording of "Miss Sarajevo" sung by Luciano Pavarotti and a local group for a war benefit. The last line always chilled Lynn, knowing that it dealt with war: "And the night is set to freeze." A copy of the popular Sarajevo daily newspaper *Oslobodjenje*, meaning "liberation," had been left on the table. They couldn't read it, but the war pictures didn't need words. The people around them spoke Bosanski and wore the shallow smiles of war, giving each other hopeless hope, knowing from experience something humanity has always known by instinct: if hope is forgotten, a bit more human goodness dies and all is truly hopeless.

"You look deep in thought, Bishop Lynn," said Bubba. "Are you OK?"

A sigh rose from the depths of her soul. "The phrase *religious war* is an oxymoron of the unreligious. The faithful mourn war as a contradiction of faith."

"Not always," corrected Galen. "I gave an address on Bonhoeffer's criteria for discernment. There are just wars."

"Not nearly as many as national leaders claim," Bubba countered with a heaviness contrary to his usual good nature.

Galen paused a thoughtful moment. "Unfortunately, that's true."

"Because the Bush administration chose to invade Iraq, my best friend from college is a paraplegic and my cousin is numbered among the thousands of Americans killed. Our soldiers deserve leaders who don't use the word *threat* for a sneak play." He paused, and when he spoke again an uncustomary cynicism edged his words. "But they're expendable, generally 'just' minorities and the poor—rarely the sons and daughters of those who run the country. It's OK to put them in harm's way."

"You are right," agreed a man at the next table, surprising them that he spoke English. He nodded respectfully to Bubba. "Leaders of nations decide to go to war. But it is the young soldiers in the nations who do the going and the dying and the living without limbs. This is true in all nations."

Bubba's chagrined expression said he hadn't expected to be understood by someone outside the U.S. For Louisianans, the Eleventh Commandment forbids talking bad about the family—immediate or national—to anyone outside that family.

"Is this your first time here?" the man asked.

Bubba nodded.

"If you drive to the Appel Quay, you will see where Archduke Ferdinand was shot. That shot started the First World War. Was that war just?" He shrugged. "The answer depends upon your view. That is the problem with war. But the result of war is clear. You can see it by looking across the street." He pointed to the BiH Center for the Blind, a War Child Project.

At that moment their Balkan Peace Mission took on life for Lynn. She would give it her very best, nothing held back.

The owner chose well from his war-limited menu. They tasted food they didn't know how to pronounce and enjoyed every bite. The driver was right—the food was delicious and they were not overcharged. He returned as promised and reloaded their roll-aboards. As he pulled away from the café,

Lynn noticed a small black car parked up the street. Someone in sunglasses sat behind the wheel. She thought of the man on the streetcar—and remembered she knew his name. Zechariah Zeller.

Every stranger in sunglasses reminds you of him, Lynn.

103

JOHN ADAMS DROVE AWAY FROM THE SARAJEVO AIRPORT IN A NONDE-script gray rental car. He would not—could not—go back to his mother's apartment. Returning here was a mistake. It made him feel like Adam Ristich again. He shook free of that persona buried long ago. One certainty in his life was that he wanted nothing to do with his past. The simple clunk of his teacup against her table, so different from the clink of a fine china cup against a saucer, had sent that certainty throbbing through his veins. He could not—would not—go back to clunks. They symbolized poverty and powerlessness.

Maintaining power was tricky. Perception played a primary role. The public empowered a man they perceived as powerful—generally based on charisma, wealth, authority, or the damaging information he possessed. But when the fickle public perceived a man's power to be waning, they cast him aside and soon forgot him. He had not clawed his way to power and prestige merely to be cast aside and forgotten at the whim of the POTUS. How he resented her capacity to affect others' perception of his power! Never again would he wade through the crumpled wrappings of those born to privilege! That would play into a system of injustice and defy his righteous calling.

From deep inside came a whisper of fear that it might also compel him to replace clinks with clunks.

He thought about his grandfather Adam who had loved him with all his heart. The memory drew him to a synagogue. He wanted a quiet place to reflect on the scene with his mother. Being in her small apartment had troubled him. Sensing that she could see beyond his facade had troubled him. Giving her Elias's medal had troubled him. Leaving his business card had troubled him. He had planned to find out subtly if his mother had Darwish's information about him, do his duty by giving her the medal, and be on his way unscathed. The cursed medal had driven him to return and now could destroy him. Even in death Elias Darwish held power over him.

As he found a place to park in front of the synagogue, his thoughts turned to the Petersons. He had watched them at the airport, recognizing the bishop from the pictures in the file Lone Star had prepared for him. When he saw her answer her cell, he'd taken a logical leap. It all fit. One, Radmila had said that President Benedict had arranged a phone appointment today with President Dimitrovski that included Bishop Peterson. His death had changed the venue. Two, the time was right for President Benedict to be taking a morning walk at the Lincoln Memorial, probably with her cell phone. Three, Lynn Peterson seemed to be expecting a call and appeared somewhat anxious about it—looking at her watch frequently, holding the phone in her hand. Four, her endeavor to cover being awestricken when she answered—a typical reaction of the common person to hearing the voice of the President of the United States. And five, her concentration and then sudden relaxed manner when she started using the name *Fay*, probably speaking into a disconnected phone. A secure call to Lone Star had confirmed his suspicions: at seven this morning his elite was sure he'd seen President Benedict's lips move during her walk—one o'clock in Sarajevo, exactly when Lynn Peterson answered her cell. He had no proof. It galled him that he still had no access to the phone the President used. But he had Lone Star and he had instinct. His logic held, and he found Lynn Peterson as guilty as Manetti, and gave her the same sentence. The Patriot commended himself for his foresight in summoning Fillmore to Sarajevo. Grievous but necessary.

At the airport, when he'd stepped around the corner to call Fillmore as planned and state the directive, he'd immensely enjoyed duping him. The arrogant man had assumed he was speaking to someone far away instead of his reactions being visible. The instructions were twofold: First, he told him to call back when he chose the site for termination. Second, he named the target, Lynn Peterson, and told him she was at the Sarajevo airport at that moment and therefore easy to follow.

But it wasn't easy to order termination. He reminded himself that the bishop was responsible for this directive, not himself. By becoming a conduit for the President, she was writing graffiti on the canvas that painted his dream for justice. God-ordained justice! Zero tolerance!

104

"Do you have other places to go today?" the jovial taxi driver asked while driving the New Orleans trio to their hotel.

"After we check in, we want to go here," said Bubba. He handed him Mrs. Darwish's name and address.

The driver looked at it carefully and nodded. "I can wait for you at the hotel and then take you there," he offered with a helpful smile. They appreciatively agreed. While he waited, the trio checked in and found their rooms.

Bubba cleaned up after his long flight. Galen changed his shirt to a blue button-down and gave his black shoes a quick buff. Lynn removed Bubba's five hundred dollars from her waist wallet and put the money in the note he had written. It pleased her that he could personally give it to Mrs. Darwish. The medal's absence faded her pleasure. More than that—it made her heart hurt.

They met in the lobby and climbed back into the taxi. Lynn noticed that the driver seemed distracted as they drove to Mrs. Darwish's apartment. He was less jovial. Perhaps they had kept him waiting too long. She knew Galen's tip would make up for that inconvenience. The driver's tension grew as they drew closer. He rubbed his palm across the nape of his neck repeatedly like a nervous tic. Not only had he lost his friendly chuckle, he'd become mute. When they reached Mrs. Darwish's street, he seemed jumpy. She glanced at his face, visible in the rearview mirror. He looked strained and stared straight down the road, frowning. His tension evoked her sense of wariness.

They stopped in front of the apartment building, and Galen paid him. "Can you return to take us back to the hotel?"

He shook his head no and looked at the generous tip without a smile. "Too much."

Galen insisted. "You have been very helpful."

He glanced up, not quite meeting Galen's eyes. "Be careful, sir." His tone sounded more like a warning than a friendly parting.

Things are not always what they appear to be. President Dimitrovski's words to her in his last phone call rang so clearly in her ears that she jumped, half expecting to see him nearby. She could not disregard the impact, like an omen. She reminded herself that she wasn't superstitious and banished it as a figment of her overactive imagination. Yet as she walked down the cracked sidewalk, she scanned her surroundings—the walls and shrubbery, the apartment buildings, the old bullet-riddled museum across the street that was just one more war-damaged structure closed to the public. She knew that assumptions and expectations limit observations, like missing a moon in the morning sky. *What am I not seeing?* she wondered. *What am I seeing that isn't really here?* Caution seized her as she moved along toward the green door of Mrs. Darwish's apartment building.

105

FRANK FILLMORE STOOD ACROSS THE STREET IN THE SECOND-STORY WINDOW of a museum still closed due to damage from the last war. He saw the taxi arrive in front of the apartment building and watched the passengers get out. He considered padding his expenses for bribing the driver, who'd earned every euro—maneuvering to pick them up, continuing to drive them, keeping him updated, and giving him the address of their afternoon destination. The advance warning gave him time to get here, locate the Darwish apartment windows, and find the best site for execution. It did not, however, allow adequate time to prepare. Successful execution required perfection. His vantage point offered him a telescopic view of the apartment window below as well as the green doorway that provided the entry/exit to the building. He watched the target walk with a self-assured air toward the green door and safely through it. Coming out would be another matter.

He'd called the Patriot as requested to notify him of the site of execution. There had been a momentary silence followed by three words: No collateral damage. Generally, the Patriot cared about success and footnoted the rest. Fillmore felt choked by the leash. He'd expected to be in South America by now, spending the bundle he'd made on the bomb deal. Remaining in the vicinity of a presidential assassination verged on suicide! He should be tucked safely away on another hemisphere in a hacienda well stocked with senoritas. Not here kowtowing to the Patriot, he thought. Frank Fillmore doesn't kowtow!

As he waited for the moment to take out the target, he reflected again on the sabotage of President Dimitrovski's plane. It should have gone down in a dive, killing them all on impact. Instead, the remarkably skilled pilot had almost made it to Mostar. He found himself wishing he had. He admired the pilot. And if the passengers were injured but alive, let them live! He had his pay. That's what mattered. He was willing to kill the President. That was his job. But he respected the man far more than the radical opposition who'd contracted him. He resented their hasty, ill-conceived follow-up plan. It was too sloppy. Too risky. It involved too many people. Besides, he'd always felt that if a target survived, fate was involved—he was too good at his job.

He'd been involved in toppling government leaders before, but not anyone like President Dimitrovski. He'd done more for peace than anyone else in Europe. Or Asia, for that matter. But peace itself was an enemy of radicals on both the left and the right. They couldn't fire up their base without an enemy to hate. And hate put lucrative contracts in the hands of operatives like himself. Conscience was a failing.

He stood at the window, alert, poised for his task. But his vision blurred, and a white and blue plane with a Macedonian coat-of-arms shattered across his mind. He shook off the image and looked through his scope into Mrs. Darwish's apartment window.

106

ZELLER'S HABITUAL PATIENCE WORE THIN AS HE FOLLOWED THE TAXI. BUT HE liked turning the tables on Peterson, stalking the stalker. He'd waited for the trio, first near a café and then near a hotel, glad it was a clear day and easy to keep their taxi in view from a safe distance. When they came out of the hotel and climbed back in, he took up the game again. The taxi stopped at an apartment building and let them out. Zeller drove on, turning right at the corner. He was ready for action, and the weather was perfect—plenty of sunlight and no wind. This neighborhood offered a strategic setting with few people on the streets. The windows had eyes, but their owners wouldn't talk. No. They were afraid to get involved. Besides, they were accustomed to gunfire and death. War helped aces. It desensitized people to violence.

He parallel parked skillfully in a too-small space. Casually, he carried his navy duffle bag down the street, just a harmless Austrian nephew from rural Tirol looking for his dear old aunt's address—should anyone ask. As he approached the intersection where he'd turned off to park the car, he noticed that a museum stood directly across from the apartment building. He ambled to the corner, scanning the museum for advantages and flaws. It looked vacant and rundown, pocked with old shellings from the last war. A good place to do business. The second story would be perfect. He searched for the best window. Wait! He caught a glint in an open one. He bent down and retied one of his running shoes to check it out. His opaque sunglasses hid his focus. Again, the sunlight glinted on metal. He got a nanosecond's glimpse of a furtive figure. Interesting. The window did indeed have eyes.

The museum would not do. No. Behind his sunglasses he scanned both sides of the street for a place with simple access and effortless escape. He decided the situation called for a triangle: himself and the other two points of interest—the apartment house door and the second-story museum window, both within range. He spotted an ideal building closed for repairs. No trees blocked his view. He rose from tying his shoe and moseyed down the street. So easy.

After snapping the cheap lock with a single blow that made a dull thud, he took the dank, scuffed stairs to the room with the best view of the other two points in the triangle. He popped his flash drive into his laptop and pulled up the Sarajevo research he'd downloaded in Vienna. A search for the apartment building revealed the list of tenants at that address. One was a woman named Rachel *Darwish*! Peterson was not innocent! No! He had just connected another Zeller dot—his final and fatal mistake!

Zechariah Zeller had no regard for a man who flaunted faith without practicing it. But Peterson was a new breed of pretender. He'd mastered the role of trailing dutifully and innocently after his wife while harboring unsuspected lethal plans of his own. Zeller had some ideas about the place of religion, and they did not include a higher power interested in his well-being. My own power, he thought smugly, is as good as it gets. Immediately he tempered his attitude. Confidence was a good thing; it freed his body, mind, and psyche for the task. But overconfidence was like a light that blinded. It could result in carelessness to details. Besides, he did not want to tempt any god that might exist to go against him.

He assembled his rifle and, curious about the glint he'd seen in the window, he looked toward it through his scope. Startled, he discovered a sniper rifle resting on a bipod, aimed toward the apartment building. Another shooter on the scene! Interesting. Probably fulfilling a contract. Who's the contractor? Who's the target?

As he continued his detailed preparations, he considered a silencer. He'd used one for Darwish and an altered one for Manetti. Today he dispensed with a silencer. He wanted the noise to throw people into panic and keep them hiding behind their blinds, assisting in an unseen escape. His excitement mounted like electricity building into a lightning bolt. He no longer minded that this was pro bono. The challenge itself was the reward.

Say your prayers and confess your sins, Galen Peterson. You are about to meet the god you've been pretending to know.

107

A GRAY-HAIRED WOMAN, HER TWO BRAIDS TWISTED INTO A BUN, OPENED the apartment door without hesitation. Her eyes were red and swollen.

"Mrs. Darwish?" asked Galen.

She nodded.

Lynn remembered her own eyes after Lyndie's death and knew that for Elie's mother the days were endless nightmares. Longing to reverse his death. To give her own life instead. Wondering how and why to go on living. There were moments when Lynn still wondered.

Galen introduced each of them by pointing and saying their names.

"Bubba Broussard," she repeated, smiling for the first time.

"English?" he asked.

"A little, please," she said modestly. "My sons moved to America. My big surprise for them." Under her breath she added, "Foolish."

"Not foolish at all, ma'am," said Bubba. "Elie appreciated it. He spoke of you often with great love and respect."

"Thank you." The heaviness of grief dulled her voice.

"We are his friends." He circled his hand to include Galen and Lynn.

"Yes, please. His letters name you, Bubba Broussard."

She invited them in, and they moved from the institutional green of the corridor to the institutional green of her three-room apartment. The south-facing windows brightened the small living room. Lynn noted the yellow flowers out her front window, dots of hope offered in the midst of despair. Neat and sparsely furnished, the living area took up the front half of the apartment. The back half was divided. The open door on the east side revealed a little kitchen with a table for two. She assumed the other room with the closed door was her bedroom.

Mrs. Darwish gestured to the two chairs. "Sit, please. I will bring more chairs." She started into the kitchen.

"I'll get them," said Galen, ever the gentleman.

Huge and sensitive Bubba followed him, eyes down, stooped by the weight of Elie's mother's incomparable pain added to his own.

"Tea, please?"

"No, thank you," said Galen, habitually prone to avoid inconveniencing anyone.

"Yes, please," Lynn said, knowing that all of them would feel more comfortable if their hands had something to hold.

Mrs. Darwish looked at Lynn and nodded with mutual understanding.

While Galen and Bubba shaped a square by adding the two wooden chairs across from the other pair, Lynn offered to help her hostess with tea. As they started toward the kitchen, Lynn noticed a small wall shelf displaying three pictures. She glimpsed the old photograph of a teenage boy and the newer one of a girl. But it was the one of Elie that caused her throat to catch. He smiled proudly in his Saints uniform. She paused. "I am so sorry, Mrs. Darwish."

"Yes."

The single syllable emitted an agony that Lynn understood. She shared softly, "I lost a child also. My daughter."

Elie's mother looked from the picture to Lynn, that terrible hurt in her eyes. Simultaneously, they put their arms around each other in the universal embrace of mothers who know what it is to lose what is most precious.

In time her trembling ceased. She straightened, gold-bar rigid, and backed up a step. Her gaze aimed toward the apartment door as though someone lingered there. After a moment she looked away. "I am sorry, please," she mumbled with a heavy sigh. "I lost both my sons, only one of them through death."

As Mrs. Darwish busied herself making tea, absorbed in her thoughts, Lynn stood nearby quite comfortable with their silence together. The space between them was filled with mutual understanding that didn't need words. But Lynn was terribly uncomfortable about the apology she must make regarding Elie's medal. Not now, she decided, putting it off. Tea first. They carried the steaming cups and joined the men sitting across from each other. Lynn sat beside Galen, Mrs. Darwish across from her beside Bubba. A briefcase stood between them. Bubba gestured toward it. "These things were Elie's. They are mementos of honor and important papers."

"I will see them later, please."

Lynn marveled at Bubba's gentleness and tenderness toward this woman he had never seen before. He was caring for her as if she was his own mother.

"Do you have someone to help you with the papers?" he asked.

"Vikolaj, my son-in-law. I practice English with him."

Bubba smiled the relief that Lynn felt, glad Mrs. Darwish had someone close. "I wrote you a letter." He placed the envelope containing his note and money on top of the white crocheted doily decorating a small table beside his chair. "You can read it later also."

But he can't give her the medal, thought Lynn. I didn't protect it. Time to begin the dreaded confession and apology. "Bubba did not know that he would be able to come here to see you. He asked me to bring you something else that was very important to Elie."

"It was lost from Lynn's pocket," Galen interrupted gently. She realized that he was being kind, not obstinate. There was no need to risk upsetting Mrs. Darwish by saying it was stolen.

Elie's mother frowned. "Lost, please?"

"Bishop Lynn couldn't help it," Bubba said with grace.

I should have helped it, Lynn thought. Somehow. "I am very, very sorry. We wanted so much for you to have Elie's medal."

"His medal, please?" Mrs. Darwish smiled.

Surprised, Lynn wondered how she could smile about the memento's loss. Evidently she didn't understand. "He wore it around his neck," she explained, demonstrating with her fingers and feeling terrible. "His name was on the back."

Mrs. Darwish rose, and they watched her walk stiffly to the kitchen table. She picked up a small box that stood on shiny purple paper, a glossy gold bow beside it. She carried it with both hands, pressing it to her heart. When she sat down with them again, she brushed her hand across the box in a gentle caress, as though absorbing the touch of the one who had touched it before her. She slowly removed the lid. With the reverence of a Catholic for a rosary, she took out something shiny and laid it tenderly on her palm. Still smiling, she held out her open hand. Two amazonite crescent moons overlapped vertically in the center of a silver circle. "You see, please? Elias's medal."

108

WHEN FILLMORE REPORTED IN AS DIRECTED, THE PATRIOT BARELY RESTRAINED hurling his cell phone across the synagogue. He learned that the elite had the target's destination, courtesy of the taxi driver, and was across the street within clear range. The information spewed hot lava into the tranquil synagogue. It was the address that slammed his world off its axis. His mother's apartment! Oh, Jahweh-Christ-Allah! Lynn Peterson had access to his mother! His *mother*, who knew too much and was not sophisticated enough to discern when to lie! This visit to his mother eradicated any remaining doubt about justification for killing this wayward bishop.

No collateral damage, he commanded and punched *End*. Fillmore would assume it was a cell phone malfunction and go back to his waiting. And now the Patriot must also wait, filled with trepidation until he received word that his nemesis, Lynn Peterson, was dead.

He rose and paced irately down the aisle, hands behind his back. The medal and his business card lurked in his mother's apartment, ready to expose him. Leaving his card had been a childish gesture of sibling rivalry. See how successful I am, Mother. She might even show it to these guests from America, a proud parent bragging about her son. One little visit could wipe out all his years of meticulous planning and progress for the sake of righteous justice. All put in jeopardy if Lynn Peterson saw Elias's medal and connected it to his shooter and his mother told her it was a gift from her son and showed her his business card. All he'd done—even the termination of his mother's other son—could prove pointless. All lost because of his compassion for his mother, a compassion that had impeded his logic.

He hated St. Sava with a passion that set his soul aflame. The ancient society had caused the problem originally with their present to him on his sixteenth birthday—the death of his father. The nightmare lingered even after all these years. His father's death cried out for the dimension of justice he valued most: vindictive retribution. He held no vendetta against the Israelis who committed the act, but against St. Sava for assigning his father to help the Christian Palestinians, an assignment that cost him his life.

St. Sava had also caused today's problem: assigning Elias Darwish to discover the Patriot's identity. The kicker should never have been born. His birth had always been a thorn in the Patriot's flesh. He faulted him on two counts: being born and committing suicide by joining St. Sava. He doubted that Darwish had any idea he was tracking his mother's son. "Irony gnaws at life with shark's teeth," she had said. His mother was wise. He had to give her that. What would Darwish have done when he put the last pieces in place, linking the Patriot to John Adams to Adam Ristich and discovering whom he was trapping? Would he have continued and broken her heart? Or backed off? Prudence forced the Patriot not to take a chance. Undesirable but necessary.

"Justice, and only justice, you shall pursue," his beloved grandfather had taught him from the Torah. He sought justice against St. Sava. Over the centuries the ancient society had always eluded official discovery. The CIA heard whispers, but without concrete evidence they gave its rumors the same level of credibility as the Loch Ness monster. St. Sava was as stealthy and smart as the CIA, but it operated from a code of honor rather than expediency. Honor kept secrets. Expediency sprang leaks. For the first time since entering the synagogue, he smiled. St. Sava eluded the world, but he eluded St. Sava.

John Adams sat back down, took some deep breaths, and focused on the synagogue's beauty, gradually calming himself. His thoughts turned to his own goodness. Despite his mother's betrayal through remarriage, he still protected her. No collateral damage, he'd ordered. He took pride in being a good son and a good man. Yet this very minute his mother might be learning that he was behind the termination of her other son. He dropped his head in his hands. "How could I bear it!" he cried out in despair. Elias dead was as much trouble as Elias alive.

109

YOU HAVE ELIE'S MEDAL!" BUBBA'S VOICE BOOMED, THUNDER ENDING A drought. He put his arm around Mrs. Darwish.

Lynn stared, dumbfounded.

Mrs. Darwish held up the medal and then turned it over. "See? His name, please. My son gave it to me."

Zeller? Surely not even Zeller could kill his own brother, Lynn!

"My first son, please. Adam."

How did he get it? Lynn wondered. Before she could ask, the bedroom door creaked open.

"*Viktor!*" said Lynn, astonished.

He bent to kiss Mrs. Darwish on the cheek. She patted his arm fondly. "This is Lynn Peterson, Galen Peterson, and Bubba Broussard," she said, gesturing to each in turn, carefully pronouncing their foreign names. "They are Elias's friends. And this is Vikolaj Machek, my Milcah's husband. They gave me two grandchildren." A smile broke through the sadness in her eyes. "Vikolaj is more like my son than my son-in-law." Her eyes lovingly embraced him. "My only son now," she muttered, the hurt back in her eyes.

Their mutual kindness and trust in each other increased Lynn's trust in Viktor. Obviously he hadn't lied about being close to Elie. Maybe everything he'd told them was true.

OK, Lynn, the little discrepancy in his name—Viktor/Vikolaj—that's understandable. But what about the little episode of scaring you to death at the safe house? Not to mention his little obsession with Elie's data.

He smiled at Lynn. "Once again Rooster Cogburn meets Baby Sister."

"Rooster Cogburn?" Mrs. Darwish looked confused but when he did not respond, she didn't pursue it. "Vikolaj was resting, please," she explained. "He has been working hard in Skopje."

"We know," said Galen affably. "We caused some of it, Viktor— I'm sorry. I mean Vikolaj."

"I go by either. Viktor is often easier for people. Most of my friends call me Vik."

"I think you will always be Viktor to me," said Lynn. "Or Rooster."

He grinned and sat down on the floor, folding his body nimbly into the lotus position.

"Have you learned anything more today about President Dimitrovski's death?" Galen asked. "Do you still think it was sabotage? Are there suspects?"

Viktor hesitated, eyeing Bubba, then spoke straightforwardly. "Frank Fillmore is at the top of the list."

Lynn sucked in air. They'd flown to Skopje on the same plane—even carried on a conversation with the man suspected of killing President Dimitrovski! She felt bone-deep shivers.

"He has skated above suspicion by governments, but St. Sava has observed that money tends to change his loyalties, and time his identities. We know he often works for the Patriot."

"Blaise Pascal's words come to mind," said Galen. "'There is an infinite chaos that separates us. A game is being played . . .'"

"'In which heads or tails must come up,'" finished Viktor. "Fillmore is a master player."

"I don't understand, please. If he does bad things and you know his name, Vikolaj, why is he not in jail?"

Viktor sighed with resignation. "That happens sometimes, Mother Darwish." He looked at Lynn and Galen. "Zechariah Zeller and the Patriot come to mind."

"And the long, massive search for Osama bin Ladin," added Galen.

"We know that Fillmore received clearance to fly to Mostar on the President's plane. He arrived early and apparently had solitary access to the cabin." Enraged, he spat the words. "Then he deplaned at the last minute! Supposedly due to illness!"

"Vikolaj," said Mrs. Darwish, concern in her eyes, "you are angry, please?"

He made a visible effort to calm down.

"Adam was angry today too." She looked longingly toward the apartment door, then lowered her eyes and said desolately, "He blames St. Sava for his father's death."

Viktor's eyes locked on her as he spoke gently to her in their native tongue.

"What harm can be done when both sons are . . . lost?" she responded in English, her voice catching on the last word. "My first husband, Iliya Ristich," she explained to the trio, "was a member of St. Sava." She closed her eyes and took a deep breath. "He died helping them with a mission. My Elias was also a member."

"I am sorry." To Lynn, death's pall draped Mrs. Darwish's life, setting joy in parentheses.

"Mother Darwish is speaking candidly and confidentially. I will speak candidly also." Viktor stood and focused on Bubba.

"Elie was close to identifying a man he considered—to use his words—the choreographer behind our international dance with death.' He did not risk sending any part of the information before completion because he feared detection. So we have nothing." He opened his empty palms. "All of his hard work is wasted unless we get his investigative results." He bent his head over Bubba and spoke with the power of conviction. "You and I both know he left that information with you."

Bubba stood also, looking down at the shorter Viktor. "He didn't tell me anything."

"He wouldn't have *talked* about it." His eyes narrowed and Lynn saw the ignitable, compact energy that could defend against four men armed with Uzis. "You play games on and off the football field, Bubba Broussard."

"Vikolaj! Please! Bubba Broussard is Elias's friend. *Our* friend." She dashed the fire with the soothing waters of five words: "He is my guest, Vikolaj."

"I am sorry, Mother Darwish. But this is very important to me. So much is at stake." He turned to Bubba. "Let me try again," he said with calm persuasion, gesturing toward Bubba's chair and sitting down again in lotus position. "If Elie began to feel worried about his safety, the procedure called for him to leave the accumulated data with someone he trusted. He would have followed that procedure. I can tell that he chose well in trusting you. Instead of using the name of a person to trust with the data, he would have used a symbol." Viktor pulled out a silver chain beneath his collar and revealed a medal identical to Elie's. "This symbol." He waited, expectant.

Bubba took a long moment to decide. He looked from Viktor to Mrs. Darwish and back again, then nodded slowly. "Elie did leave something with me that might be helpful."

Lynn understood Bubba's reaction, but she felt wary of Viktor. She had felt his pain and grief when he mentioned being

Elie's mentor. Not even Tom Hanks could have play-acted it that well. But a moment of sympathy did not automatically mean she bought his story. She looked into the eyes of a shrewd man capable of deceit. But the capacity to lie did not automatically mean his story was false. She glanced at Galen, frowning his own concern. Instead of moving toward a solution, she thought, we are going in circles like trunk-to-tail elephants.

"Where is the data?"

"Here."

A subtle shift crossed Viktor's eyes. "With you now?"

"I brought it to Sarajevo."

Viktor exhaled with a whistle of relief. "Well done! Maybe you should join St. Sava, Bubba." It was not clear whether this was a joke or an invitation. "At seven o'clock this evening I am attending a commemoration service to honor President Dimitrovski. It is sponsored by Sarajevo civil and military officials."

Commemoration service. The end of a life that was bigger than life, thought Lynn.

"I could pick up the data at your hotel on my way," Viktor suggested.

"That'll work."

"If you will excuse me, I need to clean up." Viktor rose and went into the bathroom.

No need for him to stay longer, Lynn. He's confident he'll get what he wants.

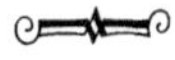

Viktor went into the bathroom and locked the door, commending himself for the hunch that Elie would have entrusted Bubba Broussard with the data. His leaving New Orleans to join the Petersons here in Sarajevo was a piece of luck. Even luckier was discovering that they were coming to Mother

Darwish's this afternoon. Luck plus patient persistence—like bugging the Skopje safe house. Viktor smiled. The discovery had given him time to arrive and plan. As expected, Mother Darwish had helped evoke their trust in him. Viktor felt a sense of urgency to get it. Soon! Very soon!

He began running water to avoid being overheard and flipped open his cell phone. Bubba Broussard had no idea what power Elie's data gave its possessor! St. Sava would value it in order to discover the Patriot's identity. And to prevent identification, the Patriot would pay an exorbitant fee to get it first.

He keyed in the code on his phone. All he said was, "I know the location of the highly sought information and will have it in hand late this afternoon." He punched *End.* Directions would be forthcoming.

110

Frank Fillmore looked at his Rolex, growing weary of the incongruence of boredom and steeled nerves. The slow minutes passed like a watch with a dying battery. Surely the target would finish her business and come out of the apartment building soon. The longer he waited, the more irritated he became with the Patriot for the directive. Though he was a crack shot, this kind of assignment demanded complete patience during idle hours of hidden observation and forced alertness—for a millisecond of action. He preferred bombs—the sound of the blast and the sight of the smoke rolling into the sky and lingering there, a celebration of damage and power.

Using his scope he watched the foursome through the apartment window: the target, her husband, their bald bodybuilder friend, and the elderly woman. Then another person appeared. Surprised, he recognized the Russian who'd talked to Lynn Peterson on Tuesday's Vienna-to-Skopje flight. Maybe the Patriot was on to something. Maybe the target was more involved in clandestine matters than she seemed. Later the Russian exited the room, leaving a foursome again.

Finally the target stood and put her hand over Mrs. Darwish's. The two men rose. Exit behavior at last.

"Come on," he whispered. "*Come on!*" He rubbed his hand across the black stock and down the metal barrel of his military issue high-powered sniper rifle resting on the bipod. No collateral damage, he reminded himself.

He put his eye carefully to the scope. With full attention and nerves of steel he aimed the crosshairs at the green door the three would use to exit the apartment building. He estimated the target's height and imagined a bull's eye on her forehead. One bullet. Nice and tidy. Fillmore stood at maximum alert, calm and ready, perfectly aimed, totally focused. He would not move again until the lovely—and soon to be the *late*—Lynn Peterson walked through the green door.

111

Lynn bent and took Mrs. Darwish's hand. "Would you like for us to pray together before I leave?" She asked the question in a neutral tone, wanting to offer if it would be meaningful but not force something that would be an intrusive obligation.

Mrs. Darwish's eyes lit up. "Yes, please."

Lynn bowed her head. The others followed. "Creator of the World, we give you thanks for the gift of Elias's life. God of Grace, we pray for Mrs. Darwish. Give her strength and comfort for her painful journey of grief. God of Love, draw her into your healing arms and hold her close." She placed her right hand on Mrs. Darwish's head. "I bless you in the Holy Name of God. Amen."

Tears glistened in Elie's mother's eyes. She rose to accompany them to the door and seemed to walk a little lighter.

They said their goodbyes, Bubba and Galen going ahead down the corridor to the building's exit. Lynn felt sad to leave, and she lingered at the apartment door. Mrs. Darwish was someone she would like to know deeply but would probably never see again. She wondered if the courageous woman felt the same, because she joined Lynn and walked beside her down the corridor, both of them dawdling. When they reached the door that led outside, Lynn opened it and was tempted again to ask how Adam had gotten Elie's medal. But she didn't. It felt inappropriate. Instead, she complimented the beautiful yellow flowers, bringing a smile to the older woman's thin face, wrinkled by time and pain. Mrs. Darwish stepped onto the threshold with her.

Things are not always what they appear to be. Those words again. A sense of unease dropped over Lynn. They hugged each other for the final time, a prolonged hug that connects two people as friends for a lifetime. Lynn watched Elie's mother reenter her apartment building and close the green door.

112

INFINITELY PATIENT, ZELLER HAD AMUSED HIMSELF BY ALTERNATING HIS FOCUS between the green door of the apartment building and the museum window. The other shooter leaned forward, and he caught him in his scope. Well, well, well. Herr Invisible from the airport—not invisible after all. No.

If Herr Invisible's target was Broussard, good riddance. If it was Peterson, he'd give him an advance chance to shoot. He had enough notches in his own belt.

Zeller shifted his rifle from the shooter in the museum back to the green door. Finally, it opened. He focused his full concentration on *Freund*. Scope, target, trigger finger merged into one. Broussard came out first and stepped down from the threshold, a perfect target beside the yellow flowers. Zeller waited. He listened for a silenced shot. Watched for Broussard to fall. Nothing!

He shifted his scope for a nanosecond. The other sniper rifle held steady in its bipod. Zeller shifted again and aimed toward the green door. After Broussard came Peterson. Another perfect target framed by the door. He reminded himself to be patient, to let the other sniper have the first shot at Peterson. Silence.

Zeller held the crosshairs on Peterson's forehead. What was the second shooter waiting for? The trigger burned against his finger. He started to ease it back. The other shooter's delay interrupted his concentration. His peripheral vision caught the glint again. Steady, unmoving, waiting. Why? Both men were open targets.

Just then Frau Peterson came out. Oh my god! Zeller shifted his rifle and glanced through his scope. The shooter aimed at her! Innocent Frau Peterson! A woman! He watched her hug the elderly woman, the two entwined.

Get Peterson, he reminded himself. Kill the stalker. The older woman stepped back into the building and shut the door. Zeller wavered, then hit his target.

113

VIKTOR HEARD THE SHOT. HE GRABBED HIS PISTOL AND SPRINTED THROUGH the apartment door into the corridor. Mother Darwish started to reopen the front door. "No!" he shouted. "Get back in your apartment! Stay away from the windows!"

"But our friends . . ."

"I'll take care of it." He jerked open the door. Hid behind it as a shield. Peeked out. Galen lay face down on the ground, his wife beneath him.

Viktor mentally replayed what he'd heard. No shattered glass. No ricocheting bullet. He scanned the scene. Eyed the museum. There! An open window on the second floor. He darted across the street. Broke through the door. Raced up the rickety stairs. Stumbled on a jagged step. Almost toppled backward. Regained his balance. Reached the second floor. Recalled the windows. Guessed the distance to the right door. Moved catlike toward it. Pistol ready. Paused behind the door a moment. Listened. Caught his breath. Heard nothing.

Slowly, silently, he began to turn the knob.

Locked! He listened again. Silence. He levered himself away from the wall. Rammed his shoulder full force against the door. The lock held. The hinges groaned. He jumped back to the side against the wall. Waited. Silence.

He rammed the door on the hinged side. It splintered open. Again he leaped back against the wall. Again nothing stirred.

He held his pistol steady with both hands. Entered. Ready to fire. His eyes swept the dilapidated room. Empty.

Except for the corpse on the floor.

114

LYNN HEARD THE SHOT. GALEN THREW HER TO THE GROUND. COVERED her. Didn't move. For a horrible instant she thought he was dead. Felt him breathe. Please don't let a bullet hit him! She lay immobilized. Terrified. Galen's arms blocked the light. His body barred the bullets. She tasted fear. The moment held in a photograph. Silence. Like the time between lightning and thunder.

Then came footsteps. Heavy feet in a zigzag sprint toward the sound of the shot. Bubba! "*No!*" she tried to shout. Galen's arm muffled her voice.

A door slammed. More steps. Shoes clicked on the street, running in the opposite direction from Bubba. Viktor?

She wanted to run away too. The single shot echoed the horror of Elie and Major Manetti. Déjà vu emotions resurfaced. Galen kept her covered, held her down. A scream rose in her throat. She summoned all of her willpower to swallow it back into the darkness.

115

IMMEDIATELY AFTER PULLING THE TRIGGER TO TERMINATE HERR INVISIBLE, Zeller returned his aim to Peterson and caught him in the scope, crosshairs once more on the mark. But Peterson lurched, hurled his wife to the ground, and covered her as a human shield. If he pulled the trigger now, the lethal shot might go through his own target into her. Shooting Herr Invisible to save Frau Peterson gained nothing if his own bullet killed her. She was fortunate that he was here today. Changing targets so abruptly to save her would cause a lesser ace to miss.

He aimed at the back of Peterson's head. Move! His trigger finger itched. But Peterson remained as a shield. A man of courage and honor, he admitted, chipping at the ice around his heart. He cleared his head. He must not allow positive thoughts about a target! No. He held his aim on Peterson. Steady!

Broussard jumped up, sprinting toward him! Not running away! The Saint zigzagged incredibly fast. In a few seconds it would be too late to shoot. Too risky. It would give Broussard his exact location. Shoot him first? Then Peterson? Broussard's courage to head into the line of fire infuriated him—but courage was not grounds for termination. No. It would be unworthy of world-class marksmanship.

Peterson's head shifted slightly, but he stayed glued to his wife. Zeller readjusted the crosshairs. Now or never.

No! He could not risk the bullet penetrating Frau Peterson. And the irritating Saint was too close. Not now but maybe not never either. Zeller lowered his rifle. "Time to go, *Freund*." It crossed his mind that the bishop's god watched over her husband as well as her. I'm getting superstitious!

With rapid, expert movements he wiped away all traces of his presence, his exit ritual as important as hitting the target. He thought about the way Herr Invisible had waited for the instant Frau Peterson appeared, held his aim on her, avoided the risk of hitting the older woman. And his own sudden clarity that Frau Peterson was the target. No! His reaction to save her had been an involuntary response from his subconscious—her face had blurred into his dear mother's face.

An honorable choice. But a costly one: it cost him the stalker. The target had saved his own life by protecting his wife.

Time to go! Zeller quickly completed his exit ritual and let himself out a door. Unseen. Unheard. Unsnared. His skill at leaving no clues equaled his aim. So easy.

116

VIKTOR MOVED CAUTIOUSLY TOWARD THE CORPSE, SLOWLY PIVOTING IN A full circle, reading the story the room could tell him. He'd expected to find the victim of the shooting—hopefully alive so he could help. But he sprawled beside the window. Viktor looked out and faced Mother Darwish's apartment building. The U.S. military issue sniper rifle had slammed to the floor, bipod attached.

He knelt close to the body. A single shot through the head. He recognized Frank Fillmore. Who had shot this man? Give him a medal! But now no one could interrogate him about President Dimitrovski's plane and who Fillmore was working for. He would have liked a crack in the interrogation room himself. Torture and drugs weren't his style, but he didn't mind fostering exhaustion that impeded controlling the tongue.

He looked out the window, seeing what Fillmore saw. The target was in the apartment building. Who? Why? And Fillmore was someone else's target. The same questions echoed. Who? Why? The obvious answer was that Fillmore could link his controller to Dimitrovski's death. But the obvious answers could screen the truth. Violent death was too complicated for simplicity.

The room offered him only one significant fact. Hitting Fillmore with perfect aim from the distance of the sound of the shot proved that the sniper was world-class—perhaps in a class by himself. Zechariah Zeller!

Fillmore's pockets were more generous. Using his handkerchief to avoid fingerprints, he found an address handwritten on a crumpled piece of yellow paper. He stiffened as he recognized Mother Darwish's apartment number. He eliminated her as the target. Himself? Perhaps. One of the Petersons? He'd noticed Fillmore talking to Galen on the plane to Skopje. Maybe it meant something. Maybe not. Broussard was also a possible target. He wondered if someone else knew Broussard had Elie's information. But shooting him before getting the data made no sense. He was anxious to get Elie's valued information this afternoon. To decode it. To trace the web Elie had discovered. He was equally anxious to get a response to the call he'd made a few moments before the shot.

Viktor focused again on Fillmore, looking for details that told him the story. He believed utterly in connections, but this time they baffled him. He looked at the words Fillmore had scribbled beneath the address: *No collateral damage.* He could have remembered that. So why did he write it down? Emphasis? Frustration? I'll never know, thought Viktor. He pocketed the note because it revealed Mother Darwish's address. She didn't need to be bothered by the police. Especially not in her time of grief.

The dead man's pockets also yielded a cell phone. It could reveal secrets that even interrogation would not expose. Hurriedly Viktor looked at the numbers in the phone memory. None. He punched *Calls Sent.* One. *Calls Received.* Three. All showed one number. He recognized it. The one written only in the Rolodex of his mind. The Patriot. Ideas began to connect like coins drawn to a metal detector. The one that stood out was *No collateral damage.* In his assignments from the Patriot that had never mattered. Why this time?

Viktor decided to keep Fillmore's phone with that valued number. Walking out backwards, he unfolded his handkerchief and swirled away his prints in the dusty floor. He'd let the police do their own detective work—minus a couple of clues.

117

GALEN HOVERED AROUND LYNN AND DEPOSITED HER INSIDE THE GREEN door, told her to stay with Mrs. Darwish and have her call the police immediately. He slammed the door behind her. Mrs. Darwish, peeking out from her apartment, called to Lynn. "I phoned the police." She gestured for her to come in. "Sit, please."

Lynn did as she was told, numbly accepting a cup of tea. And that's when she started to shake.

They sipped in silence, both too drained to speak. The police sirens wailed their approach. Mrs. Darwish brought in a partial chocolate bar and broke off two squares, giving Lynn one.

"Thank you." As the silent companionship calmed her, the question she hadn't asked earlier ran through her mind like a child's train on a circular track, refusing to be derailed by gunfire, sirens, or chocolate. "Mrs. Darwish, there is something I would like to ask." She leaned back in her chair and faked a casual tone, working hard to appear nonchalant. "Did Adam happen to tell you where he got Elie's medal?"

"After you lost it . . ." she began simply, then paused as doubt turned her explanation into a question, ". . . he found it?" Her face registered the odds against that kind of coincidence. Tears came to her eyes. "He did not stay long." She gazed toward the apartment door at an invisible image.

Lynn refused to say anything else that might cause this dear woman any more pain. They sat again in silence. Lynn finished her tea and glanced at the photographs she'd noticed earlier on the shelf beside Mrs. Darwish's kitchen door. One showed Viktor with a woman and two children. "This beautiful woman must be your daughter."

She nodded. "Milcah. And my two grandchildren."

She said the last word with such pride and love that Lynn's own heart ached. Grandchildren. With a repressed sigh she walked over to the shelf and looked at the oldest photo. "This must be Adam's picture beside the one of Elias."

She nodded again.

"He is a fine-looking boy."

She smiled. "He favors my first husband. That was taken on Adam's sixteenth birthday."

The age of Lyndie when she died. So many things opened the window to that memory.

Mrs. Darwish's smile faded, and sadness filled her eyes. "Over thirty-five years ago. Later that day his father was killed."

Lynn winced. For her. For her son.

"He left soon after that, and I did not see him again until today. My two sons—" Her voice cracked. "They did not ever meet."

Lynn looked closer at the photograph, trying to will it to tell her the story of how he obtained the medal. The boy had a look of strong determination. The camera had caught it in his eyes, in the firm set of his jaw, the lift of his chin. Strong determination to do what, she wondered. Had he achieved whatever it was?

The determined facial lines of Pasted-on-Smile at the airport came to mind, his well-tailored brown suit, his eyes following her. He may have looked something like this over three decades ago. His goatee and large, dark-framed glasses left little of his face to compare. Yet the eyes were similar.

She excused herself to use the bathroom and in privacy opened her cell phone and thumbed to the surreptitious picture she'd taken of him. He was off-center, but captured. She tried to envision a computer rendition of young Adam in the photograph, aging through time to the man in the phone photo. It was impossible. She thought about showing her photo to Mrs. Darwish but rejected the idea. It might upset her, and she had endured enough. Besides, the man at the airport had looked familiar, and she'd never met Adam Ristich. She was overreaching. Yet the thought lingered of its own volition, taking her where it would.

What if Adam got the medal from Zeller, Lynn?

As she sat with Mrs. Darwish, she tried to break off her running mental commentary. But it raced on like a steeplechase, jumping over barrier after barrier. Stop it! Adam couldn't be connected with Zeller! He killed Adam's brother and stole his medal!

Unless . . . A terrorizing conjecture trailed at the edges of her mind like a subliminal message.

Consider it, Lynn.

No! She knew where the thought would take her, and she didn't want to go there. But the pieces of the puzzle began dropping inadvertently into place, one by one. She glanced at Mrs. Darwish. Stop it! No mother could bear that! Lynn scattered the pieces again, the fleeting notion too monstrous to pursue.

"Are you all right, please?" asked Mrs. Darwish.

Nothing was all right. She took a sip of tea and returned to a casual conversation. "Three beautiful children. Elias Darwish, Milcah Machek, and Adam Ristich," she said, wanting her to know that she cared enough to remember their full names.

"Yes, please. But," she added with disapproval, "Adam changed his name." She rose and walked stiffly to the kitchen table. "I have his business card." She brought it back and handed it to her.

Lynn took it courteously, feeling its expensive cardstock. "It is an elegant business card," she complimented, dutifully reading it. When she saw the name and BarLothiun logo, she was stunned. "John Adams!" No wonder Pasted-on-Smile looked familiar! The mustache and dominant dark-framed glasses had thrown her.

"Do you know him?"

"Every American knows who he is. I think I saw him at the airport."

"Probably, please. He told me he had to hurry away because of business."

Elie had not mentioned a wealthy, influential brother. Based on what Mrs. Darwish said, perhaps he didn't even know it. The discovery felt dark, eerie, like encountering the enemy instead of the brother of a friend.

"He is important, please?" she continued.

"Very important," Lynn affirmed, shaken. "He has been a respected advisor to our presidents since the first President Bush." Adams easily crossed party lines, and his power grew over time. By the end of the second Bush presidency, it had broadened to the extent that any president would be foolhardy not to include him in an advisory capacity. He had a solid reputation of being knowledgeable, charming, and benevolent. And powerful. Better to have him inside working with you than outside against you. A line from President Benedict's letter came to mind: Fear ranch hands involved. She tingled with a sensation of connected dots, then disconnected herself from the horror they manifested. Suddenly Lynn feared for Mrs. Darwish and what she might learn about her first son. Her automatic pilot took over, and she said what every mother wants to hear, "You must be very proud of him."

118

ZELLER AMBLED TRANQUILLY ALONG THE BACK STREETS AWAY FROM THE police sirens. No one stopped him. He pretended once again to look for his aunt's address and made his way to his car toting the innocent-looking navy duffle bag that contained his disassembled rifle. But beneath his calm demeanor a storm disquieted him. He had shot another man. Pro bono. His third man in a week and two days. His thread of luck was taut. And Peterson was not dead. No. He set the duffle bag in the passenger seat beside him and gave it a fond pat. "It is time to quit, *Freund*," he said. "Not only am I getting superstitious. I am also getting soft."

He headed to his rooming house—one he'd used before in Sarajevo that neither reported all its income nor heeded passport rules. As he drove, he pondered how to resolve the Peterson problem. "Saving the life of Frau Peterson puts her husband in my debt, *Freund*," he said, brushing his hand fondly across the duffle bag. "My price will be a life for a life. He keeps his wife and in return gets out of my life. Forever. Otherwise, Frau Peterson becomes a widow."

Back in his room he first lowered the torn shade, shutting out the afternoon sun along with any observers with binoculars.

Second, he sat on the bed and placed the duffle bag beside him. Third, he carefully planned his call to Peterson, both his script and his performance. Ominous words required a tone of malice. The tone was easy, but he worked diligently on the right words. If possible, not another killing. No. He worried about too many targets in too few days. He worried about weariness leading to carelessness. He worried about luck's odds rapidly stacking against him. He sighed and glanced at the duffle bag. "*Ja*, *Freund*, it is time to retire."

Satisfied with the phone script, he practiced it only once. He must not sound rehearsed. No. He called the Petersons' hotel, eager to hear his target's reaction. He was connected immediately to their room. The phone rang several times, unanswered, until a voice invited him to leave a message. Disappointed, he broke the connection. A message wouldn't do. No. This call must be man-to-man. He would try again every half hour until Peterson returned. He stretched himself out on the bed and waited patiently, his hand on his duffle bag.

119

BUBBA SAT IN GALEN AND LYNN'S HOTEL ROOM, THE MEN TELLING HER what they'd learned from the police. "*Two* snipers!" said Bubba. "The dead one is Frank Fillmore."

Lynn was stunned.

"You remember," said Galen. "The man Viktor thought killed President Dimitrovski!"

"To quote Chief Armstrong, 'justice was served by a higher court.' The sniper who killed him got away without a trace."

"The police don't know who Fillmore was after. His bipod fell and they couldn't be sure where he was aiming. But they assume it was someone in the apartment building."

Lynn tried to make sense of the horrific afternoon and failed. She shared with them what she had learned from Mrs. Darwish: "Elie's half-brother was John Adams—*the* John Adams."

"Do you know how he got Elie's medal?" asked Bubba.

"I don't think Mrs. Darwish knows." That was the question that seared Lynn's mind also, but she didn't want to share where her thoughts had taken her this afternoon, and changed the subject. "Bubba, are you sure you trust Viktor with Elie's data?" She didn't add that he could be a disappointing new best friend.

"Elie's instructions were to give it to someone with a matching medal. Viktor has one. Besides, Mrs. Darwish trusts him, and that's good enough."

I hope so, thought Lynn.

The phone startled them. Galen answered. "Galen Peterson." He listened for a moment. Anger sparked in his eyes. "*Who are you?*"

Silence followed. A few moments later his face paled.

Lynn looked at Bubba and put her index finger over her lips, then punched the speaker button on the phone.

"Do you understand?" said the voice in a tone that chilled the room.

"It is irrational to try to understand the irrational," Galen parried.

"You are not in a position to show disrespect."

The man's clipped words and icy accent gave Lynn shivers.

"One, your wife was the shooter's target this afternoon."

Unexpected and disorienting, the words rat-a-tatted like machine gun bullets through an abbey cloister. She sank to the bed.

"Two, I saved *her* life instead of taking *yours*."

The phone cord coiled like a rattlesnake, venom slithering through the line. He'd intended to shoot Galen! She couldn't face the thought and dived quickly to the safety of denial.

You should listen to him, Lynn. A viper, yes. But he saved your life.

"And three, you owe me a debt beyond your financial means. A debt equal to the value of looking at your wife still by your side—instead of looking down at her corpse."

Galen sank to the bed and put his arm around Lynn, pulling her to him.

"The terms of repayment are nonnegotiable: *Back off.* You are to get out of my life."

The caller had intended to kill Galen, and Fillmore had intended to kill her. The reality strangled her. She couldn't breathe. Or think. But she must think. She must help Galen. She struggled to disengage from the horror.

"*Who are you?*" asked Galen again.

Desperate for a clue, Lynn focused on his pronunciations, tuning her ears to each word.

"Do not play games, Peterson. You are no match for me."

Not quite a German accent, more Bavarian German. Austria.

"With God as my witness," said Galen in a placating tone, the necessity for persuasion overriding his frustration, "I don't know what you are talking about. If I knew what I am to back off from, I would gladly do it."

Lynn mustered her wit and courage. "Thank you for today."

Galen pointed to his lips to shush her.

"Excuse me! I am sorry that you hear this, Frau Peterson."

She didn't intend to shush. Galen's life was at stake. *Excuse me.* She had heard those words in that same accent before. Where?

"I assure you that I mean you no harm," said Galen.

"Sir," she said, "you saved my life and we are grateful. You have my oath that my husband has never meant you any harm and will bring you none in the future."

"Galen Peterson, stay out of my life. Or you won't have one. This is the one warning you will get."

Lynn remembered. Excuse me. The chilling voice matching chilling eyes. Eyes hiding behind opaque sunglasses. Sunglasses being knocked askew. Belonging to a man bumping into her on the streetcar. Excuse me. Picking her pocket.

Standing at the statue in Vienna. Sitting in a black car this afternoon. Talking to Galen right now. Zechariah Zeller!

Without forethought, the searing question erupted into the air, the one that made all the difference: "How did John Adams get Elias Darwish's medal?"

Stupid, Lynn! Stupid!

Silence. The line went dead.

Bubba stared at her and slowly shook his don't-mess-with-me shaved head, disbelief on his face, the pupils of his eyes registering potential consequences. But it was the flash of fear in Galen's eyes that made her tremble.

She was the one who broke their silence, hoping that saying aloud the terrifying words would ease her fright and bring back a sense of control. Opening her cell phone, she showed Bubba the profile photos from the streetcar. "Meet Zechariah Zeller, the mime who shot Elie and stole his medal from my pocket. And intended to kill Galen this afternoon. And apparently saved my life."

120

John Adams sat in the synagogue, agitated. He glanced at his watch and frowned. Lynn Peterson should be dead by now like Elias Darwish and Major Manetti and forgotten others over the years. One's hands became soiled in the pursuit of justice.

He pulled his phone from his pocket and held it in his hand as though he could hasten Fillmore's call, like his mother watching a kettle to hurry a boil. He felt foolish but clutched it nonetheless. Again he looked at his watch. He checked the battery bars on his cell phone. He crossed his legs restlessly. Uncrossed them. Why hadn't Fillmore called?

Gradually he shifted from expecting his phone to ring at any moment to worrying that it might not ring at all. Each advance of the second hand on his Rolex intensified his angst. Finally, he stood and faced the truth. Fillmore had failed, adding this Sarajevo debacle to the Schönbrunn Palace disappointment. Twice in one week! Failure was new to the Patriot, and he didn't like it.

Zeller wouldn't have failed. He didn't fail in Vienna. Nor New Orleans. Zeller never failed.

The synagogue felt out of sync with his turbulent mood. He left and walked the streets of Sarajevo. The gloom spread around him. City smells permeated the air. The sound of gunfire rose in the distance. Children played tag nearby. Tag. To chase and be chased. The game of life. He thought of his own adored children, missing them. He would not fly home until after President Dimitrovski's funeral in Skopje. Attending it was a good public relations move, putting him in a favorable light to gain BarLothiun contracts in Macedonia. It was also an opportunity to listen around the edges for potential arms sales.

His head clearer, he walked back to the synagogue, got in his car, and drove to his hotel. He had a drink in the bar, TV blaring, thick smoke curling to the ceiling. News about a fatal shooting got his attention. He heard the name of his mother's street. The victim was identified as Frank Fillmore. His death didn't matter to the Patriot. What mattered was that Lynn Peterson, favored liaison of President Benedict, still lived. Fillmore had let himself get shot before completing his assignment. The Patriot considered a motive for Fillmore's murder, wondering if someone had avenged the death of President Dimitrovski. Justice!

In a strike-a-match flash, he saw a new approach. If Lynn Peterson were terminated, Benedict would simply find someone else. It was illogical to go after the liaison when the problem was the President.

That first scary thought about Benedict's termination, born three days ago, had continued to hover in the shadows of his mind. Now it began to unfold before him. Dimly at first. Gaining light. Brightening into a kaleidoscope of color. Expanding. Growing louder in his mind. Clearer in his sight. Like through a glass darkly, then face to face. Yes! It would work!

True honor was earned only by winning. He sneered at the barbarism of the concept of honor in the Civil War, where soldiers were slaughtered in one-to-one combat, lining up in two columns, shooting each other down in waves. One-sided wars were today's arena of honor, where disproportionate and overwhelming force from a distance smashed and bloodied the opposition and left the victor unscathed. That was the kind of war he would wage against the President. It would be over before she knew it had begun.

The . . . *promotion* of Vice President Parker would ensure that John Adams's power would not be eroded. Parker was an astute man who understood the obligation of reciprocity. The country would mourn, but it would not be harmed. He was the Patriot—he would never harm his country.

At that moment, Plan Death-of-the-President—Plan DOP—was decided. No longer scary. No longer forbidden. No turning back. Yet he distanced it from his consciousness, taking succor in the illusion that who we are is unrelated to what we do. He had intended to control President Benedict, not assassinate her. It grated against his patriotism. But he had no other choice. Abominable but necessary.

Ironically, President Benedict was aiding in her own demise through her foolhardy decision to attend Dimitrovski's funeral. Her presence was providential. Like Elias Darwish, she was placing herself in harm's way. Suicide, not assassination.

He would summon Zeller immediately to implement Plan DOP. Zeller never failed.

121

LYNN UNPACKED THE CLOTHES SHE NEEDED FOR THE RECEPTION TONIGHT, her mind on life's fragility and her own stupidity. How could she make such an irreparable mistake as asking Zechariah Zeller how John Adams got the medal!

Way to go, Lynn! Just like those dim-witted New Zealand pigeons that stick their heads right into the noose!

Now Zeller knew she could identify him and might think she knew his name. She had probably made things more dangerous for Galen and herself. She didn't know what to do, how to fix it. Or what had caused Zeller to go after Galen. And then save her. Why did someone want to kill her? Fillmore had no reason—except a contract. She shuddered. This reality was personally more threatening than Bosnia last time—her death would have been random or an accident. Was she safe now, or would a new contract be issued?

Shaken and shaking, she shifted into automatic. After a quick bath she hurriedly dressed for the pre-dinner reception and gathering of area churches, first on her Sarajevo itinerary. The day's incidents numbed her. Too many too fast like being the target of a meteor shower. Target.

In half an hour their ride would come, and she must leap from assassin's target to guest of honor, from gunfire to grace, from the sinister to celebration. A knock on the door interrupted her reverie. Fear tingled through her. Galen peeked out the Judas hole. "It's Bubba."

Not Zeller, she thought. Not yet.

"I know the army of one is early," Bubba grinned, determined to accompany them tonight, "but Viktor wants us to meet someone in the lobby."

"Did he come to get . . . what he wanted?" Galen asked.

"He's been in my room decoding it. Just finished. He has some kind of program on his laptop. It went fast."

"So he knows who . . ." Lynn found herself afraid to say *the Patriot* aloud.

"He still has to analyze all of Elie's information and compare it with their other data. Then he will be sure."

Galen frowned. "So he has everything he wanted." Though he used nonjudgmental words, his tone was void of approval.

Bubba's eyes flickered, but he merely looked at his watch and then at Lynn. "Is there time to meet Viktor's friend?"

"If we leave from the lobby," she nodded, "and don't come back to our rooms." As she stepped into the narrow hall, Bubba played guard on her right side. His shape shifted into a rampart. His huge shoulders stiffened, every nerve and muscle ready for action. Alert. Practiced. Disciplined. Galen walked on her left side. More subtle, but no less intentional. As soon as they reached the lobby, she scanned the faces for Zeller and knew the men did, too. She didn't see him, but he still loomed over her psyche.

Viktor called to them. He was in full military dress, with a chest full of medals.

Our Russian entrepreneur and St. Sava storyteller is now a soldier, Lynn. Do you think he earned the medals or bought them?

She noted his captivating presence and the respect that the hotel staff and others showed him. He was called Vik here, obviously well-known and well liked. His attention had evoked others' respect for them simply by association. "Did he forget his laptop?" she asked Bubba, noting its absence.

Viktor overheard her and responded softly. "It's safer in Bubba's room for now, Baby Sister. I'll get it later."

"I won't be here later," said Bubba.

Viktor smiled tolerantly. "I'll manage."

"Rooster Cogburn doesn't need a room key, Bubba," Lynn interjected from experience. She noticed Viktor's watchful eyes circle the lobby like a lighthouse beam. Sensing unease in this fearless man, her own uneasiness grew.

An Orthodox priest entered the hotel. Relief filled Viktor's eyes, and he motioned him over. The priest smiled and joined them. "I am sorry to be late. Introduce me to your friends, Vik."

He complied with an air of deference to the priest that surprised Lynn, a trait she'd neither seen nor expected. He gestured toward each of them. "Bishop Lynn Peterson, Dr. Galen Peterson, Mr. Bubba Broussard. This is Father Nish—whose name I am sure you recognize."

Lynn tried not to stare at Natalia's Father Nish. His manner drew them toward him, and she sensed that he was the kind of man who can lead in crises and comfort in loss.

"Father Nish," said Galen heavily, "a young hotel maid in Vienna asked us to bring you a package for her family."

"Natalia." Seeing their surprise, the priest added, "Vik told me."

"I left it with . . ."

"President Dimitrovski," Father Nish finished. "An aide who was traveling with him to Mostar telephoned me before the flight left and suggested that I arrange to pick it up there. But the crash . . ." A visible wave of grief washed over him.

"We are very sorry," said Lynn.

"I understand that it contained thousands of euros." English, though heavily accented, came easily for Father Nish.

A man in uniform hurried into the hotel. His strong build and intimidating stance commanded authority, his decorated uniform an adornment to his power, not its source.

Viktor stepped toward him and called, "General Thornburg." He saluted, and it was returned. "I was beginning to be concerned about you."

"The package," finished Father Nish, "is a loss, but inconsequential when we consider the toll that plane crash took. President Dimitrovski is irreplaceable in this region."

Grief filled the general's tired eyes. "It is a devastating loss."

"General Thornburg is here to attend a commemoration service to honor President Dimitrovski," explained Viktor. "It's for military and government officials in this area." He looked at the general. "You know that I'm driving you?"

The general nodded brusquely. "We need to discuss some things." His tone turned a casual acknowledgement into an order, his second-in-command days long forgotten.

"General, I would like for you to meet Bishop Lynn Peterson."

The general's eyes registered surprise, then dismissal, then blanked.

"And Dr. Galen Peterson, a historian. And Bubba Broussard, who plays for the New Orleans Saints. They were friends of my brother-in-law."

Were, thought Lynn. Past tense. Elie will always be my friend. Present tense.

The general extended his hand to Bubba, then Galen. When Lynn offered hers, he accepted it with veiled distaste, as though she'd forgotten her gender.

Perhaps you should have curtsied, Lynn.

"General Thornburg is in charge of NATO for the Balkans."

Marsh's general! It was Lynn's turn to be surprised.

The general gestured toward the medals on Viktor's uniform. "You are wise to place yourselves in the hands of this man of valor. I personally have decorated him twice for his work with NATO."

Oops. Sorry, Lynn. Maybe I was wrong on this one.

But maybe not, thought Lynn, still skeptical.

"Father Nish, I think you and the general have met previously," said Viktor. Both men nodded.

"You mentioned a package in the plane crash," said the general abruptly.

Father Nish sighed. "Unfortunately."

"Fortunately, I found it." A subtle shift in General Thornburg's posture put him in charge. "Please come to my room so I can get it for you." He took the priest's arm and said softly, "On the way you can tell me what you know about St. Sava."

Lynn saw Father Nish glance toward Viktor and watched their silent, unreadable exchange.

"Father—" Viktor stepped beside him. "I have a favor to ask of you as Mother Darwish's priest. This is a very difficult time for her, today especially. The shooting was by her apartment. I wonder if you might call on her. It would lift her spirits."

"Certainly."

"This evening?"

Father Nish frowned, and Lynn recognized the resignation to duty that she sometimes felt. "Certainly," he repeated.

She glimpsed a magician's sleight-of-hand as Viktor transferred something small from his own pocket to the priest's. A thought floated by and hovered like a butterfly: the amount of money in Natalia's troublesome package, Viktor's deference toward the priest, the illusive transfer of what she assumed to be a copy of Elie's decoded data. The butterfly landed: perhaps I just met the head of St. Sava.

Viktor saw her gaze and seemed to read her thoughts. His penetrating eyes and a subtle wag of his head said, Don't go there, Baby Sister.

122

AGITATED, ZELLER LAY ON THE PATCHED YELLOWED SPREAD IN HIS ROOMING house and stared at the ceiling grayed from soot. His cigarette smoke rose toward the ceiling, his free hand resting on the navy duffle bag hiding *Freund* inside. He knew that Frau Peterson would recognize his face if she saw him, but he had not expected her to recognize his voice. He had forgotten about speaking to her on the streetcar. *Excuse me.* Two common words invited uncommon danger. She linked the call and his voice to his face and the medal. At least she doesn't know my name. Or does she?

Her question echoed: How did John Adams get Elias Darwish's medal? The link also puzzled him. Obtaining the medal after the shooting had been part of the Patriot's contract with him. Perhaps the master of disguise had used it to buy a favor from Adams. He would pursue the connection between the two men. Thank you for the clue, Frau Peterson.

He reflected on Peterson's response to his accusations and pondered whether their encounters could actually be coincidence. The man's confusion was most convincing, and Zeller was skilled at reading people, an essential ingredient of his success. Only the Patriot deluded him.

His phone rang. The Patriot's voice startled him. An eerie coincidence. Another one? He made a small place in his mind for the possibility of their existence. Quickly eliminated it. No. Not coincidences, but connections. Events coming together of their own volition, like magnets.

Zeller listened to the absurd proposition. President Benedict! Shocked, he declined. "*Nein.*" He patted *Freund* on the bed beside him. "*Auf Wiedersehen.*"

"*Wait!*"

He returned the phone to his ear, puzzled. A day of puzzles. The Patriot had moved from despotic to desperate. Only a week ago he had sat at a café in Vienna, invincible. Today his voice held an unfamiliar ring of vulnerability, and his request was outrageous. Something serious had gone awry.

As the Patriot tried to persuade him, Zeller thought about the challenge. Nothing equaled it—the strategy, the skill required, the escape. He interrupted, something he would not have dared to do before the Patriot exposed his vulnerability. "Double the fee. This assignment will cost me my career."

An angry refusal followed.

"Then find another shooter," said Zeller, confident that no one else of his caliber existed. "*Auf Wiedersehen.*"

"*No! Wait!* You have to be reasonable."

"*Reasonable?*" He responded with a Zeller version of Peterson's words: "It is unreasonable to be reasonable about something unreasonable."

"Remember to whom you are speaking!" A tremor deflated the Patriot's cold malice.

Zeller hesitated, then lunged. "My terms are nonnegotiable. One, I want to be paid directly by you, the full fee in advance. Afterward I will not be able to resurface. They will hunt me forever."

The Patriot made no attempt to disagree, and Zeller continued. "Two, I want people to see you with me that morning. It will give you a vested interest in not revealing my identity."

"That's *impossible!*"

"So is the assignment. Three, I will be in the lobby of the Hotel Aleksandar in Skopje at nine o'clock Tuesday morning." In the meantime, he thought, I'll arm myself with information about the link between the Patriot and Adams.

"You are stepping over the line!"

"Those are the terms. If you want the job done, be at the Aleksandar with the fee in euros." He hung up, knowing the Patriot would tell himself he would not take orders or put up with insubordination. "But he will not risk this assignment to anyone but us, *Freund*," he said, caressing the duffle bag. "In the end, he will be there." So easy.

123

THE SARAJEVO PASTOR AND HIS WIFE ARRIVED FIVE MINUTES EARLY AND whisked the trio to the reception that began Lynn's Bosnian itinerary. First the welcoming; then the work. Lynn shook strangers' hands and offered practiced foreign greetings. Operating on remote control, she thought about the web spun on this long Friday. The flight from Skopje, President Benedict's call, Bubba's arrival, Mrs. Darwish, Viktor/Vikolaj/Vik, John Adams, Father Nish, General Thornburg, Zechariah Zeller, and the late Frank Fillmore—instead of the late Lynn Peterson. Or the late Galen Peterson.

She cut the last five words from her mind. She wasn't afraid to die. But she was afraid to lose Galen. The Zeller problem was beyond her. She did not know how to begin to resolve it.

One step at a time, Lynn. Like always.

An idea seized her. She rejected it as pointless, hopeless, daunting.

Being a bit of a coward, are we, Lynn?

The idea nagged her toward compliance. But it required the temerity to contact General Thornburg. Timidity held her back. And timing. Right now he was attending the military and government officials' commemoration service honoring President Dimitrovski. With relief she welcomed procrastination.

The reception concluded with a brief time of worship together. Candles glowed, lighting the way out of her dark abyss. They glimmered boldly, casting out the shadows of clandestine ill will. Their light brightened the world with hope and love and charity, human qualities that sometimes flickered and even blew out. But not permanently.

For the moment she was in the hands of the Church—gentler hands than Viktor's—with grassroots people who lived *in* the war, not above it. She sat amidst people whose focus on spiritual growth drew her toward the holy. Holism. Wholeness. The sinister world shrank in the distance, and Lynn regained a peaceful heart, reassured against her fear that the blossom of serenity had been plucked from the vine and left to die on the floor of the Vice President's limo. Worshiping here offered her puissance, for no contemporary word portrayed the power, strength, and force of the renewal it provided for her spirit. The tide washed away the other world, the underworld, if only temporarily.

Worship with the people brought her Home to a faith community. Where greed is tempered by generosity, real power is viewed as the power of love, and self-giving is recognized as the means to self-fulfillment. Where the magic of faith—if there is magic—is not that the people of faith are successful in living out high ideals, but that their ideals help them live on a higher plain. Where the mystery of faith—and there is mystery—is neither definable nor describable, because it is just that, a Mystery. A Mystery of Faith. Reliable. Undeniable. Viable.

Worship ended, and the hard part began. She moved into a large hall, where the fact-finding delegation had begun gathering, along with the officials from all sides of the issues. These representatives would bombard the delegation with "facts" selected to support their vested interests and actions, "facts" that some might deliberately misrepresent. The delegation's task was not so much to sift out the truth from both sides but to discern from their words and emotions how to construct a bridge, one that could begin a journey toward reconciliation. A historically hopeless task, but the vision itself must not be lost.

The meeting began with positioning and posturing. That was expected. It was also disappointing. Galen thumbed notes into his Blackberry, interested in the historical slant. Bubba stayed watchful and alert though he'd flown all night with no time since to rest. Refreshed by the worship service, Lynn buckled down to listen and discern together with the delegation how to keep hope alive for reconciliation. She listened carefully to what was said and left unsaid, and noted innuendos behind the words. Simultaneously at the back of her mind she planned her strategy to win over General Thornburg. At the break she would call him. Her stomach pitched.

124

After the commemoration service, Vik took the General back to the hotel. While there he removed his computer from its hiding place after getting himself into Bubba's empty room uninvited. He returned to Mother Darwish's and began to analyze the decoded data combined with St. Sava's accumulated information. It did not make a pretty picture.

"Is something wrong, Vikolaj?" she asked.

Not something. Everything. Elie was on the verge of connecting the Patriot to John Adams, but he hadn't discovered that the trail would lead to his half-brother. But now, Vik knew. He looked at her dear, weary face. "Everything is OK, Mother Darwish." He cared deeply for her and felt a red-glow anger rising again toward Adam Ristich/John Adams. She should have named him Cain. How could a mother bear knowing that one son had killed the other? He would see to it that she never knew. The only way to do that was to keep anyone else from knowing, including St. Sava. "You don't need to worry."

Or did she? Surely Father Nish would return the copy he'd given him. This afternoon after Bubba admitted having the data, he should have delayed the phone call to Father Nish until he'd had time to analyze it. He'd been too protective, too eager to have a copy of the decoded information in case something happened to the original. Now he had to get it back! Tonight. His request for the priest to see Mother Darwish was made only partly for her sake. Mainly it was a way to convince General Thornburg that Father Nish was truly a priest and to allay suspicions about St. Sava. He pondered how to retrieve the copy. *Casually*, he decided.

Father Nish arrived as promised. Despite Viktor's heavy heart and burdened mind, he enjoyed Mother Darwish's pleasure in the visit. Speaking Bosanski was far more comfortable for her than struggling with English, but she had met the challenge well this afternoon. He also enjoyed Father Nish's delight, his spirit obviously growing lighter as they talked.

When Father Nish stood to leave, she ignored his exit mode. "Do you know Bishop Peterson?"

A drawn-out departure, thought Vik impatiently, one of the common but understandable ploys of the elderly who live alone.

"I met her this afternoon," replied Father Nish without a hint of impatience.

"She came here today after Adam left. She prayed for me just before the shooting. I think it is the first time anyone has prayed for me in English."

"God is omni-lingual."

"Whatever the language, Father, words don't fool God. God reads our hearts."

He smiled warmly at her. "God reads a pure heart in you."

"Oh, no! I have many blemishes." She glanced toward the apartment door where Adam had come and gone.

"You handle your difficulties admirably well."

Mrs. Darwish looked at her son-in-law. "Vikolaj, we have been ignoring you! I am sorry. You will stay the night?"

"If you are troubled by the shooting."

She responded with a soul-deep sigh. "I remember my peaceful village of Biram when I was a little girl."

Rabbit-track stories—another elderly ploy, pointless but understandable. Vik rose beside Father Nish, his mind rushing ahead toward getting the copy back.

"Then the military came," she continued. "As I've grown older, I realize that men talk peace but want war. Peace brings joy to the people but only gives leaders an opportunity to make a speech. War brings fear to the people and gives leaders an opportunity to remain in office." Tears came to her eyes. "So much war! What troubles me most about this afternoon is how little the shooting troubled me. I have become hardened by violence."

Viktor stood motionless, stunned into silence. If kind people like Mother Darwish became hardened, there was no hope.

She rose stiffly from her chair. "Thank you for coming, Father." She smiled her appreciation. "You always leave me better than you find me."

"We don't ever want it to be the other way around!"

"It is a gift that you have," she said.

"You return the gift, Rachel." Her first name, rarely used by him, was said with warm regard. "I, too, am always better when I leave than when I come."

Vik patted her arm lovingly. "I need to visit with Father Nish, but I'll be back."

The priest looked surprised but asked no questions.

125

DURING THE BREAK AT THE FACT-FINDING SESSION, LYNN HEADED TOWARD the restroom, then veered off into a dark hallway. She felt her way down it until she was sure no one could hear her. She listened for footsteps. Wished she'd asked Bubba to come with her. Thought of Zeller. Shuddered. She shook off the image of his face, his eyes. Hurriedly she called the hotel. "General Thornburg's room, please." She hoped he had left for the commemoration service so she could procrastinate.

"General Thornburg here," he said gruffly on the first ring.

She felt intimidated before she began. "This is Lynn Peterson."

"I am very busy right now," he said with cold dismissal.

"Yes, sir." She continued undaunted, "The story is too long to go into, but I know who initiated the request for Major Manetti to be on our plane from Frankfort to Vienna. It was *very* high up, sir."

"I'm listening."

"President Benedict, sir." She sucked in a breath wondering if he would hang up. He didn't. "Major Manetti was her friend. Confidentially, sir, she has also befriended me, but I think, if asked, she might deny that in order to protect me."

She winced at how preposterous she sounded. Poor little lunatic! Give her a pill for paranoia.

"I'm still listening."

"I have a request of utmost importance, sir." Fear that he would consider the conversation absurd and dismiss the request brought a tremor to her voice. "Do you have the power . . ."

"Absolutely."

"I'm sorry, sir. Could you arrange . . ."

"Affirmative."

This was not going well.

Just spit it out, Lynn.

"I believe the bullet that killed Major Manetti came from the same gun that killed Frank Fillmore today. The sniper's name is Zechariah Zeller." She paused briefly. "You could check this out with a ballistics report—or whatever it's called."

Way to go, Lynn. That sounded competent.

"You base all this on what?"

Don't say intuition, Lynn.

"As I said, it's a long story. But if I'm correct, it will connect the killings and facilitate the investigation of the major's murder. I assure you that President Benedict would be as pleased as you to find out who killed him."

"Continue."

And say what? That the sniper planned to shoot my husband but shot Fillmore instead to save my life? That he also killed Elie but used a pistol instead of the rifle? And set up another man to look like Elie's killer? And I was stupid enough to let him know I recognize him? She feared the only thing he'd believe was that she had a big imagination. She made a desperate plea: "General Thornburg, even if you think I'm a kook, isn't it worth getting a ballistics report before dismissing this lead?" An interminable silence followed.

"Write up your request and give it to Vik."

Viktor again. Always Viktor. "No, sir."

Careful, Lynn. He's not used to being told no.

"I trust only you, sir. Major Manetti spoke highly of you."

He didn't click off. "Are you at the hotel now?"

"No, sir. I will slip the request under your door when I return late tonight." He gave her his room number, a welcome surprise. "Thank you, sir."

She tore a sheet of paper from the small Moleskine notebook she always carried, just like Ernest Hemingway. Her hand trembled when she wrote "Frank Fillmore," imagining a sniper rifle aimed at her. She forced the image away and steadied herself. She debated adding information about Elie's shooting and that John Adams was his half-brother.

Keep it simple, Lynn.

If the ballistics report didn't confirm her theory, the cost would be time and energy uselessly spent by the government—not for the first time. And, of course, her embarrassment and the scar on her vanity. But if it turned out to be correct, Zechariah Zeller would suffer far more than embarrassment.

But he saved your life, Lynn!

He planned to kill my husband!

126

VIK FOLLOWED FATHER NISH'S CAR TO THE CHURCH. CLOUDS HID THE STARS and moon, the darkness engulfing them. They creaked their way up the old wooden spiral stairs to the soundproof room in the bell tower, sparsely furnished with two brown leather chairs and a scarred oak coffee table. When they seated themselves, he dallied. "How did things go with General Thornburg this afternoon at the hotel?"

"I got Natalia's package from him, and he got no information from me."

"I wondered if you had met your match in him."

"And then some. I admire him, Vik. How did you fare with him after the service?"

"He shared one item of interest on the way to the service. He has received word confirming evidence of a bomb on the plane. A new security camera caught Fillmore's face when he exited the airfield in the presidential car. He was a bomb expert who frequently worked for the Patriot. The camera also showed the substitute driver whose cap was off, displaying shoulder-length hair. She got the job by posing as a man and having perfect false credentials. The police identified her. She has worked with Fillmore before. Since he was dead and couldn't be harmed—or harm her—she told the whole story to save her own skin. But you can't abet the murder of a President and go free. She'll get a permanent bedroom with bars, courtesy of the government." Vik realized nervousness was causing him to talk too much.

"President Dimitrovski's death deeply saddens me on both a personal and political level. He was the only giant of peace in this part of the world."

"Another victim of those who fear peace and peacemakers more than war." Vik sighed and changed the subject. "By the way, despite my visit-Mother-Darwish-as-her-priest maneuver, I think the general doubted that you were legitimate, but your eulogy convinced him. We agreed that you did an outstanding job."

"I do my best to dispel that old image of Balkan clergy created by a Greek bishop in Macedonia, especially when the international community is present."

"I have a cloudy memory of something sinister."

"He ordered an assassination. Actually, a decapitation."

"Centuries ago, as I recall," said Vik.

"No. Just prior to World War I. The bishop had the severed head brought back to the church to be photographed. The stain still clings to our robes, Vik." He looked away, pensive. "There are many stains."

"The sins of the bishop are visited upon the clerics?"

"Something like that."

"Your robes aren't stained."

Father Nish remained silent.

"Guilt, the great motivator, even guilt by association through having the same profession." Vik smiled at him. "Is that what motivated you to accept heading St. Sava when you already had your hands full?" He looked away for a moment, then broached the subject that had brought him here tonight. "Have you had an opportunity to look at Elie's data?"

"Not yet."

Vik tried to mask his relief.

"Since leaving the hotel, I've been basking in the luxury of idleness. Entertaining myself with a feisty general, a package filled with euros, a eulogy for the President whom I respected most in the world, contacting Natalia about never using the symbol again, and a visit to an elderly lady—one whom I truly love, by the way." Father Nish smiled. "No time yet to play with decoded data."

"The copy I gave you is inadequate." That part was true. "I had merely decoded the data, not analyzed it yet in combination with the rest of our information." Also true. "I would like to have it back and return it finalized. It will be more efficient for you."

Father Nish's eyes met his.

He sensed that the priest knew he'd deliberately left a false impression through omission. Vik was very skilled at that, but he'd never tried it with the only man he trusted. It burned a hole in his soul. He lowered his eyes.

"What has happened to you, Vik?"

Vik forced himself to look levelly at the head of St. Sava. He was determined to protect Mother Darwish from ever learning that one of her sons had had the other one killed. He was also determined to stop the dangerous megalomaniac. He was clear about his mission—get Adam Ristich/John Adams/ the Patriot—but for the first time in his career he was unclear about a plan.

Father Nish waited patiently for Vik's response, then spoke again. "You have done superior undercover work against the Patriot, especially your discovery that Fillmore worked primarily for him. The Patriot could have been behind President

Dimitrovski's death—though the operation seems closer to home. We know, however, that the Patriot is a very thorough man. It is logical for him to keep an eye on the men he hires. Since Fillmore worked primarily for him, the Patriot would have known where he was and figured out the likely reason for his presence. One way or another he could have stopped him. And he didn't."

Every word made sense. Viktor felt sick.

"You said yourself that you cannot abet the murder of a President and go free."

Viktor stood. "I need you to return that copy." There was no deference now in the lethal tone of this man who could handle four guards armed with Uzis.

"I'm sorry, Vik. You know I can't do that."

127

ON FRIDAY NIGHT AFTER FRAU PETERSON'S INTERESTING QUESTION AND THE Patriot's absurd but challenging offer of a contract on President Benedict, Zeller did some extensive research. It led him to a startling discovery about how the medal he'd wrapped in a tie box for the Patriot had reached the hands of John Adams.

First he checked Adams out on the web, photo and all, and recognized him as the man in the brown suit at the Sarajevo airport, despite his large glasses, goatee, and gray hair. He recalled the sense of familiarity and now could see all the Patriot's other disguises transposed on the face of John Adams. Wanting corroboration, he hacked into the passenger lists for Friday morning arrivals in Sarajevo. Finding no John Adams, he moved back to the previous Friday and checked the Flughafen Frankfurt passenger arrivals that correlated time-wise with his meeting at the airport where the Patriot had paid him for Darwish and issued a contract on Manetti. He ran a search for common names on both lists and for common flight origination points. He found nothing. No.

Corporate jets! Of course! The same comparison resulted in a match! A Challenger registered to BarLothiun had made both flights, and John Adams owned BarLothiun. There was indeed a connection between the two. They were one and the same! The discovery made the offer of a contract on President Benedict even more surprising. His knowledge of the Patriot's identity armed him for a surprise strike if needed in his negotiation.

Monday noon, Sarajevo behind him, Zeller found a no-questions-asked room in the old part of Skopje. He went directly to Butel Cemetery, where people busied themselves like ants, preparing for tomorrow. Crews were working on the grounds from the gate to the funeral site. Men were putting together the seating section for the VIPs. He took a careful look. That's where President Benedict would sit. *Mutter* had helped him get information about the security plans to protect that section. He had also learned that a no-fly zone would be enforced during the outdoor ceremony because of the noise and disrespect—the person the Macedonians cared most about protecting was already dead.

Zeller stayed at a distance, ambling unnoticed through the trees. He would have to be at a distance tomorrow too. But where? He ambled along, covertly searching. There it was! A black marble family mausoleum. Exactly what he needed. He guessed its size to be about eight by eight, rising ten feet, with stone parapets adding two feet more. The parapets were spaced about six inches apart to allow snowmelt and rainwater to drain from the flat roof. Narrow ornamental stones, again about six inches wide, extended diagonally from each of the four corners, stair-stepping down and angling diagonally from roof to ground. A tree grew near the back right-hand corner of the mausoleum. Its lower branches hid the ornamental stones and the larger branches draped over the flat roof. The name ZORBAS was carved above the door. He thought of Nikos Kazantzakis's *Zorba the Greek*, one of his favorite books.

He eyed the distance to the VIP section. He was too far back to concern security, and the human wall of hordes of people would separate them from him tomorrow. It would be the longest shot he'd ever made to hit a contract target. But not the longest he'd practiced successfully. He and *Freund* could do it.

He returned to his room, finalized his plans, and left again. He went for a long walk through the streets, past the marketplace, an ancient mosque, some monasteries, the bus station. The mid-afternoon sun fought unsuccessfully to warm the city's sorrow. Mourning crowds bumped him and spilled over into the streets. Thousands of people had come to the Parliament Building to pay their last respects, bringing flowers for President Dimitrovski's catafalque. Their flowers overflowed and spread out in front of the edifice like a rolling field of colorful blossoms.

A leader so loved, he thought, conscious of the void of love in his own life. The people will never know the truth, he predicted, because officially the government will continue to blame the storm. He had read carefully all the details made public about President Kennedy's assassination and had learned something important. Governments do not trust the people with the truth. No. Ergo: An assassin can terminate a head of state and simply disappear while those in power pacify the people with deception.

And the pay is good. It would be especially so for this contract.

The mobs of people would serve his interests tomorrow. After he shot his target—a single bullet to the head—he would let the crowded bedlam absorb him. So easy.

He felt confident that the Patriot would show up at Hotel Aleksandar tomorrow as invited—John Adams in some kind of disguise. It would be difficult to trap him conspiring to have President Benedict assassinated. But not impossible. During their conversation, he could fire the words *John Adams* like missiles in a preemptive strike.

Casually, in his invisible mode with lowered head and a newspaper under his arm, he entered the Hotel Aleksandar and ambled through the busy lobby unnoticed, an unhurried visitor in town for the funeral. Behind his sunglasses, he scanned the lobby for security cameras, selecting one above a bulky caramel-colored sofa, its leather cracked and worn. A matching chair completed an *L* beside it and stood in the security camera's view—a perfect chair for the Patriot, who liked to sit with his back to the wall. The camera would pick up his face and the words he shaped—words that a professional could lip-read later if necessary.

He restrained a sigh. There is another possibility: I may have underestimated the Patriot/John Adams. If so, he will have his own plans for tomorrow. Perhaps the police will arrive in his place. Perhaps another marksman will aim at me. So be it!

Zeller banked on two factors. One, desperation evidenced by this drastic assignment and the edge in the Patriot's voice. Two, the Patriot's confidence in him as an artist who drew aim with the accuracy of a brushstroke on a canvas. Zeller planned to arrive here very early tomorrow to be assured of being first. He would sit on the sofa, and when John Adams arrived, he would offer him the chair with his back to the wall—and his face to the small security camera.

Zeller rose and ambled out the door of the Hotel Aleksandar. For an instant he longed for the comfort of *Freund.* He had not wanted to risk walking around the well-secured town with a sniper rifle. But he was secure without her. Even with his jacket pocket covered by the newspaper under his arm, he could retrieve his laser-sighted pistol and dead-aim it in three seconds. So easy.

128

THE LAST EVENT ON LYNN'S BOSNIA-HERZEGOVINA ITINERARY WAS A WORSHIP service at noon on Monday in Sarajevo, where she was to do the homily. She talked about a world of faith, a world of goodness. Where *blood* is not something that runs in the streets, but the symbol of a gift. And *body* is not life snuffed out from violence, but the symbol of community. The Body and the Blood. The bread of grace and the cup of blessing. She also talked about the people of faith. Those who know that we live life at its best when we follow the teachings of faith. Abundant life—learning courage from conviction, fortitude from forgiving, and gratitude from grace.

At the close of the service she mingled with the people to share farewells. When she left for the Sarajevo airport, she felt like a refugee leaving refuge, exiled once more into the tainted world of the godless—both those who denied belief and those whose actions belied belief. Filled with the trepidation of reentry, she tucked into memory the gentle hands of the Church and tried to retain a peaceful heart.

Lynn and Galen tried to convince Bubba he could go on back to the States. Intense security for the funeral would make Skopje the safest place in the world tomorrow and then they would return to New Orleans. He agreed, with restrictions: he would remain with them at their Sarajevo departure gate until they boarded; they would arrange for Pastor Martinovski to meet their plane on arrival; and when Bubba received word that they had arrived safely, he'd fly back to the States. As they said goodbye, the trio planned to have dinner together at Commander's Palace in New Orleans on Wednesday. As Lynn thought about going home, the winds of relief lifted her like an air balloon.

Pastor Mihail Martinovski was indeed waiting for Lynn and Galen at the Skopje airport when they deplaned. He had special passes that allowed him to meet them and take them through security and customs. "As smooth as velvet drapes," said Lynn, thanking him.

He smiled. "Quite dull compared to your first arrival."

Lynn absorbed the mood of the airport shrouded in silent sadness. Even the incoming crowds were subdued. Gloom surrounded them like a Louisiana fog that refused to lift.

"This time, you stay with us," Mihail said as they walked to his car. "Elena and I insist. We will share together this sad time."

They generally declined home offers to avoid inconveniencing people. But this was a time when people needed each other. "You are very kind to have us. Thank you, Mihail."

He put their roll-aboards in his car. "You travel small. I am glad. When I offered to take you to Hotel Aleksandar last week, I had worried my car was too little. Many Amer— Many people," he courteously corrected, "have very big luggage."

"Ours is small but heavy," said Galen. "Lynn packs very much in little space."

They laughed, not because it was funny, but because laughter was something they could do together. It brought them close. Mihail is both hospitable and wise, thought Lynn. We need to be together.

As Mihail drove, he talked about plans for the next day. "Before the funeral there will be a . . . parade? What is the word?"

"A procession?" suggested Galen.

"Yes. A procession from the Parliament Building to the Arbored Walk of the Greats at Butel Cemetery. Mrs. Dimitrovski told me all about it. The casket will lead, carried by three officers on each side. They will be . . ." He looked at them, questioning. "Soldiers beside them. What is the word?"

"Flanked?" asked Galen.

"They will be flanked by soldiers with bayonets. Family members will be next, and Macedonian political and military leaders will be after them. More than five hundred people will be walking in the procession. Thousands of people will be waiting along the streets and watching from high windows."

Lynn wondered if talking about tomorrow's details, a head thing, helped relieve the pain of his personal loss, a heart thing. She had long believed that people walk each day with the sum total of their past days' actions flowing through their hearts and eyes. In Mihail's eyes she saw only amassed goodness.

"We are invited for lunch at the President's House before the procession. Mrs. Dimitrovski herself personally asked Elena and me, both of you, and Bishop Weber, who will be speaking at the funeral."

"You won't be speaking?" asked Lynn.

"State protocol says it must be the highest church official. Our bishop will do well."

Lynn admired his lack of jealousy at being passed over for this historic occasion. He was correct, however, that Heinrich would do a superb job, always faithful to the task, and an excellent ambassador for the Church.

"I accepted the lunch invitation for you," Mihail added. "That is good?"

"We are honored."

"Some people from the church and other close friends have been invited. President Benedict also."

Lynn felt grateful for a natural opportunity to meet with her as requested in her phone call.

"But she could not come. Mrs. Dimitrovski was disappointed. President Dimitrovski held her in high regard."

Lynn shared in the disappointment.

"There is much security. Agent Nedelkovski told me that your President will be well guarded by security from both our countries."

Lynn's heart skipped a beat. Surely with tight security no one would be able to assassinate the President of the United States.

As they entered the house, Lynn smelled coffee. Elena Martinovska greeted them with a smile on her face and grief in her eyes like a rose blooming on a broken stem. She had prepared delicious homemade goodies and *Tursko Kafe* in its traditional three parts. The table was set with embroidered napkins and colorful plates painted with flowers. Lynn thanked her, meaning it, knowing that some of the best parts of life is made up of such small gifts as setting the table for meaningful sharing together.

Mihail offered a blessing, courteously praying in English. A prayer too natural to have been rehearsed, too beautiful to have come from a shallow spirit. President Dimitrovski was present in their hearts as they sat around the table talking about him. Lynn realized that her profound grief over his death was partly because the world had lost one of the few leaders whose religion was not role play, for he was truly centered in the Mystery of Faith.

Her cell phone rang, surprising her. "I'm sorry," she said, stepping into the hall to answer so she wouldn't disturb them. "Hello."

"General Thornburg here." Warmth assuaged his gruff voice. "The two ballistics reports matched. You were right."

Right? Her theory was fact. But there was no *right*. It didn't change two heinous deaths. She sighed. "He was also the man who killed Elias Darwish, but he used a pistol."

"So, if you're right—and you were about this—he killed two innocents," said the general. "Darwish and . . ." His sudden pause for control said more than his words. ". . . and Major Manetti. Additionally he killed a man with a history of killing who didn't care which flag he served." Anger raised his voice. "And who caused President Dimitrovski's death. The first two deaths are unforgivable. The latter one— Well, I don't condone murder, but the world is better off without Frank Fillmore. You've been most helpful, Bishop Peterson."

"Thank you."

You're holding back, Lynn.

"He also saved my life, General Thornburg."

"Another story too long to go into now?"

"Yes, sir."

"President Benedict would like for you to be at the funeral early enough to stand close to the front between the platform and the graveside. I will find you. She wants to meet with you immediately following the service. I will get you through the crowd."

"Thank you," she repeated.

"She wants you to be prepared to report your insights about, to quote, 'the ranch hands.' I don't know what she means, and that doesn't matter as long as you understand."

"I do understand, General." She felt an inexplicable apprehension. She wasn't sure she should wait until the funeral tomorrow to unload her facts and fantasies. Whose orders did Zeller follow? She feared she knew the answer. And she began to wonder whether Fillmore had also.

The winds that had lifted her like an air balloon earlier now ceased. Her balloon crashed.

129

ZELLER AWOKE AS PLANNED AT THREE O'CLOCK ON THIS TUESDAY MORNING. He had an adrenaline high, familiar and savored. "I will miss this, *Freund*," he said, inspecting every part of his rifle once again. He scrutinized his two sets of plans: the meeting with the Patriot, a.k.a. John Adams, at the Hotel Aleksandar and the assassination at the cemetery. Perfect plans if his string of luck didn't break. It struck him as amusingly ironic that the morning meeting worried him far more than the assassination. He supposed it was because he would be in control at the cemetery, but at the hotel he would have to anticipate each of the Patriot's movements in advance. He must not make a single mistake today. No.

Each act of preparation this morning reminded him that this was his last shooting. He felt awash in melancholy, dressed in black from head-to-foot. The mourning color. "Yes, *Freund*, I will miss it."

But on the other hand, he would not miss it. How many people had he terminated? Too many. Most had earned it, but not all. He wrestled his conscience over ending the lives of people who deserved to live longer. Time and time again a perfect aim and a single bullet had turned him into a god of death. The Lord giveth and Zechariah Zeller taketh away. He would miss that kind of power.

He wondered how it all began. He knew deep down, where he seldom ventured. It took great courage to face his past and go into that space. He had not done so for a long time. With his hand on *Freund*, he dived into the sea of his own soul. There she was. Waiting. The before and the after. The beauty and the beaten. His mother lay tortured to death, tortured before his eyes, his six-year-old eyes. They had strapped him in a chair, forced him to watch, made him helpless to help her. When death finally took her away from their slow agonizing torture, they drove him for a very long time and turned him loose on strange streets in a strange city. He had been on his own ever since. Even today, he did not know who they were or why they had tortured his mother or why they had made him watch—unless to further torture her. Before his seventh birthday, he stole a gun and bullets and made a target of tin cans taken from a trash pile. He had been shooting at those men ever since. At age sixteen he received his first contract. And today was his last.

He climbed out of the soulful waters and shook off the past. "They're all dead, *Freund*. The bad and the good. It is time to bury them. I must focus on the present." And the present required him to go to the cemetery and hide *Freund* on the roof of the mausoleum under the tree branches. Afterwards he would come back here and run through the details: One, get his money in cash. Two, make a phone call. Three, set himself up at Butel Cemetery. This day would culminate his career. A day for concentration. And ultimately, he hoped, a day for celebration.

130

LYNN HAD LOOKED FORWARD TO MEETING GONKA DIMITROVSKA, BUT she hadn't foreseen the circumstances. She was grateful to be included in the intimate luncheon and for the opportunity to offer her condolences personally. Gonka greeted her warmly, as she did everyone. Her face showed the wear of grief, yet her presence was one of serenity and grace, like an alpine sunflower following the light. Meeting her friends and family was a privilege. The luncheon ended promptly at one o'clock to give the family and the Martinovskis time to go to the Parliament Building and begin the procession to the cemetery. Before leaving, Lynn's eyes swept the furnishings and décor of the presidential mansion for a final feast of beauty. It was the Bible on the mantel that stood out to her, not ornamental but well used. Her heart hurt for the family and for Macedonia.

She and Galen rode with Bishop Heinrich Weber directly to the cemetery. He mentioned that he had practiced his sermon with a translator last night. She understood why. It was an art to preach a translated sermon. It required a partnership—a dance—between preacher and translator.

She turned on her cell phone briefly in Heinrich's car. One new message. Zeller's voice brought shivers: You wondered how John Adams got the medal. A man known as the Patriot made obtaining the medal part of the contract on Darwish. The two men are one.

The voice scared her, and the message stunned her. It was like light catching illusive strands of web spun in a pattern of malice. And now the spider had a name. The one she had known she knew. The one that made reality too horrible to acknowledge. Poor, poor Mrs. Darwish! Lynn's heart agonized for her. May she never find out that John Adams issued the contract on Elie!

When they arrived at the cemetery, security stopped the car. Their driver showed the pass. Lynn understood only three words: *Heinrich Weber* preceded by a word that sounded like *episcopas*—bishop. She and Galen cleared on his coattails. They exited the car, and Heinrich took his place with the other speakers, all of whom had arrived except President Benedict. The cemetery teemed with the American and Macedonian versions of Austrian Size-Seventeens.

Lynn wanted a private moment to tell Galen about the call and get his wisdom, but General Thornburg found them immediately and greeted them warmly. He ushered them to a place close to the platform for foreign officials. Lynn peered out of the corner of her eye and saw John Adams. She dreaded telling the intimidating general about him, wishing she could skip this part of her life and fast forward herself home to New Orleans and her small life there that soared above malice and intrigue. John Adams had built a credible reputation and appeared to be highly trusted, and the general barely knew her. He would not believe her. While she was trying to figure out how to broach the subject, Galen and the general began to discuss war in the Balkans.

She was only half listening, still thinking about how best to persuade the general to take her seriously one more time, when he addressed her. "What do you think about the situation, Mrs. Peterson?"

"It sounds as though you supported President Dimitrovski's peace efforts," she responded, relieved that she had been at least partly listening.

"I am grateful when a leader puts forth as much effort, energy, and resources to avoid war as to go to war. You show me a general worth his rank, and I'll show you someone who wants war only as a last resort. It's the sissy-prissy politicians who've never served in a bloody battle who want to rush in."

No one could accuse General Thornburg of subtlety!

He moved close to her and spoke softly. "The President is not sure how much time she will have after the funeral. You are to report your concerns and insights to me in case your time together is cut short. If so, I will relay them to her."

"Yes, sir." She had an impulse to salute.

Don't, Lynn.

President Benedict's arrival brought a buzz to the waiting crowd. General Thornburg nodded toward her.

Lynn took a deep breath and began, "General Thornburg, I am deeply concerned about one of her 'ranch hands.'"

"Say more."

"That's the bottom line. It is complicated, and we have so little time."

"I see. Who?"

"John Adams."

He looked stunned. "I *don't* see!"

"He is highly dangerous."

"You are sure about this?" His tone held more amusement than concern, intimidating her.

"I feel fairly sure."

"*Feel?* Are we talking about feminine intuition?"

Lynn resented that. "Personal experience, *sir.*"

Watch it, Lynn!

Warmth and amusement evaporated. "*Fairly sure?* When you slander a long-time trusted and generous man whose advice has been respected by every Commander-in-Chief since the first Bush, I expect more than the bottom line. I demand proof, logic, and details." His words hung in the air like icicles.

She pulled her cell phone from Big-Black, retrieved old messages, and handed it to him. "Zeller called last Friday. And today he left a message."

General Thornburg listened. Disgusted skepticism changed to shock. He turned away immediately without speaking, keeping her phone. He headed directly but unhurriedly toward the small group of speakers sitting together and casually nodded President Benedict aside. He spoke briefly to her. Lynn saw her stunned look, quick recovery, and attitude of nonchalance. They could have been discussing their dogs. Nodding, she returned to her seat, and he left at a studiedly casual pace.

The regal funeral procession arrived to drumbeat and gun salvos. The family took their places on the carpet by the graveside with its black burial slab. When the officials in the last row of the procession had found their places, the military cordon opened. The Macedonian people ran into the cemetery from the hillsides, carrying flowers to put on President Dimitrovski's grave after the funeral. Lynn felt tears in her eyes. Thousands of people were running in from every direction. It was a Secret Service nightmare.

After each speaker's presentation, a Skopje choir sang hymns beautifully. Lynn forced herself never to glance toward John Adams. Heinrich preached eloquently. By the time General Thornburg returned two hours later, the choir was singing its final hymn before President Benedict spoke. He stopped at the speakers' area again and whispered something to her. Well masked, she made no response except a slight nod.

He made his way back to Lynn. He stood silently for a few moments before remarking almost inaudibly, "With the assistance of Father Nish, we received decoded data collected by Elias Darwish. Though much more time is needed, it looks like when we put everything together there is information to indict him. He doesn't know it yet, but he will be taken to the American Embassy immediately following the funeral and arrested."

Poor Mrs. Darwish, Lynn thought again.

"Vik was assisting me with the Patriot problem," said the general. "I'm surprised he failed to see the connection after decoding Darwish's data."

All of Viktor's behaviors and character traits whirled through her mind like lotto numbers turned into letters; the ones that dropped spelled *Not guilty.* "Perhaps he did identify him, General Thornburg. John Adams, he learned yesterday, is his brother-in-law."

He erupted. "That is NO REASON TO . . ."

"The heinous part is that Elias Darwish was Adams' half-brother. If this were made public, Mrs. Darwish would suffer not only the loss of her son but also the excruciating knowledge that her other son is responsible for his murder."

Despite all the general had experienced, shock registered in his eyes. "I see. But still . . ." Choosing not to voice his thought, he extended his hand. "Our country is in your debt."

"No, sir. It is in perpetual debt to you and all the other officers who keep honor and honesty alive."

"Despite the politicians!"

Only some of them, she thought. Others do their best to restore honor and honesty.

The hymn ended and General Thornburg, unnoticed in the crowd, saluted his Commander-in-Chief as she came forward to speak.

131

President Helena Benedict the final speaker, represented the international community. Lynn felt her charisma as she stood before the tens of thousands of mourners gathered on the cemetery hillsides. The innate power of her presence overshadowed her diminutive size. Her blue-green eyes were lit with compassion, a trait that partnered with integrity and energy as emerging trademarks of her presidency. Silently she looked across the masses of people, drawing their undivided attention like fireworks in a night sky. Not a whisper could be heard. She focused for a moment on the TV cameras, her welcoming gaze inviting American audiences to pay tribute to the President of the small country of Macedonia.

The hushed crowd watched her bow her head respectfully toward President Dimitrovski's family. She turned briefly toward the platform and nodded to the domestic and foreign officials. Then her eyes sank to the black burial slab engraved with Matthew 5:9 and read the verse with sincerity: "Blessed peacemakers, for they will be called children of God." Her perfect diction complemented her clear, well-modulated voice. Her shoulders lifted with a visible intake of breath. She focused on the flag-draped casket and began to speak:

> President Basil Dimitrovski, your sisters and brothers of the United States of America mourn with Macedonia. I bring a word of sorrow and condolence to your family and the people of your country. You rest under the bright yellow sun of the Macedonian flag, leaving the earth a lesser place. We grieve the loss of your bright sunlight as a peacemaker. Today's turbulent and chaotic world has lost one of its greatest presidents.

When she paused for the translation, General Thornburg muttered to no one in particular, "*She* is the greatest president this world has."

Zeller listened from his prone position on top of the black marble mausoleum. He hid within the parapets and peeked through the small gap between them. He was eager. *Freund* was ready. But not yet. No. Let her finish.

> President Dimitrovski, like my country's beloved former President John F. Kennedy, you were inaugurated at the young age of forty-three. Like him, you died an untimely death with unfinished dreams. Like him, you are mourned not only by hundreds of thousands of your citizens, but also by people all around the world.

The translator tried to convey not only the meaning of the President's words but also her magnetic style of presentation.

From his prone position, peeking through the space, Zeller saw the mob of mourners with flowers. Mourned by all but one, he thought, the one who wanted President Dimitrovski dead. If anyone ever kills the person responsible for the plane crash, he deserves the Grand Cross of Merit!

> President Dimitrovski, you vowed at your inauguration to be *everyone's* president. You traveled around the country talking with the people about their needs and concerns, visiting with artists and athletes, laborers and politicians, believers and atheists, students and pensioners, rich and poor. You drew no boundaries of economic level, religious preference, or ethnic background. You did not even bow to party affiliation. Despite the risk to your popularity in "high places," you kept your promise to be President of *all* the people!

The translation reverberated over the hillsides. Thousands of heads nodded in a tidal wave of agreement. The common people mourned the loss of one they saw not only as their President but also their trusted friend.

Zeller nodded also. He satisfied himself that he'd found a clear shot at the target. During the translation, he reran his brief meeting this morning. The Patriot/John Adams had come as expected. But unexpectedly, he appeared more confident again, in control once more. President Benedict, his last obstacle, was about to be taken out. Their meeting had gone well. Perhaps suspiciously well. One, they had been seen in public together, and the security camera had recorded it. Two, he had agreed to the full fee requested. Three, he had brought the cash with him and paid all of it in advance. A new thought strayed through Zeller's mind—blackmailing Adams after the President's death could be lucrative in the future. He checked the wind and adjusted his aim slightly to compensate, wondering if he would succumb to greed.

> President Dimitrovski, *The Wall Street Journal* identified you as a "real Balkan statesman." You were a bridge builder who held a unique vision of peaceful cooperation between nations, a vision of mutual respect for every country's sovereignty and territorial independence and internal policies. You would not let us forget our double immorality of deceit and violence. Sometimes you bore alone the burden of your vision of peace, and always you incurred political and personal risks because of it.

A low mumble filled the hillsides as the translator relayed the last sentence.

Personal risk, thought Zeller, like I incur now. For this was not only his final shot but also his farthest. He was behind the security snipers, supposedly beyond the range of accuracy. Yet it was within his range of confidence. He had practiced this distance hundreds of times over the years. He noted the winds. They had ceased. He adjusted.

> President Dimitrovski, in your inaugural address you dared to affirm love in a time of hatred and quoted St. Paul in 1 Corinthians 13, whose words describe love as all-inclusive. That worldview is dangerous to political self-interests. It counteracts a world where humanity fears differences, relishes hostilities, spreads seeds of hatred, and takes violence for granted—a world of contrived misperceptions, a world made ripe for manipulation by power mongers.

For an instant her eyes turned toward the officials on the platform and, loaded with disdain, targeted John Adams. Their glint of steel reflected an arsenal of strength. Adams stiffened. She focused again on the flag-draped casket.

> In your inaugural address, you also spoke of ideals and holy duty. But you did not stop with words. You lived them out!

"Holy duty." Now would be a perfect time, thought Zeller, a dramatic moment. No! Let her finish. She deserves that much.

> President Dimitrovski, your favorite song was "O Lord Take My Heart." You led with heart—a courageous and open heart. You repaid your enemies with understanding, your critics with compassion. You were not afraid to keep promises or make compromises. You armed yourself with political honesty, and disarmed others with your generosity of spirit and disinterest in personal power. You refused to give up on human beings. You taught us that we can rewrite our songs of hatred and destruction, and begin to join together in harmony, singing a new tune of freedom and dignity for all.

"Freedom and dignity for all." Including me? Zeller could tell the speech was nearly over. He silently positioned his rifle barrel in the canale. Held the target in the crosshairs. A single shot through the head. He eased his finger onto the trigger. Get ready, *Freund.* But not quite yet. No.

> President Dimitrovski, in honor of your memory, I commit to the international community

> that I will use all the means at my disposal to build a world of peace and unprecedented unity and justice, perpetuating your dream that one day we will live as brothers and sisters upon the earth.

The leader of the most powerful country in the world had offered homage instead of haughtiness. President Benedict nodded respectfully to the family and turned to walk back toward her place, her head bowed in humility. Her demeanor needed no translation. The watching world knew that the Superpower's reign of arrogance had ended.

Gunfire!

132

A SINGLE SHOT TO THE HEAD. ZELLER LAY DOWN FLAT. "OVER THERE!" he shouted in Macedonian above the screams. "He ran into the trees!" No one knew where the voice came from and no one cared. Some ran toward the trees. Some away from them. The cemetery was in bedlam now. People running everywhere. Every which way. Colliding with each other. Thousands of people who wanted to survive. To get away. They were focused on themselves and their loved ones, not on looking for a sniper. The sniper was the one person they did *not* want to see.

Zeller gave *Freund* a fond farewell pat and tucked a note under the barrel. He stuffed his gloves in his black suit pocket and leaped down in the tree covering into the running, hysterical, black-clad crowd. Running himself. Blending in. Getting away. Into the trees and down the hill. Running with the crowd away from Butel Cemetery. Running. Slowing. Walking. Reaching the car he'd purchased and driving out of Skopje before roadblocks could be set up. Ending his life. Beginning his life.

He had only one sadness. If he'd been a Secret Service agent, he'd be a hero instead of a murderer, a hero for saving President Benedict's life. John Adams was dead.

EPILOGUE

Wednesday, 9:45 A.M.

Three Weeks Later

AT 9:45 ON WEDNESDAY MORNING, LYNN ENTERED THE OVAL OFFICE. Awed and intimidated, she sat in a large leather chair, her feet barely reaching the floor.

"I appreciate your coming early, Lynn." President Helena Benedict's short, dark hair enhanced alert, wide-set eyes, windows into another's soul and mirrors into her own. They were the color of a blue lagoon. Opal earrings matched them, her only jewelry. She wore a trim, dark suit, tailored but not masculine. She had managed the political arena without rigidity or shallowness, a spruce tree swaying with the wind while remaining rooted. "You handled the challenges remarkably well."

Challenges. As good a word as any. "Thank you, Madam President."

"I expected my request to be a simple favor."

"I would do it again." The words came without forethought. Astonished, Lynn realized they were true.

"Knowing the dangers? Putting yourself in harm's way?"

Lynn shrugged. "I like adventure."

The President smiled. "I'll keep that in mind."

Lynn didn't feel adventurous at the moment, however. She sat forward, undersized in the oversized chair. Her thin china cup clicked on the saucer as she glanced at the old saddlebag resting incongruously on the coffee table. The light caught the **M** on the flap. Neither the saddlebag's invitation to nostalgia nor the homey aroma of cinnamon tea could dispel the aura of the Oval Office. "It is humbling to be here."

"For some. For others it evokes arrogance." The President picked up the saddlebag. "My father gave me this soon after my inauguration." Her hand tenderly brushed across the cracked leather. "He died a few weeks later."

"I'm sorry." Lynn knew all too well grief's journey, like walking barefoot on an endless path of thorns.

"I invited you to thank you personally." The President traced the **M** on the old saddlebag. "Also, because you have earned the right to hear what my father told me." She looked up sharply. "I share it in the strictest of confidence, Lynn Marie Prejean Peterson."

Normally Lynn would have been surprised to hear her second name. But the President's full-of-surprises knowledge had ceased to be surprising.

President Benedict spoke softly. "Its contents reveal family secrets."

Secrets.

"Lynn Marie Prejean Peterson," she repeated, "we share the same second name."

Lynn knew her only as President Helena Heffron Benedict. "Marie?"

"Do you know whose namesake you are?"

Lynn totally respected President Benedict, but she was confused about where this was going. Like every citizen who talks with the President at the White House, she supposed, she replied without questioning. "I am named after my great-grandfather's sister, Marie-Vincente Prejean."

"She was called Vini," said the President.

"Her married name was McGragor," added Lynn. "Vini McGragor. I recognized the name in your note to Major Manetti."

"I'm named after her also. My father was her grandson."

"I didn't know she had a grandchild! I thought her son died young and childless."

"It's far too complicated to go into today. It would take a book to tell the story." She glanced again at the saddlebag. "Suffice it to say that a family secret was kept even from me until after I became President."

Speaking of family secrets with the President of the United States made Lynn uncomfortable.

"The point is that you and I have the same great-great-grandparents—far removed from our generation. Nonetheless, we are extended family." She smiled warmly. "I wanted you to know."

"Thank you." Lynn could not quite get her mind around the fact that the President was a distant relative. She felt awkward and shifted to more comfortable conversational terrain. "Your speech at President Dimitrovski's funeral was wonderful."

"The words came easily because of my respect for him."

Lynn glanced again at the old, worn saddlebag on the coffee table and wondered if it had inspired the President's ranch hands imagery in her note to the major.

"There is something else that requires confidentiality." The President waited for a nod of agreement. "The man you identified as Zechariah Zeller left behind his sniper rifle and a note. We have kept it out of the news, but you deserve to read a copy."

Lynn read it slowly, hearing his voice as though he were speaking to her on the telephone.

FOR YOUR INFORMATION:

John Adams, alias the Patriot, hired me to assassinate the President of the United States. Proof exists on a security camera at Hotel Aleksandar. Time: 10:00 A.M. today. Computer software can cut through his disguise. A lip reader can tell you his words. In the beginning I did not know he was evil. In time I learned he was bad for his country and for the world. Offering me a contract on President Benedict proved he had become too dangerous to live. I knew if I refused, he would hire someone else. I shot him instead of her. I saved President Benedict's life and rid the world of a monster. If I were a CIA agent, you would promote me for a job well done, not try to capture and punish me. If I were a Secret Service agent, you would decorate me as a hero, not hunt me down. Consider these facts!

"The hotel surveillance video offered the proof he expected," President Benedict affirmed.

Lynn shuddered. "I can't imagine . . . if you had been . . ." She couldn't finish.

"Apparently abetting conflict and benefiting from the chaos was John Adams's strategy, financially and politically."

Lynn thought of how the flutter of a butterfly in one part of the world can create chaos in another part of the world. Yet, she reminded herself, chaos is not always destructive.

"What troubles me most," the President spoke with heavy disappointment in herself, "is that I didn't see it coming."

"No one did. But even in so short a time in office, you recognized that something was wrong. Otherwise, you wouldn't have gone outside the system." *Start with St. Sava* flashed across Lynn's mind. "In your note to the major, you mentioned St. Sava. May I ask how you know about it?"

"As a child my father spent his summers in Crested Butte, Colorado. One of his good friends was a boy named Joseph Machek."

Lynn thought of Viktor Machek.

"Joseph's father had come from Croatia as a boy to work in the Crested Butte mine, and he told my father the story. He also told him in sworn confidence that he came from a long line of members of St. Sava." The President's hand caressed the saddlebag as she gazed out the window. "My father kept that confidence until he brought me this. The story of the ancient society was one of the secrets he shared with me that day. He said I could trust St. Sava." She looked again at Lynn. "Later, during one of my conversations with President Dimitrovski, he conveyed his trust also."

Lynn recalled his comment on the phone when she asked about St. Sava: "Things are not always what they appear to be." That was the last time I spoke with him. I can never do so again. Death's finality offers no second chance for words unsaid and deeds undone.

"I'm afraid my note to Marsh wasn't clear. I meant for Marsh to begin with St. Sava, not as an enemy, but as a source of help."

Words! Bridges or chasms, depending on how they are interpreted.

"I understand that John Adams was also behind an attempt on your life, Lynn. And Zeller aborted it." The President picked up the note he had written. "Ironic, isn't it? A respected presidential advisor sought both our deaths, and a world-class sniper saved both our lives."

"Perhaps Blaise Pascal had it right," Lynn replied. "'The heart has its reasons, which the reason knows nothing about; we know it in a thousand things.'"

"Did you ever wonder why I contacted you?"

"I thought you were desperate."

President Benedict smiled. "More so than I realized. You and Dr. Peterson have done outstanding work internationally, which got my attention." The President's blue-green eyes held Lynn's. "But *family*—I trusted that."

The somber ceremony honoring Elie began at ten o'clock in the Oval Office. Loyal Vice President Parker attended. Mrs. Darwish, Viktor, Milcah, and their two children had flown on a plane arranged by the White House. This may have been the first time a member of St. Sava was in the Oval Office, but Lynn suspected it would not be the last time. She and Galen, Chief Armstrong and Francine Babineaux, Cy Bill and Bubba had flown together from New Orleans. All of them formed a semicircle around Mrs. Darwish, grown frailer. She held Milcah's hand as though her daughter also might suddenly vanish. Two sons in less than two weeks. Lynn could not imagine the extent of her pain, of doubling the suffering of one child's death. She marveled that Mrs. Darwish could rise each morning and stand erect.

Yet Zeller had spared her the toll of a long, media-frenzied trial that would have let no speck of John Adams's dishonor remain privately dormant and could have culminated in the death penalty, anyway. Very few government officials knew the truth, and the ones who did had advised President Benedict against making public John Adams's conspiracies, including his attempt to have her assassinated. They warned that it would create citizen instability and mistrust of the system. Lynn wondered, however, if President Benedict had agreed largely for Mrs. Darwish's sake. Her son's delusional malice made no headlines. Knowledge of his responsibility for her other son's death remained within a tight, closed-lipped circle. Bubba had retrieved the copy of Elie's data from Cy Bill, still sealed in the envelope, and destroyed it. Mrs. Darwish's perception of John Adams, nee Adam Ristich, as a respected and important man could remain untarnished. May it be so!

The door to the Oval Office opened, and a woman entered with two teenagers, a girl and a boy. They hung back hesitant.

Vice President Parker moved toward them, inviting them into the semicircle. "Mrs. Darwish," he said, "this is Mrs. John Adams."

"Please call me Sally, Mrs. Darwish," she said hesitantly. She pointed to herself and repeated, "Sally."

"I meet you at last, please!"

"You speak English!" Sally smiled, obviously relieved. "This is Jennifer, your granddaughter. John was right; she does resemble you. And this is David, your grandson."

Mrs. Darwish's frail arms wrapped first around Jennifer and then around David, her spontaneous love overcoming the teenagers' reticence toward a stranger.

"I have long wanted you to come to visit us," said Sally. "Since you are here, if you could spend a few weeks with us, we would like that very much."

Mrs. Darwish nodded, too moved to speak. She embraced Sally, giving and gaining strength.

President Benedict entered and warmly greeted each person by name, thanking the police chief and crime lab expert and Cy Bill (minus Ebony) for their hard work following Elias Darwish's death. She told Bubba that she had old ties with New Orleans and was a Saints fan, and she had seen him play. Her aide handed her a plaque, and she asked Mrs. Darwish to step forward. With dignity and grace she bestowed upon Elias Darwish the Posthumous Presidential Award of Merit for his brilliance, diligence, and valor in service to the United States of America, which cost him his life. The President's eyes teared but did not overflow.

The President shook hands with Rachel Darwish and then paused, extending her arms in a gesture that asked permission for a hug. Permission granted. The President of the United States and the grieving mother from Sarajevo embraced each other, two women who knew how to love, one suffering its loss and the other offering genuine compassion. Watching them brought tears to Lynn's eyes, tears that overflowed.

At the close of the ceremony Lynn spoke for a few minutes with Mrs. Darwish. "I remember your family pictures. Now you will be able to get many pictures from your daughter-in-law."

Mrs. Darwish smiled. "I have a daughter and a son-in-law and a daughter-in-law. And *four* grandchildren." She started to say something else but hesitated, her smile fading.

"Are you all right?" asked Lynn.

Troubled eyes answered. "I do not understand, please. John was important to the American government. Elias was important to St. Sava—and a football player in America. But Elias gets the high award." She looked at the plaque for a moment. "On that day when Adam came, he was . . . He did not seem . . ." With a heavy sigh she asked Lynn a question she did not want to hear. "Did he do something . . . wrong?"

Oh, God, help me choose my words wisely. "He was an advisor to the President. You can be very proud of that. His service to the country was expected. But Elie volunteered his service."

Her eyes filled with relief and gradually brightened like a rheostat lamp being turned up. "Thank you, please." She hugged Lynn.

Lynn would always be able to recall the multi-dimensions of that moment. The feel of the small, fragile woman, their arms entwined. The smell of cinnamon rolls and Turkish coffee served on silver trays. The sound of soft chatter around them, celebrating Elie's life. The glint of the Posthumous Presidential Award of Merit catching the light and forming a rainbow of colors that danced across the President's desk.

President Benedict told everyone goodbye with an old word: "Farewell. In the full sense of the meaning. *Fare well.*"

As they left, curiosity won and Lynn spoke privately to Viktor. "Over a century ago a boy from Croatia went to Crested Butte, Colorado, to work in a mine. His last name was Machek."

"Stephen. How do you know of him?"

"A friend told me the story."

"He was my grandfather's uncle. The Machek family tree goes back for generations."

Like its ties with St. Sava, thought Lynn.

Viktor glanced toward Mrs. Darwish. "What I learned from Elie's data . . ." His eyes filled with sadness. "I could not add to her hurt."

"I understand." She grinned at him. "Rooster Cogburn would have done the same thing." It was good to see him smile again.

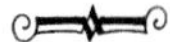

At 10:17 on Wednesday morning Lynn arrived at Café du Monde in the French Quarter and chose her usual outdoor table. Her mind was on the mystery she wanted someday to write. She scribbled on a napkin the one decided word: *Secrets* . . . She doodled flowers around the word. Then she began to doodle the St. Sava symbol around the flowers, longing to write *The Dead Saint*. But she could never tell that story.

Secrets. Secrets what? Secrets take us on a journey.

Author's Note and Acknowledgments

Like President John F. Kennedy, young President Boris Trajkovski of Macedonia was assassinated after a brief time in office. He proved himself to be one of the world's finest leaders toward peace. I met him in Oslo when he was the recipient of a World Peace Award. Macedonian President Basil Dimitrovski in this book is fictional, but the character was created in honor of President Trajkovski. While writing the first draft of the scenes set in Macedonia, my mind and heart "living" there, President Trajkovski was killed in a plane crash. I strongly felt the death of this man with the courage to envision and enliven peace. His death, like that of President John F. Kennedy, changed the future that might have been. His death also changed this book.

I am grateful to Dirk and Carol Van Gorp for escorting Bill and me through Bosnia in a UN Jeep during the NATO bombing, a personal experience of war that still burns in my heart.

To Chaplain Carl Johnston for showing us around the UN base at Zagreb, Croatia, including the MASH unit where I met a young Russian soldier who had lost both legs when a Sarajevo landmine exploded, and whom the fictional character Sasha is meant to honor.

To Bishop Heinrich Bolleter, longtime friend, for sharing knowledge and experience about Austria, Macedonia, and Bosnia-Herzegovina. To Rev. Mihail Cekov of Macedonia and Rev. Ljiljana Sjanta of Serbia for patiently answering my questions and giving me significant insight; to Macedonian missionary Carol Partridge and Rev. Dave Rieck of California for research materials providing grassroots Macedonian perspectives, and to my dear friend Dr. Annegret Klaiber from

Germany for sharing the wisdom gleaned from health work with Macedonian women.

To Bill Avera and Dirk Oden for helping me seem more knowledgeable about guns than I actually am, and to Bryant Oden for a thorough reading of the next-to-final draft and for keeping me updated technologically.

To Sgt. Cunningham, a Dallas mounted policeman, for showing me the large beautiful steeds and giving me background information.

To good friends: Bishop Dick Wilke and Julia for listening to the first scene soon after its birth; and Etta Mae Mutti, Phyllis Henry, Doug and Mary McPherson, David and Paula Severe, Bishop Dan Solomon and Marcia, and MacKenzie and Edith Thompson for listening and sharing. Dick Smith for the photograph. Thank you for cheering me on.

To more good friends who read this manuscript: Bishop Charles Crutchfield and Karen, Paul and Elizabeth Escamilla, Sandra Estess, Judy Gibbs, Sally Kelley and David Severe for wading through the first draft; Dan and Barbara Batchelor and Bill Henry for giving the second draft a go. To Bishop Sharon Brown Christopher, past president of the United Methodist Council of Bishops, for reading the final draft through the eyes of a woman in the episcopacy. My thanks to all of you for reading the novel and offering astute comments and encouragement. To other special friends in the episcopacy who are women: thank you for leading the church in an inspirational way.

To Kathleen Davis Niendorff, agent extraordinaire, and Ramona Richards, excellent editor.

To Bishop Rueben Job for guidance in my winding inner journey and, thereby, smoothing the path of my outer journey, and for steadfast interest in my writing. Thank you for bestowing confidence that invites me to swim in deeper waters.

To my husband, Bill, for our shared adventures on five continents; to Dee, Dirk, Valerie, and Bryant for the amazing adults you have become; and Angela for joining our family by marriage. My thanks to each of you for your interest, comments, and support.

And finally to Vini, heroine of my first novel, *Crested Butte*, and great-grandmother of the President in this one, who continues to peer over my shoulder as I write, asking: *Is it just? Is it fair?* Then smiling and asking the most important question of all: *Is it entertaining?* Ah, Vini, so it is!

Discussion Questions

[PART 1]

1. In the first chapter Lynn is enjoying her surroundings, and suddenly one event changes everything. Have there been times when you were enjoying yourself and something unexpected occurred that totally changed the situation?
2. For Lynn, Elie's death was like "a machete had sliced through time severing it into the before and the after." Have you experienced before-and-after life changes?
3. What do you think of Lynn's way of handling the request from the president? Would you have kept it "totally confidential"? How do you respond (verbally and inwardly) when you are asked to do something outside your comfort zone?

[PART 2]

4. During Lynn's first day in Vienna, she sees a new friend killed, forces herself to retrieve President Benedict's letter, helps the people around her, and gives an important speech that evening. Have you had days that demanded more than you thought you had the capacity to handle?
5. Lynn recognizes that one's reaction to an event (the bomb threat at the Austrian president's reception) increases or reduces its power to bring fear and be destructive. Can you think of an example?

[PART 3]

6. Lynn admires and respects the Macedonian president. What did you think of him? How did you feel after the

crash? How does the sudden death of a beloved leader affect us, both on the surface and at deeper levels?

[PART 4]

7. As Lynn enters Sarajevo, she recalls war zone experiences that indelibly touched her life. In what ways has an experience with war (personally or through someone close to you) shaped or reshaped your life?
8. Lynn speaks favorably of being in the hands of the church community and of the Mystery of Faith. Do you have a similar experience of faith (from your perspective of the meaning of that word)?
9. How did you view Zeller (the mime) in the beginning? In what ways does your perception change by the conclusion? Does hearing someone's story sometimes affect our view?
10. Did your ideas about St. Sava change as the story progressed? If you have a negative impression of a group, how does new information change your view? Can we hold such strong negative or positive impressions of a group that new facts make no difference?
11. What was the most moving or memorable scene to you?
12. At the conclusion Lynn completes the first sentence of her novel. If you were trying to complete the first sentence of your novel that began "Secrets," how would you finish the sentence? "Secrets . . . ."